Robin Hood's
WIDOW

Book II
The Robin Hood Trilogy

Olivia Longueville
J.C. Plummer

The Robin Hood Trilogy, Book 2: Robin Hood's Widow
Copyright © 2020 Olivia Longueville and J. C. Plummer
Trade paper ISBN-13:   978-1-947878-06-8
Kindle ISBN-13:   978-1-947878-07-5
EPUB ISBN-13:   978-1-947878-08-2
Audio ISBN-13:   978-1-947878-09-9

Cover design: Damonza.com
Interior design and formatting: Damonza.com

AngevinWorld.com

For my parents, Nadezda and Viatcheslav,
who are always so supportive and interested
in the work I do as a writer.

– Olivia

For Kathleen and Lesley
in heartfelt appreciation
for their support and encouragement.

– J. C.

Acknowledgments

Many thanks to our pre-readers and editors.

CONTENTS

WILLIAM THE CONQUEROR'S
DESCENDANTS

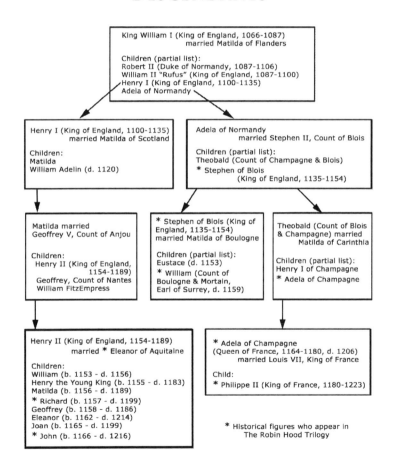

King William I (King of England, 1066-1087)
married Matilda of Flanders

Children (partial list):
Robert II (Duke of Normandy, 1087-1106)
William II "Rufus" (King of England, 1087-1100)
Henry I (King of England, 1100-1135)
Adela of Normandy

Henry I (King of England, 1100-1135)
married Matilda of Scotland

Children:
Matilda
William Adelin (d. 1120)

Adela of Normandy
married Stephen II, Count of Blois

Children (partial list):
Theobald (Count of Champagne & Blois)
* Stephen of Blois
(King of England, 1135-1154)

Matilda married
Geoffrey V, Count of Anjou

Children:
Henry II (King of England,
1154-1189)
Geoffrey, Count of Nantes
William FitzEmpress

* Stephen of Blois (King of
England, 1135-1154)
married Matilda of Boulogne

Children (partial list):
Eustace (d. 1153)
* William (Count of
Boulogne & Mortain,
Earl of Surrey, d. 1159)

Theobald (Count of Blois
& Champagne) married
Matilda of Carinthia

Children (partial list):
Henry I of Champagne
* Adela of Champagne

Henry II (King of England, 1154-1189)
married * Eleanor of Aquitaine

Children:
William (b. 1153 - d. 1156)
Henry the Young King (b. 1155 - d. 1183)
Matilda (b. 1156 - d. 1189)
* Richard (b. 1157 - d. 1199)
Geoffrey (b. 1158 - d. 1186)
Eleanor (b. 1162 - d. 1214)
Joan (b. 1165 - d. 1199)
* John (b. 1166 - d. 1216)

* Adela of Champagne
(Queen of France, 1164-1180, d. 1206)
married Louis VII, King of France

Child:
* Philippe II (King of France, 1180-1223)

* Historical figures who appear in
The Robin Hood Trilogy

Fictional Families in the Robin Hood Trilogy

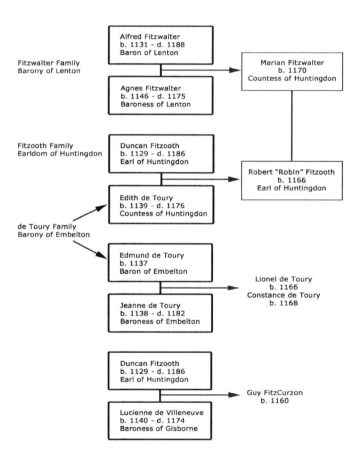

Fitzwalter Family
Barony of Lenton

Alfred Fitzwalter
b. 1131 - d. 1188
Baron of Lenton

Agnes Fitzwalter
b. 1146 - d. 1175
Baroness of Lenton

Marian Fitzwalter
b. 1170
Countess of Huntingdon

Fitzooth Family
Earldom of Huntingdon

Duncan Fitzooth
b. 1129 - d. 1186
Earl of Huntingdon

Edith de Toury
b. 1139 - d. 1176
Countess of Huntingdon

Robert "Robin" Fitzooth
b. 1166
Earl of Huntingdon

de Toury Family
Barony of Embelton

Edmund de Toury
b. 1137
Baron of Embelton

Jeanne de Toury
b. 1138 - d. 1182
Baroness of Embelton

Lionel de Toury
b. 1166
Constance de Toury
b. 1168

Duncan Fitzooth
b. 1129 - d. 1186
Earl of Huntingdon

Lucienne de Villeneuve
b. 1140 - d. 1174
Baroness of Gisborne

Guy FitzCurzon
b. 1160

ROYAL SHIELDS OF ENGLAND, 1066-1199

William the Conqueror 1066-1087
Two passant lions on a field of red

Stephen I 1135-1154
Centaur on a field of red

Henry II 1154-1189
One rampant lion on a field of red

Richard I 1189-1199
Three passant lions on a field of red

PROLOGUE
A WIDOW'S JOURNEY

9 April 1192, North of Poitiers, On the Banks of the Clain River

Bracing herself against a tree, Marian gasped for air, clutching her side as she struggled to catch her breath. She felt as though she had been running for hours.

"I think we lost that man who was following us," Much shouted over the roar of the nearby river.

Allan, who was also winded from their dash along the riverbank, followed behind as they skirted the tree line of a dense forest. Bent over at the waist and panting, he asked, "Did you recognize him?"

Much peered over his shoulder again. "No, but he looked familiar."

Finally able to speak, Marian interjected sharply, "All I care about is returning to England as soon as possible. The king commanded me to go to the court in Poitiers, and I did. I made no promises that I would *stay* there."

"We are very far from home, with few coins…" Much faltered as Marian glared at him.

"You told me you knew the way," she reminded him.

"I do," declared Much. "I traveled between Aquitaine and the ports in Normandy many times with Lord Robin."

She stared at him for a moment. The sound of Robin's name struck her like a physical blow, as if Gisborne's dagger were piercing her heart just as it had pierced Robin's. Paralyzing anguish besieged her mind until Allan's warm hand on her shoulder interrupted her descent into the black abyss of her grief.

"Much will guide us, and I will earn coins by performing in the towns along the way. It will take time, but we will be back in Nottinghamshire in a month or so."

Marian gazed into Allan's kind eyes and then Much's troubled frown. They were both looking at her with such pity that she was overcome by an irrational fury—a toxic brew of bitterness that these men lived, while Robin lay buried in the Holy Land, crushing guilt that she hadn't revealed her secret to Robin, and hatred for the men who had taken her husband from her: Guy of Gisborne, Sheriff de Argentan, and even King Richard. They all shared some blame in the tragedy of Robin's death.

She recoiled from Allan's attempt to comfort her. "We will do whatever is necessary to speed our journey," she stipulated. "Allan will sing his ballads, and if we need to steal or beg, then we will do it. Nothing is more important than returning home and avenging…" she swallowed to maintain a steady voice, "Robin's murder."

The day was drawing to a close, so they made camp. Despite the chill of the spring night, it was too risky to build a fire, since Much was still worried about the man who had followed them when they slipped away from the palace.

Fortunately, Queen Eleanor had not been in Poitiers, so security around the keep had been lax. The dowager queen had traveled to England the previous month, determined to thwart Prince John's scheme to join forces with King Philippe of France to undermine King Richard while he was away on the Crusade.

Marian had insisted on taking the first watch. She leaned against a tree at the edge of camp, hoping that she could detect the sound of approaching danger over the rustling of leaves and the whoosh of the river. At least the full moon brightened the forest, although the pale light left everything drained of color and vibrancy.

Like her life without Robin.

She willed herself to think of something besides Robin's death. Instead, she reminisced about another full moon, now over three and a half years ago, when Robin had rescued her from the sheriff. They had pledged to marry and had later become one. It had been the true beginning of her marriage to Robin.

She desperately wanted to fill her mind with joyful memories like those of that fateful, glorious night. But again and again, the happy recollections would transform into the same horrific scene, and she would relive Robin's death. The details were so vivid in her mind: kneeling in the gritty dirt, the soft texture of his hair against her cheek as she cradled him in her arms, and the sharp bristles of his short beard as they shared one last kiss. After his death, she had held his hand, clinging to its warmth and begging God to either restore his life or take hers as well.

At that moment, Marian had wanted nothing more than to join Robin in heaven. But with time to reflect, she realized that seeking death would not honor Robin or protect his legacy, and it could very well condemn her soul to eternal hellfire.

By the time she disembarked at Marseilles, she had dried her tears and resolved to resist the grief that relentlessly pulled her towards a chasm of black despair. She would not surrender her spirit to the melancholy allure of endless mourning.

Instead, she would take action. First, she would honor the blood oath she swore over Robin's body by making Gisborne and Argentan suffer for their murderous deeds. Then she vowed to devote the rest of her life to ensuring that Robin's legacy would endure and thrive. This would be her sacred mission as Robin Hood's widow.

CHAPTER 1
FAILURE IS LIKE THE SUN

29 April 1192, City of Acre, Kingdom of Jerusalem

he sound of horses approaching him from behind caused Robin to draw his dagger and pivot to face his attackers. The distinctive cadence of galloping hooves striking the cobblestone street triggered an intense memory of men on horseback, charging towards him with their swords drawn and surrounding him as he defended the woman he loved and the king he served.

At first, it all seemed so real, but when he blinked, the attacking soldiers morphed into a trio of mounted Knights Hospitaller riding past him as they hurried down the street. Their weapons were not drawn, and they did not even glance in his direction. An embarrassed Robin sheathed his dagger and continued on his journey to the harbor.

It had been two months since Guy of Gisborne had nearly killed him. During his recovery, Robin's existence had alternated between excruciating pain and lethargic befuddlement. Eventually, he had refused to take any more of the mind-numbing poppy potion, resisting the entreaties of the king's physician, Ranulphus Besace.

And when the doctor informed him that he must remain in his chamber, Robin had resolved to leave at the first opportunity.

As soon as Ranulphus was called away to an emergency, Robin had dressed, retrieved a bag of coins hidden in his trunk's false bottom, and headed towards the harbor of Acre. No doctor, not even King Richard himself, would hinder his mission.

As he walked away from the citadel, he initially felt overjoyed to be on his feet and free of his confinement. His injuries were much improved. However, as he moved through the ancient city, the tightness in his chest became a throbbing pain that frequently caused him to stop and lean against a wall to catch his breath. A sheen of cold sweat enveloped him, and his head repeatedly spun in a dizzy spiral that threatened to send him crashing onto the pavement in an unconscious heap.

Robin grimly trudged onward. At the harbor, he would board a ship where he would have plenty of time to rest from his exertions. Regardless of his pain and discomfort, there was nothing more important than traveling to Marseilles, and from there, Poitiers.

During his convalescence, the alarming discovery that King Richard had sent Marian to Poitiers dominated his thoughts. He knew that she would learn the truth, and he wouldn't be there to explain it to her. He decided to go there without delay and beg Marian to forgive him. Then, he would return to the Holy Land and fulfill his duties to Richard.

He had sacrificed enough for his king; now he would do something for himself and his wife. He smiled at the thought that Marian was his wife. Even if she was furious with him, they were still irrevocably and eternally joined.

When Robin entered the port, he noticed that it was unusually busy. The assembled men were abuzz with conversation, and many seemed angry and agitated. He pushed through the crowd, distracted by the snippets of conversation that he overheard.

"…It happened just after midday."

"The Assassins are famous for striking in broad daylight. They…"

Robin paused to listen, but the men moved away from him. He had heard of the fearsome Assassins; they were Saracen mercenaries known for their willingness to kill for hire. He tried to hear what others were saying. The disjointed fragments of sentences were both intriguing and disturbing.

"…stabbed him in the back…"

"…They captured one, the other was killed…"

"…died in agony. Count Henry left at once—"

This revelation caused Robin to stop in his tracks. These men were talking about Count Henry of Champagne, nephew to both King Richard and King Philippe, a trusted ally of Richard, and one of Robin's friends.

The other men took notice of Robin's eavesdropping, and they stopped talking as they glared at him warily. Robin averted his gaze, for he did not want to be recognized, and he continued his walk towards the ships moored along the pier. Although his curiosity had been roused, he forced himself to refocus on his mission.

Traversing the wharf, he selected the largest vessel and inquired about its itinerary. The ship was traveling to Cyprus, then Sicily, and finally Marseilles. It was perfect for Robin's needs. He informed a sailor that he wished to buy passage, and the young man left to find the captain.

After a short delay, the captain lumbered down the gangway and approached Robin, squinting suspiciously at the thin, pale young man dressed in a nondescript, hooded cloak. He brusquely demanded, "Payment is required up front. I need to see your coins." The scowling captain looked him over from head to foot. "What's the matter with you? You can barely stand. I ain't taking any sick passengers."

Robin knew the captain was within his rights to refuse passage to anyone. He cursed the wave of dizziness that briefly seized him and decided that the best course of action would be to answer honestly. "I'm not sick; I'm recovering from a battle wound." Robin lowered his voice, "I would appreciate your discretion, so please don't reveal this to anyone: I am the Earl of Huntingdon."

The captain's reaction was unexpected. For a few moments, he just stared at Robin, his mouth agape. Then he threw his head back and howled with laughter. Now it was Robin's turn to stare open-mouthed at the other man.

"Was this battle wound to your head?" The captain guffawed.

"I don't understand—"

"You ain't right in the head, and you ain't no Earl of Huntingdon. Everyone knows he was killed months ago."

Robin was flabbergasted. This made no sense. He struggled to respond, but shadows were creeping into the edges of his vision.

The captain continued, "Get away from me before I call for the guards. With the king's assassination, I have more important things to do than bother with you."

The shock of hearing such news cleared the cobwebs from his mind. Robin stepped closer to the man and questioned, "Are you telling me that someone has killed King Richard? When? How?"

The other man pushed him away, and Robin tottered before grabbing a nearby railing to steady himself.

"Get out of here, you daft fool. I'm not talking about King Richard. Yesterday, Assassins killed King Conrad in Tyre. Where have you been that you didn't know this?" The captain studied him with heightened mistrust.

Just then, a contingent of soldiers burst onto the wharves, shouting for everyone to make way. The lead guard announced loudly that they were searching for a man who had escaped from the citadel.

Robin and the captain watched with interest as the soldiers moved through the crowd, methodically inspecting each man.

Someone shouted, "What's this man look like?"

The man in charge replied, "He's a fair-haired Englishman who is thin and sickly. He's delusional and thinks he's a nobleman."

Abruptly, the ship's captain waved at the soldiers and hollered, "He's here! Look!"

Robin looked at the man in surprise, and when he looked back at the soldiers, they were now running towards him and yelling, "Hold him!"

The captain grabbed his arm, and Robin's instincts took command. He pulled away from the man's grasp while kicking him in the knee. Howling in pain, the sea captain released him.

Another pair of hands reached for him, but Robin ducked and sprinted away from the soldiers. He dashed into the maze of narrow alleyways connecting the harbor with the rest of the city. His heart was pounding painfully in his chest. His mouth had become so dry that he was coughing and retching, and his eyesight was growing dimmer by the moment.

He could hear the men behind him. They were getting closer and closer. Robin realized that he was crawling on his hands and knees, no longer able to stand, let alone run. And then an ebony oblivion descended upon him.

29 April 1192, The Royal Palace, Paris, France

Ambroise de Limours, Count de Montlhéry, glided noiselessly along murky corridors lit by flickering torches and paused at a heavy wooden door. He had attended many clandestine meetings with King Philippe in the middle of the night; however, in thirty years of service to the French royal family, he had never delivered bad news. He reviewed his strategy for managing the king and braced himself for an unpleasant confrontation.

The guard, recognizing him as dowager Queen Adela's principal advisor and a man in King Philippe's highest favor, opened the door to the king's private quarters.

Montlhéry strode into the chamber carrying a rolled map that he hoped would convince the king to finance his latest scheme to destroy the Plantagenets.

At that moment, King Philippe emerged from his bedchamber. He did not conceal his growing anger as his eyes locked with Montlhéry's. The young king was dressed in austere black attire, and his stern demeanor was intended to intimidate.

Philippe's cold and imperious voice broke the silence. "I've received word from the Holy Land. Richard is still alive, and you have failed me."

"My lord, I humbly apologize for this fleeting difficulty, but I assure you that I will never fail you." Montlhéry sank to one knee to give the king proper obeisance before standing.

"You don't have my permission to stand," the king haughtily declared.

Montlhéry dutifully dropped to one knee, despite the protests of his aging joints.

Philippe picked up a miniature porcelain lion from a nearby table and flung it across the chamber where it shattered against a wall. "I want him dead!"

Montlhéry cringed slightly. "Sire—"

"No!" roared Philippe. "For four years, I have been listening to your excuses. I have supplied endless amounts of silver, yet two Plantagenets remain, infesting the world with their foul existence."

"Sire—"

"I'm tired of waiting. When will you deliver on your grand promises of glory and power? Are you here to beg for my mercy or my silver?" Philippe's handsome features contorted in undisguised frustration.

Outwardly composed, Montlhéry seethed at having to tolerate such a scolding. "Sire, if you would permit me to explain, you will realize that I'm the bearer of glad tidings."

There was a pause as the king studied the count. "You may rise,

Ambroise, but the only good news that I want to hear is that the lion has been slain."

Montlhéry rose to his feet and grimaced from the twinge that seized his knee, silently cursing Philippe for the humiliation he had endured. He met the king's scrutiny confidently. "Sire, you will be pleased," he insisted, eager to describe the new plot to Philippe. "Although the lion still stalks the Holy Land, he has been seriously wounded."

This piqued the king's interest, and his temper cooled somewhat. "What do you mean?"

"I am happy to announce that Robin Fitzooth, the Earl of Huntingdon, and a constant source of trouble in Nottinghamshire, was killed during the regicide attempt."

Philippe's brow lifted in disbelief. "Robin Hood is dead?"

Smirking with satisfaction, Montlhéry replied, "Yes; Huntingdon will no longer hinder our plans. As one of Richard's most loyal and cunning generals, he has thwarted several schemes to slay the lion. Without him, the king will be more vulnerable to our next attack."

"This is good news, but it is not enough," Philippe admonished.

Montlhéry gave a nod. "As always, sire, your mind is nimble and wise beyond your years. You will be delighted with our brilliant new plan."

"I don't need your flattery; save such fawning for my mother," Philippe reproached him. "My cousin, Hugh of Burgundy, sent me a report that Richard has offered to meet with Saladin to discuss a pathway to peace. He could return in a matter of months."

"This new plot ensures that he will never return," Montlhéry countered.

"Travel between Outremer and England is dangerous. There would be many opportunities for a fatal accident of some sort," the king conceded.

"Sire, you haven't heard the entire plan. I vow that the Lionheart will suffer before he dies."

"I will rejoice at his demise, but it means nothing unless I can assume total dominion over Normandy, Anjou, Poitou, and all of Richard's lands on the continent, as you once promised me."

"You will have the continental lands only if you trust me, sire," assured Montlhéry.

"And if you hope to rule England as my vassal, I need to see more successes from you." Philippe imperiously glared at his advisor. "I question your competence if a renegade earl leading a small band of untrained peasants can interfere with your plans to establish a base of operations in England."

"Sire, if I may be so bold as to remind you that, with Robin Hood in Outremer these past two years, our strategy in England has seen many successes: we control Nottingham, a prosperous, fortified city, we have the complete trust of Prince John, and there are additional English nobles supporting us whose ambition and wealth far outpace their intelligence." He emphasized, "These men think they are helping us put John on the throne, and they will be quite useful to us."

"Are these nobles providing silver and men-at-arms?" Philippe observed the other man, searching for signs of deception.

Montlhéry shrugged. "Of course. But we must be cautious in our dealings with these men. Requesting too much silver from them will raise their suspicions about our true motives."

"Very well then," Philippe sighed in resignation. "What is your plan, and how much will it cost me?"

"The plan has two phases. First, we will besmirch Richard's reputation by spreading rumors, gossip, and lies that cannot be easily disproven. This part of the plan will require very little silver, only a few coins here and there to bishops, clerics, traveling merchants, and trusted nobles." Undeterred by Philippe's frown, Montlhéry persisted. "Like a plague, if the rumors are salacious and interesting enough, they will soon take on a life of their own."

The king was not impressed. "And the second part of the plan? It needs to be more deadly than idle gossip."

"The second part of the plan will require significant upfront investment. However, it promises great rewards. We will capture Richard when he returns from the Holy Land and hold him for ransom," Montlhéry announced.

For a moment, Philippe was silent. This was not at all what he expected. "That is impossible," he huffed. "We don't know when Richard will return or even where he will come ashore."

"Although we don't know when Richard will return, we can spread these rumors now while we lay the groundwork for his capture."

"You haven't answered my question: How will you know Richard's travel itinerary? This is a ridiculous plan." Philippe's eyes narrowed in annoyance; Montlhéry's schemes usually made more sense.

Montlhéry remained unperturbed. "Sire, Hugh of Burgundy will notify us as soon as he learns that Richard is preparing to depart the Holy Land. Consider all the men and military equipment that Richard must transport, and he must also find suitable accommodations for his queen and sister. The women will need a luxurious ship that provides privacy and amenities. There will be plenty of time for us to receive word that the Lionheart is returning home."

Philippe rolled his eyes in exasperation. "Even if we know the date of his departure, we won't know which port with any certainty."

"Sire, your brilliance is a constant source of inspiration for me. That is why I brought this map showing all the important Mediterranean ports." Montlhéry led the king to a nearby table where he unfurled his map and secured the corners with several small pewter plates and a silver candlestick.

He continued, "King Richard has a special talent for making enemies. His marriage to Berengaria has led to an alliance with her father, the King of Navarre. But Navarre is at war with the family which rules Marseilles, and this will prevent him from landing there."

Philippe gazed intently at the map. "That is true."

"Queen Berengaria's brother has recently attacked Toulouse. The Count of Toulouse will always support you over any Plantagenet king."

A faint smile of satisfaction tugged at the corners of Philippe's mouth. "Count Raymond is old and frail, therefore Toulouse is now ruled by my aunt and their son. The younger Raymond is devoted to me and eager to prove himself."

Montlhéry nodded. "Exactly. The younger Raymond will help us monitor all the ports of Toulouse. We can pay him to hire men who are ready to act with very little advance notice."

"What if Richard lands in Italy?" Philippe frowned. "There are excellent ports at Genoa and Pisa. The Pisans are allied with the English."

Montlhéry had anticipated this question. "The Genoese are reliable allies of the French crown, as you know. The Pisans are practical and pious. Once we have ruined Richard's reputation and supplied the Pisans with financial incentives, I am certain that they will allow our mercenaries to monitor their port."

Tapping his finger on the map, Philippe prodded, "And what of Barcelona? I have little influence there."

Again, Montlhéry shrugged. "The ruler of Barcelona is also at war with the Kingdom of Navarre, and he would gladly help us, should Richard disembark there."

Philippe rubbed chin thoughtfully as he studied the map.

"As I said, Richard's talent for making enemies means there is no safe harbor for him when he returns to Europe." Montlhéry grinned, pleased to see that the king was beginning to understand the genius of the plan.

"And there is no other way for him to return home?"

"I suppose he could cross the Alps and go through Austria or Germany. That would be quite an audacious route after the way he insulted Duke Leopold of Austria in Acre and stole Sicily from

Emperor Henry." Unable to maintain an even demeanor, Montlhéry snorted in amusement.

Philippe snickered, and the two men burst into laughter. When they recovered their composure, Philippe conceded, "You are right; even Richard would never do something so foolhardy." Sobering, he mused, "But what would be the purpose of capturing Richard? I want him dead, not in captivity. Are you planning an accident for him? As a returning Crusader, he will be under the protection of the pope."

Bowing slightly in deference to his king, Montlhéry offered, "If you wish for me to arrange a fatal accident, I will happily do it. However, there are other intriguing options which you should consider. Once Richard is within our grasp, you can charge him with any crime that suits our purposes: from robbing holy sites to sodomizing young boys. If it's a serious enough crime, the pope will not protect him."

Philippe whined, "He is popular among his people and considered a great military genius. It will be impossible to destroy his reputation."

With a knowing twinkle in his eye, Montlhéry insisted, "Sire, with all due respect, I believe you are underestimating the power of gossip."

"What if he recaptures Jerusalem? He will return a hero, and nothing we say will change that."

"If he succeeds in taking Jerusalem, we might need to adjust our strategy," Montlhéry admitted. "But he was twelve miles from the Holy City, and he retreated. I believe it is highly unlikely that even the famous Lionheart will reconquer Jerusalem."

Returning to the plan, Philippe queried, "After we capture Richard, how will you kill him without the blame falling upon France? And do you have men in place to eliminate John before he can be crowned?"

"Have you considered bringing Richard to Paris in chains? You could humiliate him in a trial where the verdict would be a foregone conclusion. You could demand a treaty surrendering Normandy and a ransom for his release."

"If he pays a ransom, then he will expect to be released. I want him dead," Philippe demanded.

Montlhéry described the final part of his plan. "While you are securing his ransom, Richard will sicken and die, just like his father and older brother. I've worked with my apothecary to perfect the poison we used on King Henry and Henry the Younger. It kills slowly and inflicts great agony on the person who has ingested it. Remember, no one has ever suspected that their deaths were anything but the result of stomach complaints."

As Philippe contemplated his words, Montlhéry continued, "As for Prince John, he will be the easiest of the Plantagenets to eliminate. There are several options for an accidental death. It could be as simple as sabotaging the strap of his saddle, just as we did with Prince Geoffrey. But first, our priority must be King Richard."

Dawn was breaking, and Philippe stifled a yawn as he signaled his approval of Montlhéry's latest scheme and dismissed him.

4 May 1192, Wallingford Castle, England

As the light of an approaching dawn painted the sky pink and orange, two men dismounted at the foot of the stairs leading into the keep of Wallingford Castle, where Prince John's court was currently residing.

The older man, Alaric de Montabard, Baron de Argentan and Sheriff of Nottingham, was in his mid-fifties, and his thinning hair was transitioning from grey to white. He was somewhat short, with a thin, slight build. His appearance was unremarkable except for the intensity of his dark eyes.

In contrast, the younger man at his side drew the notice of others everywhere he went. He was well over six feet tall, with shoulder-length, chestnut colored hair, striking pale blue eyes, and angular features that made him uniquely attractive. Sir Guy FitzCurzon of Gisborne, captain of the sheriff's guard, was only 32 years old, but he appeared tired and careworn while Argentan was energized and impatient.

"Wait here with the horses, Gisborne," the sheriff commanded. "If all goes as planned, I'll return shortly, and we will leave at once to journey north to Nottingham."

"And if it doesn't go as planned?" Guy grumbled.

Argentan cast a contemptuous glare at his captain. "You are responsible for this disaster, not me. Perhaps you would like to explain to Prince John why you killed Robin Hood instead of the king. You should be groveling at my feet, weeping with heartfelt appreciation for all that I do to protect you from your own idiocy."

Gisborne scowled, but he said nothing more, leading their mounts to a nearby trough while Argentan stalked towards the wide stairs. Prince John was demanding an account of the events in Acre, and he had ordered the sheriff to arrive at dawn for a secret meeting.

Entering the keep, Argentan made his way to the royal apartments, where he hesitated outside the large oak doors as he prepared to confront the difficulties awaiting him within Prince John's chambers. Two guards greeted him by genuflecting and opening the doors.

Argentan strode boldly to the center of the chamber. "I am full of joy to see you again, my glorious liege," he enthusiastically professed in his highly accented English. He then went down on one knee in front of the prince.

John was sitting in an over-sized chair, which resembled a throne. Despite the early hour, he was clean shaven and clothed in his crimson court attire. At the sight of Argentan, he leapt to his feet, growling, "How dare you come here, after what you have done?"

The sheriff rose and beheld him without fear. "My liege, you summoned me to appear at dawn, and I am happily submitting to your will. My life has no other purpose than to humbly and faithfully serve you."

"You said that your strategy could not fail," cried the furious prince. "You swore that I would celebrate my grand coronation in the spring."

"Yes, I promised you that," Argentan replied calmly.

John marched over to him and grabbed the front of his plain black tunic. "Well, your plan failed. I am not king, and I have most likely lost my brother's favor. And it is all your fault!"

The sheriff remained poised. "I will make amends to you, sire."

Staring into the baron's eyes, John hissed, "You have little time to remedy the situation, Baron de Argentan. I have decided to execute you. I will tell Richard that it was all your idea, and that I knew nothing about your evil scheme."

The prince released Argentan and stomped back to his throne, preparing to call for his guards to take the sheriff to the dungeons. However, the sound of chuckling made him turn in surprise.

Argentan grinned. "Sire, you almost had me worried. I have been away for so long that I forgot about your sharp wit."

"What?" Prince John was now perplexed. It was the first time he had ever received such a reaction from a condemned man. His eyes narrowed in suspicion, but he continued in a more personal manner. "Alaric, I will not be held responsible for your plot to murder my dear brother."

"Sire, how could anyone accuse you of such a wicked deed as attempted regicide? It is beyond ridiculous." Argentan walked towards the prince until he was standing very close to this young man who coveted the crown of England. In a quiet voice, he spoke emphatically, "Failure is like the sun, my lord."

John frowned as his confusion deepened. He didn't comprehend Argentan's words, yet he didn't wish to admit that the man's riddles baffled him. Bristling and assuming an impassive expression, he responded, "Of course, Alaric. I know this."

The sheriff nodded perceptively. "Soon you will be king, and the people of England, Normandy, and the Angevin lands will be blessed to have such a benevolent and intelligent man on the throne."

"But the plan failed. Richard lives, and if he blames me, he might seek vengeance," whined John, who was terrified of his formidable brother.

"Be at ease," declared Argentan, his voice soft and insistent. "Failure is like the sun, sire. Its brightness shines in the eyes of all who see it, blinding them to the successes that are hidden in the shadows."

Prince John gazed into Argentan's dark eyes, desperate to understand. "Enough of these riddles, Alaric. Tell me how this debacle could ever be considered a success."

With an air of importance, Argentan proclaimed, "The lion still roars, but he is wounded in his heart: the Earl of Huntingdon was killed by Gisborne, and he will no longer interfere with our plans."

John smiled tentatively. "That is very good news." Still puzzled, he asked, "But how will I take the throne? I cannot be crowned while Richard is alive. And I've been informed that he intends to make peace with the infidels and return home."

Beaming, the sheriff replied, "That is the best news of all, for my strategy guarantees that King Richard will never again set foot on English soil."

CHAPTER 2
THE CHARADE OF HIS LIFE

8 May 1192, The Royal Palace, City of Acre

obin was slowly regaining consciousness. A soft breeze through the chamber's sole window blew a strand of his hair across his face, tickling his nose. When he tried to brush the hair away, he could not move his hand more than a few inches. Returning to full awareness, he realized that his wrists were secured to his bed's headboard with strips of cloth.

He lifted one of his legs and discovered that his ankles were tied to the footboard.

Robin sighed. The previous day, his most recent escape attempt had nearly succeeded, and he recalled how the doctor had forced him to drink a sleeping potion while the guards restrained him.

As he examined his bindings, the sound of approaching footfalls caused him to gaze at the door in anticipation. A key clicked in the lock, and rusty hinges screeched as the aged wooden door swung wide.

He watched as his friend and mentor, Sir André de Chauvigny, burst into the room. Ranulphus Besace, the king's physician, was close on his heels.

André stood there, surveying the scene with undisguised alarm.

He cried, "God in heaven! Why is he tied to the bed? Release him at once."

Ranulphus stepped forward, wringing his hands and trying to explain. "My lord, forgive me, but we had no choice. Lord Huntingdon keeps escaping! At first we posted a guard, but he tricked the man and escaped. Then we posted two guards, and he outwitted them as well. Yesterday, he somehow slipped away again, and this time, he made it to the harbor and onto a ship. We found him just as the ship was pulling anchor. Please, you must talk to him!"

Robin grinned at the distraught physician, defiance gleaming in his eyes. André and Ranulphus untied him, and he sat up, swinging his legs over the side of the bed as he rubbed the chafing on his wrists.

"Is this true, my friend?" André asked.

The sincere concern in his friend's eyes softened Robin's anger at being kept a prisoner in the king's palace at Acre, but he still demanded answers. "Why am I a prisoner here? Either charge me with a crime, or release me. I refuse—"

"My lord," Ranulphus interrupted, "I've told you many times that you are not a prisoner."

"Yet, I am not free to leave, and I'm under heavy guard." Robin glared at the young doctor.

Ranulphus was eager to reassure Robin. "You're not a prisoner, but you have to—"

"Ranulphus, the king is grateful for your service. I need to speak with Lord Huntingdon privately." André gestured towards the door.

Ranulphus bowed low and exited without another word.

For a stretch of time, Robin and André stared at each other until André relented. "My friend, how are your wounds? If you can lead the good doctor and his guards on such merry chases, then you must be much improved."

"I am well enough. Ranulphus would prefer to fuss over me for another month, but that will not happen. I refuse to stay in a sickbed any longer. Where is the king, and what is the current strategy for retaking Jerusalem?"

"Richard is rebuilding the fortress of Ascalon. However, last month he received word from his mother that Prince John is conspiring with King Philippe. She has urged him to resolve matters here and return to England."

A surprised Robin exclaimed, "Queen Eleanor is encouraging Richard to abandon the Crusade? The situation back home must be dire. The Queen Mother has always been passionate about crusading."

André chuckled before sobering. "Have you heard about Conrad de Montferrat? Assassins murdered him, and no one knows who hired them. Hugh of Burgundy is spreading rumors that it was Richard, but that is ridiculous."

"Who will be King of Jerusalem now?" asked Robin.

"Count Henry of Champagne married Conrad's widow several days ago. King Richard is determined to settle the affairs of the Holy Land so he can leave. In the meantime, Richard has a plan for you. Everyone thinks you are dead except for a select group of knights. That is the reason you have been kept here, in this chamber and out of sight."

Robin frowned. "What is the purpose of maintaining the fiction that I am dead?"

"The king wants to send us on a secret assignment, and he believes that keeping your true identity hidden will be important to the success of the mission. I'm here to assess your readiness to return to action and to escort you to the king in Ascalon so he can explain everything. We will leave at first light, and you will travel disguised as a Knight Templar."

"André, the day is young; let's leave now. I can't spend another day trapped in this room." Robin stood and wandered to the window.

André followed him and sympathetically remarked, "You've never liked confinement."

"It's more than that; I need to set my mind free of this prison. You would not understand."

"Try to explain it to me," insisted André.

"I can no longer remain in this chamber, with nothing to do but think about every mistake I've ever made and my many poor decisions. I have no companions except for regret and anger."

"You're worried about Marian."

Resentment flashed in Robin's pale blue eyes. "Why in God's name did Richard send her to Poitiers? Why didn't you stop him?"

"I didn't think about the consequences of Marian going to Poitiers. I know that Richard sent Tuck, a Knight Templar, to follow her and ensure that she safely arrived at court. But they sailed before we discovered that you were alive."

"I'm glad that a trained knight was guarding her on her voyage, but that does not solve the problem of her going to Poitiers. I must go to her and explain everything. Then I can return here to serve Richard."

"Is that why you keep going to the harbor?" At Robin's nod, André continued, "Do you remember Sir Juan of Navarre?"

Again, Robin nodded. He remembered very well the affable Spanish knight who had long served King Richard's wife, Berengaria, in her homeland of Navarre.

"A fortnight ago, Richard sent Juan to Navarre with messages from Queen Berengaria to her family. We will rendezvous with Juan in Navarre, and then the three of us will travel to Poitiers, where we will meet with the Queen Mother and proceed with Richard's plan. He will give us more details when we see him."

Robin's mood lifted. He would reunite with Marian in a matter of weeks.

André continued, "While we are on this mission, Richard will work towards ending the Crusade. Perhaps we will be home by the end of the year."

Robin smiled wistfully at the mention of going home. But

thoughts of home also reminded him of Argentan and Gisborne, and he growled, "When we return home, we will restore justice to England."

André declared, "King Richard will execute all traitors, and the one called Gisborne will suffer before his death. The men are eager to capture Gisborne; they call him Robin Hood's murderer."

Bitterness and disgust towards Gisborne filled Robin's heart, but he knew that he could not kill his own half-brother.

André interrupted his dark musings. "I will return at first light tomorrow, and then we will travel to Ascalon. Enjoy this comfortable bed tonight, for there won't be much opportunity to rest in the coming weeks and months."

16 May 1192, Dover, England

As the first shadows of twilight arrived in the harbor town of Dover, the activities that occupied the hours of daylight—loading and unloading ships, making repairs and performing maintenance on the vessels—were giving way to the deeds of darkness which took place every night in the inns and taverns that lined the main thoroughfare.

A man in a nondescript, hooded cloak slipped into a large tavern with a wooden sign depicting a hawk clutching a dead dove in its talons. Both sailors and traveling nobility frequented this well-known tavern, and it was called *The Hawk and the Dove*.

A short, middle-aged man with greying hair sidled up to the stranger as he entered. "My lord," he beckoned, "I am Bazile, and I welcome you to my humble tavern. How may I serve you?"

The man replied, "I'm here to meet someone. I was told that I would find him in the shadows."

Recognizing the coded message, Bazile smiled. "Follow me; he is awaiting your arrival."

The stranger trailed Bazile through the maze of empty trestle tables and benches in the central room of the structure. It was still early, and the place was deserted. In the back was a small alcove, and it was indeed shadowy. The candle on the table provided only a flickering illumination, just enough to reveal the presence of a man, but not enough to see his features.

"Leave us, Bazile," ordered the man at the table.

"Yes, my lord. Let me know if you would like ale or food." The tavern owner bowed low and departed.

"Baron de Argentan, I presume?" the stranger inquired.

Argentan dipped his head in acknowledgment and said, "I am pleased to meet you. I've heard many good things about you from our mutual friends. The prince himself mentioned to me how much he values your support. Please, join me."

The other man took the vacant seat and spoke in a hushed tone. "I am eager to offer my services to support Prince John. What do you need?"

Leaning forward and continuing in a quiet voice, Argentan responded, "The prince has limited access to the treasury. We need silver to keep our efforts funded. I know that Prince John will generously repay his supporters."

The stranger frowned. "I will give everything I can, but I don't have much money."

"My plan will not require that you contribute your personal funds. I'm asking for your help in obtaining the funds of someone else."

A short time later, the two men prepared to leave the tavern.

The stranger's brow creased. "This is a dangerous game that you are proposing."

Irritation flashed in Argentan's dark eyes. "There is risk in any game that promises such a profitable reward, but since you will be in control, I'm surprised that you would hesitate."

They walked out of the tavern and into the street. The setting sun lit the building's façade, and a young nobleman hastened to Argentan's companion.

"You!" he cried. "I almost didn't recognize you. Why are you dressed like that? Are you traveling to the continent? And you're with Baron de Argentan! I didn't realize that the two of you were acquainted."

The man with Argentan grabbed the nobleman and pulled him into a nearby alleyway.

"What are you doing?" protested the noble.

Argentan waited as the sounds of a scuffle ensued. When he heard a dull thud, he peeked around the corner to see his companion cleaning his bloodied dagger on the noble's expensive cloak. The young man was lying on his back and frantically grasping at a gash that traversed the front of his neck. Blood poured out of his body, gushing between his fingers and forming an ever-widening circle in the dirt. The only sound was an eerie gurgling.

The two conspirators silently observed as the man's motions became weaker. His hands relaxed and fell away from his throat, and the crimson flow diminished. Abruptly, he stilled, and his soul departed.

Without hesitation, the other man leaned over and cut the cord that secured a leather pouch to the dead noble's belt. It was heavy with coins, and he handed it to Argentan. "Here is my first contribution," he proclaimed, grinning.

Argentan chuckled warmly. "I like how you handle yourself. Stop worrying about the plan. Organizing the abduction will be the easiest thing you ever do, and I will manage the ransom and everything else. You will never regret joining me in support of Prince John."

21 May 1192, Locksley Manor, Nottinghamshire

Dusk was descending upon Locksley. It was unusually cold and damp for May, and the village was empty as most people had already retreated into their homes for the night. A morose, solitary man approached the main entrance to Locksley Manor, its façade lit by the grey light of a clouded sunset. He paused before entering, contemplating the lantern which brightened the door with its soft orange glow, creating a sense of warmth and welcome that caused him to frown at the unintended irony. He knew that he was not welcome here.

Sir Guy of Gisborne stood at the door, brooding over the charade of his life. He had just returned from a journey into his past, and he grappled with the frustration of failing to find answers to his many questions.

During the long voyage from Acre, Guy had spent an inordinate amount of time thinking about his father—his real father—Duncan Fitzooth. He was angry at his mother for keeping the truth from him. And he was curious about this man whom he had been taught to hate from a young age. Searching for answers, Guy had traveled to the village of Gisborne, and then to the town of Huntingdon.

At Gisborne, he found that the barony was situated on lowlands along the river. Gisborne Lodge, which should have been his ancestral home, was partially collapsed and flooded. Guy did not reveal his name to the villagers, so they were naturally suspicious of the stranger with a thick French accent, and they refused to talk to him.

In Huntingdon, people were more hospitable, but they were reluctant to discuss Duncan. In contrast, they were effusive in their praise of Robin and unaware that he had died in Acre. Huntingdon was a wealthy and modern town, buzzing with activity. With bitterness and envy, Guy could not help but reflect on how the ruins of Gisborne and the splendor of Huntingdon were perfect metaphors for his life and Robin's.

If only Duncan had married his mother. Guy would have been the eldest son and heir. He would be the Earl of Huntingdon! However, as a bastard son, there was no hope of inheritance, even with Robin's death. He doubted that he could prove that Duncan was his father. Too much time had gone by, and both of his parents were dead.

After a prolonged hesitation, Guy entered Locksley Manor and was greeted by Leofric, the elderly servant who managed the estate. At Leofric's side was Elvina, an older woman who had once served Robin's mother, Lady Edith.

Guy studied them, and swallowing his pride, he decided that they were his only hope. They had both known Duncan. "Come with me," he commanded. "There is something I want to discuss with you." He led them to the hearth at the far end of the manor's great hall.

Leofric and Elvina reluctantly followed him.

"My lord, are you displeased?" Leofric inquired.

"I'm ordering you to tell me everything you know about Duncan Fitzooth."

Leofric and Elvina glanced at each other. They did not trust this ruthless, demanding man who had stolen Locksley from their beloved Robin.

Elvina, fearless and direct as always, countered, "Will we be punished for saying something that you don't like?"

Sighing, Guy knew he would need to offer them an incentive. "Just tell me the truth, and I will not punish you for anything you say. I will also arrange for all the servants to have a special meal this Sunday."

"What is it you wish to know, my lord?" asked Leofric.

"Tell me about Duncan Fitzooth. What kind of man was he? You served him; you should be able to tell me about him."

"I won't speak ill of the dead!" cried Elvina.

Guy gazed at her intently. "I wasn't asking you to criticize him; I only want the truth."

Elvina paled, realizing that she had perhaps revealed more than she intended.

Leofric clarified, "My lord, we served his wife, Lady Edith." The two servants paused and crossed themselves, as if they were speaking the name of a holy saint.

cringed at the sight. He could easily imagine everyone
.hemselves at the mention of Robin Hood after they
learned of his death in Acre.

Elvina continued, "The de Toury family of Embelton, a barony
in the north, originally owned Locksley. It was given to Lady Edith
when she married Lord Duncan as part of her dowry. Leofric and
I moved from Embelton to Locksley to serve her. She spent most
of her time here, while Lord Duncan traveled between London,
Huntingdon, and Locksley."

Guy frowned as he considered this. "Lady Edith did not live
in Huntingdon?"

Elvina explained, "She felt uncomfortable there because she was
a stranger while everyone knew Lord Duncan very well."

"Where did Robin live?"

"Lord Robin lived in Locksley when he was a child," Leofric responded. "After the death of his mother, he went to live in
Huntingdon with his father. Soon after that, he left for Poitou to
further his education."

"And you can't tell me anything about Lord Duncan?" prodded Guy.

Again, the two glanced at each other before Leofric offered,
"He was tall and very proud. Servants were invisible to him; I don't
believe he even knew our names."

A touch of bitterness colored Elvina's humorless chuckle. "All
the ladies in Huntingdon and at court found him irresistible."

Leofric cautioned Elvina with a small shake of his head.

Guy considered their words for a few moments before demanding, "Send ale and a meal up to my bedchamber." He then strode
away, mounting the stairs that led to the upper level of the manor.

After Gisborne had departed, Leofric commented, "Gisborne's
questions are unexpected. What could be his purpose?"

"I'm sure he has some evil intent. I cannot bear to see this vicious man without a conscience pretending to be Lord of Locksley," Elvina complained.

"When the Crusade is over and Robin returns, he will banish Gisborne."

Elvina smiled. "Perhaps when Robin returns, he will hold a grand feast and invite Lord Edmund and his family. Do you recall the feasts we had so many years ago? Remembering those times brings me such a mixture of joy and sorrow."

"Robin was always closer to Edmund than to his own father."

"It's odd that Gisborne is asking about Duncan," mused Elvina.

"Duncan and Robin were so different," Leofric recalled, his expression thoughtful as his mind drifted back to the days of Robin's youth. "Duncan was suspicious of peasants and servants. He believed that he needed to instill fear in us, or we would steal from him."

Elvina chuckled. "Thanks be to God that Robin never shared his father's views! He knows the name of every peasant and servant in Locksley. He cares about us." She smiled fondly. "That's why he became Robin Hood."

❦

In the grand bedchamber set aside for the lord of the manor, Guy stood and peered into a polished disk hanging on the wall. Its shiny surface served as a mirror, but his features were distorted in the uneven, poorly lit reflection. The only thing he could see clearly were a pair of pale blue eyes, so much like his half-brother and apparently just like their father.

The revelation of his mother's adulterous affair with Duncan Fitzooth had devastated Guy's world. Her deceptions aggrieved and angered him, but she was his beloved mother, and he still missed her, even though she had been dead for many years.

He was also terrified that Robin's death had irrevocably damned his soul. After all, fratricide had been the first murder ever committed, and it had condemned Cain to the eternal fires of hell.

Again and again, Guy wished he could go back and kill King Richard instead of Robin. He was convinced that Prince John would have rewarded him with titles and wealth. He would have been safe from any repercussions of the regicide.

Marian... He was bereft at the knowledge that the woman he loved was forever lost to him.

A wave of fury passed through him. All this was her fault. Had she not confessed her love for Robin, Guy would not have been possessed by the blind rage that drove him to rush forward and stab the source of his humiliation and heartbreak: Robin Hood.

He tried to decide who was most to blame for the sorry state of his life. Closing his eyes, Guy muttered to his dead brother. "It's just as much your fault too; if you had not stolen Marian from me, I would not have stabbed you."

Anger, guilt, and fear for his soul hardened his heart. Once more, he gazed into the mirror and spoke to the pale blue eyes staring back at him. "And now neither of us will have her, Huntingdon. We both lost her!" He barked out a short, humorless laugh.

Robin Hood's murderer was falling into a dark, grisly abyss. He reached for the ale that had been brought to him with his meal. Leaving the food untouched, he resolved to find relief and escape within the depths of his goblet.

CHAPTER 3
PERSUASIVE PROPOSALS

2 June 1192, Locksley Manor

uy was lost in the thick forest surrounding Locksley. It occurred to him that he should be more worried; the greenwood was a dangerous place because it was the realm of Robin Hood. Poachers and bandits could be hiding behind any tree, ready to attack.

A flash of red caught his eye. He was certain that it must be Marian, and he had to find her. He hesitated. It made no sense for Marian to be here. And she would hardly welcome his help. There was something very wrong with his situation; it did not feel real.

The icy water that cascaded over his head was certainly real.

Guy jerked to attention and raised his arms in self-defense. Through bleary eyes, he saw a dark figure looming over him, and he lunged towards his assailant. The shadowy figure stepped to the side, and Guy stumbled forward, landing on his knees.

As he shook the cobwebs from his mind and wiped the dampness from his face, he recognized that it was morning, and that he was in the great hall of Locksley manor, where he had been sitting and drinking heavily the night before, as he had been every evening since his return to Locksley twelve days ago.

A throbbing headache and nausea caused him to rub his forehead and moan.

Someone cleared his throat, and Guy squinted at the other man, only to discover that it was the sheriff who was standing in front of him and grinning with delight.

Now fully alert, Guy wobbled awkwardly as he rose to his feet. "My lord, I was not expecting you today. I apologize for not greeting you properly."

"Gisborne, I hope you enjoyed my little gift to you this morning. There's nothing like a cold bath to start the day. Isn't that right, Payen?"

Guy noticed Tancred de Payen standing behind the sheriff. The young knight's unnaturally pale skin, grey emotionless eyes, and white hair gave him a ghostly appearance, and his talent for mixing poisons disgusted Guy, who considered poisoning to be dishonorable.

The sheriff ordered Payen to wait outside, and the pallid knight slithered out the front door of the manor.

Switching to French, which ensured that none of the servants could eavesdrop, Argentan revealed, "I wish to make an important announcement. Are you listening, Gisborne?"

The mischievous glint in the sheriff's eyes put Guy on guard. He politely answered, "Yes, my lord."

"I have secured the support of a wealthy baron in our quest to place Prince John on the throne of England. There's just one problem. His daughter needs a husband."

The pounding in Guy's head intensified.

Argentan good-naturedly thumped Guy on the back. "Congratulations, Gisborne! I have arranged for you to marry this girl! Sadly, you cannot inherit the barony because the baron has an heir, but you never know, maybe his son will succumb to one of those stomach ailments that are so prevalent these days."

Guy was speechless for a few moments, staring at the sheriff and waiting for him to laugh and confess that he was joking. When the time stretched, a sickening dread settled upon him. Argentan was serious.

"I don't want to marry this girl," Guy asserted as forcefully as he could.

The sheriff's face darkened as he took a step towards Guy, who instinctively stepped back.

"When you killed Robin Hood instead of King Richard, you forfeited any right to make decisions. You *will* marry this girl."

Dismayed, Guy lowered his gaze. "I know I disappointed you, my lord, but... why do you want me to marry this girl?"

"Her father is not sufficiently enthusiastic in his support for Prince John. Having his daughter under my control will ensure his continued generosity. However, I'm certainly not going to marry her, so you will do it. You should thank me; you might receive a dowry."

The idea of additional wealth lifted Guy's spirits, especially since he might have to go into hiding once word of his involvement in Robin Hood's death reached England. Besides, the events in Acre had destroyed his hope of wedding Marian, so perhaps marrying a wealthy heiress would be a good option for him. "Who is this girl?" he asked warily.

"Her name is Constance de Toury, and her father is the Baron of Embelton. Payen and I have just returned from a trip to the north where we met the baron and his charming daughter. She will be perfect for you."

Argentan then snickered maliciously, and Guy cringed, imagining the worse. The girl was probably ugly and ill-tempered. At that moment, a niggling memory tugged at his mind. Where had he heard of Embelton?

Like the frigid water the sheriff had used to wake him, a sudden cold realization washed over him. Embelton was the barony of Robin Hood's uncle. It was the place where they had found Marian after two years of searching for her.

"But... but... this girl is Robin Hood's cousin. I cannot marry her; she is my cousin as well."

"Don't be sentimental!" Argentan scolded. "I can tolerate your incompetence but not your melodramatics. She is not related to Duncan, but to Robin Hood's mother. Therefore, you don't share any blood with her."

Guy countered, "The church does not see it that way. Canon law—"

"Don't you dare preach to me, you bastard son of an English traitor!" Argentan roared. "I am doing you a kindness. Marrying this girl will give you legal rights to Locksley."

"But I'm already Lord of Locksley. When Huntingdon became an outlaw, I was granted this estate by Prince John as a reward for my loyal service."

"Gisborne, has the ale clouded your mind? King Richard declared Huntingdon innocent of Lord Alfred's murder and pardoned him for his exploits in the woods. His titles and lands were restored to him."

Guy realized that the sheriff was right; if Robin Hood had not left for the Crusade, Guy would have lost his claim to Locksley long ago. However, because King Richard had given dominion over Nottinghamshire to Prince John, Guy had been allowed to keep the small fiefdom.

Argentan continued, "Huntingdon died unmarried and childless. Lord Embelton is his closest male relative, and he will inherit Huntingdon's titles and lands, including Locksley. Marry this girl, and I'll force him to give you Locksley as part of his daughter's dowry."

"Thank you, my lord," Guy replied.

"As you can see, my benevolence to you knows no bounds," proclaimed the sheriff. "In the meantime, your marriage to his daughter and my control over the fate of his son will ensure that the baron fully cooperates with my demands."

"How will you control his son?" Guy inquired.

"That is not your concern." Argentan cackled, enjoying the moment. "Unfortunately, your marriage bed will be crowded: there will be you, your bride, and your guilty conscience. I can hardly wait until she discovers that she is married to the murderer of her dear cousin!"

The uncomfortable truth of the sheriff's words caused Guy to pace to a nearby window. Beyond the small village, he beheld the verdant expanse of Sherwood Forest as it stretched to the horizon. The stark contrast between the splendor of the sunny, late spring day and the bleak and darkened interior of Locksley Manor reminded him of the hopelessness of his life—forever viewing distant beauty from within the shadowy confines of his enslavement to the sheriff.

Argentan joined him at the window and declared, "Emotion should never be important in a man's life. Only weak men are governed by soft, sentimental feelings."

"Yes, my lord," Guy responded woodenly as he faced his master.

"Gisborne, never forget that a woman's charms are only sweet on the surface. All women are filled with a foul poison. Look at what this viper, Marian, has done to you: she has robbed you of what little sense you possessed. But it is not too late for you to heed my warnings and follow my wise counsel." His voice hardened. "Consider the fate of Robin Hood: you saw him embracing Lady Viper, and it was his love for this obnoxious woman that led to his death at your hand."

"Indeed," Guy bitterly agreed.

The sheriff jabbed his finger into Guy's chest, purposefully aiming for his heart; the same location as his fatal attack on Robin. "You cannot love anyone, Gisborne. Love, tenderness, and sentimental yearnings are inexcusable weaknesses for a man with ambition." He laughed, and it was a vinegary, abhorrent sound. "I understand that you are a man with physical needs. Take this bride and make her a vessel to satisfy your lusts, but nothing more. Do not let the venom of a viper destroy your future."

High-pitched shrieks interrupted them.

"No! Stop!"

Guy rushed out of the manor, followed by the sheriff, and they found Payen and Odella locked in a struggle.

Odella, a Locksley servant, was a young, pretty girl with curly, dark-blonde hair and a slender build. Her father, Osmund, was a widower and the Locksley blacksmith, and he had not yet met any man good enough to marry his only child, for she was the jewel of his heart.

When Guy and Argentan arrived on the scene, they saw Payen holding Odella by her upper arms as she fought to escape his grasp. When he released her, he struck her across the face, and she tumbled into the dirt.

A roar echoed throughout the yard as Osmund, a large, muscular man, ran towards Payen with remarkable speed. He shouted, "I'll kill you, you dog!"

Before the outraged father could attack the pale knight, four guards from the castle tackled him and held him back.

Payen moved towards Odella, who was cowering on the ground, her lip and nose bloodied, but Guy grabbed him while Elvina helped the girl to her feet.

An amused Argentan silently observed the dispute.

Guy released the other knight and warned, "Touch her again, and I'll order the men to let go of her father."

Payen whined, "I did nothing wrong. This whore insulted me."

At that, Osmund bellowed at Payen, issuing a barrage of verbal abuse as the guards labored to restrain him.

Guy ignored Payen, asking, "What happened, Odella?"

Odella wiped at the tears rolling down her face and lifted her chin in defiance. "That man offered me coins for the use of my body, and I told him I wasn't that kind of girl. Then he grabbed me and told me he would just take what he wanted."

Payen scoffed. "That's a lie. We were merely haggling over price."

This instigated another cry of outrage from Osmund, and Guy

gestured for the man to be quiet before addressing Payen. "This girl is not a whore; she is a servant in the kitchens of Locksley Manor. As Lord of Locksley, I demand that you leave her alone. Don't ever touch her again."

"You're keeping her for yourself," accused Payen.

Guy rolled his eyes.

Argentan finally interceded. "Come, Payen. Our business here is finished. We must return to Nottingham before sunset."

The soldiers freed Osmund, who hurried to his beloved daughter and hugged her, hoping to comfort the teary-eyed girl.

Their horses were tethered nearby, so Argentan, Payen, and their men swiftly mounted and left.

Guy was relieved that the girl was not hurt, and he turned to walk back to the manor.

"My lord," the deep voice of the blacksmith beckoned to him.

Glancing over his shoulder, Guy looked at Osmund, who was still protectively embracing his daughter.

"Thank you." The earnest gratitude on the face of the blacksmith was a welcome change from the hostile suspicion that typically greeted Guy whenever he interacted with the people of Locksley.

Guy nodded at the man and returned to the manor.

10 June 1192, Locksley Cemetery

Guy strode towards the cemetery behind the Locksley church. Earlier, Leofric had brought him a cryptic message scrawled on a scrap of paper:

I can tell you about Duncan. Come to the cemetery at midday.

Under a large tree at the far edge of the graveyard stood a middle-aged man with wavy blonde hair that was greying at his temples. Typical for men of his age, he was becoming a bit thick around his waist, but Guy suspected that he was still adept at handling the sheathed sword that hung from his belt.

At the sound of Guy's arrival, the man looked up and announced, "I've known Leofric and Elvina all my life, and they tell me you have questions about Duncan Fitzooth."

"You have me at a disadvantage, sir," responded Guy. "Who are you?"

"I am Edmund de Toury, the Baron of Embelton."

Guy dropped to one knee to give the baron proper obeisance before rising. The two men studied each other for a few moments until Guy broke the silence. "You summoned me here, so I assume you have something to say."

Edmund marveled, "I would recognize you anywhere. You are Duncan and Lucienne's son. It is obvious."

This insight did not impress Guy. "Tell me about Duncan."

Edmund gestured at the stones in the ground. One stone was weathered, but the name *Edith* was still readable. The other one had the name *Duncan Fitzooth* carved into the surface. "My dear sister rests here. Duncan is buried somewhere in France."

Guy stared at him without responding.

Again, Edmund inspected the younger man. "You look like your mother, although your height reminds me of Duncan. And you have the Huntingdon—"

"Eyes," interjected Guy with an unmistakable impatience.

A shadow of irritation passed over Edmund's features. "I will answer your questions, but first I'm asking you to keep your relationship to Duncan a secret. Do not tell anyone, not even my daughter, Constance. Don't dishonor my beloved sister by revealing her shame to the world—that her husband was unfaithful."

"Sheriff de Argentan already knows, but he will not tell anyone, and neither will I. Frankly, I would rather be the legitimate son of Hugh of Gisborne than the bastard son of Duncan," admitted Guy.

Edmund seemed relieved to hear this, and he divulged, "You were born in Embelton, in my keep. Duncan begged me to hide Lucienne, to protect Edith from the truth. But she was no fool; she knew that Duncan was unfaithful, especially when he spent months away from her at court."

"And you agreed to deceive your sister?" Even though Guy did not know this man, it still seemed surprising that he would lie to a sister he claimed to love.

"I did not want to deceive her. However, when Lucienne was with child, Edith was also expecting. She had suffered several miscarriages, and Duncan and I were worried that the strain of learning the truth about Lucienne would endanger Edith's life and the life of her unborn babe. That is the only reason I allowed Duncan to send Lucienne to my home—for Edith's sake, not for Duncan's convenience."

Guy pondered this. "I don't remember living anywhere but the city of Montlhéry."

"You were very young when my wife and I insisted that you and your mother could no longer remain in Embelton."

"You claim that you willingly sheltered my mother. But when she gave birth to a son, a possible heir, you evicted us from your home?"

Edmund explained, "Lucienne was convinced that Duncan was planning to send my sister to an abbey, annul his marriage on some pretext, and then marry her. After all, she had borne him a healthy son, while Edith's son was stillborn. It would be another six years before Edith gave birth to a healthy baby." He recalled, "I found your mother's obsession with Duncan to be disturbing, and so did my wife. That's why I insisted that Duncan send her back to France. I was under the impression that he sent money to support the two of you. But I never discussed it with him again."

Guy contemplated Edmund's words. The characterization of his mother's feelings for Duncan as an obsession triggered uncomfortable thoughts about his love for Marian. The question of whether he had been similarly infatuated flitted through his mind, but he dismissed the idea. Only women were emotional and irrational to the point of obsession.

Guy focused on a more relevant issue. He knew that the sheriff had some kind of hold over Edmund's son, but since Argentan had refused to provide any details, he hoped to learn more from the baron himself. "Why have you switched your allegiance from King Richard to Prince John?"

Edmund protested, "I would never support that inept boy over a warrior like Richard."

"But the sheriff—"

"The sheriff has kidnapped my son, Lionel, and if I do not comply with his demands to fund the plot against King Richard, he will kill him."

This unexpected news troubled Guy, since the sheriff usually told him about such schemes and expected his help.

"Gisborne, I'm here to make you an offer. Help me recover my son, safe and sound, and I will make you a wealthy man. Land, silver, whatever you want, just help me rescue Lionel."

"My lord, I know nothing about your son's kidnapping."

"But you are Argentan's captain," countered Edmund.

Guy shrugged. "The sheriff has many secrets, and he rarely tells me everything. I can't help you."

"That's unfortunate. However, I have one more proposition for you. Surely you realize that Argentan is forcing my daughter to marry you. The marriage will not be valid because she is unwilling. Do you understand this?"

"Yes, I know this. Canon law decrees that forced marriages are invalid," replied Guy in an even tone.

"If you cannot help me rescue my son before your marriage to Constance, then the marriage, valid or not, must happen. I'm offering you monthly payments of silver if you promise to leave my daughter untouched. Do not take her to your bed, and I will pay you handsomely. In addition, when King Richard returns, I will help you leave England and escape the king's retribution. I know that Robin loves his cousin very much, and if you keep her safe, then Robin will also reward you."

Guy looked away as the blood drained from his face. Evidently, Edmund had not yet learned of Robin's death. Nevertheless, a secret source of income, hidden from the sheriff, would give him another option for escape if the sheriff's schemes failed again.

It was a persuasive proposal that he could not refuse, and he met Edmund's gaze. "My lord, I accept your offer. I only ask that you deliver the silver to me in a way that keeps Argentan in the dark. In return, I promise that I will not consummate this marriage. I have never taken a woman by force, and I swear that I will not take your daughter by force either."

Edmund had been standing stiffly during the tense conversation with Gisborne. The moment he received Gisborne's earnest assurances, he faltered, swaying slightly as one of the twin terrors abiding in his heart was vanquished. If Guy had refused to cooperate, Edmund would have been compelled to choose between the life of his son and the safety and happiness of his daughter.

After a few more words, the men parted ways.

CHAPTER 4
THE FEAST OF MIDSUMMER

24 June 1192, Sherwood Forest, Near the Fortress of Nottingham

"I think we should tie him behind a horse and drag him through the village and into the forest. That would be a miserable death," Will suggested.

Much had a better idea. "That death is too quick. I want to stab him in the stomach with a small dagger. The wound will not kill him immediately. Instead, he will live long enough for it to fester. That is the most miserable way to die."

Little John grunted appreciatively; he liked both ideas.

The day was drawing to a close, and Marian was sitting on the ground with the three men in a thickly wooded area near the fortress of Nottingham as they awaited Allan's return.

She was morbidly fascinated by the men's proposals for killing Guy of Gisborne.

"Let's cut him up, piece by piece. We'll start by cutting off his—" John stopped abruptly.

"Cut off his what?" asked Marian. When she saw John pale and Will blush, she knew the answer to her question. She also blushed.

"What is taking Allan so long?" Much hastily changed the subject.

Marian stood and walked to the tree line of the forest, and the men followed her. They were on a hill that overlooked the river, and on the far side of the river, steep cliffs jutted out of the ground. The castle walls were perched at the top of the cliffs, and beyond the walls stood the stone keep of Nottingham castle. The tallest part of the keep was the tower where Sheriff de Argentan held court.

Marian remembered only too well her visits to that tower room. She shivered at the memory and drew Robin's cloak around her shoulders. Upon her return to Nottinghamshire, she had gone to the old hunting lodge where she found a trunk belonging to Robin. His clothing was too big for her, but she had made a few alterations, and now she wore his clothes, including the hooded cloak that had been partly responsible for his outlaw name. Even though the clothing had lost Robin's scent, it still made her feel closer to him.

She also had his bow slung across her shoulder and his quiver tied to her belt. She had planned to carry his sword, but it was so long that its tip dragged on the ground when the sheath was attached to her belt. The weight of the sword was another problem, so she carried a dagger instead.

At that moment, Allan emerged from the thick brush surrounding them.

"What is happening at the castle?" Marian inquired.

"Visitors have arrived for the Feast of Midsummer," Allan reported. "I met with Kenric's friend who works in the kitchens. He says there are many wealthy nobles in attendance, and he believes it is a meeting of Prince John's supporters."

"Does he know their names?" asked Much.

Allan shook his head. "But there was something else he told me. I questioned him about Argentan and Gisborne, and he said that Gisborne is getting married the first of next month at the Locksley church."

"Really?" Marian's eyebrows lifted in disbelief. "Who would marry such a monster?"

Allan shrugged. "It's the daughter of a wealthy baron. He couldn't remember the name."

"We should kill Gisborne before the wedding," John proclaimed. "It ain't proper to make some lady a widow." He then glanced apprehensively at Marian, hoping that he hadn't upset her.

Marian's eyes shimmered with sorrow, but she did not cry.

Much angrily interjected, "We must kill Gisborne at once. He has no right to be breathing the same air as Lady Marian!"

John was formulating a plan. "We will wait along the road between Nottingham and Locksley and ambush him."

"What if his betrothed is with him? We can't kill him in front of a lady," Allan insisted.

"Let's drag him into the forest before killing him. Then she won't see it," offered Will.

The flow of ideas between the four men intensified as each gave his opinion and attempted to shout down competing schemes.

The noise became unbearable for Marian; she covered her ears and yelled, "Quiet!" She was astonished when the men stilled and gazed attentively at her. She had never commanded such obedience from men, and she was briefly frozen in shock.

Suddenly, an idea formed in her mind. It was audacious and unprecedented. But in that moment, she knew exactly what she wanted to do. Rallying her courage, she declared, "We will punish both Gisborne and Argentan, but I want them to know that their suffering is the result of what they did to Robin. And I also want to ensure that Robin's legacy is protected. Will you follow me as you once followed Robin?"

"My lady, how can you lead us? You are but a girl. What if you are captured or injured?" Little John's concerned, fatherly gaze caused Marian to swallow nervously.

Undeterred, she asserted, "Robin and his uncle Edmund taught me how to use weapons and how to think strategically. John, you will be my captain and assist me."

"We are only four men. We cannot prevail against the sheriff and his soldiers," Allan reminded them.

This instigated another round of arguing, and Marian again bade them to be quiet. She was pleased when they obeyed her without complaint. Gaining confidence, she acknowledged, "We might be at a disadvantage in numbers, but we are on the side of what is right. If we cannot use brute force to succeed, then we will outwit our enemy."

Her words impressed the men. Perhaps she could lead them in the spirit of Robin Hood.

Little John went down on one knee in front of Marian, and the others echoed his movements. The outlaw pledged, "My lady, we are ready to dedicate our lives to serving you."

Their show of devotion touched Marian's heart. Realizing that the sun was dipping below the horizon, she instructed everyone to return to the small camp they had made nearby. As they left, Marian glanced over her shoulder at the sheriff's tower. With the coming of twilight, she could see that its windows were brightly lit, and she wondered what nefarious plots were being hatched by Argentan and Gisborne.

24 June 1192, Nottingham Castle

In the sheriff's tower room, Guy stood at the window and watched as the shadows of dusk spread across the vast forest. He was thinking about Marian and wondering if she had remained in the Holy Land. Trying to distract himself from thoughts of the woman he had loved and lost, he opened the small wooden box that he held and studied the brooch that was snuggled within the folds of its dark velvet lining.

He had gone to the marketplace and searched for a suitable gift to present to his betrothed. He recalled the elaborate brooch he had purchased for Marian. It had cost him two month's wages! But there would be no affection behind this gift. With that in mind, he had selected an inexpensive brooch. It was silver, and the face was decorated with a series of interwoven concentric circles. The merchant had described it as a Celtic brooch, and the design had fascinated Guy. Nevertheless, he knew that Robin's cousin would likely find it too plain. After all, there were no gems affixed to it.

"Gisborne, your bride has arrived."

Guy jumped nervously, as the sheriff had crept up behind him while he had been lost in his thoughts. He followed the sheriff to the middle of the room and stood next to Argentan's large, cluttered desk.

The doors swung open, and Guy recognized Edmund de Toury as he strolled into the room. Behind the baron, a tall, thin woman followed. A surge of revulsion rose within his heart. Had the sheriff purposefully found a bride who was the opposite of everything he desired in a woman? Her long face was framed by hair as black as a raven's wing, and it was braided and coiled around her head like a crown. Her slender form lacked Marian's generous curves, and she was wearing an elaborately embroidered blue silk bliaut that likely cost more than the value of last season's harvest at Locksley. A necklace with a large blue stone surrounded by small diamonds sparkled as it rested on her chest, suspended by a silver chain. Guy felt embarrassed by his gift. Would she laugh at it? Clearly, this was a woman of great wealth and privilege.

Argentan graciously made the introductions. "Lord Edmund, Lady Constance, let me present Sir Guy of Gisborne."

Guy went down on one knee in front of Edmund. Rising, he bowed low before Constance.

Argentan was exuberant, savoring the control he exerted over these three pawns in his game. He announced, "Sir Guy is the son of a baron, although his inheritance was stolen from him. I have taken him under my wing, and he is like a son to me. Therefore, I'm pleased to see him settled in such a fortunate match."

There was an awkward silence until Guy mumbled, "Thank you, my lord."

"Is that all you have to say, Gisborne?" The sheriff affected mock distress. "After what I have done for you? I've secured the hand of this stunning vision of loveliness for you, and my generosity has both enriched you and protected you from harm. Where would you be without me?" Argentan's tone assumed an ominous quality.

Constance and Edmund glanced at each other uncomfortably before returning their gazes to Guy and the sheriff.

Guy cleared his throat and attempted to placate his master. "My lord, I lack the words necessary to express the depths of my gratitude."

"That's better!" cheered Argentan. "Now give the girl her gift."

Guy wished he could disappear beneath the floorboards, but there was no escape. He stepped forward and offered the small wooden box to Lady Constance as he bowed to her again. She took it from him, and he braced himself for her reaction to his inadequate gift.

Constance slowly opened the box as if she feared that its contents would jump out and bite her.

In fascination, Guy observed her brown eyes warm with unmistakable delight.

"Look, Father," Constance showed the brooch to Edmund. "It's a beautiful brooch with a Celtic design."

Edmund smiled at his daughter before remarking, "It's a thoughtful gift, Sir Guy. Elegant and lovely, just like my dear daughter."

"Of course!" exclaimed Argentan. "I taught Gisborne everything he knows about women."

Guy was speechless. He recognized genuine pleasure in the eyes of Lady Constance and her father. Somehow, he had chosen the right gift.

Argentan waved to a guard at the periphery of the room. "Escort Lady Constance to her chamber." He then addressed Edmund.

"Our meeting is about to begin, but there will be plenty of time for Lady Constance and Gisborne to become better acquainted during tonight's festivities."

After Constance's departure, a group of twenty nobles crowded into the sheriff's tower room. Guy recognized many of them, including the portly Eustace Clisson, the Earl of Bedford, and a fervent supporter of Prince John. All the men were supporters of the prince, except for Lord Edmund, whose presence had been compelled by his son's kidnapping.

When everyone was assembled, Argentan signaled for their attention and announced, "I have received alarming news from Outremer. Our king has been in secret talks with Sultan Saladin, and there are disgusting reports of him consorting with whores and sodomizing boys in the Holy Land!"

The men in the room murmured amongst themselves; this news appalled them.

Argentan continued, "But there is more: Assassins killed Conrad de Montferrat, King of Jerusalem. They interrogated one of the Assassins, and he revealed that King Richard hired them as part of a devious plot to put his nephew, Count Henry of Champagne, on the throne. Henry has already wed Conrad's widow. This disturbing news was delivered to me just days ago."

Edmund boldly stepped forward and raised his voice so that all could hear him. "I have known King Richard for many years, and these stories do not ring true. We should not spread such gossip based on the word of a hired killer—a Saracen, no less. And isn't it safe to assume that they tortured this man? How can we ascribe any validity to his words?" Edmund looked at Argentan. "We must be cautious in saying such things about our king. Slander is a form of treason."

A diabolical gleam shone in the sheriff's eyes. "I mean no disrespect. I am merely repeating the news I received from the Holy Land." He paused. "Lord Edmund, it's unfortunate that your son, Lionel, cannot be here tonight. I hope nothing happens to him while he is away. What a tragedy it would be if he were to suffer a fatal accident." Guy watched as all the color drained from Edmund's face.

Argentan resumed, "As you all know, Prince John has saved England from the evil men whom Richard had appointed to govern in his absence. John is continually striving to protect the people of England, while the Lionheart only cares for his Crusade. Tonight, in honor of Prince John, we will serve the prince's favorite English wines. The feast will begin soon, so let us all go to the great hall. Afterwards, there will be music and dancing."

The nobles filed out of the tower room, until the only remaining men were Argentan, Payen, Guy, and Eustace Clisson, who complained, "Lord de Argentan, should be I offended that you would give Lady Constance to Gisborne and not to me? She is the daughter of a wealthy English baron, and Gisborne is nothing."

Guy bristled in anger while Payen stifled a laugh.

Argentan's eyes glittered with contempt for the heavy-set earl, but his friendly grin was all that the other man saw. "My lord," replied Argentan in a soothing voice, "you deserve better than a tall, plain-faced spinster who is past her prime. Once Prince John is on the throne, he will arrange for you to wed a beautiful, young heiress with royal blood."

The earl's demeanor brightened. But then he sobered and declared, "I have been a staunch supporter of the prince for a long time, and I will expect to reap significant rewards. I provided you with a list of the lands I want annexed to my earldom. Have you discussed this with the prince? Has he agreed to give me these lands when he becomes king?"

The sheriff's smile still did not reach his cold, calculating eyes. "Certainly, my lord. The prince favors you above all others. He has great plans for you after his coronation." He redirected the conversation. "But our current priority must be to fund the new plot to capture and kill King Richard."

The Earl of Bedford paled, and with a quick inhalation, he

cautioned, "Alaric! We cannot speak treason so openly!" For all his bluster and sense of self-importance, Eustace Clisson was a coward who had avoided going on Richard's Crusade by claiming that his mother was ill and needed him at home.

"Forgive me, my lord," Argentan responded, "I did not mean to alarm you. We are confident that John will be crowned king soon, but we need more silver. I'm sure you know that John has limited access to the treasury. The prince is counting on your generosity."

"But... but," the earl sputtered, "I have already given so much! If the harvest is poor this year, my earldom will be bankrupted."

The sheriff countered, "And if you cannot support John in his hour of need, then why would he grant you the lands which you covet? Shall I report to the prince that your support is half-hearted?"

"Of course not!" Bedford's voice rose with anger.

Argentan, intending to calm the other man, purred, "You have wisely chosen to support Prince John: a man who puts England first. He will not squander the wealth of England on a foreign war. Instead, his generosity will be for those who defended him during these troubled times."

Bedford became thoughtful as the sheriff stepped closer and put his hand on the man's shoulder in a fatherly gesture. "My lord, you will be remembered and honored for your brave support of Prince John and for your commitment to a glorious future for England. Your mother, God-rest-her-soul, would be so proud."

"If only she were still here! I miss her wise counsel." The earl dabbed at the tears that had gathered in his eyes. "I will send the silver you need."

Argentan nodded sympathetically. "Go now and enjoy the feast. I believe the English wine is already being served in the great hall."

After the Earl of Bedford left the tower room, Argentan and his men switched to French, and the sheriff bemoaned, "I'd rather drink one of Payen's poisons than that swill the English call wine. The poison would most likely taste better."

Payen laughed. "I'm testing a new poison on some of our prisoners. Several said that they liked the taste. Sadly, it's fast acting. They are dead within a handful of heartbeats. When it's time to poison King Richard, I must find something slow."

"Why not use the same poison that worked previously?" asked a confused Guy.

"You do not appreciate the art of an apothecary. I relish the challenge of creating and testing the perfect poison," asserted Payen.

"Ha!" Argentan let out a laugh. "You just enjoy watching men writhe in agony as your poison takes their life."

Payen smiled sheepishly. "You know me well, my lord."

Guy rolled his eyes in disgust. He despised Payen, a man without a soul. He decided to risk the ire of the sheriff by asking a question. "My lord, did King Richard really arrange for the death of Conrad of Montferrat? I didn't see any evidence of debauchery or conspiring with Saladin when we were in Acre."

Argentan turned to his captain and sneered, "What difference does it make whether it's true? King Philippe has decreed that we spread these rumors here in England. Similar tales are being circulated in Normandy, Aquitaine, Anjou, and all of Richard's holdings in France. You are to tell these stories to as many people as possible. If necessary, pay local people to help us spread this gossip. We must undermine the reputation of the Lionheart to prepare the people for his death. We do not want him to be mourned."

Addressing Payen, Argentan commanded, "I have a new message for King Philippe that must be delivered to Dover. You will leave at first light, so do not drink too much tonight."

As soon as Payen had left, the sheriff frowned at his captain. "Gisborne, after your recent failures, I am giving you this opportunity to redeem yourself in my eyes and in the eyes of King Philippe. Do not disappoint me again. Do you understand?"

Guy sighed in resignation. "Yes, my lord."

꩜

Constance found the odd décor of Nottingham Castle's great hall disconcerting. The walls were swathed in blood red banners, and much of the furniture was also painted red. The feast had ended, and servants were carrying away the trestle tables to make room for dancing. A small group of musicians were ready to play, and she was standing alone near the far wall as she waited.

From across the expanse of the hall, she observed her betrothed, a tall, attractive man with striking blue eyes and thick, chestnut-colored hair. Although Sir Guy served the monster who had kidnapped her brother and threatened to kill him, she could not deny that he was remarkably handsome. And tall! It was unusual for her to have to look up at a man.

Her thoughts turned to Lionel. She was so anxious about him. Argentan had refused to provide any proof that he was alive beyond a short letter. Edmund and Constance had both recognized Lionel's distinctive scrawl, and it gave them some hope. She sent several quick prayers to God, beseeching Him to protect her dear brother.

She then noticed that Sir Guy was approaching her. He bowed to her, and she curtsied. He stood there, staring at her, and she searched her mind for something to say. "Do you dance, Sir Guy?"

He continued to stare at her for an uncomfortable stretch of time. Ignoring her question, he asked, "What is your favorite color, Lady Constance?"

She responded, "Blue, like a robin's egg. What is your favorite?"

He glowered at her, and she wasn't sure what she had said to offend him.

"It used to be red, but now it is black," Guy answered.

"Black?" Constance blinked in surprise; she was unnerved by the conversation and his intense gaze. Suddenly, he reached out and cradled the pendant hanging from the chain around her neck, his fingers lightly brushing her skin and making her shiver.

He demanded, "Who gave this to you?"

Constance swallowed hard and took a step back. He released his hold on her pendant. "My father gave it to me after the death of my mother. It belonged to her."

"It is not from a lover?"

Constance blushed to the roots of her hair.

Guy sneered, "Oh, that's right: you are a virtuous maiden whose innocence is highly valued. Your father is willing to pay a steep price to preserve it."

Constance's temper flared. She was not accustomed to such treatment. "You have agreed to his terms."

Guy's eyes traveled down her body before returning to her face. He lowered his voice and stepped closer. "I have not forgotten. But is this what you want? I am a man who knows how to please a woman."

Constance was still blushing furiously. She took another small step back and angrily responded, "You made a solemn promise to my father. We expect you to uphold your end of this bargain, or there will be consequences."

Guy snorted derisively. "Settle yourself. You are in no danger from me; I prefer women who look like women instead of tall, skinny boys."

She gasped, and her eyes filled with mortified tears as he sauntered away.

At that moment, her father joined her. "Are you all right? Did that man upset you?"

"No," she lied. "We were just casually conversing."

"Good. Let me know if he gives you any problems."

Constance changed the subject. "Father, did you learn anything in Locksley?"

Edmund sighed in frustration. "I spent the day with the father of Will Scarlet, one of Robin's outlaws. The man took me to their usual camp, the caves where they spend the winter, and to Duncan's old hunting lodge. In each of these places, I found evidence of recent activity, but I could not locate any of the outlaws."

"What did you hope to gain by talking to them?"

"I'm desperate. I was hoping that they had heard rumors about Argentan keeping a man prisoner somewhere nearby."

"After this sham wedding, I will work tirelessly to learn everything I can about this sheriff. Being close to his captain might give me opportunities to discover where they are keeping Lionel. It is the only advantage we have," Constance declared.

Edmund took her by the hand and gazed affectionately into her eyes. "That is true; however, I cannot bear the thought of losing both of my children, so do not take unnecessary risks. Stay alert for news from the Holy Land. I can't seem to learn anything from my usual sources, and I've sent dispatches to both the king and Robin, trying to determine if Marian arrived safely. I haven't received any news since early February."

"It's been almost five months," Constance worriedly added. "That's the longest we've ever gone without hearing something from Robin."

The sound of high pitched, squealing laughter interrupted their quiet conversation, and they looked up to see Gisborne surrounded by three beautiful women who were flirting with him in a familiar manner. He was smirking at them, and they were arguing over who would have the first dance with him. A blonde woman proclaimed that she preferred the last dance of the night, and the others laughed noisily again.

Constance's eyes widened at the double meaning of her words, and a blush darkened her face.

Edmund gently remarked, "My dear Constance, you should be relieved that Gisborne is distracted by these other women. You don't want such a man pursuing you."

Of course, her father was right, but Constance couldn't suppress the feelings of inadequacy that frayed the edges of her heart. She knew that she was too tall, too thin, and rapidly becoming too old for any man to want her hand in marriage. Nevertheless, the handsome Sir Guy of Gisborne was a landless knight with no connections to English nobility. He should have been thrilled to make such an advantageous match, even if it was only temporary. His disdain for her was particularly demoralizing, and it left her feeling as black as the color he claimed to love.

CHAPTER 5
THE ROAD TO PERDITION

24 June 1192, The Royal Palace, Poitiers

obin adjusted his helmet and hoped that its nose guard would conceal his identity from the many people in Poitiers who would otherwise recognize him as he marched behind André and Juan across the bailey and towards the palatial keep. Pondering the sense of home that he felt, he acknowledged that, while Locksley would always be his favorite place on earth, Poitiers was second in his heart.

It was within these walls that he had grown to manhood while receiving the finest education available to the noble sons of England and the Angevin Empire. His studies had included military history and tactics. Advanced weapons training had transformed him from a boy with natural talent to an undefeated champion. He had learned to honor the code of chivalry and appreciate the beauty of poetry while discovering the joys of music and dancing.

Unfortunately, those golden memories of boyhood triumphs were forever eclipsed by one of the darkest periods in his life: the months he had lived here while Richard was finalizing his preparations for the Crusade.

At that time, he had been furious with Marian for abruptly

ending their betrothal, but he had also bitterly resented the whisperings of his conscience. It kept reminding him that he had broken his promise to wed her as soon as the king had restored his titles and wealth. In truth, their estrangement had been his fault. And although he had felt guilty for choosing Richard over Marian, he had been devastated that she could abandon him with such apparent ease. The result of this seething jumble of emotions had been behavior at odds with his beliefs and values: drowning his anger in cups of ale and easing his pain in the arms of willing women.

To make matters even worse, this period of debauched living and drunken revelry had ended with unforeseen tragedy.

Looking back, he was ashamed of himself. He would beg Marian to forgive him, and he was ready to take full responsibility for his actions and poor choices. But what if she had heard the stories from the cruel courtiers of Poitiers and lost all respect for him? Could his past recklessness result in the loss of her affection? He would find out soon enough.

They entered the keep, and Robin's heart thrummed with a heady mixture of fear and anticipation. Somewhere within these thick walls, his wife was enduring widowhood not knowing that he was alive.

"Hold there! Are you here for the feast? You're late, and the feast has already begun." A guard had stopped their progression towards the main hall.

"I am Sir André de Chauvigny, and I have an important message for Queen Eleanor from the king. I also carry a message for the Countess of Huntingdon. I request an immediate audience, despite the late hour." André's authoritative voice held a touch of condescension intended to intimidate the guard, who was likely of low rank. With the Feast of Midsummer underway, all the senior soldiers and guards would be in the great hall enjoying the celebrations. It was the reason they had selected an important feast day for their arrival.

The soldier eyed them suspiciously. "The queen ain't here; she went to London months ago. I don't know any Countess of Huntingdon."

Alarm washed over Robin, but then he reasoned that perhaps the man was new to the post. How could anyone who had met Marian not remember her stunning beauty and gracious demeanor?

A second guard arrived and took command of the situation. "The Countess of Huntingdon? I know who you need to talk to. Follow me."

Robin exhaled in relief.

They marched a short distance and were shown into an empty chamber.

"Wait here," instructed the man as he affixed a bright torch to a brace on the wall near the door.

Robin could hardly contain himself. For weeks, throughout his journey with André from Acre to Navarre, where Juan joined them, and then on their travels to Poitiers, he had fantasized about his reunion with Marian, and he had rehearsed everything he planned to say to her, yet now, when their reunion was at hand, he feared he would forget his eloquent speech. He just wanted to hug her and never let her go again.

At that moment, the door opened, and a lone man entered. A jolt of recognition coursed through Robin, and he was glad that his helmet obscured so much of his face. This was the last man he would want to encounter in Poitiers.

"André," purred the man in a cultured voice. "It is such a surprise to see you. How does the king fare? We received word of the tragic death of the Earl of Huntingdon. I know he was a favorite of the king's and a friend to you. You have my condolences, of course, although I'm sure you'll forgive me if I don't join you in mourning him."

André greeted the other man with a bow. "Raimbaut de

\neuf, it's good to see you again. I'm pleased to report that
.g is in good health."

"When you asked for the Countess of Huntingdon, the guard recalled that she was my sister. I'm guessing that you wanted to speak to me. Why else would you mention Blanche? I remember that you were at the funeral with that worthless husband of hers—him feigning grief when I'm certain relief was all he felt."

Robin stepped forward, and Juan's hand shot out to grab his arm and hold him back.

André's eyes narrowed. "That's not true. Robin mourned the loss of Blanche and the babe she carried. To watch her poisoned and die in agony… it was a tragedy that deeply affected him."

Raimbaut harrumphed. "I will never forget the sight of my two sisters foaming at the mouth, retching, and screaming in pain as they rolled on the floor and begged for death. I hold Robin responsible."

"Responsible? That is ridiculous. Only the poisoner is to blame. We still do not know who sent that tainted English wine to the king. It was only the king's disdain for such wine, and the curiosity of Blanche and Clothilde in sampling it, that led to their deaths. You cannot blame Robin."

"I was told that, since the king was not drinking the wine, Robin saw no reason to have it taste-tested." Raimbaut's long repressed anger exploded. "If he had shown the same level of care for his wife as he showed for the Lionheart, my sisters would still be alive. This was Robin's fault!"

"That is unfair, Raimbaut. I was there. Within the safety of Poitiers, no one thought it necessary to test the king's food or wine."

Robin stood there, mortified, anguished, and frustrated by his inability to defend himself. He bore considerable guilt over the deaths of his first wife and her sister, despite Blanche's deceit in trapping him into marriage. But André was correct. No one had expected such an attack against the king within the walls of his most loyal keep. It was a miscalculation that Robin would not repeat during the ensuing years as he guarded the king.

André redirected the conversation. "Are you certain that the current Countess of Huntingdon is not here? Robin remarried while in the Holy Land, and King Richard sent her here with several companions after Robin's death. She is a young woman with pale blonde hair."

Raimbaut asked André to wait while he checked with his captain. Robin opened his mouth to comment, but André signaled for him to stay quiet.

Raimbaut promptly returned. "My captain told me that a woman claiming to be the Countess of Huntingdon arrived here several months ago. However, she left soon afterwards, and no one has seen or heard from her since then. That is all I know."

"I see," replied André. "The guard informed me that the queen is in London. We will pass the night here and then depart in the morning."

"I need to know the contents of the message you carry and any news from the king," Raimbaut declared.

Robin, André, and Juan gaped at the audacity of Raimbaut's demand.

"I cannot share this message with you." André directed a withering stare at the other man for his impertinence. "I'm astounded that you would request such a breach of confidentiality."

Raimbaut shrugged. "As you wish. Please go to the great hall and help yourself to any of the food or ale that remains. You can bed down with the other knights in the hall tonight. I'm sorry that I don't have a spare chamber for you, André, but it's the Feast of Midsummer, and the keep is crowded with those here to celebrate."

"Of course," intoned André. "We're weary and content to rest anywhere safe and warm."

❧

It was nearly dawn, and Robin, Juan, and André had been taking turns lying awake as they reclined on the floor of the great hall. They had chosen a spot along the perimeter of the room, away from the warmth of the fire, but close to an exit. A shadow fell over them, and a man moved noiselessly towards André's saddlebags, the only possessions they had brought with them. Robin nudged André, and they observed the stranger rifle through the bags, extracting the dispatch from King Richard with its elaborate seals. The man disappeared into the darkness with his prize.

A short time later, the shadowy figure returned and slipped the envelope back into André's bags. No doubt the seal had been expertly repaired by Raimbaut's men, although no one could completely disguise such tampering. As soon as the man disappeared, Robin and André woke Juan and the three men rose and exited the keep.

As they crossed the bailey, the sky was brightening, signaling the arrival of a long summer's day. When the portcullis was raised, and the gates opened, they departed the fortress of Poitiers and walked into the nearby forest, where they had left their horses and supplies overnight.

Once they were within the trees, André extracted the king's message and examined the repaired seal. "Very nice work," he acknowledged. "I'm not sure I would have noticed, if I had not seen them take it themselves."

Robin commented, "Of all the fish to take our bait, I would have never suspected Raimbaut. Yet, it must have been him, since the only other people aware of the message for Eleanor were a couple of low ranking guards."

"Do you think they will believe the message to be genuine?" questioned Juan.

Robin explained, "Actually, it's a genuine message, insofar as it was written and sealed by the king. It's just that the information contained within it is false. We want the misleading information to be delivered to King Philippe. We believe that his reaction will reveal whether he was involved in the plot to kill Richard in Acre."

Robin then confronted André and insisted, "I'm going to England with Juan. I'm certain that Marian heard about my hasty marriage to Blanche from the courtiers in Poitiers and returned to my uncle in the north of England." He grimaced. "I must go to her and beg her to forgive me."

André countered, "Robin, the king commanded us to find out whether Philippe was behind the regicide attempt. This ruse of the faux message was your idea, and you must proceed with our mission. Richard is counting on you. Besides, Juan has the real message for the queen, and he must be the one to travel to England. He will go to Marian after he meets with the queen."

"No!" cried Robin. "I can't allow Marian to continue thinking I'm dead, so I will accompany Juan to London."

André sighed with regret. "Robin, I understand. But you made a commitment to Richard, and we must fulfill our duties. Juan will ask Queen Eleanor to summon Marian and your uncle to London. Then the queen can explain to them that you are alive and well."

In a voice dripping with bitter sarcasm, Robin retorted, "I've made a lot of commitments to Richard over the years. I mustn't ever fail Richard! I can fail my wife, my family, and everyone else who relies upon me, but heaven forfend if I ever deny Richard his heart's desire."

"Robin—"

Ignoring André's attempt at reasoning with him, Robin heatedly declared, "The truth is, I no longer care. Facing death has taught me a lot about what is important in life. Pleasing Richard by obeying his every command has not brought meaning or joy to my life. Protecting Marian and the people of Nottinghamshire from Argentan and Gisborne is what truly matters."

"My lord," Juan's tone was compassionate. "I agree with you. Family and friends make a man's life worth living. I pray to God that He will bless me with a wife and children someday, even though I am growing too old for such pursuits." Juan smiled wistfully, his weathered face and greying hair a reminder that he had spent his adult life in service to his own king in Navarre. "But we live in a time when our kings demand that we surrender our wills to their whims and wishes. If you hope to retire to your estates in peace and prosperity, you must submit to your king."

André argued, "Robin, my friend, listen to me. I will not rebuke you for your words, although others might call them disloyal. But consider your desire to save your people from Argentan and Gisborne. These men are protected by Prince John. You cannot defeat them."

"You underestimate me, André. I'm prepared to return to Nottingham and clean the castle of these rats. This time, I will show no mercy. I will kill Argentan, and I will capture Gisborne and give him to King Richard as a prize."

"And if, God forbid, King Richard dies before he can return home and sire an heir?" André contended. "Prince John will be king, and you will be at his mercy. The best way for you to protect your people and your wife is to protect King Richard. Do whatever is necessary to ensure Richard's safe return to England. Only then will you be able to resume your life with any assurances for a secure future."

"My lord, your friend's words are wise; please heed them," Juan urged.

André's voice softened, and he put his hand on Robin's shoulder. "Let Juan go to England. I'm certain the queen will place Marian under her royal protection until we return home with Richard. In the meantime, we will follow Richard's plan to uncover the truth about the regicide attempt. Protecting Richard will protect all of us."

Robin's mind was whirling with conflicting thoughts and emotions. André and Juan had offered compelling arguments, yet he wondered if he was being manipulated, again, into doing Richard's bidding to his own detriment.

He gazed at Juan, a man who had been responsible for guarding and protecting the King of Navarre's beloved daughter, Berengaria. If a king could entrust his precious daughter to this man, then Robin could place Marian in his care as well.

With his mind, if not his heart, resigned to a course of action, Robin instructed Juan. "When you arrive in England, there is a tavern in Dover called *The Hawk and the Dove*. In the past, it has always been loyal to the crown. Go there and ask about the location of Queen Eleanor. There are several royal castles where she might be in residence. But even though this tavern has been trusted for years by the royal family, take no chances. Keep your guard up and be wary of everyone you meet. Prince John might have spies watching for anyone with news from Richard." Robin then gave Juan the name and location of his uncle, for he was convinced that Marian was in Embelton.

Juan bid them both a fond farewell and headed north towards Normandy.

∽

Soon, André and Robin spotted eight men exiting the main gate of Poitiers. Raimbaut was in the lead as the group took the road that led to Paris. Waiting until the men had passed them, Robin and André guided their horses from the shadows of the forest onto the road, where they mounted and began trailing them.

30 June 1192, On the Road South of Paris, Near the Town of Montlhéry

The sun had descended below the horizon, although the sky was still bright with the lingering glow of a long summer's day. Robin and André made camp a short distance behind Raimbaut and his men.

They could not light a fire without alerting the other men to their presence, so they were thankful for the balmy weather. At this point in their journey, they had become weary and discouraged.

As they had expected, Raimbaut traveled to Paris, where he entered the king's palace and remained overnight.

King Philippe's keep was well-guarded, so they had been reduced to watching and waiting. While in Paris, Robin and André had heard vicious rumors about King Richard and his behavior in the Holy Land. It had been frustrating to listen to such outlandish tales, yet there was nothing they could say or do to counter the gossip.

On their second day in Paris, Raimbaut had emerged from Philippe's palatial keep late in the afternoon and gathered his men before setting out on the road which would take them back to Poitiers. Robin and André were no wiser than they had been before their arrival in Poitou the previous week, and they had debated whether to stay in Paris or follow Raimbaut. They could find no easy way to slip into the royal residence, which was situated on an island in the river. Reluctantly, they chose to follow Raimbaut.

Settling in for the night, they refrained from conversation for fear that their voices would carry in the still air. They could hear indistinct sounds from Raimbaut's camp. The men were in high spirits as they headed home.

Robin contemplated their options. Perhaps they should return to Paris and infiltrate Philippe's court. They would need to obtain nicer clothing. But could they find a way into the court without being recognized or without their accents giving them away? Both he and André were fluent in French, but there would always be slight variations in their pronunciations and inflections that might betray them as interlopers.

He sighed. The answers which Richard sought could only be found at the French court. Following Raimbaut back to Poitiers was pointless.

"What troubles you, Robin?" André whispered to him.

"I was recalling my last conversation with Richard before we departed the Holy Land. I think we should abandon Raimbaut and return to Paris," murmured Robin.

"Can you disclose what the king said?"

Maintaining a low voice, Robin explained, "During the regicide attempt, Richard recognized Baron de Argentan, but not from the Poitevin court."

André leaned closer, his full attention upon Robin. "I don't understand your meaning."

"Richard was certain that he had seen Argentan at the court in Paris. I believe we will find the answers there."

His brow creased in concern, André insisted, "Tell me exactly what Richard said."

"Do you remember when Richard and Philippe were allies fighting against King Henry?"

"I will never forget it. I was serving Richard, and he was determined to force his father to declare him next in line for the throne. Even though it was ill-omened for a father and son to make war against each other, Richard was correct that England and the Angevin lands needed a clear plan for the royal succession."

Robin elaborated, "Richard went to Paris to strategize with Philippe, and he saw Argentan standing with the advisors, courtiers, and attendants along the periphery of the room. Richard's exact words were: 'Argentan was just one of many men standing in the shadows.'"

Worried that he had spoken too loudly, Robin lowered his voice. "I was shocked when the king said that, for it cannot be a coincidence."

Robin's cryptic remarks confused André. "I have spent more time at court than I care to admit. However, what he describes sounds like a typical day at court, with advisors and attendants hovering around the perimeter of the hall, awaiting a summons from their lord. What is so shocking about that?"

To clarify his meaning, Robin recollected, "Every time I have met Argentan, he has recited some absurd riddle about shadows. Gisborne even has a sword engraved with the phrase, *From Shadows to Glory*. I think shadows are a metaphor for secrets, but I'm not sure."

"You are right; we should return to Paris."

"Baron de Argentan once told me, 'Someday the sun will break through the clouds and illuminate everything around us. The truth of the shadows will be revealed.' I will welcome such sunshine," commented Robin.

With those words, the two men fell into quiet contemplation until the urgent rhythm of hoof beats disrupted the peace of the forest. André unsheathed his sword as Robin grabbed his bow and quiver, and they hastened to the nearby road.

The dark shapes of a dozen mounted men-at-arms galloped past them and disappeared around a bend in the road, and within moments, a cacophony of shouting and screaming erupted. Risking discovery, André and Robin sprinted towards Raimbaut's camp. Arriving at the scene of a one-sided battle, they retreated into the trees.

Raimbaut and his men were defending themselves from the onslaught, but they were outnumbered and had been taken by surprise. Robin nocked an arrow and took aim, but André stilled his arm and said, "Robin, we cannot endanger ourselves by making our presence known. Look; they have already defeated Raimbaut."

Robin lowered his bow and watched as the attackers lit their torches using the campfire and rode off into the shadows of dusk. They had not robbed the men, and the attack had been executed with military precision.

As soon as the assailants disappeared from sight, Robin and André rushed into the camp to check for signs of life. Robin went to Raimbaut and knelt next to him. He was still alive, but he had suffered a deep stab wound to his gut. It was only a matter of time before death claimed him. André joined Robin and shook his head to signal that the other men were dead.

"Raimbaut, can you hear me?" Robin called to him.

Raimbaut's bleary eyes focused on Robin, and then they widened in disbelief. "You! But... but... you're dead."

"There was a misunderstanding; as you can see, I'm not dead. You will be all right; we will dress your wound and find help. Do you know who those men were?" Raimbaut seemed to be drifting away, and Robin gently shook him and repeated, "Who were those men who attacked you?"

The other man struggled to speak. "Count de Montlhéry's men-at-arms... We are within his domain."

"Why did they attack you?"

Licking his lips and frowning in concentration, Raimbaut revealed, "Philippe was angry about Richard's message... He said... that I had been tricked."

Robin's heart dropped when realized that his ploy with the false message had failed so spectacularly. He couldn't dwell on that now; he had to extract as much information as possible from Raimbaut. "But why are you spying for the French king? You are Richard's vassal."

"The death of my sisters... I blamed you and Richard... wanted revenge... Why didn't you protect them? Blanche loved you." Raimbaut moaned in pain, and André pressed against his wound in a futile attempt to stop the bleeding. Robin knew that such a wound bled mostly inside the body. There was no hope of saving him.

"Raimbaut, for so long I have wanted to tell you how much I regret Blanche's death. I will always blame myself for not being more vigilant on that night. The man who murdered your sisters also tried to poison Richard in Acre. You have my solemn vow that he will not escape justice." Robin searched his former friend's face, hoping to find forgiveness.

"Make him suffer, Robin… I'm dying… you must seek justice for them."

Robin offered a truce. "Raimbaut, please let us set aside our differences and part in peace and friendship. We were once friends. Do you remember?"

Raimbaut smiled faintly. "Yes… I would like to die remembering the good times."

"Tell me, in your time at the French court, did you ever meet Baron de Argentan or Guy of Gisborne? I believe that Argentan is the man who poisoned Blanche and Clothilde. I know that he tried to poison King Richard in Acre."

"Gisborne? Yes… he serves Montlhéry." Raimbaut seemed to rally, and his voice strengthened.

"I thought Gisborne served Baron de Argentan," Robin replied.

"Gisborne serves Montlhéry… There are rumors… he is Montlhéry's bastard… don't know Argentan."

Suddenly, new suspicions about his half-brother arose in Robin's mind. "Baron de Argentan was exchanging messages with the French court; perhaps Montlhéry was the intermediary between Argentan and King Philippe."

"I'm so thirsty." Raimbaut had become very pale, and his voice faded. A strange rattle sounded in his throat. André offered him a drink from a nearby canteen, but the dying man could not swallow and started choking. He gasped. "Pray for my soul, Robin… For two years I've been traveling on this road to Perdition… I'm afraid."

Robin and André continued to sit with him, offering prayers and gentle reassurances, until Raimbaut breathed his last.

André glanced down the road. "We cannot linger here in this camp. The marauders might return and loot the dead. I will take Raimbaut's ring and send it to his family. Are we returning to Paris in the morning?"

"There is no need. We have the information we were seeking."

"And what is that?" asked a curious André.

"King Philippe was behind the regicide attempt, and I'm certain that Prince John was also involved. But now we have the missing piece of this puzzle. It is Gisborne. He is the key. I have heard of Count de Montlhéry, although I have never met him. He is a senior advisor to the French royal family. Gisborne is the connection between Argentan and Montlhéry, and Montlhéry is the connection to King Philippe. We can confidently report to Richard that Philippe was involved in the regicide attempt. It is highly likely that Philippe was financing the entire scheme; he is the only one in this group of conspirators with the resources for such a mission."

"Raimbaut mentioned rumors that Gisborne is Montlhéry's bastard. That would make sense as well," offered André.

Robin snorted in dark amusement. "It would make sense except that Gisborne is my father's bastard and my half-brother."

André's eyes widened, and he opened and closed his mouth twice before he exclaimed, "That's not possible!" At Robin's raised brow, André pressed for more information. "Are you certain? How do you know this?"

"I will explain everything as we journey back to the Holy Land. Juan should arrive in London in the next few days. Until I can return, I am forced to entrust Marian's well-being to Juan, Queen Eleanor, and Uncle Edmund."

"Perhaps by the time we return to Acre, the Crusade will have ended."

"André, we must pray for a swift end to the Crusade. There are powerful forces arrayed against our king. You were right: nothing is more important than ensuring that King Richard returns safe and sound to England. Our future, and the future of England, depends upon it."

CHAPTER 6
A WEDDING IN LOCKSLEY

Constance exited Locksley Manor and lingered near the door. She closed her eyes, tilting her head to receive the warmth of the sun upon her face. Summer had finally arrived: bright, welcoming, and adorned with the vibrant colors of the season. In her misery, Constance railed against the perfect weather. It was unfair that her long-awaited wedding day was so beautiful when it was all a charade. There should be dark storm clouds overhead. Booming thunder should drown out the priest's words, and heavy rains should cancel the wedding feast. Such a tempestuous day would match the bitter despair in her heart.

Thoughts of her brother's perilous circumstances halted her descent into self-pity, and she resolved to focus on what was truly important. The sheriff had demanded this marriage as a requirement for Lionel's continued health and safety, and nothing was more important to her than protecting her family.

With that in mind, Constance refused to limit herself to the role of a useful puppet constrained by the sheriff's manipulations. She would spy on Argentan and Gisborne, and if she discovered Lionel's location, she was certain her father and his men-at-arms could rescue him. She involuntarily shivered in trepidation. Never before had she done anything more dangerous than pull harmless pranks on her brother. She was filled with a strange mixture of apprehension and exhilaration.

Still standing in front of the manor, she observed the small church a short distance away. Several trestle tables had been set up near it, and Robin's loyal servants were dutifully preparing for the feast that would follow her wedding. She couldn't help but notice their grim, determined expressions; her future husband was not popular among the people of Locksley, and she had received many curious, even hostile, stares from both servants and villagers when it became known that she was to wed Sir Guy. Thankfully, Leofric and Elvina had revealed the truth about the marriage to everyone.

The few guests who would be in attendance were already seated in the church, and she had delayed this moment as long as possible. The manor's door opened, and her father joined her.

"Are you ready, my dear?" Edmund asked his daughter, disquiet shadowing his wan smile.

Constance adjusted the trumpet sleeves of her elegant pale blue bliaut. She had hoped to cheer herself by wearing one of her favorite ensembles. She was particularly fond of the bliaut's elaborate embroidery, and the way its silver thread shimmered in the sunlight. Reaching up to ensure that her crown of white flowers was secure, she wondered whether leaving her long, dark hair loose might be considered too casual for a wedding.

She then chastised herself for worrying about her appearance. Taking her father's arm, they strolled to the church.

Guy stood near the altar, awaiting Constance's arrival and enduring the sheriff's taunts.

"Gisborne, I hope your bride will mend your broken heart and help you forget your many past mistakes. You are moving towards a better future," Argentan proclaimed with a mawkish glimmer in his eyes.

Guy grimaced at the sheriff's reminder of Marian and his murder of Robin. He looked longingly at the door as he fantasized about running out of the church, taking the first horse he found, and galloping away without a single backward glance. Of course, that was impossible. Perhaps he could physically leave, but the hold which bound him to the sheriff was as strong as the iron chains they used on prisoners in the dungeons.

Argentan moved closer and grasped Guy's arm. Speaking quietly, he said, "Gisborne, do not forget how much your life depends on me. There is no place where you could go that I would not find you. Unless King Richard's men found you first." He pulled him into an embrace that further reinforced Guy's impression of being wrapped in heavy chains and whispered, "I am the only one who can save you."

His master's apparent ability to read his mind was unnerving. How had he known that Guy was considering running away? His fears and insecurities always intensified in the sheriff's presence. "Yes, my lord," he murmured.

Argentan released Guy from his insincere hug, but he remained uncomfortably close, insisting, "You need me. Safety is a precious commodity, as rare as diamonds. No one else can protect you for the rest of your life. Any day, word of Huntingdon's death will arrive. You will have to sleep with one eye open, since you will be surrounded by Robin's family and loyal servants." The sheriff snickered maliciously.

The color drained from Guy's face, and he stepped away from the sheriff. Just then, the doors opened. His bride had arrived.

⁂

Entering the small church on the arm of her father, Constance was relieved that so few people had been invited. Of course, Sheriff de

Argentan was there, as well as the odious Earl of Bedford, Eustace Clisson. A few local barons and their wives helped fill the pews, and in the back she noticed four men-at-arms who were there to guard the sheriff. Her gaze fell upon Guy, who stood near the altar, his bearing outwardly calm. He was dressed more formally than usual, and his fine clothes accentuated his attractive features. She felt inexplicably drawn to him, and she berated herself for being little more than a mindless moth fluttering around an alluring, dangerous flame, like those silly women at the Midsummer's Feast.

Next to Guy, Sheriff de Argentan beamed at her. Constance could barely conceal her hatred for the sheriff. That evil man loved nothing more than to perform the role of puppet master, and this wedding was just another game he was playing for his own amusement.

Her father's presence eased Constance's nervousness. She squared her shoulders and took a deep breath. She would do her duty for her brother's sake, and when Robin returned, he would help her father set the world right again by arranging an annulment of this farcical marriage. Constance gracefully glided down the aisle with all the dignity she could summon. Arriving at the altar, her father stepped away, and she felt bereft without his support. Guy moved to stand next to her, but she couldn't bring herself to look at him again.

The sheriff theatrically stretched out his arms and smiled. "My friends, we have gathered here to celebrate the wedding of my most loyal and trusted captain, Sir Guy of Gisborne." He stepped towards Constance and Guy and joined the bride and groom's hands together. "Gisborne's happiness means my own, so I bless this union, and I rejoice in his good fortune."

As she felt Guy's warm hand on hers, Constance gathered the courage to meet his gaze, and a rush of sweet emotion passed between them. At that moment, she didn't see contempt or cruelty in his pale blue eyes. Instead, there was a desperation and loneliness that could only be described as the look of a haunted man.

Continuing to stare into her eyes, Guy thanked the sheriff in a monotone devoid of real gratitude, and the sound of his voice severed their brief connection. It had been as evanescent as a snowflake captured in the hand of a child.

Edmund rolled his eyes in irritation at the sheriff's extravagant professions of joy. "Baron de Argentan, shall we begin? Or are you planning to conduct the ceremony?"

Argentan's eyes narrowed in annoyance. "We shall begin at once," agreed the sheriff.

Constance removed her hand from Guy's, and they knelt together at the altar.

A hush enveloped the chapel as the ceremony commenced. Constance and Guy appeared to be listening to the priest, but instead they were grappling with the guilt of affirming vows before the Lord that neither had any intention of fulfilling.

Argentan stood to the right of Guy, observing Edmund and becoming more convinced that the bride's father had to be watched closely. Edmund's expression revealed a resolve and intelligence that reminded the sheriff of Robin Hood. The Baron of Embelton should not be underestimated.

⌇

Led by the newlywed couple, everyone filed out of the church. The men-at-arms, who had been loitering in the back, had slipped out during the service, and they were hungrily eyeing the feast while ignoring the sullen stares of the villagers.

Guy and Constance had taken only a few steps into the church's yard when Guy tensed and abruptly stilled. Following the direction of his gaze, Constance saw the pale knight, Payen, in a heated discussion with Odella.

"Wait with your father," Guy commanded as he removed her hand from his arm and marched towards Payen.

Constance had just joined her father near the church door when a strident female voice intruded upon the peace of the gathering and demanded everyone's full attention. "Why wasn't I invited to a wedding in my own village?" A laugh followed. "I'm glad I didn't miss the feast."

Everyone startled and looked up to see five figures standing atop the furthest trestle table.

Lady Marian of Lenton, Countess of Huntingdon and Lady of Locksley, was flanked by Little John, Much, Will, and Allan. All the men held bows, arrows nocked and ready. Marian's hands were hidden behind her, and she was dressed in male clothing that hung loosely on her small frame: dark green chausses and a matching tunic under a cloak with a hood that was pushed back to reveal her face. Her long, blonde hair was loose about her shoulders.

Edmund and Constance were overcome with relief.

The sheriff remained calm, but Guy froze, and for a moment, his mind was clouded by astonishment. He could see nothing but her face: fierce in her hate and pain, but still beautiful. Longing briefly seized him before he recollected himself.

As the initial spell was broken, the air filled with whispers. The Locksley villagers stared at Marian as if she were a ghost, for they had not seen her since the arrival of Argentan all those years ago.

Marian swiftly scrutinized her surroundings and sighed with relief. There were only a handful of men-at-arms; obviously, Argentan hadn't expected any trouble. She was momentarily stunned to see Edmund and Constance. She hadn't seen Constance exit the church with Guy, and she didn't realize that Constance was the bride. In truth, such a possibility never entered her mind.

She produced Robin's bow from behind her back and nocked an arrow, pointing the weapon at Gisborne and sneering, "It's a great pity that I was not at the ceremony."

Edmund took Constance's arm and led her into the church's narthex. If arrows began to fly, she would be better protected there.

Constance implored him. "Go stop her! Those soldiers will kill her if she releases an arrow towards Gisborne or the sheriff."

"Constance, stay calm. We will wait here in the church. I promise, if Marian is in peril, I will intervene. Keep in mind that she possesses some skill with a bow. Do you remember how often she practiced when she lived with us at Embelton?"

Meanwhile, Marian was focused on Guy and the sheriff. "Guy of Gisborne! You shamelessly enter a church, even though your hands are forever stained with the blood of innocents. Your mere presence desecrates of this church!"

Argentan called to her in his highly accented English. "My dear Maid Marian, I have missed you so much! How unexpected to see you back in England. Did you enjoy your sojourn in the Holy Land? Did you visit any holy sites? Graves, perhaps?"

Payen and Bedford stood near Guy and the sheriff, watching the exchange with great interest. Guy was standing very still, his eyes trained on Marian, and his new wife forgotten.

A fearless Marian aimed at the sheriff. "I have returned to avenge Robin."

"I'm surprised the Lionheart allowed you to wander off on your own. Surely, he recognized that you are a woman in need of close supervision and a firm hand." Eyeing the weapon in Marian's hands, Argentan grinned malevolently, confident that she had neither the nerve nor the skill to use it.

Marian looked away from the sheriff and addressed the people of Locksley. "I am the widow of Lord Robin Fitzooth, Earl of Huntingdon and Lord of Locksley," she proclaimed proudly, her head held high. "Everything in this village belongs to me and my descendants."

"So you married your outlaw bird on his deathbed?" inquired Argentan cheekily.

Her pronouncement of her new title snapped Guy out of his

daze. "No," he said under his breath. He didn't want to believe that Marian had married a dying Robin.

Within the space of a few heartbeats, the implications of her words caused a stupefied hush to fall over the crowd. Many villagers gasped in horror, and some of them crossed themselves. The local nobles murmured to each other, shaken by the news.

"Robin Hood's widow!" the sheriff gleefully savored the sound. "You are in danger of following your late husband's footsteps into the shadows where outlaws reside. You have threatened me, an agent of the crown. I will be forced to arrest you and your ragged band of ruffians. This is a serious crime!"

Guy was not listening to the conversation. All he could think about was Robin's victory. Perhaps it had been a Pyrrhic victory, but Robin had claimed Marian as his wife before dying. Remembering that he now had a wife of his own, he glanced over his shoulder and saw Edmund and Constance standing at the doors of the church. Their expressions revealed how shattered they were to learn of Robin's death. Soon they would hear of his role in Robin's demise, and he could not stomach the thought of seeing Constance regard him with the same loathing as Marian. He looked back at Marian, who was still trading insults with the sheriff.

"Lady Huntingdon, do you plan to rob us today? Shall we call you Marian Hood?" Argentan was thoroughly enjoying himself as he goaded her.

"You are the criminal, Lord de Argentan. The charges I bring against you are hanging offenses," accused Marian. "Hear now, everyone: This man attempted to kill King Richard. I've also learned that he poisoned Lord Robin's men, even though they had been pardoned."

The people gathered around the forgotten wedding feast, watching the sheriff and Marian.

At the mention of the poisoned outlaws, Payen beamed with pride. Standing next to the pale poisoner, Bedford was enjoying

Argentan's taunting of Marian, a woman he had met at Embelton several years ago and had instantly disliked. He wondered why Argentan didn't order his men to take the outlaws into custody. Marian and her bow were laughable in his eyes.

Argentan dismissed Marian's accusations with a flick of his wrist, as if he were shooing away a bothersome insect. "Where are my manners? I should welcome you to our splendid celebration." He laughed nastily. "Gisborne, your former suitor, has just married a wealthy heiress!"

Marian's lips curled into a sneer. "I have to confess that I'm puzzled. Why would any woman marry this poor excuse for a man?" She scanned the yard. "Where is his bride? Perhaps she has run away in horror at the prospect of marriage to him."

The sheriff scoffed. "I think you're jealous of Gisborne. He's already forgotten you, and here you are, all alone."

A furious Marian hissed at the sheriff. "No one who knows Gisborne would want him. He's not a man but a hound at his master's beck and call."

Much's hushed voice interrupted Marian. "Tell them."

John grunted in agreement and urged, "My lady, we cannot stay here much longer. He will order the soldiers to attack us at any moment. We need a diversion."

Marian knew he was right, so she addressed the villagers and servants who had served Robin all their lives with devotion and loyalty. "People of Locksley, Gisborne and Argentan tried to kill King Richard in the Holy Land. Robin bravely saved the life of the king, but Gisborne crept up behind him like a coward, and then he... he stabbed Lord Robin in the heart!"

Everyone had been hesitant to believe that Robin was dead. But now, hearing her declare it so plainly and unequivocally, there was no escaping the truth. A pall of chasmal grief descended over the crowd, and some cried out in anguish. Many crossed themselves.

Elvina and Leofric clung to each other. A distraught Constance almost collapsed, but Edmund caught her as her legs gave way.

Argentan and Payen had the effrontery to grin at each other, amused by the intensity of the reaction to Robin Hood's death. Guy could only stand there open-mouthed and stare at Marian; the most beautiful woman he had ever known. His mind desperately sought words which would justify his actions on that dreadful day in Acre.

Little John targeted Gisborne with his bow. "Gisborne murdered Lord Robin, and he must pay for his crimes!"

"Gisborne must be put to death!" hissed Will.

Allan scowled and asked, "This wasn't the plan, was it?"

Marian snapped, "John, you agreed to follow me. Do not stray from my plan!"

Little John reluctantly lowered his bow, submitting to Marian's authority.

Argentan snickered. "Marian Hood, you are becoming tiresome! I have no interest in listening to your tirades." The sheriff lowered his voice and ordered, "Gisborne, be ready to attack them at my command."

The crowd stilled. Even those who had been weeping after the announcement of Robin's death quieted. All eyes were riveted on Marian.

Marian tore her gaze from Guy and glared at the sheriff. "Take care, Argentan," she threatened. "I am not Robin, but I am skilled with a bow. Rest assured that I will not miss."

Argentan made a peevish sound. "You might have bewitched Gisborne, but I am immune to your charms. I do not fear your meaningless threats. You have foolishly come into the open, in front of armed men. Robin Hood did not teach you well, or perhaps you are a poor student."

Marian grappled with the tangle of her emotions. Grief, hatred, fury, and fear all seemed to exist as one overwhelming weight bearing down upon her. "Argentan, do not underestimate me. I am on the side of what is right, and Robin's spirit demands justice from beyond the grave!"

The sheriff laughed in her face. "What a grand blather, my dear widowed Countess of Sherwood, not Countess of Huntingdon. I will request that Prince John strip you of your titles and lands, and he will happily do it. Then you will be nothing but a filthy forest girl."

Marian's eyes narrowed to slits. "Even if you outlaw me, King Richard will reinstate my rights!" When she saw Argentan shrug nonchalantly, apprehension seized her gut. He did not fear the return of King Richard, and that gave her pause.

Argentan observed Marian raise her bow and take aim at him. "Ha! I know women, and you don't have the stomach to kill me! You are bluffing, and I distaste a cheap bluff!" Argentan then commanded his captain. "Gisborne, arrest her and her band of forest vermin!"

Guy finally broke out of his trance, and he hastily evaluated the situation. Turning his back to Marian, he faced the sheriff and spoke urgently in a quiet voice. "My lord, she has the advantage. The guards accompanying us are not prepared for this type of battle. They are only carrying swords. Their shields and bows were left with the horses." Guy assessed the distance between their location in front of the church and their horses, which were tied to posts near Locksley Manor.

He continued, "I cannot send unprotected men to confront archers. Even if the outlaws do not have Robin Hood's skill with a bow, as close are we are, it would be suicidal to attack them. If my men retreat to retrieve their shields and bows, Marian and the outlaws will disappear into the forest before they can return."

Argentan's face darkened with rage. "You coward! Order your men to attack. I want those outlaws arrested. I want Marian Hood as my prisoner!"

Gisborne hesitated.

Suddenly, Bedford announced, "They wouldn't dare harm me;

I'm an earl. Have your men distract the outlaws, and I will capture Lady Marian." He drew his sword and stepped towards Marian.

"Wait!" cried Guy. He grabbed the edge of the nearest trestle table and tilted the top. The feast and serving platters slid off and littered the ground. He ordered the three guards behind him. "Take the top of the table and hold it in front of you to shield you from the arrows. Approach the outlaws and provide a distraction as Bedford advances towards Lady Marian."

The men promptly complied, and the outlaws shifted until they were between Marian and the advancing men. They released a volley of arrows, but the surface of the heavy tabletop shielded the soldiers. Even so, the men were hindered by its weight and forced to move at a snail's pace.

"My lady, we should retreat into the forest now, while we can," insisted John as he nocked another arrow and aimed at the approaching tabletop. The men behind it were well protected.

Marian did not want to leave yet. She had originally planned to only accuse Gisborne and the sheriff, but now she was tempted to kill them both and be done with it. Argentan's cruel taunts, and the sight of Gisborne, had enraged her.

The villagers and wedding guests scattered to find safety. Meanwhile, Eustace stalked towards Marian with his sword drawn, ready to capture her. He excitedly imagined the triumph of personally delivering her to Prince John. That would definitely impress the future king!

Marian had never liked Bedford, despite his friendship with Lionel. She watched as he lumbered towards her, his sword drawn, a sheen of sweat on his brow, and his jaw set with determination. She raised Robin's bow and aimed at the overweight earl. "Do not come any closer," she warned, while the outlaws continued releasing arrows at the slowly advancing soldiers.

Marian carefully targeted Bedford's right shoulder, intending to inflict a painful, but not dangerous, wound.

Bedford was becoming winded from his march towards her, and he panted, "Lady Marian, you look ridiculous. Surrender before you get hurt." He lurched forward, stumbling on the uneven ground just as Marian released her arrow.

It struck the earl in his throat. His eyes grew large with terror, and he dropped his sword, sinking to his knees as he extracted the arrow protruding from his neck. A torrent of blood spurted from the wound, and he frantically tried to staunch the flow with his hands. After a few moments, he slumped to the ground, dead.

The battle halted as everyone stopped and stared in shocked silence. No one could believe that Marian had killed a man in cold blood with a single, deadly arrow. The outlaws stood behind her, open-mouthed and speechless.

Allan was the first to recover. "You killed him, Marian," he said in a trembling voice.

"You shouldn't have done that," John quietly chided her.

Will looked frightened, while Much proclaimed, "Lady Marian was just defending herself."

Marian's vision narrowed until the only thing she saw was the bloodied neck of Eustace Clisson. Panic seized her, and her lungs constricted painfully until she remembered to take a breath. She had been targeting his shoulder. How could she have missed in such a lethal manner?

She forced herself to draw another arrow from the quiver at her belt, nock it, and raise her bow again, taking aim at Argentan.

In all the time that she had known the malevolent sheriff, she had only seen scorn, malice, or anger in his eyes. But now she saw a new emotion: naked, unambiguous terror shone in the eyes of the Sheriff of Nottingham as all the color drained from his face.

Marian's distress over killing Bedford morphed into an incredible sense of power. The formidable Baron de Argentan was cowering in front of her as she aimed her weapon at him.

Argentan raised his hands in surrender and stumbled backwards.

Marian drew the bow string back, and in that moment, she wanted to kill the sheriff where he stood. But a flicker of doubt stayed her hand. It was one thing to kill accidentally, but to kill while staring into a man's eyes… she willed herself to look away from Argentan's face and take careful aim at his chest.

"Marian, no!" bellowed a familiar voice.

She glanced at the church and saw Edmund and Constance emerge from its darkened interior.

The sheriff had been slowly backing away from her, and in the moment of her distraction, he spun around and sprinted towards Locksley Manor where his horse was tethered.

Disregarding Edmund, Marian once again aimed at the retreating Argentan. This time she released her arrow. Although it struck the sheriff in his hip, it merely bounced off his body and fell away.

Argentan tumbled to the ground from the arrow's impact before promptly regaining his feet and resuming his dash to safety.

A bitterly disappointed Marian lowered her bow. The arrow had probably bruised him, but she doubted that it had pierced his flesh. Her opportunity to kill the sheriff had been lost.

For now.

The soldiers who had been advancing on the outlaws dropped the bulky tabletop and joined Argentan, Payen, and the remaining wedding guests who were running towards the manor in a frenzied effort to leave Locksley as soon as possible.

CHAPTER 7
THE DARK SIDE OF HER HEART

1 July 1192, Locksley Village

A shaken Guy of Gisborne stood next to the slain Earl of Bedford and stared at his lifeless corpse in wide-eyed disbelief. Marian had murdered a man in cold blood.

Bitter sorrows of his past were nothing compared to what Guy felt at that moment, as he realized how he had utterly destroyed the gentle, beautiful young woman whom he had loved beyond reason.

Without warning, his jaw exploded in pain, and he found himself on his back and groggily gazing into the furious eyes of Edmund de Toury. His new father-by-marriage.

Edmund leaned over and grabbed him, roaring, "Tell me there's been a mistake! Tell me you didn't kill my nephew!"

The weary, resigned look in Guy's eyes must have been answer enough, for Edmund released him and stepped away in disgust as he struggled to rein in his anguish.

Guy rose to his feet only to be assailed by his wife, who pelted his chest with her fists as she sobbed, "No, no... not Robin!" Tears were streaming down her face. Guy said nothing as he endured her sharp blows.

He was grabbed from behind, and glancing over his shoulder, he recognized the large outlaw who had knocked him out cold on more than one occasion. He should have run when he had the chance.

"Bind him, and take him over there until I'm done speaking to these people," Marian crisply commanded.

Without a word, he passively let his hands be pulled behind his back as the red-headed outlaw bound his wrists. Little John spun him around, and with great satisfaction, Much pushed him with all his strength. Guy stumbled awkwardly, landing heavily on his knees. John roughly hauled him back up on his feet while Much continued to shove him until they reached the far side of the clearing, where Guy was forced to kneel in the dirt while he awaited his fate.

᪥

As soon as Gisborne had been led away, Marian adroitly unsheathed the small dagger hanging from her belt and pressed it against Edmund's chest. "What have you done?" she cried.

Edmund was confident that she would not hurt him, so he calmly stood in place.

"Marian, for goodness' sake, lower that dagger," implored Constance.

"Be quiet, *Lady Gisborne*," Marian hissed as she glared at Edmund. With horror, she had finally realized the identity of Guy's bride. A wealthy heiress, indeed.

"Marian, there is much you do not know," Edmund quietly declared.

"You've joined forces with Argentan and Gisborne!" she shrieked. "You've given Constance to a murderer!" Her voice faded into a whisper as her eyes filled with tears. "I loved you like a second father, and now you've betrayed Robin and me, and you've broken the sacred promises that you made to me."

"Marian, I didn't betray Robin or you, and I have not broken my promises to you," insisted Edmund.

Marian cursed under her breath, her expression desperate and tormented. "What have you–?" she glanced around and saw that there were villagers observing them and listening. Rephrasing her question, she continued, "How can you fulfill your promises to me if you and Constance are both here?"

Constance put her hand on Marian's arm, hoping to convince her to lower her dagger. "Marian, you are the sister of my heart, and I swear to God in heaven that we have not failed you. Argentan forced me to marry Gisborne."

Marian lowered her dagger and looked into the tear-stained face of her dearest friend. "How is that possible? How on earth could anyone persuade you to marry that monster?"

"Come, let's go into the church where we can speak privately," suggested Edmund.

Marian signaled to John to keep watch in case Argentan and his soldiers returned and then followed Edmund and Constance into the Locksley Church.

"It's Lionel. They took him." Edmund's pain was etched deeply into his face.

"What do you mean? Who took him?"

"Argentan has kidnapped Lionel, and I must financially support Prince John's schemes, or the sheriff will send Lionel back to me in pieces."

Marian gasped, and Constance's tears began anew.

"Is Gisborne holding Lionel prisoner? Is that why you've married him?" Marian's voice took on a hard edge, her hatred for Gisborne growing.

"No, I've spoken to Gisborne, and he was unaware of the kidnapping plot," replied Edmund.

Marian scoffed. "He's a liar, and you're a fool to believe him."

Edmund had to admit it was a possibility. "You might be right, but he seemed genuinely taken aback when I talked to him. Frankly, I do not believe he is clever enough to be a good liar. As it is, he has agreed to a marriage in name only as long as I send him monthly payments."

"You are paying him? He murdered Robin!" exclaimed Marian.

Constance tried to calm her. "Father is protecting me by bribing Gisborne to stay out of my bed. But consider this: now that I am married to him, I will be closer to the sheriff, and I might learn where Lionel is being held."

Marian looked skeptically at Constance and Edmund. "You are both fools if you believe you will recover Lionel. It's likely that Argentan has already killed him."

"Yes, I know that," Edmund snapped, his temper flaring with his fear that Lionel could be dead. "But imagine yourself in my shoes. If it was your son, would you be so quick to surrender all hope?"

Marian became thoughtful as she considered his words.

Constance again reached out to Marian and placed her hand on the other woman's arm. "Marian, what are you going to do now? Why did you kill Bedford?"

"Well, first I will avenge Robin's death by making Argentan and Gisborne suffer before I kill them. Then I will ensure that Robin's legacy is protected and honored." Marian sidestepped the issue of killing Eustace.

Edmund sternly advised, "Bedford was close to Prince John, and Argentan is an ardent supporter of the prince. If you continue to kill John's allies, he will send an army here with the intention of destroying you and anyone who supports you."

Marian's eyes flashed with anger. "Argentan and Gisborne must die for murdering Robin!"

Edmund gentled his voice and beseeched her. "Marian, please, I beg of you, do not kill Argentan or Gisborne until Lionel has been returned to me. If Argentan dies, Lionel's captors might be under orders to execute him in retribution, and if you kill Gisborne, the sheriff might torture or maim Lionel to avenge his captain. Please, Marian, help me protect my son."

Marian sighed and looked away as she considered her options. "You're right; I can't kill Argentan… yet. I won't kill Gisborne either. Instead, I will make his life a living hell."

Edmund and Constance nodded in relief, and Constance offered, "And we will help you!"

⁂

Marian left Edmund and Constance in the church. They needed a few moments to collect themselves and offer prayers for Robin's soul.

As Marian walked across the courtyard, the villagers were kneeling reverently before her, offering both their condolences for Robin's death and their recognition of her as Countess of Huntingdon and Lady of Locksley. As the people voiced their grief for Robin's loss, Marian thanked them, and her expression softened. It was heartwarming to know that so many people loved Robin.

She approached Will and Allan; they were standing a short distance from John and Much who were guarding Gisborne.

An uncharacteristically dark scowl marred Allan's brow. "Marian, I want to ask you something."

"Speak, Allan," Marian warily replied.

"Why did you kill the Earl of Bedford?"

Will eyed her keenly, but remained silent. He shared Allan's misgivings.

She didn't respond, and a long, uncomfortable silence stretched between them. Marian's stomach lurched, and her mouth became dry. It was not the first time she had killed a man. Just before her voyage to the Holy Land, she had engaged in a desperate struggle to escape a guard who was trying to seize her dagger. During the scuffle, her blade had pierced his thigh. There had been so much blood! She closed her eyes, and the guard's grey face and unseeing eyes still haunted her mind.

However, Bedford's death was vastly different: she had aimed a weapon at the man and murdered him. She steeled herself against an unwelcome flood of guilt. It was an accident, she kept reminding herself. She had not aimed for his neck.

Marian crossed her arms and simply stated, "What's done cannot be undone."

"You could have just wounded him, Marian," suggested Allan. "He was an earl and a supporter of Prince John. What if the prince sends his soldiers here to avenge the death of Bedford?"

Will nodded vigorously. "I'm worried about that too."

Marian bristled defensively and banished any regrets for her lethal error to the darkest recesses of her heart. She rationalized that killing Bedford was to her advantage, because her enemies would now fear and respect her as a dangerous foe. "Much is right that they all deserve to die," she stated uncompromisingly.

Allan argued, "But, if the prince—"

"Allan," she brusquely interrupted. "I don't have to explain myself to you or anyone else." She signaled for Much and John to join them. "I have a new plan."

After revealing that Robin's cousin, Lionel, had been kidnapped by Argentan, Marian explained the need for restraint. They could not kill Argentan or Gisborne until Lionel's fate had been determined. The men grudgingly agreed.

Marian offered an alternative idea. "I had always planned to make Gisborne's life miserable before killing him, and that is exactly what we will do. Lord Embelton and I believe that Argentan will keep Lionel somewhere close. We will scour the greenwood and monitor the movements of Argentan, Gisborne, and Payen as much as possible. Finally, we will resume the mission of Robin Hood. We will help the poor by demanding donations from nobles who pass through Sherwood."

John frowned. "Are you sure this man is still alive? It would be easier for Argentan to kill him than to keep him prisoner."

"I know," conceded Marian. "Personally, I doubt that he is still alive. But he is Robin's cousin, and with the loss of Robin, the family is desperate to recover Lionel."

"Are we just going to let Gisborne go? We have to do something! He must face some kind of punishment," growled an irate Much.

Marian observed Guy, kneeling in the dirt with his hands tied behind his back. "Much, you have a point. He must be punished, but we cannot kill him yet."

Will's face brightened. "I have an idea!"

~

Marian's gaze swept across the assembled people of Locksley. Edmund and Constance were standing near the church. Everyone fell silent, waiting for her to speak. She addressed the crowd in a firm, loud voice. "People of Locksley, we are united in our grief over the death of Robin Hood, my beloved husband and your rightful lord. He loved England and fought to protect you from evil men like Argentan and Gisborne." She lapsed into silence, gathering her thoughts. A lonely, fat tear trickled down her cheek. "Unfortunately, Lord Robin is no longer with us, but he will live in our hearts forever. His spirit will live in Sherwood, in Locksley, in Nottingham, and in England forever. I promise that I will continue his fight. I will protect his legacy, and we will remember Robin Hood forever!"

The peasants nodded and whispered prayers for the peace of Robin's soul. Then Leofric and Elvina delivered short speeches in Robin's honor.

Marian smiled at the villagers, her eyes shining with tears as she spoke again. "Robin Hood has already become immortal: he is a legend throughout England, and he lives in our hearts!" she proclaimed, and the people cheered her words. A glimmer of hope stirred in her heart; the people and their love for her husband would be a source of inspiration to her during the difficult times ahead.

"Today, you will witness the punishment of this criminal." She pointed at the village whipping post, where a nearly naked Guy of

Gisborne was tied with his arms wrapped around the sturdy post and bound at the wrists on the far side. He was wearing only his braies, and he stood stiffly with as much dignity as he could muster under the circumstances.

Striding purposefully towards Gisborne, Marian unsheathed her dagger and positioned herself next to the post where he could see her.

"Do you recognize this dagger, Guy?" she asked with feigned civility.

The slight widening of his eyes signaled that he did recognize it, although he remained silent.

"Of course you recognize it. This is *your* dagger; the one you used to kill Robin."

Murmuring rippled through the crowd.

Marian resumed. "You might wonder why I would carry such a morbid reminder of my loss, but I want to assure you in front of all these witnesses, that I will eventually return this dagger to you. I also promise that you will not like the manner in which I will give it to you."

She thrust the dagger towards his face, and Guy tilted his head as far from the sharp blade as his restraints allowed. Marian was grimly pleased by his discomfort. "Fear not, Sir Guy of Gisborne. I'm not going to kill you today. But mark my words: your days are numbered. You need to watch over your shoulder, because my vengeance could come at any time, day or night. You will never be safe, and you will never see the end coming until it's too late."

Guy released a long exhalation as Marian lowered the dagger.

"I recommend that you spend your remaining time on earth beseeching God for His mercy," she triumphantly concluded. "But never forget that every night I will beg God to send you to eternal damnation for the sake of Robin. And which one of us is more deserving to have our prayers answered?"

Marian was satisfied to see him blanch, his pale blue eyes filled with dread. Once again, she addressed the crowd. "Gisborne deserves death, but we cannot kill him because he is under the protection of Prince John. I dare not place you at risk of the prince's wrath. Instead, we will leave him with the stripes of our sorrow and fury." She nodded at Will, who stepped forward with the whip.

As she moved away, she reminded John. "Whip him as you see fit, but remember: do not kill him. We need him alive... for now."

1 July 1192, Locksley Manor

Constance reluctantly entered the main bedchamber of Locksley Manor carrying a tray of medicinal herbs. The long summer day had ended, and twilight was extending across the land. She could see her husband lying face down on the bed, apparently unconscious, his back bloody and raw. A servant finished lighting several candles and scurried out the door, past Edmund who was following his daughter in an attempt to dissuade her.

"Constance, you are not responsible for that man," his hushed voice insisted. "Let the servants dress his wounds."

She offered a half-hearted smile. "Father, I must disagree. I *am* responsible for him. I'm his wife, and I'm skilled in the healing arts. Besides, I do not want to force the servants to perform such a task, not when they know what he's done."

"It's not right," he grumbled.

"Papa, be at ease." With a gentle brush of her lips against his cheek, she watched him yield to her wishes and quit the room.

"Go away. I don't want your help." Guy's deep voice was ragged with pain, and he groaned involuntarily when he shifted on the bed.

"What you want is not important," she briskly informed him. "I will not endanger my brother by allowing you to die of wound fever. Therefore, I will clean your back and apply herbs to it." Constance set her tray on the low table next to the bed. She briefly left to retrieve the rest of her supplies: a bowl of diluted wine and clean linen. Dipping a cloth into the watery alcohol, she cleaned the raw welts crisscrossing his back as he hissed from the sting of her ministrations. She noticed the pale marks of old scars along his shoulders.

It had not been his first whipping.

There were questions hovering on the tip of her tongue, and she decided this was an opportunity to get answers. He could hardly walk away from her. "Why..." She faltered. "Why did you kill Robin? Was it because the sheriff ordered it?"

The silence stretched on for a long time, and just as she despaired of receiving any response, he spoke. "I wanted him to stop ruining my life."

This gave her pause. "How was he ruining your life?"

He sighed and then winced as she passed her cloth over a deep wound. "He ruined my life when he stole Marian from me."

"What? How could he steal Marian from you? I've known Robin and Marian all my life, and Marian has always loved Robin."

Guy lurched away from her and tried to get off the bed, only to collapse in pain. Frustrated that he was trapped, he growled, "You're wrong. Lady Marian had grown fond of me before Robin Hood stole her from the castle. She was going to marry me."

Initially, Constance was flummoxed by his words. He still wasn't making sense. Perhaps he was delirious. She searched her memories of the time when Marian came to live at Embelton. It had been nearly four years ago. Suddenly, she remembered something. "The poetry! You are the man who wrote those poems to Marian."

He stilled. "You saw my verses? I remember they went missing from her chamber, and I knew that she had treasured them and taken them with her that night. It proves that I am right; she favored me."

Constance was tempted to tell him that Marian had only kept the poems because of the official writing on the back of the bits and pieces of parchment. As much as she would have liked to extinguish his arrogance with a splash of cold truth, she would not reveal this to him. Her father and Robin believed the parchments were proof that the French king was interfering in England's succession. They were locked in her father's desk at Embelton.

"I see," she cautiously replied. "Although I must point out that Marian lived with us in Embelton for two years and never mentioned you."

"Are you finished? I want you to leave." Guy's voice had taken on a hostile note.

"I'm almost done. I need to put a poultice on the deeper cuts." Constance decided a change of subject was in order. "How old are these scars?"

"You are wrong about Lady Marian. There was a time when she cared for me. But how can I compete with a wealthy earl?" he whined.

Constance snapped at him in anger. "Marian is not mercenary like that. She has always loved Robin. Regardless, it is obvious that she now hates you above all others. Everyone hates you for murdering Robin."

"I don't care what people think about me." He then shifted until she could see the gleam of his eyes in the low light. "I know Marian hates me. But I still love her, and I will always love her, and no one else." He then turned his head away.

Constance finally understood his disdain for her. Marian's exquisite beauty was undeniable, and Constance, although agreeable in her appearance, could never hope to compete with such loveliness. Throughout their long friendship, Constance's better nature had battled the envy that clawed at the dark side of her heart. Even though she loved Marian as a sister, she often felt gangly and unattractive next to her.

If his intention had been to hurt her, he had succeeded. She then chided herself. This horrible man, no matter how handsome he was, had murdered her beloved cousin. Why did she care what he thought of her? Besides, he was a fool to believe that Marian had ever wanted him. Was he oblivious to Marian's lethal intentions towards him? He would be killed as soon as they rescued Lionel.

Yet, why did that thought cause a tightening in her chest? She would need to guard her heart carefully. She hurriedly finished her task and left the chamber.

⤏

When Constance returned to check on Gisborne in the early hours of the next morning, he was feverish. This was expected, and she was not overly worried. If he was still feverish the second morning, then she would have cause for concern. He had remained lying on his stomach, so she removed the soiled bandages and bathed his back in cool water.

"Maman?" gasped Guy quietly. He then mumbled something in French.

A surprised Constance paused, but said nothing. Her own mother had been French, so she knew the language well.

"Maman!" he urgently cried. He continued speaking in French, and Constance leaned closer to hear his words. "Let's run away… I do not want him to hurt us anymore." His eyes remained closed. Again he called, "Maman?"

Constance glanced around guiltily; they were alone. Her curiosity had often gotten her into trouble, but she could not resist. "Yes, my son?" she whispered to him in French.

"I love you, Maman," he murmured in his delirium. "I want to protect you." Several tears dampened the pillow where the side of his face rested.

Constance was stunned by his tender cries for his mother. He was desperate to save her from some kind of danger. She slowly finished re-dressing his welts with fresh linen as she wondered whether his mother was still alive, and where she might be living.

Returning to her own chamber, she contemplated the unsettling

100

dichotomy that her husband was a murderer who had killed Robin, but he was also a son who loved his mother.

4 July 1192, Dover, England

Juan hurried into the tavern and nimbly advanced through the throng of people. He needed to get as close as possible to one of the brightly lit torches lining the far wall. Glancing over his shoulder, he feared that his pursuers would appear at any moment.

Upon his arrival in Dover earlier in the day, he had easily found the tavern mentioned by Robin, *The Hawk and the Dove*. The proprietor, Bazile, and his sons had been welcoming, but Juan was suspicious of their eager friendliness, which had seemed forced and insincere.

Juan had lied to Bazile, assuring him he had already secured a room at another inn. He could not shake the premonition that spending the night at *The Hawk and the Dove* might prove fatal, and the vital dispatch that he carried would be stolen from him and shared with King Richard's enemies.

After inquiring about the dowager queen's location, Juan had politely refused the meal they offered him and left. Bazile and his sons had made no effort to hide the fact that they were following him as he went from tavern to tavern, desperate to find safe harbor in this busy foreign port.

He could not risk losing the message from Richard to Queen Eleanor. Positioning himself under the brightest of the torches, he pulled the sealed letter from a pouch suspended by a leather cord looped around his neck and hidden under his tunic. Hesitating, for he hated to betray the trust of the king, he broke the seal and silently read it. Frowning in concentration, he committed the words to memory.

Just then, shouting at the tavern door seized his attention, and

Juan lifted his eyes to behold Bazile and his sons aggressively making their way towards him.

The chatter and clatter of the tavern quieted as everyone was curious to see what was happening.

Juan raised the king's letter over his head and shouted, "Is this what you seek, Bazile? You will never have it!" Placing the dispatch into the flames of the torch, it instantly caught fire. He dropped the burning letter before it could singe his fingers, and it ignited the alcohol-stained rushes at his feet.

Bazile furiously screamed at him.

Juan grabbed the torch and lifted it from the brace on the wall. He then tossed it on the floor in front of the rapidly advancing Bazile. The dirty rushes covering the tavern floor flamed with an ominous whoosh, and Bazile had no choice but to retreat. When the crowd started screaming and stampeding towards the front door, they drove him and his sons backwards, away from Juan.

There was a narrow corridor near Juan, and he hastily passed through it and into a small kitchen where the serving girls were fleeing the conflagration through a back door. With a sigh of relief, Juan followed them and emerged on a side street. He jogged away from the fiery tavern and headed west.

He ducked down a darkened alleyway, only to discover it was a dead end. Pivoting, he retraced his steps and cursed the time wasted by his wrong turn. Risking a backwards glance, he was thankful that he did not see a bright glow on the horizon, which would indicate a raging fire, but he heard the baying of a hound in the distance. With dismay, he recalled seeing a hound lounging next to the hearth at *The Hawk and the Dove.*

Finally, he reached the outskirts of town, where he hoped to hide until morning when he would begin his journey to London. A small dark building loomed ahead. It was a ramshackle ruin with a partially collapsed roof, but it would provide shelter and allow him to catch his breath. Winded from his sprint through Dover, he entered the shack and struggled to calm his breathing. He had faced danger and death before, but the past fifteen years had been marked by the relative ease of serving as Princess Berengaria's personal bodyguard. He hadn't been tested like this in a long time.

Juan retrieved his grandfather's dagger from the sheath at his belt. As his eyes adjusted to the weak moonlight, he thought about the day, now nearly 30 years ago, when his grandfather, Yousef bin Hamid, had given it to him at his knighting ceremony.

The dagger had red stones and was adorned with the geometric designs favored by his grandfather's Moorish ancestors. But the most noticeable feature of the dagger was its broken tip. His grandfather had insisted that it was broken during a duel with a mischievous spirit—a *djinni*—who had bitten the blade and swallowed the tip. Yousef enjoyed making up such stories to explain the damage to the dagger, and Juan smiled wistfully at the memory of his outrageous tales.

But that was not what made the dagger special.

He reminisced in a reverent whisper, "I will never forget your wise words, Grandfather. The broken tip reminds us that only God is perfect. When danger comes, rely on God's strength, and even a broken dagger will be sufficient." A content smile graced his lips. "But if it is time for God to call me home to heaven, not even the sharpest, strongest blade will prevail."

Indistinct voices and the barking of a dog briefly distracted him. They were getting closer.

"Grandfather, before dawn breaks I will learn whether God's plan is for me to triumph or die with honor."

CHAPTER 8
BROTHER TUCK

7 July 1192, Lenton Chapel, Nottinghamshire

Marian squeezed through the gap in the back wall of her family's chapel and crawled into the vestry. She had not visited her home since the death of her father nearly four years ago. Because he had been murdered in the chapel, there were rumors that his ghost haunted it, and many considered it desecrated. Consequently, it sat empty and unused. Marian did not believe in ghosts, and she was confident that God had welcomed her dear father into heaven immediately upon his death.

She stifled the urge to cough as her movements stirred up a small cloud of dust.

Earlier that day, Marian had received word that a stranger had arrived in Lenton searching for her. This man had insisted that the chapel be opened to allow him to spend time in prayer. Her plan was to get a look at him. She would then decide whether to meet him before rejoining the outlaws, who were waiting for her nearby.

Peeking around the corner, she saw the stranger kneeling before the altar with his head bowed, and she swallowed hard as the scene resurrected memories of her father, who had spent hours in the same spot, praying and begging for God's mercy. Lord Alfred Fitzwalter had been such a kind, generous man that Marian could not imagine him committing any sins requiring such repentance.

Unlike me—I'm a murderess. The thought invaded her mind, and grief over the killing of Bedford seized her heart. She argued with the vexing voice in her head. *I'm not guilty if I didn't intend to kill.* Her troublesome conscience would not relent. *You are planning to kill, then you WILL be a murderess.*

A deep, melodious voice interrupted her mental debate. "I know someone is there. Make yourself known." The man was now standing and peering into the darkness of the vestry where she was hiding.

Cursing herself for failing to remain concealed, Marian approached the altar, genuflecting and crossing herself before facing the man.

He went down on one knee and proclaimed, "I thank God Almighty that I have finally found you again, my lady. I have despaired of ever recovering you."

Marian's brow rose in surprise, but she held her tongue as she went to the doors and signaled for the outlaws to enter. The man did not seem threatening, but Marian did not like the idea of someone wanting to 'recover' her.

John, Much, Allan, and Will filed into the small chapel, briefly kneeling and crossing themselves respectfully before turning their full attention to the stranger who stood and faced them.

He was a middle-aged man with weathered and tanned skin. Both his thinning hair and his neatly trimmed beard were streaked with grey. His long, dark tunic was belted at the waist and featured tightly fitted sleeves. In one hand he grasped a dark-colored soft cap which matched his tunic. Over his tunic, he wore a white mantle with a red cross on the left breast.

"Who are you, and who do you think I am? I assure you that I am in no need of being recovered," queried Marian, perhaps a bit more waspishly than she had intended.

"I am Brother Tuck, and I am in service to our earthly king,

Richard. You are the Countess of Huntingdon and the widow of Lord Robin Fitzooth."

Much pushed past the other men to stand in front of the stranger. "I recognize you! You were on the ship that took us from Acre to Cyprus and from there, Marseilles. I thought I saw you in Poitou as well."

"Is that true?" Marian's eyes narrowed. "You are following me?"

"Yes—"

Before the man could utter another word, Little John grabbed him, twisting his right arm behind his back and wrapping his large hand around the man's neck.

"Be at ease, my son!" Tuck exclaimed, choking a bit from John's iron grip. He hurriedly elaborated, "I have been charged with the solemn duty of protecting Lady Huntingdon. King Richard himself sent me on my mission."

"Let him go," Marian tersely ordered.

John complied, but all the outlaws stepped closer to Marian.

Clearing his throat and rubbing his neck, Tuck explained, "The king wanted to ensure that you reached the court in Poitiers safely. There are many dangers along the route from Outremer to Poitou. I am a knight and a brother of the Order of the Temple—"

"A Knight Templar!" cried Much. "I should have recognized the symbol on your mantle."

The outlaws started murmuring amongst themselves, but Marian shushed them, and they quieted.

"Why would the king send *you*?" she demanded. "I thought the Knights Templar preferred to serve in the Holy Land."

"One of our most sacred duties is to guard and shepherd pilgrims during their sojourn in the Holy Land. We also watch over the travel routes to Outremer. I believe that is why the king asked for a volunteer from amongst my brothers."

"You volunteered? Did you know Robin?" Marian became wistful. Meeting people who knew Robin always touched her heart.

"I met your husband during the march from Acre to Jaffa, where I served under Lord Huntingdon's command. He knew my name, but little else. After his tragic death, I wanted to honor him. Guarding his wife was a privilege I eagerly sought."

Much demanded a more detailed explanation. "We returned to England many weeks ago. Why did you stay hidden all this time? Have you been spying on us?"

Brother Tuck chuckled wryly. "I have not been hidden—merely lost. When you left Poitiers, you were traveling north, so I surmised that England was your destination. I knew that Queen Eleanor was in London, and I made a poor assumption that you were seeking an audience with her. So, I went to London and spoke with the queen."

"You talked to the queen about Lady Marian?" Allan interjected. Now that he had a better look at the man, he also remembered seeing him on the ship during their journey home.

"Yes. After several weeks, Queen Eleanor consented to speak with me. She rather brusquely informed me that she had never met a Countess of Huntingdon named Marian. She then commanded me to travel to Huntingdon. Of course, you were not there either, and I feared that I had failed in my mission."

"How did you find me?" asked Marian.

"The steward at Huntingdon castle told me that Lord Robin's betrothed was from Nottinghamshire, from the barony of Lenton, to be precise. So I came here." Tuck sighed in relief. "I am truly thankful that God has led me to you, and that you are all right."

Marian scoffed rudely. "I will never be 'all right' again. My husband was brutally murdered before my eyes. Did you tell the people of Huntingdon that Robin was... gone?"

"Yes, my lady. There was much sorrow and lamentations among the people of Huntingdon, but they were glad that you and Lord Robin had finally married. They said you had been betrothed for an unusually long time."

Marian did not want to linger in the chapel at Lenton for fear that word would get back to Argentan, and he would punish her people. "Brother Tuck, I appreciate your diligence, and I have no doubt that King Richard will be pleased that you completed your mission. When you return to the Holy Land, tell him I am… all right. There is no need for the king to worry about me."

Tuck countered, "My mission is to see you safe in Poitiers. I plan to escort you back there, or if you prefer, I will take you to the queen, and she can watch over you until King Richard returns from the Crusade." Taking note of her attire, he said, "I cannot leave you unprotected and living in the greenwood."

Marian bristled and looked meaningfully at John. Once again, the outlaw reached for Tuck, only this time, the Knight Templar was ready for him. With a few practiced moves, Tuck flipped the big man onto his back. The other outlaws stared in amazement.

Tuck submissively raised his hands to show he did not wish to fight. "Please, my lady, come with me, and I will let you choose between Poitiers and London."

"I choose Nottinghamshire." Marian lifted her chin defiantly.

"May I ask why you wish to remain here?"

"I wish to protect the people of Locksley and Lenton from the Sheriff of Nottingham, the man who tried to kill King Richard. I am leading these men in the fight against the cruelty and injustice of the sheriff."

Brother Tuck fell into thoughtfulness for a few moments. "My lady, I see that you are devoted to a noble cause. Allow me to escort you to safety, either to Poitiers or London. Then I will return here and lead these men in the struggles against this sheriff. I am an experienced knight. I will fight in your place."

Without hesitating, Marian refused.

"If your purpose is to fight injustice and protect the poor, I will gladly offer myself to your cause. But I cannot allow you to risk your life in such endeavors."

"Lord Huntingdon's cousin has been kidnapped. The family needs my help to find and rescue him."

"Again, my lady, I must point out that I have the necessary training to assist in the recovery of this man."

"I must avenge Robin's death. His murderers, Baron de Argentan and Guy of Gisborne, are here in Nottinghamshire. It is my right to take vengeance against them."

The outlaws nodded vigorously.

Tuck gazed steadily at Marian, compassion shining in his eyes. "Now I understand. This is the reason above all others for your desire to remain here. I feel compelled to remind you that vengeance belongs to the Lord."

"Then I will be doing the Lord's work." Marian pivoted to leave, and the others followed her.

"If you will not return to the safety of the court in Poitiers or London, then I will be obliged to stay with you, in order to fulfill my vow to the king to protect you."

Marian stopped at the door and looked back. "I don't want your help. I release you from any responsibility you feel for my well-being. Please go away."

"I beg your forgiveness for my impertinence, but it is not within your power to release me from this vow. Only King Richard possesses such authority. I will remain at your side until the king returns, or until you retreat to the safety of court."

"Marian," whispered Much as he tugged on her sleeve. "These Knights of the Temple are fearsome warriors for Christ. If he is willing to help us, then we will have the benefit of both his training and his righteousness in our fight against Argentan."

Marian glanced over her shoulder at the Knight Templar as he stood near the altar of her family's chapel. He was standing in the same place where her father's blood had pooled after his murder. She shivered involuntarily at the memory. Perhaps meeting this man here, in this sacred place, was a sign. She walked back to confront him.

"Are you willing to follow me? These men have taken an oath to obey me as their leader in this fight. I will welcome suggestions and ideas, but I will make the final decisions. You are a knight. Can you accept a woman as your master?"

A kindly smile tugged at the corners of Tuck's mouth, and he went down on one knee before her. "Lady Marian, the Order of the Knights of the Temple is devoted to the Virgin Mary. We humbly venerate all female saints for the strength of their faith in the face of their physical frailties. I pledge to follow you in your quest to protect the people of Nottinghamshire and seek justice for them. However, I will not take a life in the pursuit of revenge. Can you accept that?"

"Yes; I accept your terms. Besides, I alone wish to bear the burden of avenging Robin's death."

Marian smiled at the older man as she silently vowed to show him that women had many strengths that outweighed their physical limitations.

14 July 1192, Locksley Manor

"…Lord Duncan had come for a visit, and he was searching for the expensive horn bracer he had purchased for archery practice. Well, Lord Robin had thrown it away because it made his arm itchy and red. He preferred his old leather bracer." Elvina's eyes shone with joy as she recalled a story from Robin's youth.

"Lord Robin and Lord Duncan shared a love of archery," Leofric reminisced. "It was something they could do together without arguing."

Constance smiled indulgently. She was standing in the kitchen with the two elderly servants and listening to their wistful banter. It was a welcome respite from spending time with her brooding husband as he drank to excess while morosely staring at the crimson

111

banner which adorned Locksley's great hall. She had been told that the banner with its embroidered rising sun was Baron de Argentan's standard.

She tried to be attentive, but thoughts of her father's search for Lionel distracted her. Edmund had left with Marian and the outlaws to explore the caves near Locksley, and Constance was frustrated that she had been prevented from joining in the hunt for her brother. If Marian could traipse through the woods, then why couldn't she? She returned her attention to Elvina's story.

"...and when Lord Duncan found out—" Elvina was interrupted by a pounding at the door.

Leofric left to answer the knock. He promptly returned and announced that Argentan had arrived and would be going upstairs with Gisborne. At Constance's confused expression, Leofric explained that it was typical for the two men to retreat into the main bedchamber for privacy.

Elvina set a bottle of ale and two cups on a tray and left to deliver it upstairs.

"If only I could hear their conversation!" Constance grumbled. "But if I stand in the corridor, and they suddenly open the door, there would be no place for me to hide."

"They always speak French when they are together. Standing outside the door will not help us learn anything about their schemes," Leofric replied.

"I speak French fluently. So, I am the perfect choice to spy on them, but I have to get close enough to listen without being detected."

Leofric's face brightened. "My lady, come with me!" He pivoted and hastened to the far end of the kitchen, opening a small door and ducking down to pass through it.

Constance followed and found herself in a dark, cool storeroom stacked with barrels of ale and burlap bags of grain. Along the walls were shelves loaded with stores of food and smaller boxes filled with valuable spices.

Leofric brought a finger up to his lips to signal the need for quiet. He whispered, "This pantry is underneath the master's chamber. Maybe you will be able to hear them from here."

They both stilled and looked up at the low ceiling. Sure enough, muffled voices and the dull thuds of someone pacing above them could be heard.

"I need to get closer. Help me stand on top of one of those barrels," Constance murmured.

"My lady, that's neither safe nor proper."

Constance huffed, "I don't care about propriety. Help me up and hold my legs in case I lose my balance."

She was soon balanced precariously on top of a wobbly barrel. For the first time in her life, she was grateful for her unusually tall stature; it allowed her set one ear against the ceiling boards which also served as the floor of Gisborne's chamber. Leofric wrapped his arms around her calves, and she felt more secure.

The voices were louder, but still indistinct.

Desperate, Constance pushed against the boards above her head and discovered that one was loose. Her heart was pounding painfully in her chest as she pressed against the board with both hands. It creaked, and a shower of dust and dirt rained down upon her. In a panic, she looked down as her eyes watered and her throat constricted, an urge to cough nearly overwhelming her.

Constance looked back up and pushed against the board again. Raising up on her toes, she realized that the board was under the bed. Giddy with relief, she focused on their conversation.

"Where is your lovely wife?" The voice of the sheriff could now be clearly heard. The two men were conversing in French, just as Leofric had described.

"Lady Constance went to the kitchen to supervise the servants. Soon it will be time for the evening meal," Gisborne politely replied.

"How very domestic you have become! I told you to trust my judgment in selecting a bride for you. She is a well-born lady who will do you credit. I suggest you get her with child as soon as possible. That will strengthen your ties to the Barony of Embelton, in case something unfortunate should happen to the baron's son."

Constance's heart leapt in fear. She wanted to believe that Lionel was still alive, yet she could not deny the possibility that he was lost to them. Like Robin.

"My lord, where is Lord Edmund's son? I have not met him, and he seems to be missing."

"That is not something you need to know, Gisborne. Rest assured that I am taking very good care of your brother-by-marriage."

"Is he alive?" Guy cautiously inquired, echoing the words uppermost in Constance's mind.

"You are excessively worried about this man. Do you already have your eyes on the barony? I'm impressed with your ambition, but I'm not here to discuss Lionel de Toury with you."

Constance exhaled in relief. The sheriff seemed to be insinuating that Lionel was still alive, and she now felt certain that Guy had been honest about not knowing his location.

"Of course, my lord. How may I serve you today?" Gisborne had abandoned the topic of her brother.

Argentan's voice darkened with anger. "Instead of lazily pretending to be lord of the manor, you need to capture the outlaws and our dear Marian Hood. You are my captain, and your position will be forfeit if you continue to fail me."

"My lord, in the last few days, I have made several forays into the woods in search of Lady Marian and the outlaws. However, I have only recently recovered from the injuries I received when you abandoned me here at Locksley after the wedding."

Constance cringed at the sound of a hard slap.

"Don't you dare whine to me! Your whipping was well deserved for your many failures. You failed to kill King Richard, and you failed to protect the Earl of Bedford. Prince John was furious about the loss of Bedford, and it was all I could do to keep him from marching into Nottingham and interfering with our work here."

"How was I supposed to know that Marian was planning to kill Bedford?" Gisborne exclaimed. He then moderated his voice. "What can we do to prevent Prince John from coming here? His men would kill Lady Marian without hesitation."

"Oh, how sweet!" sneered Argentan. "You are still desperate to protect Marian Hood. Although I initially planned to kill her on sight, I now believe capturing and humiliating her would be much more entertaining. Have you made any progress in finding her?"

Guy dutifully reported, "Lady Marian and her men have robbed several nobles traveling through Sherwood. They have not hurt anyone, and they have announced their intention to help the poor by stealing from the wealthy. I'm troubled by reports from eye witnesses that there is a Knight Templar among their ranks. A man with such skills might make it more difficult to end their mischief."

Argentan scoffed. "I'm not worried about this Knight Templar. They are ill-educated religious fanatics."

"And how will you prevent Prince John from coming here?"

"I have a plan that will both placate Prince John and undermine Marian Hood's effectiveness. When the people gather to celebrate the Feast of St. Mary Magdalene, we will round up the able-bodied men from Locksley and Lenton and conscript them into Prince John's army. He's fearful of King Richard's return, so he's building a private army as a defense against his brother. In the meantime, sending these men away will prevent them from helping Marian."

Guy's voice rose in alarm. "We need those men for next month's harvest!"

"That's not my problem," retorted the sheriff.

"Does King Philippe know about this army?"

Constance gasped involuntarily. What did the King of France have to do with their schemes? She only vaguely recalled her father and Robin's speculations about Philippe's interference in the affairs of England.

The sheriff remained composed. "I will manage King Philippe. He is not your concern."

The strain of holding her arms above her head to push against the board while standing on her toes was becoming more than Constance could bear. Her arms were aching, her legs were trembling, and her head was swimming with dizziness as black spots dotted her vision. She lowered the board and collapsed into Leofric's arms.

"My lady, are you all right?" Leofric whispered as he helped her off of the barrel.

"Yes, I just could not remain standing any longer."

They retreated into the kitchen, and Constance resolved that she would be ready the next time Argentan visited Guy. "Tomorrow, when Gisborne leaves the manor to search for Marian, we will work together to loosen a board from under his bed. I want to be able to shift the board to one side without making a sound. Then we will put a sturdy ladder in the pantry so I can listen without exhausting myself or risking discovery."

Elvina brought a damp cloth and wiped the dust from Constance's face and shoulders.

"Did you understand them?" Leofric eagerly inquired.

"Yes! As soon as my father returns, I must tell him everything."

15 July 1192, Locksley Manor

"Go away! Stop tormenting me!" Loud shouts of distress in the middle of the night echoed within Locksley Manor.

Edmund and Constance rushed into Guy's chamber. The moon provided only a pale, weak light through the chamber's lone window. Gisborne was cowering on his bed, his eyes wide with terror.

He shakily pointed to the corner and cried, "Look! Tell me you see him too!"

Edmund and Constance beheld a shadowy figure standing in the corner and wearing a familiar hooded cloak while pointing a nocked arrow at Gisborne.

Edmund's impassive gaze returned to Guy. "I don't see anything."

Frantically, Guy insisted, "He's right there! Don't you see him?"

Constance moved forward until she was next to Gisborne's bed. "Sir Guy, what exactly do you see? Are you feverish again?" She placed her hand on his forehead, briefly covering his eyes as the shadowy figure stealthily exited the open door.

When Gisborne peered into the corner again, it was empty. In a frightened whisper, he asserted, "He was there... I saw him."

"Who was there?" demanded Edmund.

"The ghost of Robin Hood," Guy murmured in a hushed voice as he closed his eyes and crossed himself in fear.

Constance and Edmund eyed each other and nodded.

With her conscience prickling at her heart, Constance said, "There's no one there. You must have been dreaming. Be at ease and try to sleep."

CHAPTER 9
MARIAN HOOD

18 July 1192, Sherwood Forest, On the Road to Nottingham

uy wearily rubbed his face and yawned as the steady rhythm of his horse's plodding gait was lulling him into a light doze. He berated himself for his lethargy, brought on by too much ale and not enough sleep the previous night.

Sleep had become his nemesis. Most nights he was tormented by nightmares of the moment he had attacked Robin, only to discover that they were half-brothers. Lately, the nightmares had taken on a surreal, yet terrifying, quality. He would relive the moment when his dagger plunged into Robin's chest, only to look up and find that he had actually stabbed Marian. Some nights he would dream that he had stabbed Constance, or even his mother. Once, he even saw his own face staring back at him with vacant, dead eyes.

On the nights when his sleep was relatively peaceful, he would awaken to find Robin Hood's ghost hovering near his bed, aiming a nocked arrow at him. The apparition never spoke, and his hooded cloak shadowed his face, but Guy knew that his half-brother was haunting him from beyond the grave. The fact that no one else could see the ghost only confirmed his worst fears.

"Well, don't you agree with me?" demanded his companion.

"Yes, of course, Sir Gervase," Guy dutifully answered.

Sir Gervase Rainecourt was Prince John's envoy, and he had been dispatched to Nottingham to meet with Argentan. He was the same age as John, and he was eager to remind everyone of his position as a confidant of the prince.

Guy had been tasked with meeting him at the border of Nottinghamshire and escorting him to the sheriff. Guy had also collected a bag of silver from their contact at the tavern in Dover, and he had noticed that the monthly bags of silver had decreased in weight since their return from the Holy Land.

Stifling a yawn as he endured yet another story about Gervase's close relationship with the prince, Guy felt some gratification knowing that the sheriff would also find the man insufferable, but he would still have to curry favor with him.

The sheriff was desperate to keep Prince John from interfering with the affairs of Nottinghamshire, and Guy was desperate to keep the prince's soldiers away from Marian. As long as he was in command of the sheriff's men-at-arms, he could protect her, but he would have no control over the men who served John.

Diverting John's interest from Nottinghamshire was becoming increasingly difficult. Nearly every noble traveling to Nottingham during the past fortnight had been robbed. Marian and the outlaws took anywhere from a tenth to a quarter of whatever valuables they found, and no one had been injured since her lethal attack on Bedford.

Gervase was still droning on and on about something Prince John had said or done; Guy had stopped listening several miles back. He glanced over his shoulder at Gervase's men-at-arms as they marched behind the two mounted knights. The royal envoy had brought a dozen men with him, and they easily outnumbered Marian's outlaws.

Looking forward, he tensed at the sight of two dark figures ahead. He was relieved to see that it was just an elderly couple hobbling along the road. They were swathed in tattered hooded cloaks and leaning heavily on walking sticks. Tomorrow was market day in Nottingham, and it was likely that they were on their way to sell whatever was wrapped in the bundles tied to their backs.

"Make way; we're on the sheriff's business," he shouted.

The man bobbed his head, and they shuffled into the marshy ditch and tall weeds that bordered the old Roman road.

After scanning the forest on both sides of the road, Guy looked up, as if he expected Robin Hood to drop a net upon the soldiers from heaven. Sighing, he acknowledged that he needed to get more sleep.

"Look!" Gervase exclaimed.

Some thirty yards down the road, the red-headed outlaw who had accompanied Robin to the Holy Land stood at the tree line. On the opposite side of the road was the boy with the red scarf.

"Murderer!" roared Much. "You will be punished for killing Lord Robin!"

Will Scarlet said nothing, but he grinned at them and waved his scarf over his head.

"After them!" Gervase ordered. "Divide up, and bring me that forest vermin, dead or alive!"

His men eagerly started after the outlaws, who fearlessly stood there, easy prey for such trained wolves.

"Wait! You can't send all your men after two outlaws," insisted Guy.

Gervase agreed, and he sent three men after Much and three after Will. Once the soldiers drew near, Much and Will vanished into the forest.

Guy grew concerned that half of their men were now chasing after outlaws. "My lord, we should not tarry here."

Before Gervase could respond, they heard a shout behind them. Turning, they saw Little John laughing and pointing his staff at them. He was at least twenty yards away, and the two elderly peasants were fearfully crouching in the ditch between the soldiers and the outlaw.

Once again, another outlaw stood across the road. He was playing a lute and loudly singing:

A rooster is a proud bird;
He tells everyone he's king.
But although he rules a roost,
He lacks land and can't take wing.

Guy suggested that they ignore the outlaws and hasten down the road, but the song's insults to Prince John incensed Gervase. Much to Guy's exasperation, he sent all his remaining men after Little John and Allan-a-dale.

Once again, when the soldiers drew close, the outlaws entered the forest, and Gervase's men disappeared as they pursued them.

Guy glared at the other man in disbelief. "Who taught you military tactics?" he thundered. "You've sent all your men into the woods. Who will protect the sheriff's silver?"

"Get off your horses and kneel on the ground. Place your hands on top of your head," commanded a dulcet feminine voice.

Guy saw that the 'old' couple had dropped their burdens and pulled back their hoods. It was Marian and the Knight Templar, and they were aiming nocked arrows at them.

Guy and Gervase grudgingly obeyed.

"I am here to take your silver," Marian announced as the Templar bound Guy's hands behind his back. "It is needed by the people who are suffering under Sheriff de Argentan's taxation."

Gervase disdainfully sneered, "So, *this* is the Countess of Huntingdon? You look like a dirty peasant, although I can see that you have a pretty face. After you are captured, I might request a turn with you, as soon as you've taken a bath, of course." He then licked his lips suggestively.

Scowling, Tuck bound Gervase's hands behind his back before pulling the man up onto his feet. He then marched him to the side of the road, spun him around, and gently pushed him backwards. Gervase landed on his backside in the muddy ditch with a loud squishy splash, ruining his white silk surcoat with the prince's heraldry.

"You will not speak to Lady Huntingdon in such a manner," Tuck sternly admonished.

Gervase sputtered indignantly, "Who are you to dare put your hands on me? Don't you know who I am?"

"I'm Brother Tuck, an obedient servant of King Richard, who personally commanded me to guard Lady Huntingdon. You are a man whose clothing now matches his unclean thoughts."

Guy stared at the ground, attempting to hide his smug grin at Tuck's fitting punishment. He was also comforted and thankful that a trained knight was protecting Marian.

"Gisborne, where is the silver?" Marian had lowered her bow and was pressing his old dagger, the one he had used to kill Robin, against his chest.

Swallowing hard at the sight of that cursed blade, Guy confessed, "It's in my saddlebags."

Gervase grumbled at Guy's passivity and made several derogatory comments about his manhood.

As Marian retrieved the bag of silver, Guy ventured hopefully, "I thought you only took a portion from travelers."

Marian laughed, but she did not sound amused. "Not when I'm stealing from the sheriff. I have a message for your master: return Lionel to Edmund unharmed, and I will return this silver to Argentan, unspent."

Tuck then graciously offered to carry the bag for Marian, and the two disappeared into the forest.

Gervase awkwardly struggled to climb out of the ditch with his hands bound behind his back, but he slipped and tumbled backwards again. Guy labored mightily to suppress his laughter and assume an even demeanor. The other man was soaked in mud.

Just then, Gervase's men returned to free them. They confessed that the outlaws had lured them deep into the woods only to disappear. Their sense of direction had become confused in the thick forest, and they had found their way back to the road by retracing their own steps. After they had mounted their horses and resumed their journey, Gervase reproached Guy. "This is *your* fault! I expect you to buy me a new surcoat to replace this one. And why did you send all my men away when they were needed to guard Argentan's silver?"

Guy sighed and spurred his horse towards Nottingham.

21 July 1192, Sherwood Forest, The Meadow

Constance arrived at the forest meadow near Locksley. After dismounting and wrapping her horse's reins around a shrub, she observed Marian as she practiced with her bow.

Again and again, Marian drew an arrow from the quiver at her belt, nocked it, and released it towards a crude target in the center of the meadow. The target was shaped like a man, and its exaggerated height could only mean that it was a stand-in for Guy.

Constance was worried about her dear friend. She had lost weight and looked exhausted. Her once beautiful pale blonde hair was dull and tangled, and there were smudges of dirt on her cheek and forehead.

At that moment, Marian saw her and waved.

Forcing a smile, Constance marveled, "Your expertise with a bow astounds me; I wish Robin could see how skilled you have become!"

Marian scowled. "Are you certain that no one followed you?" she demanded.

"Yes, of course. Guy is in Nottingham with the sheriff." Constance strove to hide her annoyance. Marian asked her that same question every time they met at the meadow.

Marian led Constance to the oak with her and Robin's initials carved into the trunk, gesturing towards a blanket spread upon the ground.

"Do you have any news?" Marian inquired after they were comfortably seated in the shade of the great tree.

"Nothing has changed. Tomorrow's Feast of St. Mary Magdalene will be held at Locksley, and the people of Lenton have been invited to attend. Guy, Payen, and another knight, Sir Gervase, will choose young, healthy men for Prince John's army and take them to Nottingham along the main road. Only men from those two villages will be taken. The sheriff believes they are more likely to protect you and conspire with your band of outlaws."

"I will not allow Argentan to conscript these men, forcing them to risk their lives to serve Prince John," Marian vowed.

"Are you ready to carry out your plan?" asked Constance.

"Yes; it took a little longer than I expected, but more men arrived to help, and we finally finished yesterday."

Constance chuckled. "I wish I could be there to watch."

"Will the sheriff be there?"

"No; he will await the men's arrival in Nottingham before they are sent south to serve the prince. However, I think you will find this amusing: I overheard Guy and Payen speculating that Argentan is afraid of you. Since the wedding, he rarely leaves the castle unless he has many guards surrounding him. He also rages about how he should have killed you years ago, and how he plans to humiliate you when you are captured."

"Interesting," commented Marian. "He should be afraid of me because if it wasn't for Lionel, I would have killed him already. Is Gisborne suffering?"

Constance wanted to rebuke her friend for speaking so freely of killing, even if it was the sheriff, but she held her tongue. "Guy is drinking too much, eating too little, and he's plagued by nightmares, even on those nights when the 'ghost' of Robin Hood does not appear. If your plan was to kill him slowly, then you are succeeding."

"Good; maybe he will commit suicide in a fit of despair."

"Marian! Don't say such things! He would have no hope of heaven or redemption."

Marian snorted derisively. "He doesn't deserve redemption. If God is just, he will never allow Gisborne into heaven alongside Robin."

"In all the years I've known you, I've never seen this side of you. You've never been cruel. Please don't dwell on such things." Constance's voice was pleading as she tried to steer her friend away from such vindictive thoughts.

"You will never understand! I watched that monster stab Robin in the heart! When Robin's heart was pierced, mine was too. Our love created an eternal connection that can never be severed. And why are you worried about Gisborne's soul? You should feel the same as I do!"

"Perhaps if I had seen him kill Robin, I would feel the same way." Constance paused as she gathered the courage to speak her mind. "I haven't forgiven Guy, but I believe he feels remorse. If he confesses his sins and sincerely asks for mercy, he could be reconciled with God."

"No! God mustn't let him into heaven with Robin. Stop defending him! You know I hate him!"

"Marian, please, don't be angry with me. I share your grief for Robin's death. But Guy is my husband, and even though we don't sleep together, I spend a lot of time with him. I see him suffering, and I believe that he feels genuine regret over killing Robin." She tried to grasp Marian's hands, but Marian pulled away.

Constance persisted. "I'm actually surprised that he is so troubled; I mean, it's almost as though Guy feels some type of connection to Robin. I don't understand it, but I see it. Perhaps it's because both of them loved you."

"Gisborne knows nothing about love. It's impossible for such a man to feel love."

Constance knew this was not true. She had seen him cry out for a mother whom he loved, and she believed that a man who loves his mother cannot be truly heartless. "I think you're talking about the sheriff, not Guy," she suggested. "Argentan is an evil man incapable of tender feelings, but Guy is not like that. The sheriff is very cruel to Guy. I've noticed it when I've been spying on them."

"I agree that the sheriff is evil, and if he is cruel to Gisborne, then I celebrate it. I'm just sorry I can't watch."

Constance sighed. "My dear Marian, I don't think you mean these things you are saying, and I don't want to upset you, but please, don't be so eager to wish for his eternal damnation—that's not for you to decide. I think he's trying to be a better person."

"Ha! That's ridiculous. Why would you think that?"

Constance carefully weighed her words. "I see him attempting to stand up to the sheriff. He tried to dissuade him from rounding up the men for Prince John's army. And…"

"And what?"

Constance blushed as she remembered a strange incident. "A few days ago, a woman approached me at the castle. She was irate and called me a witch, saying I had put a spell on Guy to keep him faithful. It was awful! But Guy saw her talking to me, and he intervened. He told her that, because he now has a virtuous, proper wife, he no longer wants her or any other woman. I was astonished to hear him say that since we don't have a real marriage."

"Don't you dare defend the man who murdered my Robin!" Marian gasped. She then dissolved into tears.

Constance scooted closer and wrapped her arms around her bereft friend. "I'm so sorry, Marian. I know you are still mourning him."

Marian fought to settle herself and stem the flow of her tears. Drying her face with her sleeve, she confessed, "Sometimes I feel as though time stopped at the moment of Robin's death. Or rather, that time should have stopped. It seems wrong that life goes on without him. There are times now when I realize that I'm enjoying something, or that I'm happy about something, and then I'm crushed to realize it. How can I be happy about anything if Robin is gone? I'm disrespecting his memory when I'm happy, and I hate myself for it."

"No! Please, Marian, listen to me. I remember losing my mother when I was fourteen, just when I felt I needed her most. And I had similar thoughts: how can life go on as before when everything is different? How can I enjoy anything in life after watching her die from a painful, lingering illness? But I realized that, if I'm trapped in my grief and forever mourning, then I'm not living *my* life. And I'm not honoring my mother's memory because she would want me to be happy. You have to move on from grief to live your life fully."

Marian indignantly shifted away from Constance's embrace. "How can you expect me to forget Robin and live without him? I will never love again, and I'll never be fully alive again."

"I'm saying you have to live the life that God has planned for you. You can't give up on *your* future just because Robin's was stolen from him."

"I was going to kill myself, but I feared that God would never let me join Robin in heaven," Marian whispered.

Constance crossed herself and exclaimed, "Marian! Don't even *think* about doing such a dreadful thing!"

"Don't worry, the only reason I'm able to continue living is to protect Robin's legacy. Still, when I feel happy, I despise myself."

Constance again hugged her friend, and the two women wept together.

When their grief had subsided, Constance commented, "I will never forget my mother. I think about her often. I wonder what she would think of Guy, and how she would suggest I handle this situation."

Recognizing that her offhand mention of Guy had irritated Marian, Constance hastened to add, "I would never ask you to forget Robin. You should keep him alive in your heart and your memories. But you also need to look forward to the future. And when you are happy about something, welcome that happiness knowing that Robin would celebrate any joy you feel, if he were here to witness it."

22 July 1192, Sherwood Forest, On the Road to Nottingham

Something was very wrong.

Guy kept scanning the sides of the road and glancing over his shoulder. Behind him, twenty young men dutifully shuffled along, their wrists bound before them, and a rope securely looped around each man's waist, connecting them and preventing their escape as they walked to Nottingham. Sir Gervase was riding next to him, while Payen brought up the rear.

Two dozen foot soldiers, their shields up and their swords drawn and ready, flanked the captives and presented an impressive display of power.

Yet, Guy could not help but worry about the lack of resistance from the peasants. It was almost as though they had expected the arrival of Guy and his men at the Feast of St. Mary Magdalene. And when Sir Gervase announced that he would select young, healthy men to serve in the army of Prince John, there was little more than some murmuring among the assembled villagers of Locksley and Lenton.

Guy had expected screaming women and desperate men running for their lives, but it was nothing like that. The women had merely observed as the men stood for Gervase's inspection. They had allowed themselves to be bound, and they had obediently started marching to Nottingham, where the sheriff planned to make a speech about the importance of supporting Prince John.

Guy had been tricked by Robin many times, and this had all the earmarks of a trap. Marian was remarkably cunning, just like Robin, and Guy knew better than to underestimate her.

A shout rose, and the young outlaw with the red scarf waved at them from the tree line.

Gervase scoffed. "If he thinks we will chase after him, he's as stupid as he looks!"

Ignoring Will, they kept moving.

"Indeed, but we must hurry to Nottingham. These men are healthy; let's have them run the rest of the way," suggested Guy.

"Nonsense," Gervase argued. "They have a long march south beginning in the morning. I will not fatigue them today."

At that point, the road widened, and it was bordered by fields. Guy breathed a sigh of relief that they were no longer surrounded by the dark forest.

That's when he saw them.

Marian and her outlaws were standing in a large, fallow field next to a barrel and a number of buckets. None of the men had drawn bows, or even swords. They just stood there, silently watching from a position at least a hundred yards away. Behind them, Guy noticed several huge mounds of fresh dirt. Did they intend to use the dirt as a defensive barricade? That wouldn't be very effective.

"Halt!" cried Gervase. Everyone stopped and stared at the outlaws.

Since the man was Prince John's envoy, Guy had allowed him to take command. However, after the debacle of a few days ago, he felt he should offer some advice. "Sir Gervase, may I suggest the men start running now? I suspect a trap."

Gervase regarded him with utter disgust. "What kind of man fears a woman and a handful of peasants? You are pathetic. Can't you see this is our opportunity to capture them for Prince John?"

Before Guy could respond, Gervase ordered the bound peasants to sit on the ground while his soldiers moved to a position between them and the outlaws.

Marian loudly proclaimed, "I will not allow you to take these men away. They will never fight for Prince John and against King Richard as long as the spirit of Robin Hood is alive!"

"Argentan knew that you would come, Marian Hood. But we are ready for you, and you cannot stand against us," Gervase confidently asserted.

Marian smiled. "I predict that it is you and your men who will be unable to stand. Release the men of Locksley and Lenton, and I will allow you to leave peacefully."

He laughed at her and leaned towards Guy as he lowered his voice. "Women have no sense of tactics or strategy. This is too easy. Watch me triumph over these enemies of the prince."

Guy looked between Gervase and Marian. Once again, he was certain that Marian should not be underestimated, but he also knew there was nothing he could say that would convince Gervase that retreating was their best option.

Gervase addressed his men. "Round up Marian Hood and her outlaws. Argentan wants her alive, and he'll give ten silver pieces to the man who captures her."

"Are you sending all your men, Sir Gervase?" Guy cautiously asked.

"You and Payen will stay here and guard these peasants."

Gervase ordered his men to attack, and when they started running towards the outlaws, he spurred his horse to follow behind them.

A cold sweat broke out on Guy's brow as Marian and her men calmly observed the soldiers surge forward. They made no move to run into the forest or take refuge behind the piles of dirt. He was about to call to her, to beg her to run away, when the soldiers unexpectedly disappeared. Gervase's horse abruptly leapt over something, and he fell backwards off his mount, also vanishing from sight.

Guy blinked, and he heard Payen swearing behind him.

Just then, shouting erupted, and Guy urged his horse towards the noise, with Payen at his side. Their horses became skittish and refused to move forward, so the two knights dismounted and warily advanced.

Marian and her men remained in place, only now they were armed with their bows.

It was then that Guy saw a great gaping hole in the ground. Gervase and his men were furiously yelling as they recovered from their sudden plunge into the earth. Bits of burlap hung in shreds along the edges, and Guy could see that the hole had been concealed under sacks that had been stitched together and covered with a thin layer of dirt and debris. The rough fabric had given way from the weight of the men running across it.

"Hold there!" commanded Marian, who was aiming a nocked arrow at him.

Guy submissively raised his hands in surrender and ordered Payen to follow suit.

At the bottom of the hole, Gervase was screaming at Guy to attack her, but now it was Payen and Guy who were outnumbered.

With interest, Guy noticed that there were small buckets along the edge of the hole. Whenever Gervase or one of his men tried to climb out, an outlaw would pour water from a bucket down the side of the hole, transforming the dirt into slimy, slick mud. The man would helplessly slide back. The hole was about six feet deep, and when some men clambered onto the shoulders of others, the outlaws would throw clumps of dirt and stones at them until they lost their balance and fell. A few men were moaning in pain at the bottom of the pit; they likely had broken legs.

"What do you think of my little surprise, Gisborne?" Marian's icy voice cut through his musing.

"Impressive, Marian. Was this your idea?"

"Of course, this was my idea. Although I'm sure you believe that women aren't as smart as men."

"I have never thought that, especially in regard to you," he asserted.

"Jump in, or I will have one of my men push you."

Guy sighed. "Why don't you tie me up instead? I think I would prefer that to spending time in a dirty hole."

Marian laughed, and when Guy saw Little John striding towards him, he went to the edge of the hole and lowered himself into it. At least he had the satisfaction of seeing Little John shove Payen into the muddy trap.

The outlaws then emptied the remaining buckets and the barrel into the hole until the sides were saturated, and the bottom was flooded.

The soldiers were shouting; Gervase and Payen were cursing, but Guy quietly stood there. He was the only man tall enough to see out of the hole, and he watched as Marian and her men freed the captive peasants and led them into the forest.

⁂

Marian's favorite meadow had never been so crowded. Edmund, the outlaws, and all the rescued men stood around, talking excitedly about their amazing rescue.

Marian mounted Edmund's horse so that everyone could see and hear her. The men quieted and looked at her expectantly. "Men of Locksley and Lenton! The spirit of my late husband, Robin Hood, is with us today, and I know he would rejoice that you have been spared from serving under the pretender to the throne, Prince John."

Everyone let out a cheer. Some shouted "God Bless Robin Hood!" while others proclaimed, "Long Live Robin Hood!"

Marian raised her hand, and they hushed. "Let's all say it together: Long Live Robin Hood!"

The crowd chanted it several times before Marian signaled for them to stop. "We must keep the memory of Robin Hood alive. You cannot return to your homes, because the sheriff will come for you again. Who would like to join me and fight against Argentan and Prince John?"

Every man in the meadow shouted that they were ready to fight.

She nodded with satisfaction. No longer would the outlaws be so outnumbered in their struggles against the sheriff. She continued, "I know Robin Hood would be proud to call every one of you a member of his merry band. I've discussed this with Lord Edmund and Little John. The forest can only sustain a certain number of men. We must be able to feed you, shelter you, and hide you from the sheriff and his soldiers. Our plan is for half of you to stay here, while the rest travel north to the Barony of Embelton. There you will receive training in weapons and fighting. After a couple of months, the two groups will exchange places. Your military training will ensure that, when King Richard returns, we will be ready to defend him from Prince John and his minions."

She contemplated the enthusiastic, excited faces of the young men. With a twinge of sorrow she was reminded of Robin's eagerness to fight for his king, and she knew it was a masculine trait that she could use to her advantage. She didn't care much for King Richard, but he was preferable to the odious Prince John.

She exclaimed, "Are you ready to fight for King Richard?"

"YES!" the men cried out.

"Are you ready to fight for justice in the name of Robin Hood?"

"YES!" again the men chorused.

Marian smiled, although it did not reach her eyes. "Everything I do, I do in the name of Robin Hood. Robin Hood will always be a symbol of what is good, just, and right. Will you follow me?"

The men heartily pledged their loyalty to Marian as they resumed chanting, "Long Live Robin Hood!"

CHAPTER 10
THE BATTLE OF JAFFA

2 August 1192, Outside the Walls of Jaffa, Kingdom of Jerusalem

obin squinted against the bright sun as he gazed up at the heavily damaged wall of Jaffa.

Because the Crusader army had been delayed at Caesarea, Count Henry of Champagne, the newly crowned King of Jerusalem, had assembled an elite group of men and sailed south to provide support for King Richard as he awaited the rest of his army. Robin, who was still disguised as a Knight Templar, had joined him.

After disembarking on the beach, Henry, Robin, and their men had made their way through the war-ravaged city to the location of a large breach where Richard and his senior knights were assisting infantrymen and stonemasons in its repair.

Apparently, the Lionheart hadn't needed their help. He had recaptured Jaffa from a force of 7,000 Saracens with only eighty knights, four hundred crossbowmen, 2,000 Pisan and Genoese marines, and exactly three horses. Robin couldn't comprehend how that was possible, so he sought André de Chauvigny, while Henry conferred with Richard.

His friend was in high spirits, energized by their incredible triumph. "Robin! You missed all the fun yesterday. I daresay you will forever regret your decision to help Henry lead the army south instead of joining us for our little cruise along the coast."

Robin chuckled warmly. "Tell me about this miraculous victory of yours—although I fear I will be forced to hear about it from you over and over for the rest of our lives."

Smacking Robin good naturedly on the back, André guided him to a shady spot. He had been working on the wall all day and welcomed the opportunity to rest.

"Our ship arrived in the middle of the night, and when dawn came, it was obvious that Jaffa had fallen to the Saracens. Their standards were flying over the city, and the beach was swarming with them. Our hearts fell, and the king knew there was nothing to be done until Henry arrived with the army."

"They should arrive in a sennight," Robin remarked.

André continued, "While the king was considering his options, we saw a man leap from the citadel into the sea. I thought the poor bastard was committing suicide to avoid capture, but then we realized that he was swimming towards us. We fished him out of the water, and he told us that, although the city was controlled by the Saracens, the citadel was still in Christian hands. And so, the king went ashore."

"What do you mean, 'the king went ashore?'" asked an alarmed Robin.

"After ordering the galley to make for the beach, he took off his leg armor, slung his shield around his neck, grabbed his battle-axe, and jumped into waist-high water to wade ashore. The rest of us followed him. The crossbowmen on deck gave us cover, but Richard's audacity in running onto the beach was so unexpected that the Saracens failed to mount an effective counterattack."

"When I am not with the king, *you* are in charge of Richard's safety," Robin sharply admonished him. "How could you have allowed him to do such a foolhardy thing?"

"Allowed?" André regarded his friend curiously. "Robin, how

do you suggest I constrain the *king* from doing as he pleases? Surely you know Richard better than to think anyone could dissuade him from a course of action once he has committed himself to it."

Robin sighed. He had regretted his angry words from the moment they left his mouth. Lately, he had been struggling to check his emotions. Little things would set him off in a rage, and he had lost his temper on more than one occasion since his return to the Holy Land after his mission to Poitiers and Paris.

"My friend, forgive me; you are right. I confess that I haven't been sleeping well, and you know that I'm not much of a sailor. The voyage from Caesarea has me out of sorts."

"Be at ease, Robin. I share your dislike of sea travel. It has a similar effect on me."

"Tell me the rest of the story."

"We rapidly cleared the beach and entered the city. Later, we learned that Sultan Saladin had lost control of his men. They were so preoccupied with looting the town that few of them were aware of our arrival. Many of the Saracens believed that the citadel had already fallen, so when they moved to attack us, our men in the citadel were able to strike them from the rear. Soon the enemy was in such chaos that they abandoned the city and their loot and fled to Saladin's main camp."

"Incredible," marveled Robin. "I see we are rebuilding the wall, yet the king is camped outside the city."

"The city is filled with rotting corpses, and the stench has become unbearable."

"I could smell it when we came ashore. At first, I thought it was from the dead bodies littering the beach, but when we passed through the city, I realized that death is everywhere in Jaffa. I can understand your desire to avoid breathing such foul air, but we cannot provide adequate security for the king outside the walls."

"We have no choice. We don't have enough men to maintain a proper watch along the wall while also guarding the galleys in the harbor and protecting the king. Have you spoken to Richard yet?" asked André.

"No, we only just arrived. Henry was impatient to apprise Richard of the army's status, so I decided to give them privacy and speak to you instead."

"Let's go see the king; he will be pleased that you are here, and he will be eager to tell you the story himself. I noticed that you are still disguised as a Templar."

"I'm tired of this charade. It seems rather pointless, given that so many men have recognized me since our return from Paris. I've sworn them to secrecy, of course, but it's widely known that I survived the attack on the king."

André nodded sympathetically. "I have good news: Richard has again entered into negotiations to end the Crusade. He is very close to an agreement with Saladin. The only sticking point is Ascalon. Saladin demands that the fortifications be torn down, and Richard insists that they must stay."

5 August 1192, Outside the Walls of Jaffa

It was early morning, but dawn was still a couple of hours away. Robin abruptly woke, panting and sweating from yet another nightmare. He quietly rose from his makeshift bed, careful to avoid waking André and the other men sharing their tent. As he ducked out from underneath the tent's flap, he observed the men guarding the king and was pleased to see that they were awake and alert.

He greeted them and wandered away, seeking to clear his mind of the dreams that haunted him nearly every night. Visions of battles, blood, headless corpses, of women and children weeping over husbands, fathers, sons, and brothers—it all seemed so pointless.

Richard and his senior advisors, including Robin, were convinced that conquering Jerusalem was achievable, but keeping it would be impossible. But how to save face and exit gracefully? How could they ensure that the Christian controlled areas remained safe from Saracen attack? With this in mind, the king was forever negotiating an end to the Crusade, claiming that he was impatient to return home, yet there was always some obstacle that prevented a final agreement with Saladin.

Robin walked towards the horses. Richard's small force had gathered fifteen of the valuable beasts, and they were tethered to posts between the tents and the city's wall.

All too often, his mind seemed to roar with the din of battle, even in the still of the night, and he had discovered that spending time with the horses seemed to settle his mind and soothe his tormented soul. As he drew near, they greeted him with quiet nickering, and he smiled.

Sorting through a haphazard pile of tack, he found a brush and approached an aging gelding. Robin rubbed his palm from the horse's forehead to his muzzle, and the horse nodded, nibbling at his fingers.

"Sorry, old friend, I didn't bring any treats," Robin apologized in a low voice as he stepped to the horse's shoulder and began brushing his back and side while the animal made appreciative guttural sounds.

Again and again, Robin moved the brush across the horse's muscular body. The uproar in his mind—screams of dying men, shouts of the enemy, the whoosh and boom of a trebuchet delivering its missiles—faded, and a sense of calm enveloped him.

As his mind cleared, he could concentrate on the memories that kept him sane during his long absence from Marian: riding along a forest path with Marian; sitting with her in the cool shade of the great oak in their meadow. He wondered if their initials could still be seen in the tree's trunk after almost four years. How was it possible that so much time had passed?

Robin's exhausted mind drifted to earlier times. He reminisced about following his mother into the forest as she searched for the herbs and plants she used in her healing potions, and he was struck by the realization of just how much he still missed her gentle spirit and kind nature. She had been so patient with him! She always understood when he simply could not sit through another lesson, and she never discouraged his energetic disposition or his boundless curiosity.

If only his father had shown such patience or had been interested in Robin as a person instead of an heir. Duncan had expected Robin to be little more than a copy of himself in every way. It was a great source of contention between father and son during those rare times when Duncan visited him and his mother at Locksley. His father had always been more interested in spending time at court with the king instead of with his family.

A twinge of guilt twisted in Robin's heart. Hadn't he been guilty of the same thing? He had chosen to follow Richard instead of keeping his promise to Marian. He didn't deserve her, but now that they were married, he would spend the rest of his life trying to make amends for his mistakes.

Thankfully, she was safe with Uncle Edmund. Robin was certain that she had gone to Embelton upon leaving Poitiers. After all, she didn't know anyone in Huntingdon or London, and both Locksley and Lenton were under the control of Argentan.

Robin closed his eyes and rested his forehead against the shoulder of the horse. He could feel and hear the pulse of the animal's strong heart: steady, calming, reassuring...

He fervently wished he were in Embelton with Marian, Uncle Edmund, and his cousins, Lionel and Constance. Robin recalled those happy times when his mother had taken him to visit her brother and his family. Uncle Edmund had always been there for him; Edmund valued his wife and children above his court connections, and he always put them first in his life.

Robin wanted to be like Edmund... He wanted to return home

and start a family with Marian. Never again would he let Richard become the center of his world…

Memories of a carefree past… playing games with Lionel and Constance… Edmund teaching him to fish…

Robin's breathing evened out, and he leaned heavily against the side of the horse. The brush fell from his hand and thudded on the ground as he slipped into a light doze.

Something pushed against his leg, and Robin was instantly alert. He drew his dagger and spun around, wobbling a bit from the speed of his actions.

No one was there.

A soft whine caused him to look down where a small dog was sitting at his feet. His tail was tentatively moving from side to side as he assessed whether Robin was friend or foe. He had foxlike ears and a short, dark coat with a white splotch on his forehead. The top of his head barely reached Robin's knee.

Returning his dagger to its sheath, Robin grinned and gently admonished, "Don't you know better than to startle an armed man?"

Something in the shadows distracted the little mutt, and he trotted off into the darkness. Robin remembered that he had several pieces of dried meat in a pouch tied to his belt, which explained the dog's interest in him. He followed the dog and found him near the edge of the camp.

Robin squatted on the ground and held out the jerky for him. The little dog took the offered morsel, his tail wagging enthusiastically. As the dog chewed happily on his prize, Robin began petting him and rubbing behind his ears. The same sense of calm he had experienced with the horses came over him, and he resolved to take the dog back to camp.

He noticed that the dog was clean and well-fed; this was no street mongrel but someone's pet. With sadness, he surmised that the dog's owner had likely been a Christian who had been killed when the Saracens invaded the city. He knew that the Saracens' beliefs did not allow them to keep dogs as pets.

A rustling in the bushes caused his heart to speed, and he swiftly rose to his feet and drew his dagger.

To his relief, a man in the garb of a Genoese sailor stepped forward into the weak moonlight. He must have been attending to personal business.

Robin relaxed, put away his weapon, and greeted him in Italian. Luckily, the man spoke French, since Robin's knowledge of Italian was limited.

"Are you one of the Knights Templar who arrived a couple of days ago?" the man inquired.

"Yes, I am Brother Robin. Were you part of Richard's assault on the beach?"

The man proudly affirmed that he had participated in that remarkable victory, and the two men spoke for a while, sharing stories and getting to know one another.

A soft glow in the east signaled the approaching dawn, but it would still be more than an hour before daybreak. Without warning, the little dog's hackles rose. He moved away from Robin, growling with surprising menace and slinking low to the ground, as if he were preparing to attack.

"What's wrong with your dog?" the Genoese man asked.

Robin shrugged, and the two men followed the dog, peeking between the gnarled olive trees that lined the edge of the camp.

For a moment, Robin saw nothing but a shadowed landscape. Then he heard the beat of hooves striking the ground. The shadows morphed into mounted men moving in formation. The massive Saracen cavalry was stealthily approaching the Crusader camp, where King Richard was peacefully sleeping in a simple tent with only a small contingent of men guarding him.

❧

An hour later, the sky had brightened considerably, although the sun had yet to peek above the horizon. Robin watched as King Richard, bare-legged and dressed only in a long chain mail shirt over his nightclothes, rode along the defensive array to verify that his strategy had been implemented according to his detailed instructions.

For the first time since spotting the Saracen cavalry as it advanced towards their small camp outside the walls of Jaffa, Robin had hope that he might survive the coming battle. He had been amazed at the speed with which Richard had sprung into action and the brilliance of his impromptu plan.

Between the camp and the enemy, Richard had created a long, thin line of defense. In the front, infantrymen knelt side by side, their shoulders touching. Their left arms held their shields, creating a low barrier that stretched the length of the line. In their right hands, they steadied a spear. The butt of each spear was anchored in the ground, and the shaft was aimed diagonally up at an angle that would place their sharp points at the chests of oncoming horses.

Archers with crossbows were positioned behind the infantrymen, staggered so they were aiming over the kneeling men's shoulders. Behind each archer, a second man with another crossbow and a stack of bolts stood ready to reload. This would allow a nearly continuous release of bolts, as the archer would only have to pause long enough to exchange his discharged crossbow for a loaded one.

The line of defense might have looked thin, but the lethal combination of spears and crossbows would be impenetrable, as long as the men held firm.

The king was, of course, mounted, and that left only fourteen horses for 80 knights; therefore, Robin would have to supervise his section of the defensive array on foot.

The Saracen onslaught could begin at any moment, so Richard was moving along the line and encouraging the men. Approaching

Robin and those under his command, the king paused to address them. It was likely the same speech he had given to each group, but his dynamic delivery and charismatic assurances of success made it sound spontaneous and heartfelt.

The king proclaimed, "A few days ago, God granted us a glorious victory when we liberated Jaffa by boldly attacking our enemy, even though we were vastly outnumbered. Today, by the power of God, we will fearlessly defend this Christian city. I know we will be victorious if we have faith in our cause. The Saracens cannot defeat us, but we can defeat ourselves if we lose heart and abandon our fellow Christians in this moment of testing. And we *will* be tested this morning. God sent us here to die if need be; shame to anyone who holds back now. If any man breaks the line and flees, I will personally cut off his head and toss it to the enemy. If you desert your post, you will have to explain to God Almighty why you failed Him today."

The initial wave of Saracen cavalry had arrived with the first rays of sunlight streaming across a clear cerulean sky, but the Crusader phalanx held strong, and the charge was broken. Again and again, hour after hour, the enemy charged towards Richard's prickly defense, and those mounted men who did not veer off at the last opportunity were either taken out by a crossbow bolt or lost their horse to a spear point.

The sun had journeyed from the east, to its zenith, and was now falling towards its destination beyond the western sea. After suffering heavy casualties and losing over a thousand horses, the Saracen cavalry refused to mount another charge. Faced with mutiny, Saladin gave the signal to withdraw.

A shocked Robin watched in dismay as Richard seized his lance and boldly rode out from behind the safety of his defensive array. He paraded along the entire Saracen line, challenging any man there to come out and fight him. So terrifying was his reputation among the enemy that not one man dared face the Lionheart. A triumphant Richard returned to his men.

The Crusaders had decisively won the Battle of Jaffa.

5 September 1192, The Citadel of Jaffa

It felt good to laugh and joke with his friends, Robin mused.

He was standing in the great hall of the Citadel of Jaffa with André, Sir Baldwin de Béthune, and Sir William de l'Etang. It had been a month since their victory outside the city walls, and there was much to celebrate. The city had been cleared of rotting bodies; the wall had been repaired, and although all four men had fallen ill after the battle, they were now recovered. Only the king remained unwell. Ranulphus had despaired that the king might die, but eventually Richard had rallied. He was weak, but he would survive.

Perhaps it was the fruit and ice sent by Sultan Saladin; Robin remembered eyeing the exotic treats with longing. Saladin had also sent two fine stallions as a grand gesture because he had noticed that Richard was riding an inferior mount during the battle. But the greatest gift from the Saracen leader had been a conclusion to the negotiations.

Richard had finally agreed to demolish the fortifications at Ascalon, and Saladin had granted Christian pilgrims access to Jerusalem's holy sites. There had been a number of other agreements, and on the 2nd of September, the final truce between Richard and Saladin had been formalized. The truce would last three years, and then Richard had every intention of returning to resume his efforts to retake Jerusalem from the Saracens. Negotiations had been held through intermediaries, so Richard never had the opportunity to meet Saladin face to face, and it was a source of disappointment for the gregarious king.

Robin was briefly distracted as he gazed out a nearby window to admire the deep blue sea and the bright, clear sky. He prayed that they would soon be on a ship and headed for home.

."Robin, are you listening?"

"My apologies, Baldwin. My mind was elsewhere."

Baldwin repeated his question. "What do you think of Bishop Walter's plan to lead a pilgrimage to Jerusalem?"

André interjected, "The king refuses to go, and he's hinted that he doesn't want any of us to go either."

"I don't understand that," admitted Baldwin. "I think Richard should go as well, but if he refuses, then why would he want to prevent us from going? I have dreamed of visiting the holy sites all my life."

Robin was certain he knew the reason. "Richard was not bluffing when he said he would return in three years. First, he wants to thwart King Philippe and Prince John's ambitions, and then he plans to sire at least one heir with Berengaria."

"I still don't understand why it would matter to him if we went to Jerusalem," countered Baldwin.

"He wants us to serve him in the next Crusade, and if we've completed our pilgrimage, what incentive is there to return?" William speculated.

"Exactly," agreed Robin. "Speaking for myself, nothing short of Richard threatening my family would induce me to take the cross again. I've already informed the bishop that I will accompany him to Jerusalem. This will be my only opportunity; I will never willingly return to this land of endless war and death."

The other men concurred with Robin's sentiments, and they decided that the four of them would travel together with the bishop. For a while they discussed their plans, and soon they fell into their usual routine of teasing one another.

Robin's dog trotted over to them and sat at his new master's feet.

"If you keep feeding that dog, you will never get rid of him," advised William.

"Why would I want to get rid of him?" responded Robin. "He saved our lives when he alerted me that the Saracen cavalry was marching towards our camp."

Baldwin knelt down to pet him. "Is he coming with us to Jerusalem?"

"Of course," Robin replied.

André asked, "Have you chosen a name for him?"

Robin gazed down at the reddish-brown mutt. After the battle, he had been relieved to find that the dog had remained safe in his tent. "I thought about calling him 'Jaffa,' but then I decided that the fewer memories of this place, the better. Instead, I've settled on the name Jack."

"That's a good name," opined Baldwin.

A thought occurred to William. "Are you taking him back to England? There are lots of dogs in England, and they're bigger and better looking."

"But they're not as smart as Jack," insisted Robin.

A round of objections to such a sweeping generalization led to a light-hearted debate over the relevant merits of the various dog breeds typically found in England, Normandy, and the Angevin lands.

Robin reminisced, "Marian had a little dog that was about this size when she was a young girl. I think she will like him."

It was time for the evening meal, so Baldwin and William left to wash up, as they had been keeping watch along the city wall earlier in the day.

Robin could tell that André had something he wanted to say, so he demanded, "Well? Spit it out. What's troubling you? I can read that look on your face."

Closely observing his friend, André questioned, "Are you really planning to take that dog back to England and give it to Marian?"

"Yes. Why do you care?"

"You misunderstand; I'm glad you're taking him, but I question whether you should give him to Marian. At night, I've noticed that the dog moves close and calms you when your sleep is disturbed. Recently, you seem much better rested."

Robin's eyes narrowed in displeasure tinged with embarrassment. After an awkward pause, he replied, "I told you he was a smart dog." Pivoting, he summoned his new companion. "Come, Jack. Let's see what the cook has for you tonight."

CHAPTER 11
PROOF OF LIFE

15 September 1192, Locksley Village

onstance observed her husband and her father as they supervised the harvest. There was a certain desperation that hung in the air; both Lenton and Locksley were short of able-bodied men, and the crops would spoil if they weren't harvested soon.

The remaining peasants were working together in an effort to save as much of each estate's crops as possible. The previous sennight had been devoted to Lenton's fields, and today marked the beginning of the harvest in Locksley.

At the moment, Edmund and Guy seemed to be arguing. Ever curious, Constance moved closer to hear what they were saying, only to discover that they were debating the relative merits of cow manure versus pig manure as fertilizer. Crinkling her nose at the thought, she wandered away, intending to return to the manor. When she recognized the familiar rhythm of her father's energetic gait approaching her from behind, she paused.

"Constance, can you bring me a cup of water? I'm thankful for the fine weather, but it's unusually warm today."

She promptly complied and soon found herself next to him as he took a long drink of the cool water she had fetched from the well.

"Will you be able to save the crops?" she asked.

"I believe so; the question now becomes whether there will be enough. A healthy estate needs both supplies to keep on hand and a surplus to sell at market in order to purchase items not produced locally."

"Do you find it odd that Guy is so interested in managing Locksley?"

"For a knight like Gisborne, acquiring land is vital to accumulating real wealth, and it provides an entrée into the lower ranks of the nobility."

"That must be why Locksley is so important to him," Constance concluded.

"I assume that's the reason. Although, I'm surprised by the intensity of his drive to make it a success. He must realize that he will lose Locksley as soon as King Richard returns and restores it to Marian."

They continued watching as Guy moved from one group of workers to another, exhorting the men to hurry and even occasionally lending a hand. He was covered in sweat, and his clothes were smeared with dirt.

Edmund grudgingly confessed, "I hate him for taking Robin from us, but I cannot deny that he's doing a good job. I wish your brother would show this kind of interest in the management of Embelton instead of his endless fascination with court gossip and fashion trends."

Constance murmured her agreement.

Sounding a hopeful note, Edmund declared, "When Lionel is returned to us, I will insist that he take a more active role in learning the skills he will need as Baron of Embelton."

Constance's voice dropped to a whisper. "What do you think of Marian's latest plan?"

"There is a risk, but I gave her my consent."

Just then, the ground shook as the sheriff and his large contingent of armed bodyguards galloped into the village.

Edmund leaned close to her and spoke in a low voice. "I believe Marian has put her plan into motion. Pray, Constance. Pray for success."

Guy had also seen the arrival of the sheriff, and he joined Constance and Edmund as they stood near Locksley Manor. He was hastily brushing the dirt from his tunic, and he used the sleeve of his shirt to wipe the sweat from his brow.

As soon as Argentan's bodyguards fanned out in a defensive formation encircling the courtyard, he dismounted and marched towards them. Constance curtsied, her father sketched a short bow, and Guy briefly dropped to one knee.

With an unmistakable iciness, Argentan mocked his captain. "Evidently, you have missed your calling. Instead of wasting the funds that were spent training you to become a knight, you should have been sent to the fields as a peasant. Your mother would be so proud to see you covered in dirt like this."

Constance studied Guy's reaction; it was the first time she had heard any mention of his mother since his delirious ramblings.

And to her utter shock, the sheriff eyed Edmund and asked, "What do you think, my lord? Would Lucienne approve?"

Constance's mind whirled in confusion. Guy's mother now had a name, and not only did Argentan know her, but apparently, Edmund knew her too.

"Father, how do you—" she began, but he shook his head at her, and Guy talked over her.

"My lord," Guy replied in an equally chilly voice. "Locksley is short of men. I warned you that I needed those men for the harvest before you tried to conscript them into Prince John's army."

Argentan snarled, "Are you talking about the men who escaped because of your incompetence? I had to hire Welsh mercenaries to meet my quota of men for Prince John's army—money I'm taking from *your* wages, by the way. And now I have to deal with that woman. I should have killed her years ago; I knew she was trouble from the moment I met her."

Gisborne glared at his master.

Edmund's voice dripped with disdain. "My lord, is there a reason you have ventured forth from the safety of your tower? Are you seeking Gisborne or me?"

The sheriff's eyes narrowed. "I've come for both of you. Marian Hood has requested a parley. I'm to bring Gisborne, and no one else. However, I've decided that you will come with us. I have no doubt that you are in contact with her. You can deny it all you want, but when I find proof, I will have Prince John strip you of your barony!"

Edmund had the audacity to laugh. "Neither you nor Prince John have the power to take Embelton from me. John has no authority in the north, and the Great Council will not consent to such an action against me."

Constance again tried to speak up, only to have her father shush her, and her husband shake his head at her. Her temper flared; Edmund had coached her to ask a specific question, hoping to establish the fiction that they didn't know Marian's plans. She crossly interjected, "Why is Marian asking for a parley?"

"Gisborne, control your wife, and tell her she doesn't have permission to address me," Argentan crisply commanded.

"Permission?" Constance's voice rose in disbelief.

"Constance, please go into the manor," implored Guy.

"Ha! I always knew your manhood was a tenuous thing!" cried the sheriff. "That's what happens when boys are raised by their mothers."

"Leave my mother out of this conversation," demanded Guy. "And I'd also like to know why you are having a parley with Marian."

"Your wife isn't keeping you informed? Why don't you tell him, Lady Constance?" Argentan's hateful stare was overwhelming, and Constance sought Edmund's help.

Edmund was very convincing as he lied. "Constance and I are

not in contact with Marian. We would never risk Lionel by causing problems for you."

Argentan looked skeptical, but he deigned to answer. "Marian is offering to give back half of my silver, if I can provide proof of life for Lionel. Gisborne and Lord Edmund will accompany me. My soldiers will hold Lady Constance hostage until I return safe and unharmed. If anything happens to me, she will be tonight's entertainment for my men."

Before Edmund could react, Guy had grabbed the front of the sheriff's tunic and was lifting him off the ground. "No! No one touches my wife!"

Edmund stepped between the two men and insisted, "Gisborne, release him." He then tried to reason with the sheriff. "Argentan, this is unnecessary. If Marian has offered you parley, she will not betray you. Why not let Constance come with us? If I thought it was dangerous, I would not propose it."

The sheriff adjusted his tunic and stepped back, out of Gisborne's reach. "Constance will stay here with my men; it's not up for negotiation." He then leveled a menacing glare at Guy. "Don't you dare put your hands on me again! I've given you everything you have, including Locksley and this horse-faced wife of yours."

Constance recoiled at his cruel remark and covered her mouth with her hand.

The sheriff's tirade continued as he stabbed his finger at Guy. "I've also allowed you to live despite your repeated failures. What I've given, I can take away. I know Payen would happily step into your shoes as Lord of Locksley and into Lady Constance's bed as her new husband. At least he isn't losing his mind and seeing ghosts in the middle of the night."

Edmund struggled to contain his temper as he snapped, "Enough! I won't tolerate your insults and threats against my daughter. Listen, I'm willing to come with you to the parley, but I need assurances that Constance will be safe in my absence."

Rolling his eyes, Argentan declared, "Nothing will happen to your *lovely* daughter as long as nothing happens to me during the parley."

Guy suggested, "Constance, you can lock yourself in my chamber. Ask Leofric for the key."

Mortified by the sheriff's unkind words and fearful of his threats, Constance did not want anyone to see the tears that were blurring her vision as they pooled in her eyes. She shielded her face by hugging her father before dashing into the safety of the manor without acknowledging Guy or even looking at him, while the sheriff's soldiers took up positions surrounding it.

15 September 1192, Sherwood Forest

Marian's patience was wearing thin. She was already in a foul mood from having to spend the previous day arguing with Little John and Tuck over her plan to meet with the sheriff. Little John had questioned the prudence of parting with any of the sheriff's silver when the people of Locksley and Lenton faced the possibility of starvation because of the poor harvest.

Tuck had contended that it would be impossible to ensure her safety if she adhered to the terms of the parley by keeping the outlaws away from the meeting place. After all, Argentan and Gisborne would be there, and they weren't honorable men.

She explained her ideas and defended her plan several times, but Tuck and John would take turns shifting the debate to another point, until the three of them were arguing in circles. In a moment of clarity, she recognized that they were acting in concert, intending to wear her down until she abandoned her plan to offer a parley.

With the success of her earlier schemes, Marian had gained confidence, and she knew it was time to remind them that she was in command. Although she was seething inside, she affected an air of composure as she informed the men that the discussion was over:

Tuck would accompany her as her second, while John and Much would stay out of sight, but nearby, to sound a warning if the sheriff broke the parley by bringing additional men.

To her utter relief, Tuck and John had relented and submitted to her leadership. Now the wisdom of her idea to talk to the sheriff would be put to the test.

Perched on a low branch, she heard John's bird call, alerting her that Argentan and Gisborne had arrived, and that they were following the trail of white cloths tied to shrubs and tree limbs which led to the small clearing below her.

A small parade stumbled through the underbrush littering the forest floor. First, Edmund shuffled into view. Argentan was using him as a shield by walking closely behind him, one hand grasping the neckline of Edmund's tunic while the other pressed a dagger against his back. Following on the sheriff's heels was his trained hound, Gisborne, his sword drawn and ready.

She was surprised to see Edmund, but then she concluded that his presence worked to her advantage.

Marian snickered as she realized that the rumors were true: Argentan was frightened of her. She rejoiced in the pale and anxious expression on the sheriff's face. For a moment, she wished Robin could see it too, but then she forced herself to refocus on the task at hand. Thinking about Robin had a way of consuming her mind and rendering her unable to function. For this confrontation, she would need to be in complete command of her wits.

As soon as they entered the clearing, John sent her another bird call, indicating that there were no other soldiers trailing the sheriff.

Gracefully dropping from the tree, Marian found herself face-to-face with Sheriff de Argentan. Brother Tuck stepped forward as Marian's second.

"The parley specified that each side was allowed only one man as a second," admonished Tuck.

Ignoring the Knight Templar, Argentan addressed Marian. "Do

you expect me to believe that your forest pets are not hiding nearby and watching us? Really, my dear Countess of Sherwood, I'm disappointed that you think I'm so gullible." The anxiety that had been evident on the sheriff's face had now morphed into his usual haughty demeanor.

"There are many words that come to my mind when I think of you, Sheriff de Argentan, but gullible isn't one of them. I have every intention of honoring the parley. We will both leave this meeting alive and well," asserted Marian.

Still gripping Edmund's tunic, the sheriff shifted his dagger, so that Marian was sure to notice it. He lamented, "You haven't thanked me for bringing your dead husband's uncle to you. I thought you would be pleased to see him, but perhaps you are seeing him so often these days that meeting him in the forest is unremarkable."

Marian feigned confusion. "Are you speaking in riddles again? I have not seen Lord Edmund since the wedding. Of course, I'm always pleased to see Robin's uncle. But when you are threatening him with a dagger, my fears for his safety outweigh my desire to offer a casual greeting."

"It's good to see you at last, Marian," Edmund declared. "Constance and I have been worried about you. Are you in good health?"

"Yes, thank you. How is Constance?" Marian replied.

"Please spare me the theater of your tender reunion," jeered Argentan. "I might not have proof of your collusion yet, but such illicit business cannot remain in the shadows forever."

Without reacting to the sheriff's accusations, Marian asked, "Did you bring proof that Lionel is alive and well?"

Argentan released Edmund, sheathed his dagger, and reached inside the pouch he carried to retrieve a letter. He proclaimed, "I visited Lionel and verified that he is in excellent health. However, if you continue stealing from me, the poor boy might have to go hungry." Argentan then handed the letter to Edmund. "You are familiar with his manner of writing. Examine this letter and confirm to Marian Hood that it is authentic."

Edmund broke the seal and read the letter. The time seemed to stretch unbearably, but finally, he looked at her. "Marian, it is his writing; I recognize it."

"And the words? Does it sound like Lionel composed it?" Marian inquired.

"Yes; but it is addressed to you, so you should read it for yourself." Edmund grimaced. "Marian, please remember that he's being held captive, and I'm sure he's enduring difficult circumstances."

The sheriff, Gisborne, and Tuck watched as Edmund gave the letter to Marian, and she silently read it.

Dear Marian,

Are you trying to get me killed? I thought you cared about me and my family. Have you considered what my death will mean to my father and Constance? Do you want them to be mourning me when they are already grieving for Robin?

I'm surrounded by dangerous men, and my life is in the hands of Sheriff de Argentan, yet you are deliberately stirring up trouble for him.

You are behaving in a selfish, reckless, and foolish manner. You are not honoring Robin's memory. He would be ashamed of you, and I'm certain my father agrees.

I was told that I must prove to you that I am still alive. After the feast of St. Mary Magdalene, you used a hole in the ground to trap Prince John's envoy and his men, thereby preventing the men of Locksley and Lenton from serving in the prince's army.

Please, if you care about me and my family, surrender to Sheriff de Argentan at once. He has assured me that you will be treated according to your station as Countess of Huntingdon, and he has sworn to guarantee your safety on his sacred honor.

Lionel de Toury

"Well?" asked the sheriff. "Are you ready to put an end to this nonsense and surrender? I will personally escort you to London, where you will be placed under the dowager queen's protection until King Richard returns. That sounds more than fair, considering the trouble you've caused everyone."

Marian's eyes had become watery with Lionel's stinging rebuke. She had never been close to him, but she knew that Robin was fond of him, and of course, she loved Edmund as a second father, while Constance was the sister of her heart.

Why couldn't Lionel understand the gravity of the situation? Didn't he realize that powerful forces were contending for the throne of England, and that he was merely a pawn in a dangerous game? He always saw himself as the center of everything. But for him to believe that the sheriff would treat her kindly if she surrendered… it was ludicrous.

She shifted her gaze from the letter to Argentan. "This only proves that he was alive in late August. I want proof that he is alive now."

"This is all the proof you're getting," proclaimed the sheriff. "You're lucky I agreed to allow him to write to you. Apparently, he's very disappointed in you."

Marian observed Edmund's worried face. "I think this sounds like Lionel, but you know him best. Do you believe that Lionel wrote this?"

With resignation, Edmund confessed, "I have no doubt that he wrote this. I think we can accept this letter as proof that Lionel is alive."

"Are you ready to surrender?" Argentan repeated.

"Lionel is naïve if he believes your promises. I will never surrender to you."

The sheriff shrugged. "Regardless of whether you surrender
today, or I capture you in the future, the result will be the same: you
will join your husband and your father in the shadows. My silver?"

Marian disclosed, "You will find it on the path as you return to
the road where you left your horses."

When the sheriff took a menacing step towards her, Tuck, Guy,
and Edmund all moved closer to Marian. Scowling at the other
men's obvious desire to protect her, Argentan refocused on Marian
and swore, "I promise, if you dare to ask for proof of his life again,
the proof I bring will be a few fingers, an ear, or some other body
part. Do you understand?"

"Perfectly," Marian snapped.

Argentan pivoted to leave, and Edmund and Guy fell into step
behind him.

Marian made a small gesture with her hand behind their backs,
and as Argentan walked away, Little John and Much pulled a length
of twine from opposite sides of the path, catching the sheriff at the
ankles and sending him tumbling into an inelegant heap on the
cluttered forest floor. Much promptly yanked the twine from the
path, removing the evidence of their prank.

Gisborne rushed to the sheriff and was helping him up as Argentan cursed and batted away his hands.

Marian hurried over and offered her assistance. "My lord sheriff,
are you all right? If you're not accustomed to walking in the forest,
it's easy to trip on the uneven ground."

Argentan staggered to his feet and yelled, "You! You did this!"

"Me? How? I was standing over there. Maybe you stumbled
on a rock." Marian studied the ground and stirred the leaves and
sticks with the toe of her boot as if she were searching for the cause
of his fall.

Argentan couldn't argue with her; he also looked at the ground and saw that it was uneven and covered with debris. Cussing and sputtering in outrage, he grabbed Edmund again and forced him to walk in front of him.

Edmund glanced over his shoulder and bid her farewell with a sly wink.

Marian and Tuck realized that Gisborne was still standing there, and Tuck shifted his position to stand protectively between them.

Guy acknowledged Tuck with a short nod, but he grinned at Marian and asked, "Should I be on the lookout for any more twine between here and the road?"

Tuck smiled and responded, "Go in peace, my son. The way is clear."

As Argentan bellowed for him to hurry, Guy declared, "Thank you, Marian. I know you didn't do it for my benefit, but I thoroughly enjoyed the sight of him falling on his face."

Before she could respond, he hastened to the sheriff's side.

9 October 1192, Mansion of the Templars, City of Acre

Standing at a window in the Mansion of the Templars, Robin gazed out over the vast sea and watched as the sun sank below the far horizon. His last day in the Holy Land had ended.

Although that thought comforted him, he was plagued by a sense of dread when he considered the long, dangerous voyage ahead. They were leaving very late in the season, when even the most experienced seamen were reluctant to sail. For that reason, it had been difficult to hire a ship for the journey.

There was also unrest among the people who remained in the newly christened Kingdom of Acre, an acknowledgment that Jerusalem would remain under Saracen control for now. The people of Acre did not want Richard to leave, so the king and his men planned to steal away in the middle of the night.

Robin touched the small lump under his tunic. Once again, he possessed his mother's silver ring, the one he had given Marian only to have her return it when she ended their betrothal. It hung on a chain, nestled against his chest and over his heart, where an ugly scar would always remind him of how close he came to dying at the hands of his half-brother.

In his mind, the silver circle represented his past, present, and future. If not for the ring, he would have died months ago, and there would have been no present and no future for him. As an inheritance from his mother, he treasured it, but its true significance in his heart was as a symbol of his future with Marian.

He closed his eyes and focused on memories of her, and a recollection of standing with Marian next to his parents' graves came to mind. The sun was shining on her pale blonde hair...

The sound of rusty hinges and laughter broke the spell as Baldwin, William, and André entered the chamber, and William announced, "Our baggage has been loaded on a small boat and sent to the buss that will take us home. I think the people of Acre will be surprised when they discover that we are gone."

Baldwin commented, "I was walking in the market, and I overheard several people claim that Richard would not risk his life by leaving so late in the season."

Chuckling, Robin declared, "We've been here sixteen months, and despite our failure to retake Jerusalem, Richard has achieved some incredible victories, yet the people still underestimate his belief in his own invincibility."

The other men heartily agreed.

André pointed to a strange assortment of short wooden poles, canvas, and leather straps lying on the floor at Robin's feet. "Is that yours? What in the world is it?"

Robin grinned. "I purchased it in the market to take on the trip home." He leaned over and deftly spread apart the poles, revealing that the canvas formed an inverted cone, similar in shape to a basket. He then tilted it on its side and whistled.

The men watched as Jack trotted over and entered the opening. Robin then lifted the contraption and slung it over his shoulder, tying the leather straps across his chest to secure it on his back. From over Robin's shoulder, the little dog peeked at the bemused men, and they burst into laughter.

Baldwin was the first to recover his composure. "I thought we were traveling disguised as Knights Templar, but I see you will be disguised as a peasant woman with an extraordinarily ugly baby."

A confused William asked, "What is the purpose of this? Has the dog become lame?"

Robin explained, "Jack might be swept overboard in rough seas, so in bad weather, I will use it to secure him. I know we will be traveling through winter storms with our late season departure."

"That's actually a good idea," conceded André. "But you still look ridiculous. Does the king know that you're bringing that dog with us?"

"Richard is quite fond of Jack," asserted Robin. "After all, if Jack hadn't alerted me at Jaffa—"

Baldwin rolled his eyes. "Please, not again! You can't give all the credit for our victory to a dog."

"True," agreed Robin. "Nevertheless, he's coming with us, and I will carry him if conditions warrant it."

André warmly admitted, "I like Jack, even if he is too small to be a proper dog. I was told that these dogs are good at catching vermin and small prey."

"I hear that Queen Berengaria asked for a dog like Jack. Richard searched high and low, and he was able to find a pair of similar dogs for her," disclosed Baldwin.

William added, "I saw the dogs just before she left Acre. The queen was very pleased with them, and someone joked that there might be both puppies and babies in her future."

"Speaking of Berengaria, I hear she gave you a gift, Robin. Is that true?" asked André.

Robin took off his canvas contraption and set it down, but Jack seemed content to snooze within its depths. Grasping at a glint of silver around his neck, Robin pulled the chain out from under his tunic and showed them the queen's gift.

"It's a ring," Baldwin remarked.

"Not just any ring," Robin explained. "It's the ring that belonged to my mother; the one I gave to Marian when we were betrothed. She returned it to me before we left on Crusade."

"I don't understand," confessed William. "Why is the queen giving you a ring that already belongs to you?"

André had told Berengaria about the ring, and he reminded Baldwin and William. "Don't you remember? The ring saved Robin's life because he wore it on a chain over his heart, and when that traitor, Gisborne, stabbed him, the ring prevented the dagger from going too deeply into Robin's chest."

"It was a miracle," exclaimed Baldwin. "Praise God for His endless mercy!"

Everyone concurred, crossing themselves at the wonder of it all.

Robin continued, "Gisborne's dagger badly damaged the ring, and when the queen heard the story of how it saved my life, her romantic nature inspired her to have it repaired and returned to me." He briefly pressed his lips to the ring before tucking it back under his tunic.

He proclaimed, "I'm not much of a sailor, and I dread the thought of winter storms and rough seas, but to return home and finally reunite with my wife makes any hardship worthwhile."

The other men chorused their agreement. They expected to arrive home by Christmas, and each man looked forward to reclaiming the life they had left behind when they embarked on Richard's Crusade.

CHAPTER 12
SHADOWS OF THE PAST

23 October 1192, Locksley Village

At the sight of Locksley Manor in the distance, Guy reined in his mount and took a moment to savor the feeling of home that the small estate inspired in his heart. Perhaps it was the warm fire in the hearth or the aroma of delicious food that would greet him upon his return. More likely, it was the intelligent, kind-hearted wife who awaited him.

He needed to suppress his growing attachment to Constance; she would never be a real wife to him. Yet, he could not deny how much his life had changed in four months of marriage. Constance and Edmund had become fixtures at Locksley, although Edmund spent part of each month in Embelton to attend to his affairs there.

The three of them had quickly fallen into a pattern of spending evenings together, first to enjoy a meal and then to sit around the hearth conversing. As the sheriff had mockingly said, it was all very domestic. And although the sheriff had spoken derisively, Guy had to admit that it was a balm to his soul. Not since the death of his mother had he experienced such pleasant companionship.

Edmund and Constance reminisced about past events, told humorous family stories, or discussed more pressing issues such as the Crusade. Edmund often spoke about the Anarchy of King Stephen's reign, which had begun two years before his birth and dominated his childhood recollections. He also recalled the rebellion against King Henry that had been led by Eleanor and their sons. He had fought in several of those skirmishes as a supporter of Henry.

At first, Guy had just sullenly observed their affectionate, familial banter. Gradually, he had gained the courage to ask a question or offer an opinion. To his utter amazement, they had not laughed at him, or sneered at him, or ignored him. No one had called him an idiot who was too stupid to understand what they were discussing. Instead, they had answered his questions and listened to his opinions. They had shown him kindness and respect that he did not deserve.

After all, he had cruelly murdered a beloved member of their family.

Guy knew that Robin's death had caused them great sorrow. He was astonished by their treatment of him, but like a thirsty man crawling across the arid plains of an unending desert, he accepted their cup of good will and drank of it greedily.

Knowing that he was in a precarious situation—either Marian, the outlaws, returning crusaders, or the sheriff himself would soon end his life—he was determined to spend the remainder of his time on earth enjoying the comforts of Locksley and the companionship of Constance and Edmund.

He spurred his horse into a trot.

Edmund was away again, so it would be a cozy dinner for two. He would tell Constance about Marian's latest caper, and he looked forward to hearing her musical laugh.

Yesterday, Marian and her men had robbed yet another of Prince John's supporters as he made his way through Sherwood Forest. But she didn't just steal from the man, she left him as naked as the day he was born and tied to a tree on full display for anyone to see. The nobleman's guards and companions had also been bound, but they had been left fully clothed. Understandably, the man had been howling for Marian's head, so Guy had spent the day following the tracks that led away from the scene of the robbery.

During the search, one of the man's guards had divulged that the noble had enraged Marian by claiming that Robin had bedded every available woman in Poitiers before the Crusade, and now that he had seen Marian, he could understand why her late husband had preferred the charms of the cultured, beautiful women at court.

Guy wouldn't mention that part of the story to Constance, and he wasn't sure what to think of the man's scandalous gossip, but he had no doubt that such allegations had ignited a fire of indignation within Marian.

Just then, his musings were interrupted by the sight of a familiar horse tethered to the post next to Locksley Manor.

Payen.

The despicable poisoner was at Locksley, even though Guy had warned him to stay away. He dismounted and tied his horse next to Payen's. Bursting through the door, he found the great hall of the manor empty, with only the crackle of a welcoming fire to greet him.

Leofric's calm, patient voice intruded upon the silence. "My lord, the evening meal is not ready yet. Shall I serve you ale while you wait?" When he noticed Guy's distracted manner, he added, "Lady Constance is resting above stairs until the meal is served."

"Where is he?" demanded Guy.

"Who?" asked a perplexed Leofric.

"Payen, of course."

Understanding dawned on the older man's face. "My lord, he has already left. He arrived earlier with a message from the sheriff. I told him you weren't here, and I offered him a drink while he waited, but he just gave me the letter and left. I'm surprised you didn't pass him on the road."

"His horse is still tied to the post out front." Guy searched his mind. Where else would Payen have gone? If he had planned to wait for Guy's return, he would have remained in the warmth of the great hall enjoying an ale.

Leofric was also confused. "Does he have any other business here in Locksley?"

Before Guy could respond, Elvina entered the room and addressed Leofric. "When Odella returns, tell her to come to the kitchen. I don't know what's taking her so long."

Suddenly, a cold fear seized Guy, and he knew. Memories of his mother, beaten and ravaged by Montlhéry, flashed in his mind, and they were so clear and so real that he briefly experienced the same panic and helplessness that he had felt as a boy. But he was no longer a boy, and although Odella was just a servant, she was *his* servant, and he was responsible for her as Lord of Locksley.

Without another word, he rushed out of the manor only to find Payen untying his horse and smirking to himself. There was a smear of blood on his cheek, and his hands were soiled, as if they might have blood on them too.

"What have you done?" Guy roared.

The other man startled and pivoted. Fear flashed in Payen's grey eyes at the sight of Guy, but he quickly recovered and declared, "I've delivered the sheriff's message. I gave it to that old man; didn't he tell you?"

Guy grabbed Payen by the front of his tunic and growled, "I'm asking you where you went *after* delivering the sheriff's message. Whose blood is on your face?"

Payen's eyes fleetingly shifted to the left, before he refocused on Guy and admonished, "Unhand me, or I'll tell the sheriff that you are aiding and abetting Marian Hood and the outlaws. Then he'll give *me* Locksley and your rich wife."

Guy tossed Payen to the ground like the garbage he was. Following Payen's glance to the left, he saw Osmund's home with its door ajar. Filled with dread, Guy ran in that direction, as Payen mounted his horse and galloped away.

Cautiously entering the open door, Guy froze in horror, as memories from long ago were resurrected in his mind. Odella was lying unclothed and bleeding on the floor.

When she moaned and tried to move her hand to cover herself, he snapped out of his trance and hastily pulled off both his tunic and his shirt. Dropping to his knees next to her, he draped his tunic over her to preserve her modesty, and he used the softer fabric of his shirt to wipe the blood from her face and hands.

Odella had a gash on her cheek and cuts on her forearms and hands. She had valiantly fought Payen, but even though the slender knight was a small man, he could easily overpower a woman, especially since he had been wielding a dagger.

She whimpered and began thrashing, her mind still in the throes of the terror of the attack.

Without thinking, he softly murmured in French. "Shhh, you'll be all right, Maman." Mortified by what he had said, he switched to English. "Odella, you'll be all right." She was pushing him away as he tried to help her, but he persisted.

Elvina arrived and knelt on the other side of Odella. "My lord," she beseeched, "please fetch Lady Constance. She'll know how to treat these wounds."

Guy agreed and was about to leave the girl in Elvina's care, when the small home shook with a deafening cry of fury and pain. Glancing over his shoulder to see the source of that inhuman sound, Guy looked into the crazed eyes of Osmund, and he instantly realized how everything must appear to the girl's father.

Odella, bleeding, naked, and trying to move away from Guy.

Guy, his hands stained with blood, naked from the waist up and kneeling on the floor next to her.

"No!" he shouted, but in the next moment, he was briefly airborne before he crashed into the wall, and the entire building trembled.

Dazed, Guy lurched to his feet, his head swimming. "I didn't—" Again he found himself tossed across the room like a child's rag doll.

He landed with a thud and rolled under a trestle table, knocking one support askew. The heavy top teetered, and Guy braced it with his hands to prevent it from falling on his head. He was now wedged between the tilted top and its remaining support.

Abruptly, the world around him morphed into his childhood home, where he had often cowered under the trestle table while Montlhéry beat and abused his mother. He felt small and helpless, and he hated himself for his failure to protect his mother from the monster who had ruled their lives without mercy.

Large hands were reaching for him, and in his mind, he was facing another beating from his mother's abuser. The hands were dragging him out from under the table, and a distant voice was screaming something, but he was so befuddled that he had no idea what was said. He struggled to escape the grasping hands, and that's when he saw it: a knife had fallen from the table during his beating and was within reach.

This was his opportunity to kill the man who had hurt his mother, and he ignored the small voice in his mind that begged him to return to the present.

He grabbed the knife and staggered to his feet, only to be slapped hard across the face in the same manner as Montlhéry had slapped him, over and over again. He reeled back, but he did not fall. Then he slashed at his attacker, deeply slicing the front of Montlhéry's neck.

Thick, hot blood sprayed Guy's face and chest, and the shadows of the past faded away, revealing the horror of the present. Montlhéry was nowhere to be seen. In front of him was Osmund, clutching the gaping wound across his throat in a futile attempt to stem the flow of blood as he dropped heavily to his knees. He collapsed on the floor face first, and an ever widening circle of blood spread beneath him.

Odella fainted, and Elvina stared at Guy in shock.

Constance arrived, and she shrieked, "What kind of monster are you to rape an innocent girl and murder her father!"

Guy was still disoriented. He dropped the knife, swaying on his feet and rubbing a lump on the back of his head as he stammered, "I... I... Payen..."

He could not bear the look of horror and disgust on his wife's face, so he stumbled out the door and limped to a nearby well to wash away the blood that seemed to cover him from head to toe.

～

Despite the late hour and chilly temperature, Constance continued to search for Guy. He had been seen exiting Locksley Manor in a clean set of clothes shortly after the death of Osmund, but his horse was in the stables, and no one knew where he had gone.

Constance was determined to find him and apologize for accusing him of raping Odella. Elvina had explained to her that it was Payen who had attacked Odella, and that Guy had only just arrived home and was trying to help her. Osmund had also wrongly assumed that Guy was the villain, and Elvina confessed that she had been afraid that the burly blacksmith would beat Gisborne to death.

Constance knew that the people of Locksley were outraged and heartbroken by Gisborne's cruel slaying of Robin and several other peasants whom he had killed when he first arrived in Nottinghamshire. And now, he had murdered one of the village's most beloved men.

But if Gisborne died or were sent away, Payen would likely take control of Locksley, and no one wanted that. As her father liked to remind everyone, *better the devil you know than the one you don't.*

Leofric and Elvina had also told her that Gisborne's temperament had significantly improved since his marriage, and Constance was quite pleased to hear that she might have had a positive influence on Guy.

However, in the end, the only happy resolution would be for King Richard to return and restore Locksley to Marian.

Finding herself at the Locksley cemetery, Constance lifted her torch to brighten the area. She saw nothing but forlorn headstones shrouded in shadows.

In defeat, she decided to return to the manor. If only her father were here! But he was searching for Lionel in York after hearing a rumor that Argentan had traveled there prior to the parley. Constance loved her brother, but she was irritated at him for the tactless, hurtful letter that he had written to Marian.

Just then, she noticed a flickering glow between the slats of the chapel's shuttered windows. Tentatively opening the door and entering the narthex, she tiptoed to the inner door that led to the sanctuary. It was open, and she observed Guy kneeling at the altar with his head bowed, apparently in prayer. She was about to leave when he spoke.

"Are you searching for me, Lady Constance?"

"How did you know–?" she sputtered.

He shrugged but did not answer or turn to look at her.

She placed her torch in a nearby bracket and approached the altar. After genuflecting and crossing herself, she sat in the first pew, and he sat next to her.

Still staring at the altar, he asked, "How is Odella? Were you able to tend to her injuries?"

Constance briskly replied, "Her physical injuries will heal, but she is very distraught; her innocence has been stolen, and she has no family because *you* killed her father." As soon as her accusatory words left her mouth, she wanted to take them back; her intention in seeking him was to apologize, not antagonize him.

"I didn't steal her innocence. I have never taken a woman by force, and I never will," he avowed with surprising intensity.

"Elvina told me what happened, and I'm sorry that I accused you of such a terrible crime. But why did you kill Osmund? Why not explain to him what happened?"

Guy's gaze dropped to his hands. "It was not my intention to kill Osmund; he was a good man." He sighed. "But what's done is done."

"Not your intention? How can you unintentionally take a knife and nearly behead someone?" Constance heatedly countered.

He reluctantly confessed, "Sometimes my emotions overpower me."

Constance harshly rebuked him. "Are you saying that you couldn't control yourself? Are you a man or a child? I've noticed that young children have little control over themselves." Her voice hitched and became a whisper. "Is that why you killed Robin?"

"Are you here to condemn me because I killed Osmund or Robin?" retorted Guy.

Constance paused and acknowledged, "Both, I think. Do you blame these uncontrollable emotions for your attack on Robin, too?"

For the first time since she had joined him in the chapel, he looked at her. One eye was almost swollen shut and a large bruise darkened his cheek. His other eye was assessing her angrily. Constance realized that no one knew where she was, and she was alone with a man who had just admitted that he had little control over himself. She stood to leave.

He reached out and grasped her wrist. "Wait; don't go. I won't hurt you."

Against her better judgment, she sat back down and stared at him expectantly. Finally, she prodded him. "Well? Are you going to answer my questions? Why did you kill Osmund? And Robin?"

Guy again averted his gaze, and he seemed either embarrassed or unsure of what to say. After an awkward silence, he revealed, "You spoke the truth. Today, I was a child, or rather, I was reliving a memory from my childhood."

"I don't understand."

"When I was a boy, there was a man…"

"Was he your father?"

"No, he was not. But my mother, she was a widow, and…" Again his voice faded as he searched for the right words.

"She was his mistress?"

Guy appeared stunned that Constance had deduced the truth so readily. With an exasperated huff, she declared, "I'm not naïve, and I'm not here to pass judgment on your mother. Just tell me what happened."

At her words of encouragement, Guy continued, "This man beat my mother and me, and because I was a boy, I could not protect her. I often saw my mother in a state similar to Odella's—"

Without intending to interrupt him, Constance let out a distressed sound at the thought of a boy seeing his mother beaten and abused.

He concluded, "When I killed Osmund, I thought I was killing this other man who had hurt my mother. My mind saw him and not Osmund. I know it sounds absurd, but it's the truth."

Constance considered his explanation for a few moments. Then she asked, "Is that why you killed Robin? Because of this man from your past?"

"No." He studied his hands again. "I was angry because Marian chose Robin. That's why I attacked him. I know you won't believe me, but I am sorry for what I did. I wish, more than anything, that I could go back in time and choose a different path."

Although Constance had felt sympathy for him and his mother, her grief for Robin overwhelmed her heart. Robin's untimely death was a tragedy from which his family would never completely recover. "I will never forgive you for murdering Robin," she fervently declared.

"I'm not asking you to forgive me for what I did to Robin," he replied evenly as he once again focused on the altar.

Constance was indignant at his choice of words. "For what you 'did to Robin?' That's an odd way to describe it. You didn't steal his horse or accidentally step on his toes—you murdered him!"

Guy sighed and met her irate gaze. "You have a valid point; let me rephrase it: I'm not asking you to forgive me for murdering Robin."

They fell into silence until Constance asked, "Is your mother still alive?"

"She died from a stomach ailment when I was fourteen summers, just as I was promoted from page to squire."

Constance felt a kinship with him for his loss. "My mother died when I was the same age. I still miss her."

"I miss her, but I'm also angry at her for the lies she told me."

"What did she tell you?"

"I don't want to talk about it." His guarded tone held a note of warning.

Constance did not want to push him to say more, so instead she suggested, "Sometimes mothers deceive their children to protect them from the truth."

"Perhaps."

There was another pause in their conversation, and Constance was debating whether to leave when he eyed the simple altar of the Locksley chapel and announced, "My mother wanted me to become a priest."

An unladylike snort escaped from Constance, and she slapped her hand over her mouth, mortified. To her relief, Guy was not insulted; he laughed as well. She realized that it was the first time she had ever seen a genuine smile light up his face.

He abruptly caught his breath and put his hand against his ribcage, grimacing in pain.

Constance frowned, concerned about the injuries he had sustained at the hands of Osmund.

Without warning, he clasped her hand. Startled by this sudden contact with him, she tried to pull away, but he would not release her, so she allowed him to hold her hand. His intense scrutiny caused a fluttering in her stomach.

"There is something I've wanted to say to you for a long time," he revealed. "I know you will never forgive me for killing Robin, but I would like to ask for your forgiveness for the things I said when we first met. I was furious with the sheriff, and I directed my anger at you instead."

Constance remembered his words only too well, but she wanted to be certain that he was talking about the same conversation, so she replied, "I don't understand."

"I'm sorry for the unkind things I said about your appearance. I was just trying to hurt your feelings. It's another example of me behaving like a child. In truth, you are lovely in every way that a woman can be lovely. Please, ignore the sheriff. He hates all women and knows nothing of beauty."

Constance glanced away self-consciously as an image of Marian's exquisite beauty rose in her mind. "Thank you. I will accept your apology, but I've always known that I'm not as beautiful as... some women. Nevertheless, I appreciate your kindness."

He released her hand. "There is one more thing I must say while we have privacy. Tell your father I'm trying to discover where Lionel is being held, but I've not had any luck. I've questioned the sheriff, but he refuses to tell me anything, and I'm worried he'll become suspicious of my motives if I persist. I've also searched through his papers and letters, but I can't find any reference to your brother."

She was astounded by this unexpected disclosure. "Why would you take such risks to help us?"

He made a dismissive gesture with his hand, as if he were shooing a fly. "It's the least I can do. You and your father have been very kind to me, and you've shown me respect that I don't deserve, considering what I did to Robin. I will help you if I can, regardless of the risk."

Constance swallowed nervously as her conscience was pierced by the knowledge that she and her father had been feigning friendliness in order to put him at ease so they could spy on him and his interactions with the sheriff. They had also been secretly helping the 'Ghost of Robin Hood' torment Guy and make him miserable.

Placing her hand on his forearm, she earnestly replied, "My father and I thank you for your help." She paused and studied his haggard features. "Are you still having difficulty sleeping?"

Guy contemplated her hand as it rested on his arm, lost in his thoughts.

Constance gently, but firmly, insisted, "Come to the manor. I have a sleeping draught that will help you find respite from your nightmares. I would also like to bind your ribs and apply a poultice to your bruises."

11 November 1192, The Port of Corfu, In the Ionian Sea near Greece

Robin stood on the deck, his bow drawn and aimed at the captain of a pirate galley bobbing in the water alongside King Richard's buss. Robin and six of the king's best archers were lined up, targeting the pirates in case they made a move against Richard, who was negotiating with them to charter two galleys for the next leg of their journey.

Even in the mild November air, sweat was dripping down the side of Robin's face, and his arm was trembling from the strain of holding his bow at the ready. He felt weak from the hellish month he had already spent at sea, and the swaying of the boats made him question his ability to strike his target.

On the galley, the pirate captain was arguing with Richard over the king's plan to sail north, along the east coast of Italy. Finally, Richard gave the signal that they had reached an agreement, and an exhausted Robin lowered his bow.

"I think your prayers have been answered, Robin," Baldwin speculated as he stood nearby.

An incredulous Robin stared at his friend. "You mean my prayers that we spend a month wandering back and forth across the Mediterranean during winter?"

Baldwin laughed. "I meant your prayers to never again set foot in the Holy Land. If Richard had been unsuccessful in chartering these galleys, we might have had to return to Cyprus or Acre until spring."

Robin thumped his friend on the back good-naturedly as they

watched Richard, André, and William leave the pirate galley and return to the buss. He conceded, "I guess I hadn't thought about it that way. But after sailing as far west as Sicily, the fact that we have returned to an island off the coast of Greece feels as though we are back where we started."

Baldwin sighed. "So many nights I have lain awake and tried to think of another way for us to go home, but I can't think of a better alternative."

"When the king announced that we would sail up the Adriatic, then go overland through hostile territory as we travel to Saxony, we all argued with him long into the night, but to no avail," Robin recalled.

"The king can be quite stubborn, once he has a plan in mind," remarked Baldwin.

"That's certainly true," agreed Robin. "But in this situation, I believe his plan is our only hope of reaching home without waiting until next spring. When we landed in Sicily and learned that bands of mercenaries were patrolling all the ports from Italy to Barcelona with the single goal of capturing Richard, we were left with few alternatives."

Baldwin commented, "If Richard were to be captured by an agent of King Philippe, he could lose everything: Normandy and the Angevin lands, even the crown of England and the Duchy of Aquitaine."

Just then, André and William joined them, and William offered his assessment. "These pirates are willing to take us north, and they seem very impressed with the king."

"Everyone is impressed with Richard upon first meeting him," André interjected.

"Just the first meeting?" questioned Baldwin. "I'm still impressed by his audacious schemes and fearless disregard for his own safety, and I've known him for years."

They all chuckled.

William added, "Admiral de Turnham examined the galleys and pronounced them sound, so we will transfer our cargo to them as soon as possible."

"How many men will Richard take with him?" Robin asked.

André explained the king's plan. "Only twenty men will continue with us, and we'll be divided into two groups of ten. The four of us will remain with the king, along with six more hand-picked men; Richard wants his favorites at his side. The other men will be on the decoy ship."

As his friends continued discussing the plan to sail north, Robin wandered away to stand at the railing and stare longingly at the western horizon. He was so far from home, and he wouldn't be getting closer any time soon. His hopes to reunite with Marian by Christmas were fading.

In the month since they had left Acre, he had passed the time imagining the moment when they would be reunited after their long separation, and he always seemed to picture her as she appeared at the May Day celebrations where their betrothal had been announced. He also wondered how she had reacted when Juan delivered Richard's letter, announcing that Robin was alive and would return to her when the Crusade ended.

These were the thoughts that filled his mind when he wasn't puking over the side of the ship. This passage, in rough winter seas, had been nightmarish and nothing like the other sea voyages that Robin had previously taken. At least Jack had proved to be a good sailor. Robin grinned at the thought of introducing his little dog to Marian.

As his gaze drifted to the pirate galleys, he couldn't help but notice how small and fragile they looked next to the larger, heavier buss.

CHAPTER 13
DEFIANCE

12 November 1192, Sherwood Forest, The Outlaw Camp

The outlaws were gathered at one of their favorite campsites, the one next to the hunting lodge that Robin's father had built. The small structure was used to protect their supplies from the elements, and it provided privacy for Marian and Odella.

Odella had refused to return to Locksley where she would have to face her father's murderer every day, not to mention the possibility that her assailant could arrive at any time on the sheriff's business. Marian had been hesitant to let her live in the camp, but she understood her desperate need to escape from Gisborne and Payen, so she had grudgingly yielded to the girl's tearful pleas.

At the moment, Odella was cooking a pair of coneys on a spit, and her presence in the camp had dramatically improved the outlaws' meals, much to everyone's delight.

The day was ending, and Marian pulled her cloak tightly around her shoulders to ward off the increasing chill. The shorter days and cooler temperatures were a harbinger of autumn's impending transition into winter, and the outlaws would soon need to relocate to the caves near Locksley.

Leaning against the side of the lodge at the edge of the

camp, Marian pretended to be relaxed when, in truth, she was silently fuming.

To the casual observer, the camp appeared cozy and peaceful, but Marian knew better. Edmund's plan to train the men at Embelton had been reasonable in theory, but the practical effect had been to undermine her position as leader.

A fortnight ago, the ten men who had originally gone to Embelton arrived at the camp, while the men who had remained with Marian left to go north. She had been pleased with the trained men's proficiency with swords and bows, but she quickly realized that they had no allegiance to her.

Even now, as she watched the camp, she could see the result. Aside from the fire where Odella was cooking, the camp was evenly divided into two groups huddled around separate campfires.

At one fire, Tuck was holding court with six of the new outlaws, regaling them with stories of the Holy Land, the Crusade, and the Battle of Arsuf, where King Richard had prevailed against the Saracen cavalry shortly after his brilliant end to the siege of Acre.

Robin had played a role in both the victory at Acre and the Battle of Arsuf, so she had been captivated by these stories as well. Or rather, she had been interested in them the first two or three times she heard them. However, the men seemed to never tire of discussing every detail of these battles.

Marian observed how the men sat at Tuck's feet, leaning towards him and hanging on his every word. *Again.*

At the other fire, John, Will, and Much were sitting with four of the new outlaws, who were lifelong friends of Will's and were of a similar age. They were equally enthralled with Little John's tales of living in the forest and his anecdotes about the people of Locksley.

The new outlaws had been courteous to her, and they had said all the correct things. But she could see it in their eyes: they had no respect for her. They were tolerating her.

Thankfully, John, Much, Will, and Allan were still devoted to her. Surprisingly, Tuck had also been a reliable defender of her role as leader, although he was the one most likely to advocate for his own ideas. Nevertheless, in the end, he always deferred to her.

But the new men? Several times she had caught them muttering and complaining behind her back. She had overheard both John and Tuck castigate them for not following her orders.

The sound of someone approaching drew everyone's attention, and several of the men grabbed their bows and moved to the periphery of the campsite. John whistled loudly, and the answering bird call caused everyone to relax.

Allan rode into the camp on their lone horse. It was still his role to perform reconnaissance in the neighboring villages and towns. One of Will's friends tended to the horse while everyone else gathered around Allan to hear the latest news.

He revealed, "Queen Eleanor has posted a proclamation announcing that King Richard has left the Holy Land and is on his way home. I overheard someone say that the queen expects him to be back in London by Christmas!"

The men cheered and excitedly discussed this momentous news with each other.

Allan made his way across the camp to Marian, and she greeted him warmly. After spending months traveling together, she thought of him as the brother she never had. He was kind to her, but he was also unreservedly honest. If he disagreed with Marian, he always let her know in a way that was candid, yet respectful. She often relied on him more than Tuck or Little John, but she didn't want the other men to know that.

"What do you think of King Richard returning?" Allan asked her.

Marian glanced away, noticing that the men had resumed their positions at the campfires, only now they were more animated and energized.

"I welcome his return. I'm certain that he will arrest and execute Argentan and Gisborne. And with the king's support, I know that

Robin's legacy will live and thrive; he promised me as much when I last saw him."

Allan studied her closely. "What's the matter, Marian? I can see that something's bothering you."

She sighed. "It's the men who just arrived from Embelton. I can tell that they do not accept me as their leader."

"They all swore fealty to you."

"Oh, I believe that they were sincere when they took their oaths. But their hearts are not in it. They would prefer to follow Tuck. A few of the younger Locksley boys look to John for leadership."

"John was in charge for a long time; at least that's what I've been told. Robin was already leader when I joined. Do you remember the night we met?"

Marian beamed. "I will never forget that night. It was the night when Robin and I pledged our lives to each other. You were our witness, and now that we're friends, I'm glad you were there."

Allan gestured towards the other men. "Maybe Tuck and John need to talk to them and tell them to listen to you."

She disagreed. "I think that would just reinforce in their minds that Tuck and John are their leaders, not me. I need to find another way. The problem is, I don't understand men."

Allan laughed. "Men are very simple creatures. Give us good food, good fun, and most importantly, make us feel needed and respected, and we will happily serve you."

Marian considered this. "Are men really so easy to understand? What about their obsession with battles and fighting? Or with hunting?"

"Well, you just answered your own questions: hunting leads to good food. Fighting is good fun to most men and winning battles earns respect."

"Do you think fighting is 'good fun?'" she questioned.

"Fair point. I prefer performing. Although if my audience doesn't like my music, I might throw a few punches." He laughed again. "Just remember, men are like little boys, only taller and stronger. Think about how you deal with a young child—"

"I suppose I could imagine that." She grinned at the thought. Sobering slightly, Marian inquired, "Was there any other news?"

Allan slapped his forehead. "I almost forgot! Sir Gervase is on his way back to Nottingham. He was in Mountsorrel earlier today, and he will pass through Sherwood tomorrow."

"And his escort?"

"He's got at least a dozen, maybe fifteen, soldiers with him. If he's that heavily armed, he might be bringing more silver to Argentan."

"Call Tuck and John over, I want to discuss my plan for tomorrow with them."

"I will get them for you now. Do you need me? I'd like to see if Odella needs help with anything," he requested hopefully, and Marian noticed a new sparkle in his eyes. She smiled knowingly and sent him on his way.

13 November 1192, Sherwood Forest, On the Road to Nottingham

Marian stood next to Tuck as they surveyed the road, waiting for Sir Gervase and his men to appear. The outlaws were concealed within the tree line on either side of the road, and she mused that they were divided up in the same way as the previous night around the campfires.

The newer men were wearing scarves over the lower half of their faces to hide their identities in hopes of protecting their families from the sheriff's retribution. Argentan probably suspected that many of the outlaws were men who had escaped conscription into the prince's army, but Marian didn't want to give him definitive proof. The people of Lenton and Locksley were suffering enough as it was.

After deciding that she would need to evaluate the strength of Gervase's force before attempting an ambush, Marian had given all the men strict orders to wait for her signal. Tuck and John had agreed with Marian that the men should not take unnecessary risks since King Richard was due to return soon.

Finally, several dark shapes crested the hill: a mounted knight and three guards on foot. It was Sir Gervase.

Marian muttered a mild curse.

"My lady?" a curious Tuck whispered.

"Something's wrong," she explained in an equally hushed voice. "Allan said Gervase was traveling with at least a dozen men."

Tuck considered this for a few moments. "Perhaps Allan was mistaken."

Marian had great faith in Allan's talent as a spy. She replied, "This doesn't feel right. I trust Allan. Send a man down the road to see if more soldiers are following him."

"Good thinking," commented Tuck, as he signaled to the nearest man and commanded him to do reconnaissance by backtracking Gervase's route.

To Marian's surprise, the other man quietly argued, "But there's only four of them! We should attack now."

Tuck firmly scolded the younger man. "Lady Huntingdon wants you to check down the road, and that's what you'll do. It's not your place to question her."

Grumbling, the man walked south as instructed, only to stop and say something to his companions. Marian couldn't hear what he said; everyone was carefully modulating their voices.

Gervase and his men had moved just beyond the position of the outlaws, and Marian took the opportunity to make eye contact with John as he waited on the other side. With a slashing gesture, she signaled that the attack had been aborted, and he nodded in understanding.

Suddenly, a loud cry shattered the morning stillness, and the man to whom Tuck had given orders rushed out onto the road, followed by four of his friends.

Marian opened her mouth to call them back, but it was too late. The foolhardy men were standing on the road behind Gervase and his men, aiming their bows at them and demanding that they relinquish their valuables.

On the far side of the road, John sought Marian's notice; he was confused by the unexpected appearance of the outlaws without her signal. She gestured to John to stay put, and he obeyed. They all listened as Gervase taunted the young outlaws.

"Are you going to use that bow, or are you just playing games? I have no intention of handing over my coins to anyone except the lovely Marian Hood. Where is she?" Gervase scanned from one side of the road to the other, and he bellowed, "Marian Hood, come out, and face me!"

The leader of the renegade outlaws released an arrow, intentionally sending it wide of Gervase's head. The envoy was not impressed.

"Get off your horse," demanded the outlaw.

Gervase laughed at him.

The outlaws standing in the road nervously glanced at each other in confusion.

These reckless men had forced her hand, and Marian was just about to signal to the other outlaws to attack, when a dozen additional foot soldiers appeared and broke into a run towards Gervase. Some were brandishing swords and others carried bows.

It had been a trap, and there was nothing she could do to rescue her men. Full of dread, she watched as they spun in a circle and realized that they were surrounded. She could see them searching the tree line where she was hiding with Tuck, as if they expected the Knight Templar to perform a miracle and deliver them from their hopeless predicament.

Calmly drawing his sword, Gervase maneuvered his horse into position, and impaled the leader of the maverick outlaws. The other four outlaws dropped their bows, fell to their knees, and raised their hands in surrender.

Much to her dismay, Gervase had noticed the men's focus on the section of trees where she was located. As the rest of his soldiers arrived, he pointed in her direction and shouted, "Search there! Ten silver coins to the man who captures Marian Hood!"

"My lady, we must go now!" exclaimed Tuck.

Knowing that John would lead the remaining outlaws to safety, Marian pivoted and sprinted away from the road with Tuck at her side.

⊷

Marian had barely caught her breath when John and the other outlaws entered their camp near the old hunting lodge.

John demanded, "What happened? Why did you send them onto the road while keeping us in the trees?"

Before Marian could answer, Tuck explained, "Those fools disobeyed me."

Sharply correcting him, Marian snapped, "No, they disobeyed *me* by attacking when I had not given the signal."

"Of course, you are right, my lady," a contrite Tuck admitted.

Marian shifted her focus to her next priority. Summoning the five remaining new outlaws, she commanded, "As swiftly as your feet can move you, I want two of you to go to Locksley and the other three to Lenton. Find the families of the men who were captured and the family of the man who was killed. Tell them to gather their possessions—whatever they can carry—and bring them all here. There's no time to waste."

She then instructed Will. "Go to Locksley Manor, but take care that Gisborne does not see you. Find Constance and tell her that her father must come here as soon as possible."

Will and the other men left, running at full speed to their destinations.

"We have to go back and rescue them!" Much frantically insisted as he tugged on Marian's sleeve to gain her attention. "They're still on the road to Nottingham, and we can intercept them before they arrive at the castle."

Marian's eyes narrowed in aggravation. "Are you proposing that the five of us ambush Gervase's force of fifteen? His men are armed with swords, shields, and bows, and they have the expertise of seasoned soldiers. Our priority must be to save those men's families."

"But... but," stuttered Much. "We can't leave those men to die a horrible death at the hands of the sheriff. We must save them!"

John was murmuring his agreement, while Tuck and Allan seemed dismayed by Much's outburst.

"Those men knew the dangers of joining our band of outlaws, and despite the training they received, they willfully disregarded my orders," a grim Marian reminded him. "They are already as good as dead, and there is nothing we can do—"

"No!" howled Much. "We have to do something. Robin would have—"

"Robin?" echoed Marian, her voice rising in indignation. "Are you suggesting that Robin would have sent his men to certain death in a futile rescue attempt? Much, we have known each other for a long time, but I swear to God—"

"My lady!" a scandalized Tuck interjected at her lack of piety.

"Quiet, Tuck! I don't want to listen to one of your sermons right now," she snarled.

To his credit, Tuck fell silent, while John and Allan attentively followed every word.

Continuing where she had left off, Marian censured Much. "I appreciate your long friendship with Robin, but you don't get to lecture me in Robin's name. If I want your opinion about how Robin might have done something, I will specifically ask you. Otherwise, if you ever use Robin's name to manipulate me again, you will have to leave."

"Leave?" Much was taken aback by Marian's stern rebuke.

"That's right; you will no longer be welcome here if you try that again. It doesn't matter what you *think* Robin would or wouldn't have done. To my heart's everlasting sorrow, Robin isn't here. He's gone forever. But I'm here, and I'm the leader. You, along with these other men, swore a sacred oath to follow me. If you can't abide by your vow, leave now. You can remain at Embelton until King Richard returns."

"No... no," moaned a distraught Much as his eyes filled with tears. "Marian, don't send me away; my life has no purpose beyond our fight against Argentan and Gisborne. Please, I'm sorry..."

Marian resisted the urge to console him; she had realized that such feminine impulses just emphasized to the men that she was a woman. She had never seen the men comfort each other with hugs or reassuring words, so she remained aloof and subtly reminded him of the difference in their rank. "Much, I won't send you away if you will show me the same deference you showed Lord Robin."

"I promise Lady Marian, I won't do it again; just let me stay," begged Much.

Satisfied that she had made her point, she addressed John, Tuck, and Allan. "As soon as the families arrive, we need to make them comfortable until Lord Edmund can send them north. As for the remaining five men who recently joined us, I will speak to each of them to determine whether I can trust them to obey me in future raids. If I have any misgivings about a man, I will send him north. Besides, it sounds as though the king will return by Epiphany. In the meantime, we will curtail our banditry. As long as we are frugal, we have enough to help the people through the winter."

The men nodded in agreement.

Marian scrutinized each man. "If any of you have doubts about following me—if you are not willing to obey me as your leader, I want you to leave with Lord Edmund as well."

At once, Tuck, John, Much, and Allan dropped to one knee at her feet and affirmed their unwavering allegiance to her.

2 December 1192, The Shores of the Adriatic Sea, Near Aquileia

The unrelenting wind blowing over the roiling waters and across the bleak, rocky shoreline was icy. Robin pulled a blanket snugly around his shoulders to keep warm and observed Jack as he happily played on the beach, digging in the sand and barking at the waves that intermittently lapped at his paws.

Lifting his eyes to the leaden clouds that shrouded the sky, he guessed that it must be midday. Unbidden, a memory of one of Argentan's riddles echoed in his mind:

You are like a man lost in the twilight of a wintry day; the clouds have obscured the sun, and the abundance of shadows has confused your sense of direction.

The sheriff's riddles plagued Robin during times like this, when he was alone with his thoughts. He now understood that some were referring to the fact that Gisborne was his half-brother. Others were likely allusions to the sheriff's ties to the French court and the mysterious Count de Montlhéry. The connections between Argentan, Gisborne, Montlhéry, and King Philippe were undeniable.

Robin's gaze shifted to the wreckage of the galley, lying on its side and wedged between the rocks lining the shore. Fractured memories whirled in his mind like the churning, wrathful sea: holding Jack tightly against his chest with one arm while clinging to a mast on the deck of the galley with the other; the shock of cold water slapping him in the face as it surged over the railing and across the deck; the tossing of the ship as it rocked back and forth until it was nearly capsized; the galley screeching and groaning like a wounded man crying for help as the wind howled like a fiendish beast from the abyss pursuing its quarry. And finally, the deafening boom as the vessel crashed against the rocks on the beach, followed by a desperate escape to the shore through frigid waist-high waters.

Never again would he nonchalantly embark on a sea voyage, even if he was only crossing between England and Normandy. Perhaps, since all his estates and properties were in England, he could avoid future sea travel after his return home. He could only hope.

"I see Jack has recovered from our little adventure last night." King Richard commented as he joined Robin on the beach.

"Sire, it's good to see you up and about and looking well," replied Robin, who briefly sank to one knee.

"No formalities, Robin. You must refrain from showing such deference to me as we travel in disguise."

"You are right, of course," conceded Robin. "With all due respect, do you really think people won't recognize you? Few men are as tall as you, and even fewer have the manner of a warrior king who is accustomed to immediate obedience."

"My pride is pierced that you have so little confidence in my acting abilities," cried the king in mock distress.

"I'm glad you are in such good spirits, sire, and I'm sure you will prove me wrong as we travel north. Have the other men returned from securing supplies for our journey yet?"

Richard, his back to the sea, scanned the horizon. "Aquileia is an old Roman city, and I've been told that it is mostly in ruins. It's only a handful of miles inland, so they should return before sunset."

"Are you certain of our location?" Robin cautiously asked. He felt utterly disoriented on this foreign beach, *a man lost in the twilight of a wintry day,* as Argentan had put it. He knew that the pirates manning the galley had either drowned or run away during the night. The second galley had disappeared, and everyone feared the worst for those on that ship.

"Again, you doubt me?" the king continued in a light-hearted manner. Sobering slightly, he explained, "As the storm intensified last night, I spoke to the captain. He knew these waters well. We are between the Republic of Venice to our west and the Kingdom of Hungary to the east. Actually, I believe God placed us here, in this desolate spot, to facilitate the secret nature of our travels."

Robin took advantage of the king's good mood to press for more information. "Your plan to travel in disguise, as vassals of our friend, Baldwin de Béthune, is sensible. However, we are in a strange place, without maps, and none of us speak the local languages."

"We are traveling as returning Crusaders and Knights Templar. The people whom we encounter will be happy to help us. And we are carrying a large supply of Venetian ducats, the preferred coinage for this area. Don't worry so much, Robin. My plan is brilliant, and we will reach my dear friend and brother-by-marriage, Henry the Lion, in Saxony before the end of the month."

"From Saxony, how long will it take to reach England?" Robin inquired.

"I see you are eager to reunite with the lovely Lady Marian." Richard grinned knowingly. He then frowned. "I don't understand why she disobeyed my orders to wait in Poitiers for my return. Nevertheless, I'm in a good humor, and I forgive her for her defiance of my wishes."

"Marian and I appreciate your benevolence, sire. I'm concerned that she might have heard about my marriage to Blanche. You know the cruelty of the court gossips in Poitiers."

"True," agreed Richard. "You must tell her how Blanche manipulated both of us. First, she lured you into her bed, and then she used her rank as a royal cousin to force my hand and demand that you marry her. It's a mystery of the ages how a woman can present herself as a harmless, gentle lamb while securing an advantageous marriage with the ruthless cunning of a wolf."

Robin barked a short laugh, although he wasn't particularly amused by his memories of that dark time in his life. He contended, "I believe that Argentan was responsible for the poisoned wine that killed Blanche, our unborn child, and her sister. We know for certain he attempted to poison you in Acre with tainted wine."

"When I return to England, Argentan and Gisborne will be executed for treason. Then I must punish Philippe. My mother has written that his aspirations in Normandy have been clearly exposed in my absence."

"My liege, are you planning a new campaign in Normandy?" Robin's heart sank with despair at the thought that he would soon be fighting another long war. The old saw *from the cauldron into the fire pit* came to his mind.

"A war with Philippe is inevitable."

Robin noticed that the king was closely assessing him, and he feared that he had unintentionally revealed his reluctance to join such a fight.

"You would be a great asset to me in such a war," Richard remarked. "However, I have decided that you will serve me in Huntingdonshire and Nottinghamshire. I need experienced, loyal men, like you, in England, if I am conducting a campaign in Normandy."

Robin released a breath he had not realized that he was holding and gratefully thanked his king. "Sire, I would be honored to serve you in England."

"You have always served me well, Robin," acknowledged Richard. "If you want a quiet family life, you will have it. As for me, my queen and I must start a family as soon as possible. Only the birth of a healthy son will curb John's ambitions."

Robin nodded and offered, "I pray you will have many sons."

Richard fell silent for a few moments. "As my father learned, sons can be both a blessing and a curse. John was always his favorite, just as I was favored by my mother. I'm older than John, and I don't know him well, but it still troubles me that my own brother would scheme to have me killed."

"Do you believe that King Philippe and John were working in concert?"

"We already know there are ties between Argentan, Gisborne, and Philippe. John has dominion over Nottinghamshire, so Sheriff de Argentan answers to him. I have no doubt that John is actively plotting with Philippe to take my throne. At the same time, I wonder what John has promised Philippe in return. Would my brother be so foolish as to sacrifice Normandy on the altar of his ambitions?"

"What will you do with John, if I may ask, sire?" Robin knew his question was impertinent, but he still dared ask it.

"I can't execute him; he's my brother, and it would break my mother's heart to lose yet another child. I haven't decided what I will do. If you had a brother, Robin, you would understand."

Robin looked away as he debated whether to reveal the truth about Gisborne. Unfortunately, Richard had observed his reaction.

"Tell me, Robin," the king demanded.

"It's a long story, sire," Robin demurred.

Richard gracefully swept his arm over the desolate beach in front of them. "How else shall we pass the time until the others return? This is the perfect opportunity for you to tell me a long story without any interruptions or distractions."

CHAPTER 14
AN UNEXPECTED ALLIANCE

10 December 1192, Lenton Village

Allan decided that he would compose a song about the brave, beautiful girl walking alongside him as they entered the village of Lenton.

He had first noticed her four years ago. At that time, Marian was living in the hunting lodge, and Odella would bring food for her from Locksley. After Robin took Marian to Embelton, Allan had lamented the end of Odella's frequent visits to the camp, and when he returned from his long journey to the Holy Land, he had rejoiced at the news that she was still unmarried. Unfortunately, there had been few opportunities for him to talk to her when she was living in Locksley, but now that she was residing in the outlaw camp, he sought her company as often as he could.

Outwardly, she was recovered from the brutal attack she had endured. There were small, pink scars on her forearms, hands, and left cheek. Allan believed that each scar was a testament to her indomitable spirit, and he admired her courage in resisting a man armed with a dagger.

Despite her attempts to appear unscathed by what had happened, sometimes he saw her despondently staring off into the distance, profound sorrow etched upon her lovely face. Occasionally, Allan had approached her, hoping to spend time with her, only to find that her eyes were puffy and red from crying. She would hastily wipe the dampness from her face and smile, greeting him sweetly and never complaining.

To see her struggling with her grief and pain had made him both sad and outraged. Thoughts of killing Payen rose in his mind, but he knew that revenge was like a virulent plague that infected everyone involved and left no survivors. He resolved that, instead of risking the hangman's noose for the crime of murder, he would find ways to make Odella happy. Maybe he could help her forget.

Therefore, he had been ecstatic when she had cheerfully offered to help him deliver food to a sick family in Lenton. After their arrival at the modest home, they distributed the food, and Allan entertained the family with several songs. He was pleased that Odella knew the songs too, and her soprano was the perfect complement to his tenor.

As they left the family, he boldly took her hand in his, and she allowed it with a shy smile. It occurred to him that the phrase, 'falling in love' was an awful description. Love felt more like soaring than falling. Song lyrics filled his mind, and he whistled a happy tune, exhilarated by the warmth and genuine happiness in her eyes.

However, falling into despair was the perfect description of how he felt when they were surrounded by men on horseback, and he gazed up into the cold, hateful glare of Sir Gervase.

"I recognize you. You're the one who thinks he's a troubadour. Perhaps I will take you to London, and you can entertain Prince John with your song about roosters," Gervase sneered.

Allan quickly recovered his wits and countered, "My lord, lots of men look like me, and you're mistaking me for someone else. I ain't no singer."

"Odd that I could hear you and this girl singing in that shack over there." Gervase signaled to his men, and several soldiers hurried over to him. "Arrest these two—"

"Wait! I don't know this girl, and she has done nothing wrong. Let her go, and I'll come with you quietly," begged Allan.

Gervase laughed. "You're in no position to bargain. If you don't know this girl, why are the two of you singing love songs and holding hands?"

Allan opened his mouth and expected something clever to emerge, but for once in his life, his mind went blank, and he couldn't talk his way out of his predicament.

Gervase gave instructions to the soldiers to bind them and take them into Lenton Manor. A small crowd had gathered, and the people were worriedly murmuring. Noticing the villagers congregating around him, the royal envoy loudly proclaimed, "Tell Marian Hood that I have caged her songbird. If she wants him back, she must come here today, because tomorrow I will deliver him to Nottingham where the sheriff will hang him for his crimes!"

10 December 1192, On the Road to Lenton

Constance was not accustomed to riding her horse at full gallop, and she struggled to keep pace with Guy, who was pushing their mounts hard as they rode to Lenton.

They had been enjoying their midday meal when a panicked Elvina stumbled into the hall and announced that Sir Gervase had taken Odella prisoner. Elvina sobbed that she feared the girl was facing more abuse at the hands of both Gervase and Payen. That was all Guy needed to hear as he leapt from the table and dashed to the stables with Constance close on his heels.

Finally, they arrived at a fork in the road—one path led to Nottingham and the other to Lenton—and Guy slowed to a trot. When he abruptly halted, Constance's horse pulled up short, and she nearly tumbled out of her saddle. Guy reached over and grabbed her elbow to steady her.

She was about to ask him why they had stopped, when she noticed he was staring straight ahead and frowning. Following his gaze, she saw Marian standing in the road; her bow drawn and aimed at Guy. The outlaws were with her, and they were also targeting her husband.

"Dismount, and walk towards me with your hands raised," commanded Marian.

Both Guy and Constance dismounted, and she rushed to Marian and breathlessly explained, "Marian, please, we have to go to Lenton. Gervase has captured Odella."

"I'm aware of that, Constance," Marian responded in a tight voice.

Will and Much took Guy's sword and dagger, and he lowered his hands as he stared impassively at Marian.

"I'm holding you responsible," she proclaimed.

His brow rose in surprise. "For what, exactly, am I responsible? Are you blaming me for everything bad that happens? Do you really believe that I have such god-like power?"

To Constance's dismay, Marian slapped him for his impertinence. Unlike the slaps she had seen him receive from Argentan, the force of this strike had no effect on Guy as he stoically stood there.

Tuck stepped forward. "My lady, please, let's ask him to explain himself before we assign guilt."

Marian reluctantly agreed, and she ordered Will and Much to look after the horses while John and the others kept watch along the road. She then escorted Tuck, Guy, and Constance to a small clearing within the safety of the greenwood.

"Marian, he had nothing to do with Odella's capture," Constance asserted. "We've been at Locksley all day and only received word when Elvina told us what had happened."

"Both Allan and Odella have been captured by Gervase," Marian revealed. "He announced to the people of Lenton that if I wanted them back, I would have to come and get them."

Guy stated the obvious. "It's a trap."

"Of course, it's a trap! What is your role in this scheme? I find it highly suspicious that you're here." Marian glared at him.

Tuck was calmer than Marian, and he remarked, "You expect us to believe that the moment you heard that Odella was captured, you rode to Lenton. That seems odd."

"That's exactly what happened. When we heard the news we left at once," Constance affirmed.

"I don't care about your minstrel," claimed Guy. "If you want him back, you can have him. I only want to take Odella away from Gervase and Payen."

"My scouts in the village tell me that Payen was there briefly, but he has returned to Nottingham," Marian replied.

"Thank God," Guy sighed in relief before answering. "I have not had contact with Gervase recently. I'm sure you're aware that he has been staying at Lenton." After a pause, he informed her, "Prince John has offered him the Barony of Lenton, if he captures you."

Constance observed Marian sway as if she had been dealt a physical blow. Lenton was her legacy and childhood home, and it was dear to her heart.

"Why are you worried about Odella?" Tuck questioned. "She's not your responsibility."

Guy disagreed. "She is a servant of Locksley, and even if she's living with Marian in the forest, she is still my responsibility, especially now that she has no family."

Marian ripped her dagger from its sheath, pointed it at his heart, and shrieked, "And you're the reason she has no family! You butchered her father in front of her! Tell me why I shouldn't end your life now and avenge both Robin and Osmund."

Constance was shaken to her core by the mask of hatred on

Marian's face. Evidently, Guy's killing of Osmund had revived Marian's intense anguish over the murder of Robin.

"Marian, please!" she cried. "This is not the time. We must focus on Odella and Allan."

Marian frowned at Constance. "What are you doing here, Constance? Did Gisborne force you to come? Is he using you as a shield to hide behind, like the damned coward we all know him to be?"

Tuck, Guy, and Constance all started talking at the same time, but for once, Constance managed to shout everyone else down and declare, "Guy didn't force me; he tried to stop me from coming. He only relented when I pointed out that Odella would not be comfortable leaving with him, and if she's been assaulted again, I need to be there to help her."

"It's true, Marian. I've never forced Constance to do anything she doesn't want to do," Guy insisted.

Tuck inquired, "What was your plan, Gisborne?"

"Constance and I were going to Lenton to demand that Gervase release Odella to me," he explained.

"That's your plan?" challenged an incredulous Tuck.

Constance gave Guy a hard look, and he reluctantly elaborated. "I also have a small bag of silver that I was going to give him in exchange for the girl. Marian, if you take my silver, I won't be able to bribe him for Odella's safe release."

"Marian will not take our silver," Constance contended. "Isn't that right, Marian?"

Marian scowled at Constance, but spoke to Guy. "You can return to Locksley, and take Constance with you. My men and I will rescue Allan and Odella."

Now it was Guy's turn to be skeptical. "Do you plan to walk into Lenton Manor, past Gervase's large contingent of men-at-arms, and just take Odella and Allan away from him?"

Marian scoffed. "Do you expect me to divulge my plan to you?"

Tuck was assessing Guy. "Will you help us by creating a diversion?"

"We don't need his help! He will betray us," Marian exclaimed.

"My lady," Tuck's voice was gentle and calming. "We have the same goals. I don't believe Sir Guy would have knowingly exposed his wife to danger. I believe he speaks honestly about his intentions to rescue the girl."

"You're a fool; everything Gisborne says is a lie."

Constance recognized that Marian's emotions were spiraling out of control, but she didn't know what to say, or how to comfort her.

Unexpectedly, Guy redirected the conversation, his voice solemn and respectful. "Lady Marian, please listen to me. Nothing must happen to Sir Gervase. He is Prince John's close confidant. You've already killed one of the prince's favorites, Eustace Clisson. If anything happens to Gervase, if he's killed or even sustains a minor injury, no one will be able to protect you from John's wrath—not your men, or this Knight Templar, or me—none of us will be able to protect you."

Marian hissed, "I don't need *your* protection, and Prince John's men will never find me in the forest."

Guy's expression was grave. "I don't think you understand; Prince John's army wouldn't waste time marching through the greenwood searching for you. They would simply burn Locksley and Lenton to the ground and kill every man, woman, and child in both villages."

Marian paled, and Constance felt the blood drain from her face as well. For once, Marian was speechless, so Constance suggested, "Guy, you can't mean that. Surely, you are exaggerating."

Tuck was not as shocked, but he pressed Gisborne for more. "Are you certain of this?"

"The only reason that the sheriff hasn't burned both villages to the ground is the tax revenues that they generate. He wants to drain as much wealth from Locksley and Lenton as possible. I have worked hard to keep Locksley profitable because I know the taxes will keep the sheriff happy. But Prince John won't care about the tax revenues from two small villages. They will mean nothing to him, and if he wants to demonstrate his absolute authority over Nottinghamshire by destroying these villages and executing the villagers, he will do it."

Marian turned away, shaken by this news.

Constance walked over to her and gently offered, "Let us help. We only want to protect Odella from another attack. Guy's not interested in arresting Allan or anyone else. Please, Marian."

The time stretched on as Marian considered her options. To Constance's profound relief, Marian regained control over herself and approached Guy.

"Will you follow my instructions without deviation?"

"That would depend, Marian. Gervase can't know that I'm helping you. The sheriff already suspects that my attempts to capture you have been half-hearted. And if something happens to me, Payen will take control of Locksley, and Constance will be in danger."

"My plan does not require you to confront Gervase. I want you to carry out the plan you originally had: go to Gervase, and offer him silver for Odella. If possible, strike up a conversation with him. We need you to distract him while I implement my plan."

"What is your plan?" inquired Guy.

"You don't need to know my plan," Marian briskly informed him. "The less you know, the more genuine the surprise on your face. Just play along with what happens and keep Constance safe."

10 December 1192, Lenton Manor

Marian surveyed the rear wall of Lenton Manor. She wished she could move closer, but the winter landscape was bereft of leafy cover. Gervase had men stationed on each side of her former home. There were two doorways into the manor: the main entrance at the front, and a side door leading into the kitchen. At each doorway, five men stood watch. Although there was no door on the side opposite the kitchen, there were several large windows through which a grown man could pass into the main part of the house. Four men guarded that side.

The rear wall had only two windows: one near the ground and one leading to an upstairs room that had served as Marian's bedchamber. And towering over the back of the manor was a large oak, its branches gracefully hugging the rear corner of the house where that small window was located.

Childhood memories of Robin teaching her how to climb that tree were bittersweet. How young and innocent they had once been! She refocused on the task at hand. There were only three men guarding the back of the manor. As she had hoped, the two rear windows hadn't been considered much of a security risk.

She handed Tuck her bow, quiver of arrows, and dagger. Lowering her hood so that there would be no question as to her identity, she emerged from her hiding place, holding her hands above her head in surrender.

The three guards immediately saw her and drew their swords, taking several steps in her direction, but maintaining their proximity to the manor.

She could hear one man offer to get the captain, and her heart sped to a dizzying tempo. The success of her plan hinged on limiting the number of soldiers involved, and her biggest fear had been the possibility of these men calling for assistance. To her relief, the oldest of the three hesitated. Marian dropped to her knees and summoned them. "Help me; I'm hurt, and I want to surrender."

The older guard grinned and said, "Let's arrest her ourselves; there's ten pieces of silver on her head. If we call the captain, he'll keep the bounty for himself."

They drew near, and Marian submissively held out her hands, allowing one of the men to tie her wrists with a small cord. The men sheathed their swords, and they were already planning how they would spend their unexpected windfall.

With feigned confusion, Marian asked, "How will you divide ten coins between three men?"

They paused briefly. One replied, "Well, that's three each, and we'll have to share one."

The older man countered, "No, I'm the one who saw her first, and I get the tenth coin."

The third man claimed that he had seen Marian first.

They became completely absorbed in their argument, and Marian rose to her feet as a signal. Her movement drew the men's attention and allowed John, Tuck, and Much to creep up behind them. They overpowered the soldiers, gagging and binding them before they could sound an alarm.

Tuck cut the cord around Marian's wrists while three of the younger outlaws exchanged clothes with the soldiers and took their positions along the back wall of the manor.

Marian reviewed the plan. "Tuck, wait out of sight with John and Much while I climb the tree with Will. We're the only ones who can fit into the smaller window."

John asked, "Are you sure you'll be able to open the shutter on that window? From here, it looks locked."

With a mischievous twinkle in her eye, Marian explained, "It only *looks* secure. I disabled the lock years ago, and I've passed through that window many times. However, the lower window's shutter has a strong lock, and I'll open it for you, Much, and Tuck."

She addressed the remaining two outlaws. "As soon as we're inside, go to Gisborne and Constance, and tell them to proceed to the front door of the manor. Then return here and keep watch over these soldiers to ensure that they do not break free of their bindings before we are ready to leave with Odella and Allan."

⇜

Marian and her men were in the kitchen of Lenton Manor. The servants had been overjoyed to see her, and they had nearly exposed her with their welcoming cries. After Marian had quietly explained her purpose, they had obediently allowed themselves to be locked in the pantry. John and Much blocked the door that led to the garden with the heavy top of a trestle table. No soldiers would be able to come to Gervase's aid by entering the manor through the kitchen.

From the shadows of the short corridor that connected the kitchen to the great hall, she observed Gervase unnoticed. Similar to Locksley Manor, the great hall of Lenton was little more than a large, open space with a dining area on one side and a seating area with a hearth at the other.

Gagged and bound at their wrists and ankles, Allan and Odella sat sullenly on the floor. Aside from his prisoners and the servants who were now secured in the pantry, Gervase was alone. He had put all his men on watch outside the manor.

A vigorous pounding on the door heralded Gisborne's arrival. Marian's stomach lurched; he would serve as a useful distraction, as long as he didn't betray her. Bile rose in her throat, and she nervously swallowed.

She could clearly hear the loathsome Gisborne and the vile Gervase as they greeted each other.

"What are you doing here, Gisborne? And you've brought your lady wife. I'm always pleased to see you, Lady Constance."

Gisborne bowed, and Constance curtsied, offering Gervase the utmost courtesy.

"Thank you, Sir Gervase," Constance replied sweetly with a smile.

"I received word that one of my servants is here. I've come to request her release; she's a simple girl," Guy politely explained, "and I'm certain she's done nothing wrong."

"Are you referring to that girl over there?" Gervase gestured towards his captives.

Marian observed as Constance walked towards Odella, only to have Guy hold her back by grasping her arm. She was incensed by the sight of Gisborne touching Constance with the same hand that had killed Robin... Again, she forced herself to come back to the present.

"Yes, Sir Gervase, I respectfully request her return," answered Gisborne with somewhat exaggerated deference.

"She was in the company of a known outlaw. That makes her an outlaw, too. I plan to take her to Nottingham tomorrow. The sheriff can decide."

Guy suggested, "Sir Gervase, she's a young girl, and this notorious outlaw likely deceived her. I don't think we need to bother the sheriff—"

Gervase laughed in his face. "You're talking about her as if she were a child. She's a grown woman, and according to your friend, Payen, she's a fine ride. I'm thinking she will warm my bed tonight."

A terrified Odella whimpered as tears rolled down her cheeks while Allan frantically tugged at his bindings in a futile attempt to loosen them.

Between gritted teeth, Guy declared, "Payen is no friend of mine." He untied a small pouch at his belt and dropped it on the table. "Take this for your trouble and give the girl to me."

Gervase took the pouch and weighed it in his hand. "Hmmm. Now that I think about it, I seem to remember that Payen has expressed an interest in the girl as well. Perhaps, I will sell her to him. As you said, why bother the sheriff? He will be happy enough to hang this outlaw."

"This girl belongs to the Locksley estate. You've no right to sell her to anyone," Guy asserted.

Gervase grinned. "This is very interesting. Why do you want her so badly? I doubt that you'd be ransoming a mistress in front of your wife."

Constance finally entered the conversation. "I'm a healer, and I've been training this girl in the healing arts. She's very talented, and that's why we beseech you to have mercy and release her to us. We will take responsibility for her and ensure that she does not consort with any other outlaws in the future."

Rubbing his chin thoughtfully, Gervase admitted, "Normally, I would want to please a fine lady such as yourself, Lady Constance, but I've already received an offer from Payen." Dismissively dropping Guy's bag of coins onto the table, he announced, "This isn't enough."

Marian noticed Gisborne's jaw twitch as if he were grinding his teeth.

"I will double what Payen is offering you," Gisborne proposed. "Release her now, and I will return tomorrow with more silver."

Marian gave the signal, and Tuck crept into the great hall from the kitchen. Gervase's back was to him, and with the two men engrossed in their haggling over the girl, only Constance noticed Tuck's silent approach.

Again, Marian's stomach roiled. This was the moment when Gisborne would likely betray them.

Constance clutched Gisborne's forearm and pretended to swoon, distracting both men. Guy caught her before she crumpled to the floor while Gervase watched in surprise. In that same moment, Tuck grabbed Gervase from behind, trapping the man's neck in the crook of one arm and covering his mouth with his other hand.

Marian and Will burst into the room with their bows aimed at Gisborne and Gervase. Guy meekly raised his hands in surrender, and Marian felt as though she could breathe again.

John and Much gagged and bound Gervase and Gisborne, and then they forced them to sit on the floor, back-to-back, as a heavy rope was wrapped around them, securing them together. Gervase was red-faced, and his muffled cries were too loud for Marian's comfort. Heeding Gisborne's warning, she was careful to ensure that the prince's envoy was unhurt. Constance was loosely tied to a chair, and Marian winked at her, pleased to see a small smile on her friend's face behind her gag.

As soon as they freed Allan and Odella from their bindings, the girl rushed to Marian and threw her arms around her, weeping with relief.

Allan also approached Marian and confessed, "This was all my fault, and I'm sorry."

Marian gently unwound Odella's tight hug and delivered her into Allan's custody as she advised, "We can talk later; we must leave at once."

Sauntering to the table and retrieving Gisborne's bag of coins, Marian gleefully observed Guy's eyes widen in surprise and then narrow in annoyance. His muffled protests joined Gervase's, and Marian snickered at him.

She then led everyone to the rear window where they exited with the help of the disguised outlaws who were standing guard.

With a brief backwards glance at her beloved childhood home, Marian led her band of outlaws into the sheltering embrace of Sherwood Forest.

CHAPTER 15
THE LION IS SNARED

18 December 1192, City of Vienna

The midday sun was valiantly striving to warm the crisp, wintry air, but the overcast skies were hindering its efforts.

Robin and William de l'Etang were standing within the shelter of a tree-lined ridge overlooking the city of Vienna. It was nothing like London or Paris, although it was also situated on a great river. The city lacked a proper wall, and it was arranged around a confusing mosaic of islands and channels connected to the River Danube. The buildings—or perhaps they were better described as hovels—were mostly low wooden structures with smoking chimneys. In the distance, the duke's castle stood watch over the city, and it was the only stone edifice in view.

Their original goal had been to avoid Vienna at all costs. Duke Leopold's hatred of the Lionheart was legendary and had been birthed in Richard's insulting treatment of him following the end of the siege of Acre. Robin recalled the king's order to tear down the duke's standards from the walls of the recaptured city. Several of his advisors, including Robin, had urged him to refrain from offending Leopold, but Richard had been in one of his exhilarated moods, when he was least receptive to the counsel of others.

If Richard had shown Leopold some respect and had allowed the duke some portion of the glory, they would now be headed towards the warmth and comfort of that castle.

Instead, they faced the bitter harvest of Richard's hubris: no food, no shelter, and no respite from the fear of capture. Powerful, wealthy rulers such as Duke Leopold, King Philippe, and Henry VI, the Holy Roman Emperor, controlled vast networks of loyal, enthusiastic vassals ready to do their bidding, especially since it was well-known that a generous bounty would be paid to the man who ensnared the Lionheart.

Philippe's influence had prevented them from landing in the ports of Toulouse and Provence. Fear of retribution from Emperor Henry over Richard's interference in Sicily had made the Italian ports dangerous. And now, they must contend with Leopold's animosity in their journey towards Saxony.

From the time they had left Aquileia, their lives had been a frenetic sprint from one town to another. Again and again, they would settle into rooms at a comfortable inn, only to discover that the villagers had easily seen through Richard's nonexistent acting skills. The people would inform the local officials that the elusive but much sought-after King of England was within their grasp. This would necessitate yet another hectic flight, leaving warm beds and nourishing food for a grueling exodus through freezing temperatures with exhaustion and hunger as their only escorts.

Three days ago, they had left everyone in Friesach, where Baldwin would act as a decoy by pretending to be the king. He was ordered to spend lavishly and attract the attention of the local ruler while Richard, Robin, William, and Ioldan, the boy who was their interpreter, embarked on a frantic race to their destination: the lands of Henry the Lion, the king's brother-by-marriage. They were now only fifty miles from their first safe harbor since their departure from Acre over two months ago.

Ioldan, who was perhaps twelve or thirteen summers, joined

them on the ridge and said, "Herr Wilhelm, King Richard is calling for you."

Robin and William returned to where they had left the king to rest. He was propped up against a sturdy tree, his long legs splayed out in front of him, his hair a matted mess, eyes closed, and his breathing shallow and ragged. Robin had often seen Richard sick during the Crusade. He had been very ill after the end of the siege of Acre, and his health had never completely recovered, as bouts of severe sickness plagued him again and again during their sixteen months in the Holy Land.

However, it occurred to Robin that his liege lord had never looked so gaunt and haggard. Richard was feverish, and Jack was curled up next to him to keep warm.

William grabbed Robin's arm and leaned close to him, whispering, "Robin, what if the king dies while he is in our care?"

Hearing William voice those words made Robin finally confront the possibility that King Richard could die. The consequences of the king's death—to England, to Normandy, to the continental holdings—would be devastating. But the threat to Robin and his family from a wrathful King John and his minion, Argentan, would be lethal.

That's assuming that Robin and William escaped immediate execution for delivering the body of a dead Richard to either Duke Leopold or Henry the Lion.

If Richard died, how could Robin protect Marian and Edmund? What about the people of Huntingdon and Locksley? He was so fatigued from the lack of sleep and food during their desperate dash across central Europe that his mind could only focus on the ruin he would suffer if the king perished, and he could not think of what to do next.

Fighting his exhausted daze, Robin asked, "Ioldan, have you been bathing the king's face with snow to help soothe his fever?"

"Yes, Herr Robin, I've been doing that since we arrived."

Richard mumbled something, and Robin squatted next to him and prompted him to repeat what he had said.

"Mother... the walls... very hot... where am I?" He was delirious.

Robin sighed. "Sire, we're on the outskirts of Vienna."

"Vienna? No, no... need Henry... Lion. Lions... help each other..." Richard chuckled under his breath, but then he grimaced in pain, leaning to the side and heaving unproductively, since none of them had eaten in several days.

Robin stood and gestured for William to follow. Walking a short distance away, he admitted, "I have not wanted to face the truth, but you are right: the king could die if we continue. After three days of riding day and night, without food or sleep, I confess that I'm struggling to think clearly, but perhaps if we found a small inn, we could rest tonight and resume tomorrow."

William agreed, and they returned to the ridge overlooking the city. Focusing on the edges of the sprawling metropolis, he pointed towards the east. "Look, Robin, there's a ferry crossing, and that cluster of buildings will probably include an inn. Tomorrow morning we could use the ferry to traverse the river and continue to Henry's domains."

"I'm not sure Richard will be able to stay seated on his horse," commented Robin. "I will have to sit behind him and hold him upright."

"The only other option is to drape him over the saddle, face down," suggested William.

"If Richard ever found out that he entered Vienna for the first time with his arse in the air, our lives wouldn't be worth warm spit," Robin gravely speculated.

William stared at him curiously, but when Robin's lips twitched as he fought to suppress a grin, the two men burst into laughter, imagining the proud Richard carried on his horse in such a humiliating position.

It felt good to laugh and enjoy a moment of levity as they faced the dangers of entering a city that was second only to Paris in the perils it held for their liege lord.

Robin lingered in the shadows between two market stalls. He was reminded of something Argentan had said during their first meeting, when the sheriff had arrested him for Alfred's murder:

For too long, Huntingdon, you have enjoyed the blessings and warmth of the sun. It is time for you to dwell in the shadows where you will finally see everything that the sun has hidden from you.

Could the riddle refer to hiding in plain sight? Robin was standing in the shadows, but he was not fully concealed from view. He had pulled his hood forward to hide his face, but anyone in the nearby market could still see him standing there. Several people had glanced in his direction, but they had not really looked at Robin. Their gazes had slid past him, focusing instead on the next merchant's stall.

His mind drifted, and he rubbed his face to rouse himself as he refocused on his purpose. He was in the small market of Erdberg, the village near the ferry they had spotted from the ridge. Richard and William were safely ensconced in a clean, warm room at an inn, while Robin had accompanied Ioldan to the market for food.

He planned to stay a short distance from the boy, so that no one would know they were together. If the boy found himself in a dangerous situation, Robin could rescue him. Or, if the boy betrayed the king, Robin could take the necessary actions to protect Richard. He prayed the boy would remain true; he had never killed a child, and he wasn't sure he could do it.

The boy, with his strange accent and foreign coins, was attracting a lot of notice from the locals. Unfortunately, exotic Syrian coins were the only currency they had left because Richard had insisted that Baldwin keep the remaining bags of Venetian ducats to bolster the fiction that Baldwin was the king.

From his observations, Robin realized that the boy was enjoying his notoriety—people were crowded around him, and he was the center of attention. This was dangerous, and Robin would have to rebuke him for his conceit.

If only he could comprehend more of this strange language! Some German words were similar to the Old Saxon dialect, but identifying a few words would not help him understand whether the boy was following the script that Robin had rehearsed with him. Ioldan was to profess to be the servant of a rich merchant named Hugo who was coming to the city in three days.

Still exhausted and hungry, Robin's mind wasn't as sharp as usual, and he had to admit that he wouldn't know for certain if the boy had kept his promises until it was too late.

Soon, Ioldan was carrying several containers of food and walking back towards the inn.

Robin loitered in the market, watching to see whether anyone would follow the boy. Although a few men took note of the direction in which he was headed, no one made a move to pursue Ioldan, so Robin left the market and returned to the inn.

He was now focused on two things: food and sleep. Tomorrow he would be more coherent.

21 December 1192, City of Vienna

Robin tossed a small piece of cheese over Jack's head, and the dog energetically leapt up, twisting midair to catch it in his mouth. Richard roared with laughter while Robin and Ioldan chuckled at both the dog's antics and the king's enthusiastic response.

It was the morning of their third day in Erdberg, and the king was much improved. He had more color in his cheeks, and he was holding down food. More importantly, he had regained both his wits and his good humor.

Jack had proven to be an excellent diversion for the king, a man who loathed inaction and empty hours. Robin felt the same way; it was something the two men had in common. To pass the time, they had taught Jack tricks, reminisced about the past, and composed songs. Richard was a talented troubadour, and Robin enjoyed singing the king's songs with him as they bided their time, waiting for William's return.

After their first night in Erdberg, William and Robin had realized that the king would be unable to travel for several days. With that in mind, William had left for the lands of Henry the Lion, intending to bring a few of Henry's men-at-arms back to escort Richard to safety. They would still have to maintain secrecy, as the arrival of Henry's soldiers in Vienna could be interpreted as an aggression against Leopold, but at least they would have fresh horses and be in the company of trustworthy men who knew the area and spoke the language.

Robin yawned and rubbed his eyes. He was not getting enough sleep as he spent each night standing guard over the king. He would nap during the day while Ioldan stood guard, but he had little faith that the boy understood the gravity of their situation. Robin still shadowed him during his trips to the market each day, and to his consternation, the boy's fame had not diminished. Too many people were watching him and asking him questions. Robin did not need a translator to interpret the skepticism on their faces.

"As your liege lord, I'm ordering you to rest, Robin," the king proclaimed. "Now that I'm feeling better, it will do us no good if you become ill. We must be sharp-witted and ready to flee as soon as William returns."

Robin knew that Richard was right. Without further comment, he stretched out on the chamber's smaller bed, and Jack joined him, snuggling close to his side as Robin relaxed and slipped into a dreamless sleep.

⁊

"Robin, wake up," summoned Richard, who was jostling Robin's shoulder to rouse him.

"Sire?" Robin slowly emerged from the hazy, shadowy land of a deep and restful sleep. He sat up and swung his legs over the side of the bed, stretching and willing himself to full consciousness. "Do you need something?"

Richard paced within the confines of the small chamber. "I'm concerned that Ioldan has been gone too long. I sent him to the market, and he's not returned."

This revelation cleared Robin's mind of any remaining cobwebs. "Sire, how long ago did he leave?"

"It was soon after you went to sleep. It's now midday, and I don't believe he's ever needed this much time when you took him to the market. I want you to go find him," commanded Richard.

Robin stood and reached for his hooded cloak. "Will you be all right while I'm gone? Lock the door behind me and don't open it for anyone except me or William. It's likely that he will return today."

"I'm not a child, Robin," the king chided. "I'm capable of managing myself for a time while you're gone."

"Forgive me, sire, I know this. I will return shortly."

"Damn!" muttered the king.

Robin gazed at him expectantly, waiting for him to elaborate.

"It's a bitterly cold day, and I was going to insist that you take my gloves, but I just remembered that I already lent them to Ioldan."

Robin was reaching for the door's latch when the significance of Richard's words dawned on him. He stared at his king and prayed that he had misunderstood. "Sire, are you saying that Ioldan was wearing your gloves? The ones embroidered with gold thread and the royal insignia?"

"Well, it's a frigid day, and the boy seemed cold."

Robin's heart dropped. With all the attention that Ioldan attracted each day, there was no way that the gloves had gone unnoticed. "Sire, we need to pack our things and find a different inn." Robin grabbed the nearest saddlebag and stuffed his belongings into it.

"I think you're overreacting, Robin. No one will notice a servant's gloves."

"If a servant is wearing gloves fit for a king, I'm absolutely certain it will be noticed."

The king fell into thoughtfulness. "You might be right, Robin. Go to the market and find Ioldan. I will gather my things, and as soon as you return, we will move to a different inn."

Robin slung his saddlebag over his shoulder and gathered the harness he used to carry Jack. With a final backward glance at Richard, he left the inn with Jack at his heels and went to the market.

It was a perfectly ordinary day at the small market. The usual groups of people were there, buying and selling the goods that made life in a city possible.

But Ioldan was not there.

Robin had no idea where the boy could have gone. He had resolved to return to Richard when Jack let out a low whine and started sniffing the ground. To Robin's surprise, Jack trotted off, away from the market.

He almost summoned the dog, but instead, he trailed after him.

At the edge of Erdberg, behind a stack of firewood, Robin found Ioldan's body in a snowbank turned pink with blood. He had been beaten, and a few of his fingers were missing, an indication of torture. Searching his body, Robin did not find any of the coins the boy would have carried to the market, and Richard's gloves were nowhere to be found.

Had the boy been robbed by someone who wanted his money and expensive gloves? Or had he been tortured by someone who suspected that his master was King Richard?

There was no time to waste, and he ran back to the inn.

❧

Robin stood behind the soldiers surrounding the inn. Several hours had passed, and on this day, the winter solstice, the afternoon was rapidly fading into twilight. Unable to understand what anyone was saying, he was forced to wait and watch along with the throng of villagers that had gathered.

The soldiers were milling around, and he assumed that Richard was trapped in the inn. Robin became increasingly agitated. He had failed to protect his liege lord, and visions of doom crowded his mind.

Finally, Duke Leopold arrived to take Richard into custody, and the king emerged from the inn. He had cleaned himself up, and he proudly strode down the street, his golden-red hair illuminated by the weak sunlight, and his bearing every inch the dignified monarch.

When he was face to face with Leopold, Richard theatrically handed his sword to the Duke of Austria and surrendered.

"Robin!" a loud whisper behind him beckoned. It was William.

Robin joined him, and they discreetly abandoned the dramatic scene as Duke Leopold snared the Lionheart.

"I've just returned with six of Henry's men," he explained. "What happened?"

Robin described the morning's events, and they decided that William, Robin, and two of Henry's men would follow Richard to discover the location of his imprisonment. They would then go to Henry's lands before traveling to London to inform Queen Eleanor that her son had been captured by one of his many enemies.

25 December 1192, Locksley Manor

Marian paused and took a steadying breath before walking through the front door of Locksley Manor for the first time in over four years. Since her return from Acre, she had only entered through the kitchen door as she haunted Gisborne during the night as Robin's ghost, but to cross the threshold of Robin's childhood home gave her an immense sense of triumph.

The great hall was filled with so many people that most of them would have to stand as they enjoyed the feast. When they saw her, everyone dropped to one knee, recognizing her as the Lady of Locksley and Countess of Huntingdon.

"Thank you for your welcome," she announced with a broad smile and joy shining in her eyes. "Today, we have so much to celebrate! It's the Feast of the Nativity, when we commemorate the birth of our heavenly King. Lord Embelton is in London, where our earthly king, Richard the Lionheart, is due to arrive today. But we also have a third reason to celebrate." Marian gestured to the door as the bride and groom entered, their faces flushed with excitement.

Marian continued, "We rejoice in the union of two people who are very dear to all of us: Allan-a-dale and Odella."

Everyone applauded the newlyweds, and Allan embraced his new wife and gave her a quick kiss on the cheek. This prompted a chorus of cheers and whistles from their audience, and Odella blushed.

As soon as the feast was underway, Marian stood back and watched the people of Locksley as they enjoyed the festivities. If only Edmund and Constance could have been there as well.

Constance had planned the entire event, knowing that she could not join Marian. Instead, she was in Nottingham with Gisborne, helping him host the Feast of the Nativity at the castle. Once again, Argentan had left Guy in charge as acting sheriff. It was a surprisingly frequent occurrence, as the sheriff and Payen disappeared for days, or even weeks, at a time.

With Argentan away and Gervase in Cardiff with Prince John, Nottinghamshire was calm and peaceful.

Her gaze drifted to Allan and Odella. Their simple wedding, with Leofric standing in for Osmund and Marian as a witness, had been intensely emotional for her, and she had been embarrassed by her tears.

She wondered if weddings would always affect her so. Perhaps it was regret over the fact that both of her weddings to Robin had been unconventional. First, there had been their clandestine wedding on the night of her escape from Nottingham castle. Neither of them had known that canon law decreed that a formal declaration of an intent to marry, followed by consummation, constituted a valid marriage. She remembered Edmund explaining it to her, following her mortified confession to him that she had been intimate with Robin.

She didn't like to think about their second wedding, as Robin lay dying in the dirt of a distant land. It hadn't been necessary, since they were already married, but there was no time to explain it to Robin, so she had agreed to the hasty exchange of vows.

Previously, Marian had believed that Robin's death was the moment when everything in her life had changed forever, but a new thought occurred to her. The day of her father's death had also been transformative. She reminisced about the first part of that fateful day: talking to Robin about his parents and her father and then spending time in their favorite meadow as he joked and made her laugh until her side hurt. By the end of the day, she was an orphan, and Robin was a prisoner.

On that tragic day, they had been forced onto a bewildering path that would inexorably change the course of their lives, and that innocent and carefree girl of her memories was now a stranger.

Elvina brought her a small plate of food, and she politely declined. She was worried that there wouldn't be enough for the villagers and servants.

Marian was ashamed to admit that, before her return from the Holy Land, she had never given much thought to the servants and peasants around her. She had never considered what their lives were like or how they lived day to day. She had been focused solely on her own needs and wants, and of course, her future with Robin. Now, as Countess of Huntingdon and Lady of Locksley and Lenton, she would be responsible for many hundreds of men, women, and children.

That so many people would soon be relying on her good judgment filled her with an odd mixture of trepidation and anticipation. Edmund had offered to teach her the basics of governing her estates, and she had gladly accepted his help. A few years ago, she wouldn't have wanted such obligations. She would have been focused on having children and managing her household.

But now everything had changed. She had achieved things she had never imagined doing, not even in her wildest flights of fancy. She had triumphed over incredible odds, and she was confident that she would succeed as Countess of Huntingdon. Furthermore, she would be in a position to provide a better life for her people.

She could hardly wait. King Richard would quickly set everything to rights, and this spring would be the beginning of her new life. The king would also help her protect Robin's legacy.

Oh, Robin! Her brave hero, her handsome husband—smart, witty, kind, and generous—no man could ever replace him in her heart, and she resolved to remain a widow. She was proud to be Countess of Huntingdon, but no title would ever mean as much to her as the one she had now: Robin Hood's widow.

At that moment, an unexpected insight lit her mind with such force that she swayed on her feet. She was so overcome that she left the great hall and exited the manor through the kitchen door. Fortunately, everyone was so happy and occupied with the feast that no one noticed her departure.

She strolled towards a small clearing separating the manor from the great forest surrounding Locksley. The forest Robin had loved; the place where he had felt at peace. She gazed towards heaven, knowing Robin was somewhere beyond the dark sky with its bright points of light. Her breath created wispy clouds that rose before disappearing into the cold night air.

"I'm sorry, Robin," she whispered. She had realized that, for the first time since his death, she had been eagerly anticipating the future, even though it would be a future without Robin. And it was also the first time she had felt at peace knowing she had a future, even though he did not.

To understand why she felt that way, she contemplated the life she had led before the murders of her father and Robin.

When Robin returned from Poitou and proposed to her, he had become the center of her existence. Her world had consisted of Robin and her father. Everything and everyone else in her life were just embellishments, like the embroidery adorning her favorite bliaut.

However, that was no longer true. Although Robin's legacy would always be a part of her life, she was now, by necessity, a person separate from Robin.

The heartache of losing Robin had forever scarred her soul, and her sorrow would never completely disappear. But her life was now defined by more than her grief, and she could finally imagine a life without Robin at her side.

She realized that Constance had been right: because Robin had truly loved her, he would want her to live a long, full life. He would want her to experience joy and happiness. And by living her life fully, she would honor Robin's life and legacy.

This would be her purpose going forward, not as Robin Hood's widow, but as Marian Fitzooth, née Fitzwalter, Countess of Huntingdon and Lady of Locksley and Lenton.

CHAPTER 16
ROYAL INTRIGUE

10 January 1193, Sherwood Forest, The Meadow

Marian had become very adept at moving through the forest, and on this bright, wintry day, she was with Tuck and Allan as they jogged towards the meadow.

Earlier, a servant from Locksley had arrived at the caves with news that Constance had requested an urgent meeting. Marian was euphoric, certain that Constance was delivering good news from London, and she was distracted by fantasies of Argentan and Gisborne's arrest by agents of King Richard. Maybe Argentan had been gone so long because he feared the king's return. But why had he left Gisborne in Nottingham? These thoughts circled her mind as she spotted Constance standing next to the great oak.

Swiftly crossing the expanse of the meadow, she was slightly out of breath when she greeted her friend with a wide smile.

Her smile collapsed into a frown of dismay when she saw Constance's red-rimmed eyes and tear-stained cheeks. Marian felt as though she had been punched in the gut as she whispered, "What happened? Is it Lionel? Your father?"

A sob escaped Constance, and she wiped her face with her sleeve, revealing, "Oh, Marian! I received a message from Father this morning. King Richard never arrived. Father is still in London, hoping the king has only been delayed, but he wrote that the city is abounding in rumors. People are saying that Richard drowned in a shipwreck, or that pirates killed him, or that King Philippe captured him. No one knows what has happened, but it's almost certain that *something* has happened. He should have been back by now."

For a moment, Marian's mind struggled to comprehend the gravity of Constance's words. When Allan and Tuck each grabbed of one of her elbows, she realized they were fearful she might faint. With no small amount of irritation, she shrugged off their grasp.

Tuck requested, "Do you have the letter? Would you allow me to read it?"

Constance pulled the crumpled message from a pouch tied to her belt and wordlessly gave it him.

Allan asked, "Is there any news of your brother? What about the sheriff? He's been gone since before Christmas."

Marian still could not speak, so she was grateful that Allan had voiced the questions uppermost in her mind.

"We haven't heard any news about Lionel. I'm so afraid for him, and I have no idea what this might mean for his captivity. I was at Nottingham Castle with Guy yesterday when the sheriff finally returned from his mysterious trip. He was gone for a month! They went to the tower room, and I'm unable to listen to their conversations there—it's not like when they meet at Locksley." She sniffled and dabbed at her face again.

Tuck offered Marian the letter, and blinking back her own tears of despair, she skimmed it. There was nothing beyond what Constance had already disclosed.

Recovering her voice, she commented, "Edmund does not say when he will return."

"I believe he'll return as soon as he learns the truth of what has happened to the king."

Tuck, who had lived most of his life in Outremer, asked, "Are you certain John will inherit the throne if Richard is dead? I heard that the king has a nephew who is considered in the line of succession because he is the son of a brother older than John."

Marian didn't know; such royal intrigue meant little to her. Whenever her father and Robin had engaged in political debate, she had just left the room for fear that she would doze off if she had to listen to such talk.

In contrast, Edmund had often discussed politics with both of his children, and Constance had always paid close attention to these conversations. "My father says Richard's nephew, Arthur of Brittany, should inherit," she answered, "but that might be wishful thinking since he dislikes John. Regardless, Arthur is only a boy, and John is well established here in England."

Tuck nodded perceptively. "Lady Marian, please allow me to escort you to London," he implored. "You need to be under the protection of the dowager queen."

Marian looked at him skeptically. "Would the queen protect me from her own son? If Richard is dead, then we all know that John will be crowned king. I've never met the queen, so why would she help me against the wishes of a King John?"

"Maybe because you're the Countess of Huntingdon?" speculated Allan.

Constance confidently asserted, "King John will force Marian to marry one of his favorites in order to transfer the wealth of the Earldom of Huntingdon to a trusted supporter. Despite her outlaw activities and the bounty on her head, I don't think he would risk the public outcry of executing a woman and the widow of the people's hero."

"Never will I consent to such a marriage!" cried Marian as her stomach churned with panic.

Constance grasped Marian's hands and stared meaningfully into her eyes. "You need to return to Embelton. You will be safe there, and it's the only place where you will have the leverage and the power to establish your rights. You know this is true."

Tuck frowned. "What are you talking about, Lady Constance?"

Marian continued to gaze into Constance's eyes as she answered Tuck. "I understand her meaning, and that should be enough for you."

Stepping away from Constance, Marian announced, "I will wait until we hear from Edmund. If we learn that John is to be crowned king, I will go to Embelton at once. Until then, I must put my affairs in order here." She abruptly pointed at Allan. "Do not break the solemn vow you made to me."

Constance's brow rose in surprise. "He knows?"

Tuck, his voice taking on an uncharacteristically hard edge, demanded, "I am tasked with protecting you. I need to know about this."

Marian was unyielding. "If there comes a time when you need to know, I will tell you. Until then, we need to return to camp and tell the others what has happened."

With a final hug, Marian instructed Constance. "Return to Locksley and send word as soon as you hear anything from your father."

⁂

Marian was sitting at the mouth of one of the caves near Locksley, staring morosely into the flames of a campfire.

No wonder Robin had insisted that she go to Embelton all those years ago. Winters in the forest were miserable, and she acknowledged that she had been counting on the king to return and rescue her from spending the rest of the winter sleeping in a damp, dirty cave. She knew her thoughts were little more than childish whining, but she decided that she didn't care.

Like a fool, she had been making grand plans for her life—plans that required the return of King Richard. Relying on a man for anything guaranteed disappointment, she bitterly groused to herself.

Except for Robin, of course. He wouldn't have disappointed her.

Except that he *had* let her down when he didn't return to her after he was cleared of the charge that he murdered her father.

She tossed more kindling into the fire and drew her cloak tight around her shoulders.

What kind of wife would still resent her husband when he was gone and couldn't defend himself? She remembered how Robin had begged for forgiveness when he was dying, and she had forgiven him. So why was she still angry?

Because she was a terrible person.

Maybe she didn't deserve happiness.

Maybe it had been wrong to fantasize about the happy future she had anticipated following Richard's return.

The tears that blurred her vision only made her more frustrated and resentful. She had to be strong, and she couldn't lose hope.

She would return to Embelton, but first, she would finally avenge Robin's death. She owed that to him.

Argentan was beyond her reach, as he rarely left the castle without a heavy guard. Besides, she couldn't risk the wrath of Prince John, especially since it was likely that he would soon be crowned king.

But Gisborne? Apparently, Argentan could barely tolerate him, so she was certain that Gisborne meant nothing to Prince John.

She decided that the time of Gisborne's reckoning had arrived.

11 January 1193, Tower of London

Edmund's outward demeanor was calm, but he hadn't been this nervous in many years. The dowager queen, Eleanor, had summoned him for an audience, and he couldn't imagine why she would want to speak to him.

As a loyal vassal of King Henry, he had met Eleanor occasionally, and he had found her to be the most intimidating woman of his acquaintance. The last time he had seen her had been the Christmas feast of 1172, just before she led her older sons in a rebellion against

Henry. When the attempted coup failed, she had been captured and imprisoned, and after sixteen years of confinement, Henry's death had finally set her free. Since then, she had ruled the Duchy of Aquitaine and played an important role in managing Richard's lands in his absence.

An attendant escorted Edmund into a brightly illuminated royal chamber and left him there alone. With nothing to do but wait upon the queen's pleasure, he examined the impressive tapestries that adorned two of the walls. There were scenes from the life of Christ, and one depicted the Capture of Jerusalem during the First Crusade. In the corner, an ornate throne presided over the chamber on a raised dais.

A second door was next to the throne, and when the latch rattled, and the door started to swing open, Edmund dropped to one knee and remained there, his heart beating so hard in his chest that he silently reproached himself for feeling like a page attending his master at court for the first time. He focused on the floor in front of him.

The shuffle of a light step and the rustling of fabric announced Eleanor's arrival as she entered the room and moved to sit on the throne. "Arise, and greet me, Edmund de Toury, Baron of Embelton." Even after all these years, her voice was recognizable, although it now held the quaver of old age.

He rose, and when his knees complained, he acknowledged that she was not the only one to have aged in the last twenty years. Meeting her steadfast gaze, he could see that the fire in her blue eyes had not dimmed, although her beauty had faded, and wrinkles marred her once flawless skin. Her hair was covered by a wimple, and her elegant red bliaut was embroidered with gold thread. She looked perfectly at ease sitting on the grand throne.

Attending the queen was a monk who was wearing a cloak with an oversize hood that shadowed his face.

Edmund cleared his throat and declared, "Your grace, I am honored to greet you, and I'm at your service."

"Where do your loyalties lie, Embelton?"

Evidently, there would be no social pleasantries.

Edmund paled, revealing the extent of his guilty conscience. He had spent the past eight months funding John's ambitions in a desperate bid to keep Lionel's kidnappers happy. He vehemently affirmed, "King Richard is my liege lord, and I stand ready to support him whole heartedly."

"A trustworthy man described you as honorable. He was mistaken; I know you're lying to me," asserted Eleanor in a voice like steel sheathed in velvet.

"Your grace, I—"

"Although I have been very busy managing Richard's fiefdoms while he is on Crusade, your treachery has not gone unnoticed—"

"It's not as it seems—"

"You will refrain from speaking unless I give you permission," she coldly informed him. "As I was saying before your rude interruption: Considering the time that you've spent in Nottinghamshire, which is under John's dominion, the unusual flow of funds from your wealthy barony for unknown purposes, and your attendance at several meetings of conspirators attached to John—all these facts point to only one conclusion: you have abandoned your true liege lord for the empty promises of my youngest son. Whatever he has offered you, he does not have the power to grant it."

Edmund's mouth was dry, and his heart thrummed painfully in his chest. He was in an impossible situation. Dropping onto both of his knees, he begged, "Your grace, I'm not denying your allegations; you evidently have impressive sources of information. But I beg you to allow me to explain."

"I'm not interested in hearing your excuses. I've already determined that you are a disloyal liar."

His heart collapsing in despair, Edmund had no choice but to risk the queen's displeasure by offering his explanation, regardless of whether she wanted to hear it.

"They have my son."

Silence reigned in the chamber for an uncomfortable length of time.

"Explain," the queen demanded, her tone as sharp as a new blade.

"My only son and heir, Lionel, was kidnapped last May. His life is forfeit if I do not make payments to these men who serve Prince John." He hastily added, "Forgive me, your grace, it's not my intention to speak ill of your son."

Eleanor scrutinized him, and he felt like a small child who had been caught stealing biscuits.

After another extended silence, she alleged, "You claim to fear for your son's life, yet you did not request my help. If your allegiance to Richard is true, why not come to me? I could have demanded the return your son. Instead, you have recklessly given John the resources that might allow him to steal the throne."

Edmund had never considered seeking Eleanor's assistance. He explained, "Your grace, I am humbled to know that you would have helped me. However, because I actively supported King Henry in the... dispute between the two of you that led to your long confinement, I did not expect your magnanimity in this matter."

"Dispute? Well, I guess that's one way to describe it." An amused Eleanor chuckled before resuming. "I have a long memory, and I never forget a betrayal. Nevertheless, your support of Richard would have outweighed any lingering resentment over your previous choices. And now, your funding of John has endangered Richard."

"I understand, your grace. Perhaps my knowledge of the situation in Nottinghamshire would be helpful to your cause. I have been monitoring the actions of the man who kidnapped my son, Baron de Argentan, the Sheriff of Nottingham."

"Argentan?" She frowned. "He must be ancient by now. I remember spending Christmas at the castle in Argentan over twenty years ago, and the baron was elderly then. What is he doing in Nottingham?"

"I believe the man you remember has long since passed from this world. Baron de Argentan and I are the same age. He is a widower who is baron by right of wife."

Her brow creased in thought, she commanded, "Tell me what you have learned. Convince me that the information you've gathered in Nottinghamshire is more valuable than the monies you've provided to John."

Edmund described the scraps of official documents from the French court which were in his possession, and how they proved that the Sheriff of Nottingham was in communication with the King of France. He mentioned the flow of silver that periodically arrived from Dover, and he speculated that it originated from a wealthy continental source such as the French court. Argentan's frequent and mysterious disappearances, sometimes for a fortnight or longer, were unusual for a sheriff, and Edmund commented that he had grown suspicious that Argentan might be traveling to a distant location, such as Paris, on these occasions.

He revealed that his daughter, Constance, had overheard the sheriff and his captain discussing King Philippe in a way that corroborated his belief that they served the French king.

Finally, he concluded by relating what Marian had told him about the events in Acre: Argentan had journeyed to the Holy Land, where he had attempted regicide against Richard and had evaded capture. Edmund surmised that such an expensive and audacious undertaking would have required funding and support that only King Philippe could have supplied.

He finished with, "I don't know whether this information is helpful. Much of it I gathered as I searched for my son, hoping to rescue him." Edmund realized that the queen was leaning forward, closely attending to his every word.

"I am most interested in the connections you have discovered between Sheriff de Argentan and the French court." She gestured towards the monk and ordered, "Show him the letter."

The man passed through the nearby door and promptly returned with a thick piece of parchment, which he handed to Edmund.

Carefully studying it, Edmund was flabbergasted as he realized its significance:

Henry, by the grace of God, Emperor of the Romans and ever august, to his beloved and special friend Philippe, the illustrious King of the Franks, health and sincere love and affection.

Inasmuch as our imperial highness does not doubt that your royal mightiness will be delighted, we have thought it proper to inform your nobleness that while the enemy of our empire and the disturber of your kingdom, Richard, King of England, was crossing the sea for the purpose of returning to his dominions, it so happened that the winds brought him to a place which lies between Aquileia and Venice, where, by the sanction of God, the king, having suffered shipwreck, escaped, together with a few others.

A faithful subject of ours, Count Meinhard of Gorz, hearing that he was in his territory, and calling to mind the treason and treachery and accumulated mischief he had been guilty of in the Holy Land, pursued him with the intention of making him prisoner. However, the king escaped.

Shortly after, the king proceeded to Friesach, where six of his knights were captured.

The king, with only three attendants, hastened on by night in the direction of Austria.

The roads, however, being watched, and guards being set on every side, our dearly beloved cousin Leopold, Duke of Austria, captured the king so often mentioned in a humble house in a village in the vicinity of Vienna.

Inasmuch as he is now in our power, and has always done his utmost for your annoyance and disturbance, we have thought it proper to notify your nobleness, knowing that this is well pleasing to your kindly affection for us, and will afford most abundant joy to your own feelings.

Given at Creutz, on the fifth day before the calends of January.

"God in heaven!" exclaimed Edmund. "Are you certain this is authentic? How were you able to get a copy of a letter between Emperor Henry and King Philippe?" He then realized the impertinence of his outburst and implored, "Forgive me, your grace, I was overcome by astonishment, as never in my life have I seen such a letter."

"I'm feeling generous, so I will answer you. During my imprisonment, I found it necessary to cultivate useful diversions. Accordingly, I formed a network of people who keep me apprised of this type of intelligence. In this particular instance, Emperor Henry sent several copies of this letter to Philippe to ensure that at least one arrived safely. My good friend, the Archbishop of Rouen, secured this copy for me."

She continued, "I have another source of information, a trusted man who traveled with Richard. He told me that all the ports under Philippe's influence were overrun by mercenaries ready to take my son prisoner. Likewise, the ports of Italy were also filled with peril for Richard. That is why he ended up in Austria."

"Your grace, I am aghast that these men would capture a returning Crusader and keep him prisoner. Have they forsaken the Truce of God?" Edmund shook his head in disbelief. "I pray for Richard's safe return. He is the rightful king, and I'm eager to serve you in any way that you ask. We both have beloved sons who have been unjustly imprisoned. I only beg your consideration that whatever you require of me does not further endanger my son."

"I have one question, Lord Edmund," she declared.

He was startled that she had deigned address him in a less formal manner. "Yes, your grace? I will answer it if I can."

"Measure your words carefully. I am contemplating whether to show you mercy and accept your supplications. Answering honestly is your only option, because I will know if you are lying."

"Of course, your grace. Please, ask me, and I will answer honestly."

"In the past six or seven months, have you received any messages from Richard? Perhaps a dispatch delivered by a knight from Navarre?"

Edmund frowned in confusion; this was not at all what he expected her to ask. "I've never met anyone who claimed to be from Navarre, and I've never received a direct message from King Richard. In the past, I received letters from my nephew, the Earl of Huntingdon, who served under Richard, but he was killed in Acre nearly a year ago."

To Edmund's surprise, his response seemed to please the queen. She almost smiled.

"Well, Lord Edmund, I have good news for you." Her gaze slid to the monk, and she nodded.

The man pulled back his hood.

"It's good to see you again, Uncle Edmund."

The chamber darkened, and Edmund collapsed on the floor.

CHAPTER 17
THE TASTE OF BITTER FRUIT

11 January 1193, Tower of London

It had been three days since Robin had returned to London, bearing both the shocking news of Richard's capture and the outrageous letter the Archbishop of Rouen had surreptitiously obtained for Eleanor. At the same time, Robin had been horrified to learn that Juan had never arrived at court the previous summer. Edmund and Marian had been left believing he was dead.

Eleanor had blamed Edmund, reasoning that Juan had gone to him before coming to London, and that Edmund had killed him because he had thrown his support behind John. Robin knew her theory was ludicrous, but the queen was not easily dissuaded. In the end, she had decided to interrogate Edmund to discern the truth.

It all made sense now, and Robin could breathe easy knowing for certain that Edmund had not betrayed Richard. Instead, he was under duress, with Lionel's life in the balance.

Robin had arranged for Edmund to be carried to the chamber where he and Jack had been staying since his return. Standing at the foot of the bed, he watched as Jack licked Edmund's face, rousing him at last. He shooed the dog away and helped his uncle sit up and swing his legs over the side of the bed.

When Robin sat next to him, Edmund tentatively laid his hand on Robin's chest, as if he were searching for his heartbeat. "Are you real? Am I dreaming? How can you be here?"

Robin smiled warmly. "Uncle Edmund, I'm really here, and you're not dreaming. I didn't die in Acre."

Edmund stared at him.

"I grew a beard in the Holy Land," Robin admitted as he rubbed the short bristles on his chin. "I could shave it off if that would help you recognize me." He laughed at the absurdity of it all.

Edmund reached up and cupped Robin's cheek as tears filled his eyes. "I would recognize that laugh anywhere, and although you are quite thin, and you look exhausted, no beard can hide the truth." Edmund pulled him into a tight embrace, resting his forehead on Robin's shoulder and sobbing unreservedly.

Robin had never seen his uncle cry, not even after his aunt's death, and the intensity of the moment brought tears to his eyes as well. He patiently cradled Edmund in his arms until the older man regained control over his emotions.

The two of them stood and moved to the chairs next to the hearth. They sat quietly together for a while, as Edmund either gazed at him in wonder or wiped his face with his sleeve as tears trickled down his cheeks.

Robin became concerned. "Are you all right?"

Chuckling, Edmund replied, "Someday, when you reach my age, you will understand. There is something about getting older that makes you more susceptible to your emotions. It becomes more difficult to control them, and at a moment like this, it's impossible. But I'm all right." He beamed. "I'm better than all right! After the misery of the past year, I have hope again."

"I'm so sorry you had to suffer under the belief that I was dead. Although King Richard wanted to keep my survival a secret, he wanted you and Marian to know the truth. That's why he sent Juan."

"Is he the knight from Navarre whom the queen mentioned?"

"Yes."

"But why did the king want people to think you were dead?"

"He wanted me to conduct a clandestine investigation of Argentan and his associates. Richard believes that my time living in the forest has taught me valuable skills of stealth. In June, he sent me to Poitiers and Paris, where I covertly gathered information for the king concerning Philippe's involvement in the regicide attempt."

"So, there is a connection between Argentan and King Philippe?"

"There is no question in my mind that Philippe is the mastermind behind the attacks on Richard. I also believe Philippe was plotting to capture or kill the king as he returned from the Crusade, and that Emperor Henry is conspiring with him. You saw the letter."

"You were in Paris? In June? Why couldn't you have come to England?" The surprise in Edmund's voice was strongly colored with shades of displeasure.

"I wanted to come to you, but Richard was impatient to receive the proof of Philippe's treachery. Besides, I assumed that Juan would deliver the news to you, and I never imagined that it would take so long to end the Crusade and come home."

"And now you are finally home! We can head north tomorrow," cried a joyful Edmund.

Robin stood and paced. "Well, not exactly."

Edmund sobered. "Tell me."

"Would you like to join me for an adventure? The queen is sending me on a short mission, and the sooner I satisfy the queen's demands, the sooner I can go to Marian. In the meantime, the queen will keep my return a secret, so that Marian will not hear it from a stranger. Although, I imagine it takes a long time for news to travel from London to Embelton." Robin was embarrassed to realize that he had been nervously rambling.

Edmund was studying him closely. "What is this mission? And why can't someone else do it?"

Robin sat down again. "The queen is distressed about Sir Juan.

She was fond of him, and she knows that Queen Berengaria was quite attached to him as he had been her personal guard since early childhood. I'm the only man in England who knew him, and I can describe him to innkeepers along the way. She wants me to backtrack from London to Dover to discover what happened to him."

Frowning, Edmund declared, "I don't understand the urgency. Of course, the loss of a trusted knight is a serious matter, but it's been so many months I doubt you will be successful."

"That's true, but there's something else: Eleanor believes the method for sending royal communications between the continent and London has been compromised. If there are traitors, she wants them eliminated."

"That makes sense," conceded Edmund. "I would be honored to join you for this mission; perhaps it will help restore me to the queen's good opinion."

Robin agreed, and added, "And then we will make haste to Embelton—even if I have to board another damn boat and sail up the coast—so I can reunite with Marian. I'm outraged that she's been mourning me all these months." Bracing himself as he imagined her overcome by grief, he asked, "Edmund, how is Marian? Is she all right?"

Edmund looked down at his lap, and after an excruciating pause, he confessed, "Marian's not in Embelton. She's in Nottinghamshire."

Robin blanched. "What? I thought Argentan and Gisborne were in Nottingham. Is she a prisoner?"

Edmund raised his hands as if he were surrendering, and his words tumbled out in an anxious rush. "She's living in Sherwood Forest as leader of the outlaws, and she's helping us search for Lionel."

For several heartbeats, Robin grappled with the dissonance between Edmund's revelation and his heart's carefully constructed fantasy of Marian at Embelton, practicing her embroidery and organizing feast day celebrations with Constance.

He grabbed Edmund by the front of his tunic, lifting him from his chair and shaking him with unrestrained fury. "You were supposed to take care of her and protect her!" he yelled. "How could you allow her to risk her life in such a foolish manner?"

"Robin!" exclaimed Edmund. "Release me, now!"

Robin let go of him, and the older man fell back into his chair.

Jack whined and cowered under a small table as Robin commenced pacing across the chamber. He was muttering, "This is ridiculous… impossible…" Glaring at Edmund, he jabbed his finger at him and snarled, "Why are you allowing her to behave so recklessly? Is Lionel so precious to you, that you would sacrifice Marian?"

"I know you're upset, but that's an unfair allegation," Edmund responded heatedly. He then argued, "Are you seriously accusing me of *allowing* her to take risks? Robin, we're talking about Marian! What makes you think that I, or anyone else, can control her? She's always been strong-willed. I will remind you that she set sail for the Holy Land with only one man to guard her—a minstrel, no less, not a knight—and she certainly didn't seek my permission first. She's *your* wife; you should understand her nature better than anyone else."

Robin defensively retorted, "Well, she's always been obedient to me. I don't know what you're talking about."

Edmund scoffed. "I remember a certain letter where you informed her that you were taking the cross, and you instructed her to await your return. Her 'obedient' response was to end your betrothal and return your ring."

Robin collapsed into the nearest chair; he remembered Marian's letter only too well. He absentmindedly reached up and touched the front of his tunic, reaffirming that the ring was still there, suspended on its chain and resting over his heart.

Both men struggled to check their emotions.

Sighing, Edmund lamented, "I just wish the two of you had been able to talk when you were reunited in Acre. Marian told me everything that happened leading up to your, uh, supposed death. And she told me there hadn't been time to tell you the things you needed to know."

A niggling memory tugged at Robin's mind. He was lying on his back, severely wounded, and Marian had wanted to say something. But his memories of that time were so hazy and jumbled that he wasn't sure what was real and what was imagined. Robin prodded, "What was she planning to tell me?"

"It's not my place to say. You will be with her soon, and she can tell you herself. But there is one thing you should know ahead of time. It's something I didn't realize until I arrived home after delivering Marian's letter and ring to you."

Edmund gathered his thoughts and took a steadying breath. "When I returned home without you, Marian was devastated. She honestly believed that sending you the letter and ring would persuade you to travel to Embelton at once to make amends and beg forgiveness. She made a dreadful miscalculation, and I told her so. But by then, it was too late. You had already left England."

Robin somberly considered this. In retrospect, it made more sense than believing that she had lost all affection for him. A thought occurred to him. "Edmund, did she say anything about her stay in Poitiers?"

"No. She told me she was only there for one night."

Robin was relieved to hear that no one had told her about his hasty marriage to Blanche or the shameful behavior that led to it. But then he realized that he would have to tell her himself, and he had no idea how she would react. Feeling a bit like a coward, he hoped she would be so overjoyed to see him that nothing else would matter to her.

"I will seek an immediate audience with the queen and tell her that someone else must investigate Juan's fate. If Marian is in danger, I must go to her now," he declared.

"Between the onset of winter and the expectation that Richard will return any day, the outlaws have suspended their banditry," stated Edmund. "Marian is safe, although I know living in the caves near Locksley is unpleasant for her. Let's proceed with your original plan. I suspect that gaining the queen's favor would be a worthwhile endeavor for the two of us during these uncertain times."

Robin agreed. "With the king in captivity, I don't know how either Eleanor or the Great Council will curb John's ambitions, especially if he joins forces with Philippe. Nevertheless, I'm convinced that pursuing the queen's favor is a wise strategy." He paused and gravely proclaimed, "Everything is at stake: our families, our lands, and our very lives. We must be ready for the possibility of civil war."

12 January 1193, Sherwood Forest, The Meadow

Marian was painstakingly re-carving her and Robin's initials on the great oak. It was something she did periodically to ensure that they were always readable. And it was especially important on this day that the carving look as close as possible to its original appearance, because this was the day she would avenge Robin's death by killing his murderer.

At the sound of an approaching horse, she sheathed her dagger and picked up her bow, nocking an arrow and aiming towards the path that led to the road.

Gisborne emerged from the forest and scanned the unfamiliar meadow with interest as he dismounted. When he saw Marian, he stilled.

"Take off your sword and your dagger, and leave them on the ground," she commanded.

To her consternation, Gisborne examined the ground, and after a short delay, he removed his belt, to which his sheathed weapons were attached, and looped it around the pommel of his saddle.

Nearly groaning in frustration that he wasn't obeying her, she ordered, "Tie your horse up over there, and then walk slowly towards me."

He draped his reins over a shrub and cautiously approached her.

As soon as he drew near, she hissed, "I told you to put your sword and dagger on the ground."

He sighed. "Marian, my sword is my most valuable possession. I refuse to leave it on the damp ground."

Realizing that arguing over this was pointless, she demanded, "Tell me what has happened to King Richard. Is Argentan somehow involved in his disappearance?"

To her surprise, Guy readily answered her. "The Holy Roman Emperor has taken King Richard captive. He's somewhere in either Germany or Austria. That is all the sheriff has told me. However, it's unlikely he will ever return to England."

Her heart sank; he was confirming her worst fears. She would need to leave for Embelton as soon as possible. Tossing her bow on the ground, she grabbed her dagger—or rather his dagger, the one he had used to kill Robin—and pointed it at him as she gestured towards the tree with her other hand.

"Do you see what's carved on that tree?"

He squinted and took a few steps closer. For several moments, he studied the tree.

She impatiently asked, "Well? I'm assuming you can comprehend its meaning well enough."

"Yes, Marian, I see it. I'm guessing you have carved this to commemorate your affection for Robin."

"No!" she cried. "*Robin* carved this, not me. I have kept it looking nice, but Robin carved this after he rescued me from the castle. It proves that we loved each other even then."

He remained composed and said nothing.

"What you don't know is that we were already married when he carved this over four years ago. The night he rescued me, we entered into a clandestine marriage at Saint Mary's Church in Nottingham. So, now you know: I would have never married you. I already had the most perfect husband any woman could want."

He looked at her, and she was mortified to observe something akin to pity in his eyes. She did not want or need his pity! She wanted him to be shattered and to beg for his life!

"Marian, I congratulate you on your marriage to Robin. I don't know what else you want me to say. I'm here because you sent me a note that Constance is in danger, and you needed my help. How can I help you protect Constance?"

"*You* are the danger that Constance is facing."

"Me?"

"You have tricked her into believing that you're a human being instead of the monster that I know you to be. I must remove you from her life."

"What has Constance said about me?"

Marian was aghast at the hopeful note in his voice. "Nothing! She loathes you just as much as I do!"

"Have you finally decided to kill me, Marian?"

He was still too calm, and it infuriated Marian. She poked him with the dagger and demanded, "Turn around, and put your hands together behind your back."

He obeyed, and she retrieved a sturdy rope from the ground at her feet and bound his wrists. This seemed too easy. "Now face me again," she continued, "and kneel."

As soon as he complied, she gazed down at him. With his great height, she hadn't seen him from this angle, with his face tilted up, since her imprisonment in the castle. She remembered him kneeling at her feet, declaring his love, and she also recalled how vulnerable she had felt at that moment. But now she was in control, and she had the power of life and death over this heartless murderer of her Robin.

Extending her dagger until it was pressed against his chest, she hoped he would not notice the slight tremor in her hand. She wanted to hurt him like he had hurt her. She wanted to see him in pain.

Poking him until he winced, she declared, "I know your marriage to Constance is not a real marriage, not like the one I had with Robin. I don't believe you're capable of genuine feelings, so why are you trying to deceive her into believing that you care about her?"

He sighed again, and at first she didn't think he would answer, but then he confessed, "I do care about Constance. I believe that anyone who spent time with her would grow to care for her. She's clever and kind-hearted, and she will make some fortunate man an excellent wife."

"But not you. You're not good enough for Constance."

"I know that, Marian. I realized that a long time ago. But I appreciate the kindness and respect that Constance and Edmund have shown me, regardless of whether I deserve it."

She sneered, "You are probably too stupid to realize this, but Constance and Edmund despise you. They're only pretending to like you, and their kindness is not sincere. It's simply a ruse to extract information from you about Argentan and hopefully, Lionel's location."

His eyes widened before his gaze dropped to the ground at her feet, and his shoulders slumped. For the first time since his arrival, he looked defeated.

She wanted to jump up and cheer; she had finally wounded him, but in that moment, it was strangely unsatisfying.

Still staring at the dirt, he replied, "I'm sure you're right. I considered that possibility, but then I decided I didn't care. To a starving man, even bitter fruit tastes delicious."

His words shocked her, and he seemed human, even vulnerable.

Abruptly, he changed the subject and lifted his gaze to hers. "Marian, I must warn you that the sheriff is planning something. He hasn't revealed any details to me, which makes me think it might concern you. Please, be careful."

"I'm not afraid of the sheriff, and I'm always careful."

She raised her dagger, and when she peered into his pale blue eyes, she thought of Robin. She was horrified that looking at Gisborne reminded her of Robin. Had her memories of Robin's appearance faded? It hadn't even been a year since his murder.

As her dagger hovered over him, she taunted, "Aren't you going to beg for your life?"

"No, Marian. My life is in your hands. You must decide my fate."

"Close your eyes."

"No."

Through gritted teeth, she repeated, "Close your eyes, or—"

"Or you'll kill me? Marian, either kill me now, or let me go. I'm here, and I'm not fighting you. Has it occurred to you that I'm nearly twice your size? That I could break the cord around my wrists, overpower you, and easily take that dagger from you?"

He moved his arms, and to Marian's dismay, he brought his hands forward, showing that he had broken free of his binding.

He continued, "I've never struck a woman, and I'm certainly not going to start by hitting you when I've already done so much to hurt you. I'm submitting to you. I'm putting my life in your hands. You decide. You are within your rights to seek vengeance against me for the wrong I have committed against you."

This was nothing like she had imagined when she had fantasized about killing him.

"The 'wrong' you have committed?" she shrieked. "You've destroyed my life. I'm no longer a complete person because half of my heart is buried in a foreign land. I can't even visit Robin's grave!"

She flinched when he moved his hand, but he was only wiping away a bead of sweat rolling down the side of his face.

When he met her gaze again, she was confounded by the way his eyes reminded her of Robin. A thought intruded upon her agony. Was it possible that God was sending her a sign that He did not want her to kill Gisborne?

Guy interrupted her tormented reverie.

"Marian, when I murdered Robin, I blamed him for what I had

done. I blamed the sheriff. I even blamed you for choosing Robin instead of me. But I've had a lot of time to think about what happened, and I'm prepared to take responsibility for murdering your husband. If that means my life is forfeit, so be it."

This was the final nail in the coffin of her lethal intentions. She tossed the dagger away as if it were ablaze and dissolved into tears, burying her face in her hands. From the corner of her eye, she saw him stand and tentatively reach for her, presumably to console her, but she shied away and stumbled over to the great oak, falling to her knees and sobbing uncontrollably.

She had failed to avenge Robin. She could lead the outlaws; she could outsmart Gisborne and the sheriff, but she couldn't intentionally kill a man.

"Thank you for sparing my life, Marian. Take comfort in the knowledge that you are not a killer. I've killed… too many times. I've killed when following orders; I've killed without thought or care, and I've killed in the heat of anger. Be glad that you can't look a man in his eyes and kill him—even a man who has taken the life of someone you loved—because there is one thing that killing has taught me: no matter who it is that you've killed, a small part of your soul dies as well. And eventually, there is nothing left of your soul but an empty husk."

Marian had recovered some, and she reached out to caress the initials on the tree. "I will never forgive you," she quietly avowed as she touched the *R.*

"I don't deserve your forgiveness. But I am sorry for what I've done to you. I will never forget the moment when I first saw you riding along the road encircled by your father's men-at-arms. You were the most beautiful woman I had ever seen. And now, after watching you lead the outlaws all these months, I'm certain that you're the most intelligent woman I have ever met."

Marian tearfully studied the initials without responding.

"Robin was fortunate beyond measure. I will always be envious that he was worthy of your love, and I acknowledge that I am not."

After a short wait, he implored, "Will you grant me permission to leave?"

She did not answer him, and after a pause, he pivoted and walked back to his horse.

12 January 1193, Locksley Manor

Constance was sorting her medicinal herbs in the pantry when she heard a noise above her head and realized that Guy had returned. She wondered where he had gone when he left earlier.

The pantry door creaked, and she startled.

"My lady," Elvina whispered. "Gisborne sent me to find you. He said he wanted to speak to his wife forthwith."

"Did he give a reason?" Knowing that he was just a few feet above them in his chamber, Constance's voice was hushed as well.

"No, my lady, but he's in a bad temper."

A cold dread seized Constance's heart. Had he discovered that she was spying for Marian? Did he have news of Lionel? So much time had gone by since his abduction that she was losing hope.

She hastened up the stairs, and when she entered Gisborne's chamber, he was pacing, muttering to himself, and visibly agitated. As soon as she closed the door, he halted and scowled at her. His eyes glittered with what she imagined was rage, and his expression was dour.

Constance looked down, unable to endure the intensity of his scrutiny.

"I'm an idiot," he stated in a flat monotone.

Constance's heart sped, and her stomach churned. He must have realized that she and her father had been helping Marian and the outlaws. Trembling with fear, she heard his heavy steps approach her.

She braced herself for the worse and flinched as his hands gripped her upper arms. Alarmed and confused, she tilted her head up only to feel his lips crash against hers. She reflexively tried to move away, but he pulled her closer, embracing her and deepening the kiss.

And to her everlasting shame, she wrapped her arms around him and returned his kiss as the rest of the world vanished from her consciousness. When he released her and backed away, she felt the moment had ended far too soon. Embarrassed by such thoughts, she concealed her mortification by calmly asking, "What do you mean?"

He nervously ran his fingers through his long, dark hair. "The sheriff is always telling me that I'm an idiot, and today I proved him right. Again."

"What did you do?" Constance's apprehension grew.

He chuckled, but it was a grim sound. "I almost died today. I was facing the sharp end of Marian's dagger as she prepared to claim her vengeance."

"You're still not making sense. Why does that make you an idiot? If you were afraid to die, that would be understandable."

"Of course, I'm afraid of dying. And although I doubted that Marian would kill me, I knew it was a possibility. And when she raised that dagger over my head, did I beseech God to grant me His mercy and allow me into heaven? Did I beg for His forgiveness for my many sins? I did not because I'm an idiot." Guy mirthlessly barked out a laugh. "Instead, all I could think about was you. I saw your face in my mind, and I prayed that I would not die before I had the chance to taste the lips of my sweet wife."

"Oh!" Constance was completely taken aback.

"I'm ready to die now, for I have kissed you and found you to be everything I would have desired in a wife but can never have."

"I... I don't know what to say."

"You don't have to say anything. I apologize for kissing you, as I'm sure you do not welcome such attentions from me. It will not happen again, because my time grows short. I suspect that my usefulness to the sheriff is ending. If King Richard returns, he will execute me. If John takes the throne, I'll be killed for knowing too much. You will soon be free of me, and I know that your next husband will be a vast improvement."

He marched from the chamber and slammed the door.

Constance collapsed into the nearest chair, buried her face in her hands, and wept. Constance knew that Guy was likely right. Either the sheriff would kill him, or King Richard would execute him for murdering Robin and committing treason. He deserved to die, of course. But why did the thought of his death cause her heart to constrict painfully?

He's a monster, she told herself. But that wasn't true. She had seen him hesitate, and sometimes even recoil, from the sheriff's evil plans. She believed that he could have captured or killed Marian on several occasions, including, she was certain, today. Guy was tall and strong. If Marian had threatened him with a dagger, he could have overpowered her.

Constance also believed that he was sincerely remorseful for killing Robin and Osmund.

He's a puppet and weak. This was undeniable, as Argentan seemed to have some strange hold over Guy. She didn't understand why he tolerated the humiliations and mistreatment that he endured at the hands of the sheriff. Perhaps it was because he was a landless knight. But why not find another lord to serve?

She didn't understand Guy, but more troubling, she didn't understand herself. From the moment of their first meeting, she had found him irresistibly attractive, and she had been instinctively drawn to him. No other man had ever inspired such feelings in her heart. But those nascent, smoldering flames of desire should have been extinguished by the revelation that he had murdered her beloved cousin.

Constance faced the truth: she was just as weak as Guy. It was inexcusable for her to feel affection for Robin's murderer. She should rejoice that he would be dead soon, and she would be free to find a real husband.

Intense memories of their kiss overwhelmed her. She hadn't wanted it to end.

Again, she became disgusted with herself. She shouldn't have these feelings. What was wrong with her?

She thought about the times she had seen compassion, vulnerability, and decency in Guy. He had treated her with respect over the course of their marriage. Apparently, he had been faithful to her and had not humiliated her by consorting with other women. He had also trusted her with personal stories about his troubled childhood, even though she suspected that there was much he had left out.

She could no longer deny that she genuinely cared about Guy.

In the end, Guy's fate was in God's hands. She did not want him to die, but she couldn't save him either. In her anguish, she prayed for guidance from the only One who truly controlled their fates.

CHAPTER 18
SECRETS AND LIES

14 January 1193, Sherwood Forest

Marian allowed herself one last look at the cave where she had spent many uncomfortable, sleepless nights over the past two months. Soon, she would be back in Embelton and sleeping in a real bed, but that wasn't the only reason for her light-hearted mood.

She picked up the saddlebag containing her meager belongings and walked out into the crisp morning air. The wispy clouds overhead were not threatening, so she expected an easy journey north. Tuck, who still saw himself as her protector, would accompany her, and Little John would resume his role as leader of the outlaws during her absence.

Everyone had gathered to wish them safe travels, as Tuck held the reins of two horses that had been borrowed from Locksley, courtesy of Constance. Marian spoke to each man, thanking them for their efforts and assuring them that she would return as soon as she could.

Hugging Odella, she inquired, "Where's Allan?"

"A messenger came before dawn this morning, and Allan left with him. He promised to return before you left," replied Odella.

As if summoned by their conversation, snapping twigs and the thudding of hooves heralded Allan's arrival. He leapt off his horse and ran to Marian.

Out of breath, his face flushed from exertion, Allan exclaimed, "Marian, it's Lionel!"

Everyone crowded around, eager to hear the news.

Allan continued, "Very early this morning, I received word from our man in Lenton that Lionel was there looking for you. I was skeptical, but the messenger said that the steward at Lenton knows Lionel, and he recognized him."

"I don't believe it," groused John. "It's too convenient for him to appear after all this time."

"It sounds like a trap," Tuck remarked. "Perhaps this is related to Gisborne's warning."

Before Marian could answer, Allan explained, "I thought so too, but when I got to Lenton, I learned that Gervase is not there. He's still traveling with Prince John. Lionel is hiding in the Lenton chapel. He begged the Lenton steward to find you, and he said he fears for his life if the sheriff finds him first."

Marian agreed with Tuck and John; this was all very suspicious. But what if it was Lionel, and he needed her help?

After considering her options, she devised a plan.

❧

Marian and Tuck were concealed within the trees as they observed Lenton Manor and the small chapel located about thirty yards from the main house. Everything seemed calm and perfectly normal.

After a long wait, John joined them and reported, "Will and Much went to the village of Lenton, and there are no soldiers there. Allan took one of the horses and surveyed both of the roads that lead here. He didn't see any guards along the road. The rest of the men have been combing through the forest surrounding both the village and the manor. There are no soldiers hiding in the woods."

Marian nodded, deep in thought. "I talked to the steward, and he swears the man is Lionel. He arrived late last night, begging for food and shelter and requesting that someone find me so that I could help him reunite with his father."

"Where is Lord Embelton?" asked Tuck.

"He's still in London, waiting for news about the king," responded Marian.

A worried John disclosed, "It appears to be safe, but the hairs on the back of my neck are telling me that something's not right."

"I agree with you; this feels wrong, but if Lionel is there, and he needs my help, I must help him," declared Marian.

She then decisively commanded, "Have the men wait here, inside the tree line closest to the chapel. Allan will stay with the horses." She pointed down the road. "He should head in that direction, and he will find a place where he can hide the horses behind a row of pine trees."

She shrugged out of her cloak and gave it to John. "Tell Will to wear this as a decoy. If the sheriff's men appear, our men should make a lot of noise as a diversion and lead them on a chase through the forest."

Facing Tuck, she ordered, "You will enter the chapel through the main door, and I will enter through the back."

As soon as everyone was in place, Marian squeezed through the small opening at the back of the chapel and crawled into the dark vestry. When she heard raised voices, she scrambled to her feet and hurriedly made her way to the door that led to the sanctuary.

"Lady Huntingdon sent me here to escort you to safety."

"I don't know you. Go find Marian and bring her here at once."

She sighed, recognizing Lionel's voice and wondering why he couldn't be more gracious to someone who was trying to help him. She walked into the sanctuary and said, "No need, Lionel. I'm here."

"Marian," he cried, a broad smile lighting up his face. "Aren't you a sight to be seen; what are you wearing?"

She hid her irritation as she queried, "Lionel, what happened? How did you get here, and where have you been?"

"Who's this man?" he demanded, pointing at Tuck.

"I'm Brother Tuck, and King Richard honored me with the duty of watching over Lady Huntingdon and protecting her."

Lionel had the temerity to laugh. "That's a thankless chore, to be sure. Don't you know she thinks she's a knight? She likes to play with bows and swords."

Tuck's eyes narrowed. "I believe the lady asked you several questions, and I humbly request that you show her the courtesy of answering."

Lionel shrugged. "Sorry, Brother Tuck; I'm just so glad to be free that I'm a bit giddy. I was abducted during a visit to court in May, and since then I've been a prisoner. Yesterday, my captors were moving me to a new location, and I recognized that I was near Nottingham. When they fell asleep, I escaped."

"Thank God," breathed Marian. "Lionel, we've been so worried about you. We almost gave up on ever finding you."

Tuck wasn't satisfied, and Marian noticed that he was intently studying the other man. "How did you escape your guards?" he asked.

Lionel glanced between the two of them. "Don't you believe me? After what I've been through, this is the greeting I get? Oh, very well, the guards were young and inexperienced; this was the first time I had ever seen them. Last night, they were drinking heavily and passed out, and that's how I escaped."

"I see you were well fed during your captivity." Tuck persisted like a hound following a scent.

Marian reluctantly acknowledged that Lionel looked more like a man returning from a sojourn at court than a former prisoner on a desperate flight to freedom.

Lionel's smile disappeared. "I don't appreciate your tone. Argentan ordered the men guarding me to treat me well, so long as

Father made ransom payments. Are you disappointed that I'm not in ragged clothes and half-starved?"

"Of course not, Lionel," interjected Marian. "We can't stay here; it's too dangerous. We can talk more once we're safely away."

"Marian, take me to Embelton. I want to go home."

Lionel's plaintive plea and tear-filled eyes touched Marian's heart. "We will leave now and ride to Embelton." A realization struck her. "Wait! We have to go to Locksley and get Constance." She saw a flash of irritation on Lionel's face.

"We don't have time to go to Locksley," he asserted. "When my guards woke up this morning, I'm sure they started searching for me. They might have already sent word to Argentan. The first place the sheriff will send his men is Locksley. That's why I came here; I thought it would be safer for me than Locksley."

"You have a good point." Marian pulled Tuck aside, and in a low voice, said, "Tell Much to make haste to Locksley. He can escort Constance to Embelton since he knows the way. Lionel and I will wait for you with the horses."

Thankfully, the steward at Lenton had provided them with a third horse. Marian and Tuck tried to maintain a brisk pace, but Lionel kept falling behind, and he protested that they were pushing their mounts too hard considering the distance to Embelton.

"Please, Lionel; it's imperative that we leave the sheriff's jurisdiction as quickly as possible," beseeched Marian. Just then, she sharply reined in her mount as several birds took flight from a copse of trees up the road.

Tuck had seen them too, and he pulled up short next to Marian. They both silently studied the road ahead, looking for signs of danger.

Marian nearly jumped out of her skin when Lionel rode up behind her and loudly questioned, "If we're in such a hurry, why are we stopping?"

Tuck shushed the younger man, who resentfully complained, "I don't answer to you. You will show me the respect due my station."

Marian was growing increasingly impatient with Lionel. He had always been demanding and full of himself, and she had hoped that his months of imprisonment might have taught him humility.

Again, Lionel asked, "Well? Why are we stopping?"

"I thought I saw movement up ahead," Marian explained.

"I don't see anything," a petulant Lionel countered.

Tuck commented, "Something startled those birds."

"I think we should go around this section of road," Marian suggested. "The forest is dense here, so we'll have to walk the horses until it is safe to return to the road."

"Walk?" cried Lionel. "That's ridiculous. Look," he pointed down the road. "There's no one there. There's not even another traveler on the road with us. It's the middle of January, and it's cold. If we're going to reach the next inn by nightfall, we can't start traipsing through the woods because you're afraid of a few birds."

"Lionel, we can't risk—"

Before she could finish, Lionel spurred his horse into a fast trot and proceeded down the road.

"Wait!" Marian shouted. She and Tuck urged their horses forward as Marian kept calling him and begging him to stop.

At last, he halted and turned his horse to face them and await their approach.

As Marian and Tuck drew near, she admonished him. "Lionel, please to listen to me. There are dangers on the road—"

At that moment, mounted knights and foot soldiers streamed out of the trees lining both sides of the road, and before Marian and Tuck could react, they were surrounded by at least three dozen men.

To her utter horror, Sheriff de Argentan, Payen, and Gisborne also emerged from the trees, and the sheriff casually maneuvered his horse alongside Lionel's.

"Now do you believe me, Alaric?" Lionel beamed. "I told you my plan would work."

"My friend, I'm very impressed," replied the sheriff. "If only Payen and Gisborne were half as clever as you, I could have put a stop to her bothersome antics months ago."

Marian was so staggered that she struggled to speak, or even think. She glanced from Lionel to Argentan and then from Payen to Gisborne. They were smiling and laughing, except for Gisborne, whose eyes were focused on the ground. Tuck's distraught expression likely mirrored her own.

She was still on her horse, and a mounted knight rode up beside her. He took her dagger from its sheath, seized her bow and quiver, and tightly bound her wrists, leaving them in front of her so she could hold on to her saddle's pommel as he took control of her horse's reins. Tuck was also disarmed and bound.

As soon as she was secured, a triumphant Argentan rode up to her and sneered, "Your reign of mischief has ended."

Marian kept her eyes trained on Lionel, and she refused to look at the sheriff.

He leaned in close to her and lowered his voice. "If I had my way, I would personally send you into the shadows to join your husband and father. Nothing would give me more pleasure than watching the light in your eyes dim." He reached up and wrapped his hand around her throat, just as he had done on the day of Robin's hanging.

She could feel each finger and his heavy ring. Maintaining an impassive expression, she stared straight ahead.

An alarmed Gisborne implored the sheriff. "My lord, what about your promises to the prince?"

That seemed to break the spell, and Argentan released her. He remarked, "Unfortunately, Prince John has other plans for you. But at least I'll have the opportunity to host you at the castle. Sadly, your original chamber is unavailable, so I must put you in the dungeons."

Marian glowered at Lionel and questioned, "What have you done?"

He smirked at her without responding.

"I've also invited a special guest who will join us tomorrow," Argentan excitedly divulged. "It will be such a surprise! I can hardly wait."

When Marian finally looked at the sheriff and saw the malevolent gleam in his eyes, her heart collapsed.

He knew.

❧

As they rode back to Nottingham Castle, Guy was fuming. He was annoyed at Marian for not heeding his warning. He had known that the sheriff was planning something, but he hadn't learned the details until they were on their way to the location of the ambush. There had been no opportunity for him to send word to Constance in hopes of alerting Marian.

Most of all, he was seething at that pompous fool who was his brother-by-marriage. How could Lionel have betrayed his father in such a reprehensible manner? Edmund was a good man, and he was a loving father. Over the past six months, Guy had often felt envy that Lionel had a father who loved him so much that he would do anything to secure his freedom and keep him safe. In contrast, Montlhéry had been the only father figure that Guy had ever known.

And what of Constance? She loved her brother so much that she had submitted to a sham marriage with a man who was far beneath her station. Not only did she risk her personal safety— another man might have insisted on his marital rights—but she had also compromised her future options for an advantageous marriage. High-ranking men seeking a wife often disdained widows and women with annulled marriages.

The sheriff interrupted his disheartened musings.

"Gisborne, I've sent men to Locksley to escort your wife to Nottingham first thing tomorrow. What touching reunions we will witness at the castle!" Argentan laughed smugly as he spurred his horse to the front of the line next to Lionel.

Guy took this opportunity to move alongside Tuck and quietly disclose, "Tell her I didn't know the truth about Lionel until this morning."

Tuck nodded, acknowledging that he had heard him.

15 January 1193, Nottingham Castle

Constance was apprehensive as she climbed the winding staircase towards the sheriff's tower room.

The previous day, she had been preparing to flee to Embelton with Much when Locksley Manor was suddenly surrounded by the sheriff's men-at-arms. They had guarded her through the night—perhaps the longest night of her life—before escorting her to Nottingham. And now she was about to face Argentan, and no one would tell her why.

From Allan and Much, she had learned that Lionel had escaped, and that Marian was accompanying him back to Embelton. She could only guess that the sheriff was furious at the loss of his hostage, and she feared that he might be planning to take her captive instead. She wondered if Guy would protect her, but after months of watching the sheriff control and manipulate him, she didn't believe that he had the courage to defy his master.

Her stomach was churning as she entered the tower room where the sheriff was standing in front of his messy desk, waiting for her.

Guy was staring out a window, but at the sound of her arrival, he promptly walked up to her. To her surprise, he leaned over, as if he were affectionately kissing her cheek, but instead, he whispered into her ear. "I'm sorry; I swear I didn't know."

When he straightened up, she saw that he was tense, and his eyes were shaded with worry.

"How touching!" mocked the sheriff. "I should have known that Gisborne would make quite the docile husband."

Constance grudgingly looked at the sheriff. His exhilarated manner did not bode well for anyone ensnared in one of his games. But her gaze immediately slid past him to Marian, who was standing on the other side of the room, her wrists bound in front, her face smudged with dirt, and her hair disheveled.

With a cry of alarm, Constance hurried to embrace her. "Marian, oh, Marian! What happened?"

Argentan was ecstatic. "Gisborne, this is the first of several tender reunions we'll be witnessing." Addressing Constance, he explained, "I captured her along the road, and that's the reason for her gloomy demeanor. Poor Marian Hood!"

Marian's eyes were filled with despair. Unintentionally, she echoed Guy. "Constance, I'm so sorry."

Constance was taken aback; why were they sorry for her? Then a cold fear seized her; if Marian had been captured, and Marian had been with Lionel...

She spun around, glancing between Argentan and Guy. "Lionel? Is he... all right?"

Guy looked down, and Argentan chortled.

"My dearest Constance," declared Lionel as he sauntered into the tower room. "I'm heartened that you are worried about me, but I assure you, I am very well on this beautiful winter's day."

"Lionel!" she cried before sprinting across the room and launching herself into the arms of her long-missing brother. "I've been so afraid that I'd never see you again. Praise God that you are safe!"

Abruptly, she realized that something was wrong. She released Lionel and stepped back. Lionel wasn't bound. He was moving about freely and perfectly at ease. Had Marian traded her freedom for Lionel's?

A confused Constance beheld his smiling face. Then she glanced at Marian, only to see her staring uncomfortably at the floor. Her gaze shifted to Guy, and it was unnerving to see him mirroring Marian's posture. Apparently, neither of them could look her in the eye, while the sheriff's eyes were alight with excitement.

"I don't understand. What has happened? Are you releasing Lionel, but taking Marian prisoner instead?" she questioned.

"You might say that," offered the sheriff cryptically.

"Constance, have you heard about the king?" asked Lionel.

She cautiously answered, "I heard that he is a prisoner somewhere in Germany."

"That's right," concurred Lionel. "Richard will not be returning to England, and John will soon be crowned king."

"No!" exclaimed Constance. "I don't believe that. Since King Richard is a Crusader, the Holy Father will insist that the Truce of God be respected, and they will have to release him."

To her dismay, Argentan and Lionel chuckled. Guy and Marian were still examining the floor at their feet, and she was growing impatient with their silence.

Argentan asserted, "King Richard will never return. He will stand trial for the crimes he committed in the Holy Land, and since he is guilty, he will be held accountable, regardless of the protections usually afforded to returning Crusaders."

Constance opened her mouth to argue, but before she could speak, Lionel insisted, "John *will* become king. I told Father that Prince John is the future, but he stubbornly clung to the Lionheart. Now, I have forced his hand. Over the past eight months, it's become common knowledge that the Baron of Embelton is supporting Prince John. This will inspire others to join our cause."

"You 'forced his hand?' You mean…" She could not speak the words; it all seemed so unreal.

"Eight months ago, I met with Baron de Argentan, and we formed this plan. Prince John's strategy was faltering from a shortage of funds. Father refused to listen to me; he was completely unreasonable. So yes, I forced Father's hand, and the coffers of Embelton have played an important role in positioning the prince so that he can finally take the throne."

Argentan added, "Lionel, the prince is exceedingly grateful to you. I know your position will be elevated to favorite advisor and close companion to the new king." He paused, as if he were debating whether to continue. "I'm not supposed to say anything, but I heard your name spoken in discussions regarding the Earldom of Bedford. Eustace had no living relatives, and the title has reverted to the crown."

"Did you hear that, Constance? An earldom!" Lionel triumphantly proclaimed. "I would outrank Father and help King John rule England!"

Constance recognized that the sheriff was encouraging Lionel's exaggerated opinion of himself. Tears blurred her vision, bile rose in her throat, and she was overcome with alternating waves of disgust, heartbreak, and fury. When she thought about how she and her father had been so frightened for him, and how they had fervently prayed to God for his safe return, she wasn't sure whether to weep in despair or shout in anger.

Instead, she quietly stated, "You're not an earl yet, and John has not yet been crowned. Father always said, 'don't sell your crops until they have been harvested,' and you should heed his wise counsel." Unable to bear the sight of him, she pivoted and moved to stand at Guy's side.

Lionel had become a stranger to her.

"You will see that I'm right, and when I'm an earl advising the king, you and Father will bend your knee at my feet and beg me for favors," Lionel angrily responded.

Argentan, who was enjoying the familial drama, then explained, "Even now, John is in Paris, swearing fealty to King Philippe for Normandy and the Angevin lands. Philippe has sent a letter to

Richard, severing all ties and declaring war on the Lionheart for his many crimes. This afternoon, I'm traveling to Tickhill Castle, where the northern supporters of John are meeting to plan our next moves. While I'm gone, I'm appointing Lionel as acting sheriff."

Constance looked at Marian and grew fearful. What would happen to her?

Argentan seemed to have read her mind, because he announced, "Prince John is still short of funds. Therefore, he is accepting bids for the hand of this lovely creature." He gestured at Marian, clearly mocking her unkempt state. "The highest bidder will become Earl of Huntingdon by right of wife. There's only one small complication."

"No!" gasped Constance. She saw Marian's devastated expression and knew that Lionel had betrayed her in the worst possible way.

"I believe we need one more person to make this gathering complete," proclaimed Argentan.

A horrified Constance watched as Lionel strolled out of the tower room. He was gone for a short time before he came back carrying a fair-haired toddler with pale blue eyes.

As soon as the boy saw Marian, he squirmed and cried, "Mama!"

When Lionel set him down, his little legs swiftly carried him to Marian, who knelt on the floor as the child approached her.

Guy strode over to Marian and cut the bindings around her wrists so she could embrace her son. He then returned to stand with Constance, who thanked him.

Lionel then revealed the secret of Robin Hood's widow.

"In June 1189, shortly before the king and Robin left on their Crusade, and seven months after Robin brought her to Embelton for safe-keeping, Marian delivered this child. She christened him 'Robin,' and she calls him 'Robbie.' She claims he is Robin's son—"

"Claims?" Constance indignantly interrupted. "Anyone looking at this child knows he is Robin's son. Enough of your insinuations. Haven't you already done enough? You should be ashamed of yourself."

Lionel smirked and extended his insincere regrets to Guy. "Sorry about saddling you with this sanctimonious, towering scold. But at least you get Locksley."

Guy bristled, but Constance grabbed his forearm to keep him from reacting to Lionel's taunt.

Marian, with tears rolling down her face, was still hugging Robbie, who was chattering about riding on Cousin Lionel's big horse.

Laboring to control his temper, Guy heatedly contended, "This boy is now the Earl of Huntingdon, and Marian is his guardian. At most, the crown could assume the role of guardian, but Marian cannot confer the title to a husband."

"A bastard cannot inherit," retorted the sheriff.

"He's not a bastard!" declared Marian. "Robin and I entered into a clandestine marriage before he was conceived."

"Where is your proof?" asked Argentan.

"Both the priest and a witness can attest to the marriage and the date: the 8th day of September, in the year of our Lord, 1188."

A sudden realization prompted Constance to interrupt. "Why are you asking for proof?"

The sheriff's eyes narrowed. "I need to interview the priest and any witnesses to corroborate her claims, of course."

Constance stared meaningfully at Marian, who nodded that she understood. The sheriff would kill anyone who could testify to the validity of her marriage.

Marian countered, "I will only give the names to an impartial person, such as..." She was briefly lost in thought until an idea brightened her expression. "Queen Eleanor!"

Argentan and Lionel rolled their eyes and laughed at her.

The sheriff replied, "I don't care about these witnesses. This child will never be the Earl of Huntingdon. You can return to the dungeon and spend one last night with your bastard son. I've arranged to send him to Normandy, where a childless noble family will adopt him. Even though you will never see him again, do not fret; he will be well cared for, and he won't suffer the stigma of illegitimacy."

Constance and Marian chorused their vigorous opposition to the sheriff's plan.

Argentan took several steps towards Marian, who fell silent and hugged Robbie close, shielding him from the sheriff. "You will either marry a man of the prince's choosing," he growled, "or you will suffer an unfortunate accident that might involve me choking the life out of you."

CHAPTER 19
A HERO'S LEGACY

15 January 1193, Nottingham Castle

Constance's patience was at an end.

After the meeting in the tower room, Guy had escorted her to his personal chamber in the keep, and he had beseeched her to stay there until he returned. Standing at the window, she had watched the afternoon advance from the brightness of midday to the lengthening shadows of twilight. And now the forest beyond the castle walls was shrouded in the murkiness of dusk.

She regretted her promise to wait, and she wondered if she could visit Marian and Robbie in the dungeons.

At last, the latch rattled, and the door opened. Guy had returned, and he was carrying two bundles, which he deposited on the bed.

Curious, she went to inspect them, but he gently took hold of her arm and led her to the corner of the room farthest from the door. In a hushed voice, he asked, "Who knows about Robin's son?"

"Besides myself, my father, and Lionel, only the household servants at Embelton and the sisters at our local abbey where we hid Robbie when I was forced to come here to marry you. Oh, and Allan-a-dale knows."

"The minstrel?"

"Yes; he traveled with Marian to the Holy Land, and I guess she told him. The king also knows."

"King Richard?"

"Of course, what other king could it be?" she irritably snapped, before attempting to settle herself. "I'm sorry, it's just that I'm so beleaguered by what has happened. How can everything go so wrong all at once?" Without waiting for him to respond, she recounted what she knew. "After Robin died, Marian told the king about their clandestine marriage and Robbie's birth. He gave her strict instructions to keep Robbie a secret until he returned to England and proclaimed his legitimacy."

"Constance, the king will not return. There are powerful forces arrayed against him, and he will not prevail." He then disclosed, "Marian recently told me about this marriage, and she mentioned that it was at Saint Mary's Church. After I left you, I went there and gave the priest a bag of coins and ordered him to go into hiding. Earlier, Marian spoke of a witness. Who was the witness?"

Constance studied his expression, her eyes narrowing. He seemed sincere, but how could she trust Guy when she couldn't even trust her own brother? "I can't divulge his name; if the sheriff finds him, he will kill him to undermine Robbie's claim to the earldom."

Frustrated by her reticence, he implored her. "Just tell me whether the witness is safe."

"He is safe. Have you seen Lionel? Do you know what he is planning now?"

"Argentan has already left to go to Tickhill, so Lionel has assumed the duties of sheriff."

Constance snorted, not caring if she sounded bitter. "I suppose he'll expect everyone to obey him. He'll love it."

"How could your brother turn his back on Lord Edmund? To have such a father... doesn't he realize that such a father is worth more than money or power? If only..." He glanced away, momentarily lost in his thoughts.

Constance recognized that he was reflecting on his own father-less childhood, and her heart went out to him. Reminded of Robbie's predicament, she asked, "When will the Norman couple arrive to take Robbie away? Is there anything we can do to stop this from happening?"

He guided her to a chair near the hearth and insisted that she sit. Dropping to one knee in front of her, he grasped her hands. "Constance, there is no Norman couple."

"I don't understand."

"The sheriff was lying to you and Marian. He will not let Robbie live. The risk is too great."

Constance cried out in horror before covering her mouth to muffle the noise. "He's going to kill him?" she whispered. "No! We can't let him—"

"I won't let him hurt Robbie. I've taken his father from him and destroyed Marian's happiness, but I won't allow the sheriff to take that boy's life. I have a plan, but the less you know, the better. Actually, I can't believe our good luck. With Argentan away, and Lionel in charge, I have great confidence that my plan will work. Lionel isn't familiar with the castle or the usual routines for the night watch."

"Is there anything I can do to help?"

He paused, regarding her intently.

"Please?" she insisted. "I want to help. Marian is the sister of my heart, and I've been helping raise Robbie since his birth."

"There is something, but I think—"

"I would do anything for Marian and Robbie."

"It's something that would help me."

Constance felt annoyed by his extended reluctance. "Well, I can't read your mind, so you need to ask me."

"They will discover that Marian is missing during the changing of the guard at dawn, if not sooner. The captain of the watch will then immediately come to this chamber to notify me because I'm second in command to the sheriff. I'm asking you to share my bed, so that when he arrives, we will be found together, and if Lionel accuses me of helping Marian, you can swear that we were together all night, and the captain will confirm that you were here. Of course, I will not impose myself on you."

Constance stood and walked to the hearth. Holding her hands out to feel the comforting warmth of the flames, she questioned, "Why would anyone suspect you?"

He rose to his feet and followed her. "My infatuation with Marian is well known. Initially, I will be under suspicion. However, Lionel is inexperienced and over-confident, so I think he can be convinced that the Knight Templar was the mastermind of the escape."

"You are right about Lionel. He's completely out of his depth." Turning to meet his gaze again, she noticed a resolve that previously had been missing in him. He was ready to risk everything for Marian and Robbie, and Constance's heart swelled in admiration. "I will do it; I'll say that we were together all night."

"Constance, are you certain? Do you realize what this will mean?"

"You promise that you will not assert marital rights? You will only be lying next to me on the bed?"

"Yes, on my honor, I give you my word. But if they find us sharing a bed, and you tell everyone that we were together all night, it will not matter whether we were just sleeping; you will sacrifice your ability to obtain an annulment. And even though I don't expect to live a long life, you will be forced to remain as my wife."

He reached out and took her hands, looking into her eyes as he earnestly avowed, "I will implement my plan regardless of your decision. I will not be angry if you choose to spend the night in the guest chamber down the hall."

Constance had understood the implications of her offer, but to hear him say it out loud was daunting. She was also dismayed by her yearning to be close to him. She could imagine reclining with him in bed as he embraced her, and such thoughts made her ache with desire.

Striving to dismiss these wanton impulses, she considered his steadfast resolve to rescue Marian and Robbie. Never before had she seen such strength and determination in him, and she was impressed. At that moment, she decided to help him. "You are risking your life to save Marian and Robbie, and I'm only risking my reputation. No matter the consequences, I will help you."

In the hearth's glow, she saw gratitude shining in his eyes. He gathered her in his arms, and although he did not kiss her again, he held her for a short time, and she reveled in his warmth.

When he released her, he went to the bed and collected his bundles.

She inquired about them, and he revealed that he had procured a warm cloak for Marian, a blanket for Robbie, and a dagger for Tuck.

"Did you bring food?"

"I'm sure Marian and Tuck can wait until they are safely away from the castle before eating."

Constance grinned. "You don't know much about children, do you?"

"I don't know anything about children."

"Well, Robbie is three and a half years old. Little children that age are always hungry. And food is a great way to keep a child quiet and content."

Guy acknowledged, "A quiet, content child could be the difference between life and death as we move through the corridors of the keep."

"I thought so; I have some cheese and bread that a servant brought to me earlier. I will cut it into bite-size pieces and wrap it in a cloth."

She promptly prepared the food and gave it to him. He was

walking to the door carrying his bundles, and she was overcome by the notion that he might never come back.

"Wait," she demanded, and he stopped and looked at her curiously.

Constance hastened to him, raising up on her toes and kissing him on the cheek. Gazing into his eyes, she whispered, "Godspeed, Guy."

16 January 1193, Nottingham Castle

It was after midnight, and Guy paused near the door that led down into the bowels of the keep. He leaned against the wall, closing his eyes and taking a steadying breath.

No one, except for Edmund and the sheriff, knew the truth: he was that little boy's closest male relative. Robbie was his nephew, and Guy was responsible for protecting him until he grew to maturity. He felt the unbearable weight of his guilt, for he had taken Robbie's father away from him forever. Considering how growing up fatherless had affected his own life, he was devastated by remorse.

He was also overwhelmed by what had just transpired with Constance.

Guy thought about Marian, and how she loathed him. He now recognized that her friendliness all those years ago had lacked sincerity. During his adult life, he had known many women, and most of them had regarded him seductively, their eyes half-lidded and smoldering with lust. These women had only been interested in the thrill of an illicit tryst and the pleasure he could give them. In contrast, when he had first met Constance, she had been distant and disapproving.

But the look on Constance's face as he was leaving—it was something he wanted to see again and again. Her eyes had been shimmering with admiration and genuine affection. Guy had walked away feeling as though he could defeat an army single-handedly. He would rather die than ever disappoint her again. He would save Marian and Robbie, and Constance would see that he could be... his mind stumbled on the word, for it was an idea he had never before considered: he could be the hero for the first time in his life.

Marian sat on an old, battered bench in her cell, gently rocking back and forth to comfort Robbie. He was cold and hungry, and after crying himself to exhaustion, he had finally drifted into a fitful sleep.

In her mind, she kept searching for a way out. She observed the guards and whispered ideas to Tuck, who was in an adjoining cell. It soon became obvious that they were utterly and completely trapped.

She gazed down at her precious son. It was his existence that had given her life a purpose after her return from Acre. Robin's legacy. That's how she had thought of him during all those lonely nights in the forest. It broke her heart that he would never know Robin, but Edmund had offered to be his surrogate father.

Once a month, Edmund had secretly escorted her to the abbey near Embleton so she could visit Robbie for a few days. These visits had been healing and inspirational, and she would return to the outlaws determined to ensure that Robin's legacy, Robbie, would live and thrive in a world free of tyrants like Argentan and Gisborne.

And now the sheriff was going to take him from her. She had already lost half of her heart when Robin died. How could she possibly face a future without Robbie?

There was a noise in the corridor leading to the stairway, and she was dismayed to see that it was Gisborne. He spoke briefly with one of the guards, and then walked up to their cells, carrying two bundles.

"I've brought a blanket and a warm cloak, and Constance has sent food for your son," he disclosed.

Then Guy drew close to Tuck's cell and whispered something to him. Marian saw Tuck reach through the bars and remove a dagger from between the folds of the blanket. She set Robbie down on the bench as Guy slid both the blanket and the cloak between the bars of her cell. She pulled the cloak around her shoulders and wrapped her son in the blanket.

Guy quietly ordered her to shield Robbie's eyes, and she instinctively obeyed.

"Who's on watch here?" Guy brusquely demanded.

The two guards on duty hastened to Gisborne. The older one asked, "Sir Guy, is there a problem?"

"Look at this lock; it's not secure! Who's responsible for this?" Guy was angrily pointing at Tuck's cell door.

The two men bent over to get a closer look, squinting in the low light of the dungeons.

Marian watched as Guy unsheathed his dagger and nodded at Tuck. In a swift, practiced motion, he grabbed the man closest to him from behind and slit his throat. Simultaneously, Tuck reached through the bars, seized the other man by his hair, and shoved his dagger deep into his neck.

She held Robbie close, hoping that he could not hear the macabre gurgling sounds of the men as their lifeblood pooled on the stone floor. Guy left to retrieve the keys to the cells, and soon Tuck, Marian, and Robbie were free.

"We were suffering in misery and hopelessness, but God has answered our prayers by sending you," a grateful Tuck proclaimed.

Tuck's lavish praise of Gisborne annoyed Marian, but she could not deny that it was the truth. The noise and movement had woken Robbie, and he was on the verge of another bout of full-throated wailing. She urgently requested, "Where is the food Constance sent?"

Guy loosened a pouch tied to his belt and gave it to her as he revealed, "I have a plan to get you out of the castle, but we cannot linger here. I've already cleared the way of soldiers, but we must hasten before the next watch begins."

He added, "Marian, if you can keep Robbie quiet and cover his eyes—"

"What is it you don't want him to see?" she asked suspiciously.

Guy looked at her gravely and confessed, "The trail of dead bodies that I've left between here and the main corridor of the keep."

❧

They hurried through the dungeons and up the rickety stairs that led to the keep. Marian held Robbie and kept him distracted with tidbits of food, while Tuck carried a torch to light their way. And throughout their furtive flight to freedom, Guy efficiently and lethally dispatched any unlucky guard who was in the wrong place at the wrong time.

They passed through the kitchens and into the bakery. Guy stopped and sheathed his sword. He then removed a leather cord with several keys from around his neck and led them to an oak door at the rear of the bakery. Marian noticed that the door was new and unusually sturdy for a pantry, but since some spices were more precious than silver, perhaps it wasn't so remarkable.

He unlocked the door and shepherded them into a room chaotically packed with crates, barrels, and miscellaneous items. Once they were inside, Guy closed the door behind them, and Marian was instantly alarmed. They were in a small, windowless space with one door. She met Tuck's gaze and recognized that he was worried too.

"Hold the torch over here so I can see better," commanded Guy.

Marian and Tuck watched as Guy moved two crates that were stacked against the wall. Then he dropped to his knees and slid his hand across the floor, evidently searching for something. In the low light, Marian couldn't see what he was doing, but she heard a sharp click, and a trap door in the floor swung open, revealing the top of a ladder descending into dark depths.

"What is this, Gisborne?" Tuck demanded.

"This is a tunnel that leads to the brew houses beyond the outer bailey walls."

"How do you know about this?"

"I supervised its construction," Guy explained. "Shortly after we arrived in Nottingham, the sheriff designed and planned this tunnel. After several years of digging, it was completed last summer."

Marian surmised, "He wanted a way to escape in case King Richard returned."

"I think it's more likely that he just wanted an escape route, regardless of who might be pursuing him. Please, do not tell anyone about this tunnel. There are only three people who know it's here: the sheriff, Payen, and myself. Argentan will know that I was the one who betrayed his trust, and he will execute me."

Marian scoffed at Guy's fears. "One of the workers has probably already gossiped about the existence of this tunnel. I'm sure you didn't dig it yourself."

For several heartbeats, Guy stared at her, and she realized the truth. She whispered, "The men who dug this... are they...?"

In a detached, even voice, Gisborne replied, "The men who dug this tunnel will never divulge its existence, thanks to Payen's talent for mixing ale and poison."

Tuck drew their attention back to the matter at hand. "What's the plan, Gisborne? With all the bodies you've left in our wake, time grows short before one of them is discovered."

"You, Marian, and Robbie will go through the tunnel. It ends inside a brew house at the foot of the cliffs. Earlier this evening, I tied two horses to a post in the building. Take care—the room was barely big enough to hold the horses, and when you open the trap door, your unexpected appearance will startle them." He then untied another pouch from his belt, and it jingled with coins. "Please, take Marian and her son somewhere safe."

Tuck frowned. "The plan is sound, but when it's discovered that we are gone, and no one can figure out how we escaped, Argentan might suspect that you showed us the tunnel."

"I thought of that. As soon as you are in the tunnel, I'm going to the postern gate and kill the guards there. We're lucky that there's no snow, and the ground is dry. Otherwise, it would be difficult for me to create a believable trail to mislead Lionel."

Marian approved. "It's a good plan. Robin took me through the postern gate all those years ago, and it would be a natural assumption that I used the same route again."

Robbie had eaten all the food and was fussing. Marian set him down as she prepared to enter the tunnel, and to Marian's consternation, Guy knelt in front of her son.

"Lord Robbie," he respectfully addressed the little boy. "You must obey your mother if she tells you to be quiet. Do you understand?"

The boy's pale blue eyes studied the tall stranger for a few moments, and then he timidly smiled and nodded.

Gisborne stood, and Tuck shook hands with him. "Thank you, Sir Guy. God bless you for your courage and efforts on our behalf. We will keep the tunnel a secret."

Marian stared at her nemesis. "You have sacrificed many small pieces of your soul tonight," she observed as she recalled what he had told her about killing.

"You're assuming that there's a part of my soul that remains to be sacrificed," he suggested, somewhat casually.

"There is one thing that I've learned tonight, and it's that you still have a soul to sacrifice. Thank you."

With that, Tuck climbed down the ladder, and Marian lowered Robbie into his waiting arms. With one last glance at Guy, she followed the Templar into the tunnel. Guy crouched above them and handed the torch to Tuck. And then they were gone.

16 January 1193, Dover, England

Robin and Edmund sat at a private table in an alcove near the back of the tavern. *The Hawk and the Dove* was not very busy on this cold night, as few people traveled during winter. Most of the patrons were returning Crusaders, and they were clustered together discussing the fate of the king. Several prostitutes sat glumly at a separate table, realizing that the men's preoccupation with the missing monarch would result in poor earnings for the night.

Edmund despondently declared, "We are at the end of our search. No one between London and Dover recalls Juan. Too many months have passed, and we have wasted our time."

"It's likely that you are right," Robin conceded, "but I specifically gave Juan the name of this tavern."

"This tavern has been forwarding messages between England and the continent since before you were born," Edmund reminded him.

Jack whined, unhappy that they were ignoring him as he sat under their table. Edmund picked him up from the dirty tavern floor and held him on his lap. He had also grown fond of the little dog.

Robin was discouraged, but he was not ready to admit defeat. He signaled to a serving girl, requesting more ale and asking to speak to the proprietor.

A short, middle-aged man with grizzled hair arrived at their table with their drinks. A younger man, barely into adulthood, shadowed him.

"My lords, I am delighted to greet you. This time of year there are few nobles traveling," he remarked as he took note of the quality of their apparel. "I am Bazile, the owner of this tavern, and this is my youngest son, Udo."

Following the script they had practiced during the past few days, Edmund announced, "I'm the Baron of Embelton, and I'm here on the queen's business." He retrieved a folded document from inside his tunic and gave it to Bazile. "Can you read?"

"Yes, my lord," replied Bazile as he scanned the letter they were carrying from Queen Eleanor, stating that Edmund was conducting royal business and must be shown every courtesy and receive unconditional cooperation.

Edmund explained, "The queen is searching for a Spanish knight who is missing. He arrived in Dover last July, but he disappeared shortly after that."

"July? My lord, that is so long ago! For many months, the port has been crowded with returning Crusaders and foreigners. He might have been here, but I just don't remember."

Robin studied the man and concluded that he was sincere. Just then, Udo leaned forward to get a better view of the queen's letter, which Bazile was still holding. Something shiny caught Robin's eye, and he looked at the hilt of the sheathed dagger hanging from Udo's belt.

His heart dropped, and he asked, "What kind of dagger is that, Udo?"

The younger man beamed with pride. "It's a Saracen dagger. I, uh, I bought it from a returning Crusader."

"May I see it?" requested Robin.

Udo handed it to him, and Robin examined the familiar heirloom that Juan had long cherished. It was easily recognizable with its broken tip, red stones, and the exotic, geometric designs that gracefully adorned it.

Robin offered, "I will buy it from you. How much?"

Udo was startled by Robin's unanticipated proposal, but Bazile's expression remained guarded as he demurred. "My boy is fond of this dagger. It's not for sale." The avarice in his eyes said otherwise.

Robin kept his bag of money hidden as he retrieved a coin and laid it on the table.

Udo reached for it, but Bazile stayed his hand and repeated, "It's not for sale."

Robin stacked two more coins on top of the first.

Bazile grinned with delight. "It's a rare dagger from the Holy Land."

"It's broken," remarked Edmund.

Bazile countered, "The stones are genuine, and the design is unique."

Robin added three more coins, doubling the amount on the table.

A bewildered Edmund stared at him, while Bazile was closely studying Robin, trying to gauge how much more he might be willing to spend. But before Bazile could negotiate a higher price, his son triumphantly grabbed the six coins and cried, "It's yours!"

Bazile angrily thumped his son on the back of his head and cursed at him.

Robin took the dagger and wedged it into the same sheath as his usual blade. He gazed meaningfully at Edmund and said, "My lord, shall I give him the queen's dispatch?"

Edmund's eyes widened in surprise; it was the first time they had progressed to this part of their scripted ruse. He revealed to Bazile, "Queen Eleanor has an important message that must be taken across the channel and delivered to the Archbishop of Rouen. She directed that I come here for your assistance."

"My lord, anything for our good queen. I will send Udo to deliver it. In fact, my other two sons will return from Rochester tomorrow, and they can accompany him as well. I've noticed that there are many urgent messages traveling between England and Normandy these days. Do either of you have news of the king?"

Robin announced, "The queen says he will arrive from Germany within the month."

The tavern owner's carefully schooled expression faltered, and his son looked confused. Recovering his wits, Bazile professed, "That's good news."

Robin placed the sealed dispatch and a few coins on the table to cover both the cost of sending the letter and their drinks.

Meanwhile, Edmund rose and thanked Bazile for his hospitality, expressing regrets that the hour had grown so late.

As soon as they were out of the tavern, Edmund demanded, "What's going on, Robin?"

"We found Juan, or I should say, Juan's dagger. This was his most precious possession, and he would have never sold it. Therefore, I'm certain that Juan is dead, and that Bazile, or one of his sons, killed him."

"What is the plan?"

"We will see what Bazile does with the queen's message. Hold on to Jack and give him some jerky to keep him quiet."

They stealthily made their way to the back alley and discovered that the tavern had a small courtyard behind it, which was hemmed by a low wall. They hid in the shadows formed by the wall and an adjacent building.

Bazile and Udo emerged from the tavern. Udo placed a lit torch in the bracket next to the door, brightening the area.

"You fool! I think he would have given more for that dagger, if you had only let me do the talking." Bazile was loudly castigating his son.

"What if he changed his mind and decided that he didn't want it?" Udo whined.

"He would have paid anything for that dagger; I could see it in his eyes. But that's not what worries me."

"It was my dagger to sell," groused the son.

Again, Bazile thumped his son on the back of his head. "I should have never allowed you to keep it. That man was asking about the Spaniard, and he obviously recognized that it was his dagger."

Bazile opened the queen's dispatch and held it high, angling it towards the torch as he read it.

After he had finished, he lowered it and exclaimed, "I can't believe it! This wasn't supposed to happen. Queen Eleanor has already reached an agreement with Emperor Henry for the king's release. We've got to notify Argentan as quickly as possible, so you'll need to head north at first light."

"Shouldn't we send word to Prince John?"

"He's in Paris, and he'll probably hear the news before Argentan can contact him."

Robin nudged Edmund, and the two men's eyes met in understanding. The queen's message was a subterfuge, of course, but it was the sort of news that would cause John's supporters to panic.

Robin slid his bow off his shoulder, nocked an arrow, and took aim.

Thwack. Udo collapsed, an arrow protruding from the center of his chest. Bazile instinctively pivoted to see from whence the arrow had come.

Robin immediately released another arrow, which found its mark in Bazile's chest.

Edmund and Robin entered the courtyard and hurried over to them. Udo was dead, but Bazile was lying on his back and attempting to cry for help. Robin retrieved the queen's false message and gave it to Edmund.

"Bazile," Robin beckoned to the dying man. "Why have you betrayed the king?"

The light in the man's eyes was rapidly dimming. "I serve Prince John... Who...?"

"I am Robin Hood, and I serve King Richard. I recommend you make your peace with God."

A long exhalation followed by an abrupt stillness marked the end of Bazile's life.

"We must notify the local sheriff that I executed these men for treason, and we'll use the queen's letter to avoid arrest," Robin declared. "The sheriff must also arrest the two remaining sons when they arrive tomorrow."

"How do we know that this sheriff is trustworthy?" questioned Edmund.

"We don't. We are facing an uncertain time when everyone's loyalty must be tested and proven."

As soon as the ambitious under-sheriff of Dover saw the queen's letter, he did not question Robin's summary execution of Bazile and Udo, and he vowed to arrest the other sons forthwith. The man promptly volunteered to escort Bazile's sons to London, along with a sealed dispatch from Robin. For a minor local official, it would be a once in a lifetime opportunity to meet the legendary Queen Eleanor and make a positive impression on a powerful royal.

The sun had just risen over the horizon as Robin and Edmund strolled to their waiting horses. Jack trotted up to them, his tail wagging.

Gazing north, Robin knew that no matter what difficulties lay ahead, and no matter what fate befell King Richard, he would be facing the future with Marian at his side, and ultimately, that was all that really mattered to him.

Robin Hood had returned, and he was going home.

End of Part II

The Robin Hood Trilogy, Part III:
Robin Hood's Return

Robin and Marian are finally reunited as they confront an uncertain future.

While an increasingly reckless Prince John pursues the throne, Queen Eleanor collects an unprecedented king's ransom. Social unrest and ruinous taxation threaten to tear England apart.

As opposing forces battle for control of the English throne, the King of France and his sinister advisor, Montlhéry, conspire to end the Plantagenet dynasty forever.

Dark secrets and unexpected revelations could destroy the future of England. The course of history hangs in the balance.

Robin and Marian must save both King Richard *and* Prince John. But can they prevail in the ultimate battle between the future and the past?

If you enjoyed this novel, please leave a review at Amazon. It really helps!

Visit our website to learn more about upcoming releases for the Robin Hood Trilogy. You will find bonus materials relating to this book and articles about this fascinating, exciting time in history.

www.AngevinWorld.com

Glossary

Achilles' heel

From Greek mythology, a small, but fatal, weakness; a vulnerability in an otherwise invincible opponent which will lead to the opponent's downfall. It can refer to any type of weakness—not just a physical vulnerability.

Angevin

Originating from or belonging to the County of Anjou in France. Henry II's father had been Count of Anjou, and Henry ruled both England and vast continental territories, including Anjou. For this reason, Henry II, Richard the Lionheart, and John are referred to as the Angevin Kings of England, and their holdings are called the Angevin Empire. John lost control of these continental lands; thus, he is considered the last Angevin King of England. These three rulers are also referred to as the first Plantagenet kings.

antechamber

A chamber that serves as a waiting room and entrance to a larger room.

apothecary

A person with specialized knowledge of herbs, spices, and medicines. An apothecary would also be knowledgeable about poisons.

bailey

The courtyard of a castle. It's an open area enclosed by the castle wall.

berm

The area between the castle wall and the moat.

bliaut

A long outer tunic worn by both men and women. The bliaut had a full skirt, a fitted bodice, and sleeves which were fitted along the upper arm while flaring between the elbow and wrist. The lower part of the sleeve sometimes flared into a trumpet shape. The length of the men's version varied, but the women's bliaut would have been full-length. Women's tunics were also called gowns or kirtles.

bodkin

A long, narrow arrowhead designed to pierce chainmail.

bow *(bōh)*

A weapon that propels projectiles (arrows).

bow *(rhymes with how)*

1) Bending at the waist towards another person as a formal greeting. Typically performed between men of equal rank.

2) The front of a ship.

brace

In addition to the usual architectural meanings, a brace also refers to a pair. The phrase, "a brace of coneys," refers to two wild rabbits.

bracer

A bracer is wrapped around the forearm of an archer in order to protect the arm from the bowstring. Bracers were made from leather or horn.

braies

An undergarment that was made of linen and worn by men. Although underwear as we know it today was not worn, these would have been similar in that they were worn under other clothing.

brocade

A heavy fabric woven with an elaborate, raised design or pattern. During this time period, brocade fabric was the height of luxury and very expensive.

brooch

A clasp or ornament with a hinged pin and a catch to secure the point of the pin on the back. In the 12th century, there were no buttons or zippers, so a brooch was an indispensable piece of jewelry for securing clothing, especially cloaks. Elaborate, jeweled brooches were a sign of wealth and status. Brooches were popular gifts.

buss

A large, fully decked ship with two masts. These ships were capable of carrying nearly 1,000 men, 75 crewmen, horses, and equipment (such as disassembled siege engines).

by right of wife (jure uxoris)

During this time, a man could assume a title of nobility when he married a woman who held the title in her own right. He would also become the legal possessor of her lands.

Carentune

A town east of Nottingham which was mentioned in the Domesday Book of 1086. Today, the town is a suburb of Nottingham, and it is called Carlton.

causeway

A road or path that is raised in order to cross a moat, marshland, sand, or similar impediments to travel.

chausses

Leggings or stockings. They could be made of either cloth or chainmail.

Circe

In Greek mythology, Circe was a witch who turned men into pigs by giving them a drink from her cup of enchantment. With the help of Hermes, Odysseus was able to defeat her magic and force her to restore his men to human form.

clandestine marriages

Before 1215, a couple could declare their intention to marry in front of witnesses, and if these vows were followed by consummation, canon law considered the couple to be legally wed.

coney

An older term referring to wild rabbits or hares.

courtesan

A woman who seeks financial support and security from noblemen and men of wealth in return for companionship and sexual favors.

courtier

An attendant at court, especially a person who spends a great deal of time attending the court of a king or other royal personage.

cross guard

For swords and daggers, this is positioned crosswise to the blade and between the grip and the blade. It protects the user's hand. See also: hilt, pommel, and grip.

curtain

Another name for the castle's outer wall surrounding the bailey.

curtsy

A formal gesture of greeting and respect made by women and girls consisting of bending the knees to lower the body while slightly bowing the head.

destrier

A large, strong war horse. Only wealthy lords and knights could afford them.

djinn / djinni *(jin / jin-ee)*

Also called jinn and genies, djinn are supernatural creatures. References to djinn can be found in both pre-Islamic and Islamic mythology and theology. They can influence men to either good or evil. Sometimes they are described as "mischievous spirits," and that is the definition used in this book. Djinn is the plural form of the word, and djinni is singular.

dowager

A widow whose title was obtained from her deceased husband. Adding this modifier to a title distinguishes the widow from the wife of the man who currently holds the title.

dowry

Money or land given by the bride's family at the time of her marriage. If the girl entered a convent instead of marrying, the dowry would be given to the convent.

drawbridge

A bridge that can be raised to prevent access or lowered to allow passage of vehicles or pedestrians.

empyreal

Heavenly; pertaining to the highest heaven.

Ernehale

A town northeast of Nottingham which was mentioned in the Domesday Book of 1086. Today, the town is a suburb of Nottingham, and it is called Arnold.

ewer

A large earthenware jug or pitcher with a wide mouth.

fallow field

A field that has been left unseeded for one or more growing seasons in order to restore its fertility.

fealty

Loyalty that a vassal owes to his lord. This often refers to the actual loyalty oath, as in "an oath of fealty."

Feast of St. Andrew

This was celebrated on November 30th. It was considered a major feast that was observed as a holiday and required fasting on the previous day.

Feast of St. John the Baptist

Also known as Midsummer; it was celebrated on June 24th. It was considered a major feast that was observed as a holiday and required fasting on the previous day.

Feudal System

This land-based economic and social system determined the rights and obligations of men. See also: fief, vassal, lord, liege, homage, and fealty.

fief

Land granted to a vassal for his use. In return, the vassal provided loyalty and service to the owner of the land. A fief could also be a payment instead of land.

fiefdom

Land owned by a noble or knight.

field

In heraldry, the background color of a coat of arms is called the field.

fleur-de-lis

In heraldry, a stylized representation of an iris, consisting of three petals. This heraldry represents the royal family of France.

forthwith

An old word that actually dates to the 13th century. It means immediately, at once, without delay.

fortnight

A period of two weeks, or fourteen days.

galley

A type of ship which used rowing as its primary method of propulsion. These ships also had sails. With two methods of propulsion, galleys were versatile and popular for both warfare and trade. Early galleys can be traced as far back as the 8th century BC, and they remained in use throughout the Middle Ages.

gatehouse

A complex system of gates and towers which protected the entrance to a castle. See also: causeway, drawbridge, and portcullis.

genuflect

Briefly dropping to the right knee before rising. This was a formal greeting performed when in the presence of a man who is of superior rank. It is also performed towards the altar when in church.

great hall

Known as the heart of the living space in a castle, it was the location of feasts, and it was often the area where business was conducted. In earlier times, it was also where people slept.

grip

The part of sword or dagger that is gripped by the hand. See also: hilt, cross guard, and pommel.

Hades

1) In Greek mythology, the god of the underworld where the dead lived.

2) A name for hell. This use is not capitalized.

hauberk

A chainmail shirt or tunic that protected the upper body, especially the neck and chest.

heathen

1) A person who does not worship the triune God of the Bible.

2) An irreligious, uncultured, or uncivilized person.

high table

An elevated table in the great hall where the lord, his family, and important guests were seated during feasts.

hilt

The handle of a sword or dagger. It is comprised of the cross guard, grip, and pommel (see the entries for these words for additional information). Hilt is often used interchangeably with grip.

homage

A declaration of loyalty from one man to another. The man declaring his loyalty would typically receive a fief in return. The first step in becoming a vassal is to pay homage to the lord.

homily

A sermon, usually on a Biblical topic.

Hospitaller

See: Knight Hospitaller.

humors

The fluids in the body. In ancient Greece, Rome, and the medieval period, humors were thought to be closely tied to health. Balancing your humors was vital to good health.

infidel

For Christians, a person who is not a Christian. For Muslims, a person who is not a Muslim.

jousting

A tournament competition where two mounted knights rode towards each other with the goal of unhorsing their opponent using blunted lances. This contest was conducted in a highly formalized manner, but it was still very dangerous.

keep

The living area inside of a castle complex. It was a heavily guarded and fortified building or tower. The great hall would be located in the keep.

Knight Hospitaller

A member of the "Order of Knights of the Hospital of Saint John of Jerusalem." A religious charitable organization founded circa 1096 to provide aid to Christian pilgrims traveling in the

Holy Land. In the last half of the 12th century, they became more militaristic. Plural is Knights Hospitaller. Also spelled Hospitaler.

Knight Templar

A member of the "Poor Fellow-Soldiers of Christ and of the Temple of Solomon" (simplified to "The Order of the Temple of Solomon" in this book). A religious military order founded by Crusaders in Jerusalem around 1118 to defend the Holy Sepulcher and Christian pilgrims. Plural is Knights Templar.

Lent

A Christian season of fasting and penitence in preparation for Easter, beginning on Ash Wednesday and lasting 40 weekdays to Easter, observed annually.

leprosy

A devastating illness that destroys skin, flesh, and bones. During the Middle Ages, it was considered divine judgment for a sinful life.

liege lord

A feudal lord who is entitled to allegiance and service from his vassals.

lord

A landholder, typically a noble or the king, who granted fiefs (the use of land) to vassals (who were often knights, or even other nobles).

lute

A stringed musical instrument that is plucked to produce sound. It has a long, fretted neck and a hollow, pear-shaped body.

Maman

French word that translates to momma, mommy, mum, and similar informal versions of mother.

mantle

A long, loose cloak or cape usually worn over other clothing, similar in function to a modern overcoat.

Mass

A Catholic Church service which includes Holy Communion.

men-at-arms

A general term for trained soldiers. Typically, they were trained like knights, but not all men-at-arms were knights.

Mère

French word that translates to mother. More formal than Maman.

Michaelmas

The Feast of St. Michael was celebrated on September 29th. It also marked the end of the harvest season. It was considered a major feast that was observed as a holiday and required fasting on the previous day.

Midsummer

Also known as the Feast of St. John the Baptist; it was celebrated on June 24th. It was considered a major feast that was observed as a holiday and required fasting on the previous day.

millstone

A heavy disc-shaped stone. Grain was placed between two millstones, and they were rotated against one another in order to grind the grain into flour.

minstrel

An entertainer. Minstrels were primarily performers. Although some wrote their own songs, they often sang songs composed by others, notably the troubadours. Minstrels also performed acrobatics, juggled, told jokes, and recited poems.

Moor

The name given to the Muslim people who invaded Spain in the 8th century. The Moors were from northwest Africa, and they were of mixed Arab and Berber heritage.

Morpheus

In Greek mythology, Morpheus was the god of sleep and dreams. The phrase, "in the arms of Morpheus" simply means that the person is asleep. Today, the narcotic morphine can trace its name to Morpheus.

Mount Olympus

In Greek mythology, the location where the gods lived.

obeisance

Giving proper respect and deference to someone of superior rank. Typically this would require kneeling (see genuflect), bowing, or curtsying.

Odysseus

In Greek mythology, Odysseus was the King of Ithaca, who was called by his High King, Agamemnon, to wage war against Troy. Known as "Odysseus the Resourceful," it was his strategy of the Trojan horse that resulted in the victory of the Greeks over Troy. Odysseus was anxious to return to his wife, Penelope, but his voyage home was fraught with fantastical dangers and adventures. His story is known as the Odyssey. He was gone from Ithaca for twenty years, and many believed that he was dead. He returned in disguise and defeated the men who were pursuing his wife by winning an archery contest where he demonstrated his amazing skills with a bow that only he could string.

Orpheus

In Greek mythology, Orpheus was a talented musician and poet. While still living, he descended to the underworld in hopes of rescuing his dead wife, Eurydice, from Hades. He was given permission to lead her back to earth, as long as he did not turn around to look at her. At the last moment he looked, and she was lost to him forever.

Outremer

A French word meaning, "overseas." Used as a name for the Crusader States, especially the Kingdom of Jerusalem, after the First Crusade.

page

A boy in training to become a knight. He would progress from page to squire to knight.

palfrey

A horse used for everyday riding. These smaller horses were often ridden by women.

parchment

Animal skin that has been processed to use as a writing surface. It was typically sheepskin, and it was also used to cover windows before the widespread use of glass.

passant

In heraldry, a beast walking, with the right foreleg raised.

Penelope

In Greek mythology, the wife of Odysseus. She faithfully waited for her husband and refused to remarry when everyone else was convinced that Odysseus had died and would not return. Pursued relentlessly by a band of unwanted suitors, she delayed any decision to remarry by weaving a shroud for her father-in-law by day, only to unravel her work at night. When her ruse was discovered, she devised an archery contest that only Odysseus could win. He returned just before the contest and won it before slaying the unwanted suitors.

physician

A university educated doctor.

pilgrimage

A religious journey to a holy place.

Plantagenet

This became the family name of Geoffrey V, Count of Anjou. Reputedly this name was given to him due to his habit of wearing a sprig of yellow broom blossoms (in Latin: *planta genista*) in his hair. Geoffrey's descendants would rule England from 1154 to 1485 as the Plantagenet dynasty.

Poitevin

Originating from or belonging to the County of Poitou in France.

pommel

1) A knob attached to the end of the grip in swords and daggers. It provided a counter balance to the blade, and it helped the user maintain a better hold on the weapon because it prevented the hand from sliding off the grip. See also: hilt, cross guard, and grip.

2) A knob at the front of a saddle.

portcullis

A heavy gate that was raised and lowered to control entry into the grounds of a castle. It was part of the gatehouse. A portcullis was composed of crossed bars, forming a grate or grille. The bottom edge consisted of spikes.

postern gate

A small door hidden in the castle wall that allowed soldiers to enter and exit the castle grounds without using the main gate. This was useful during sieges. Typically, a postern gate was only large enough to allow the passage of one man at a time.

Pyrrhic victory

A struggle that ends in the ruination of the victor. The cost of victory is so devastating that it is tantamount to defeat, and it outweighs any benefit that accrues to the victor. The phrase originated with stories of King Pyrrhus of Epirus and the battles of The Pyrrhic War (280–275 BC).

rampant

In heraldry, a beast standing on its hind legs, the right foreleg raised above the left.

relics

Sacred objects which were associated with a saint or holy person. It was believed that relics could work miracles. Relics included objects that the saint might have owned or touched. Physical remains of a saint, including blood and bones, were also considered relics.

Saint George and the Dragon

This legend was very popular during the 12th century. A dragon had nested in a village, and he would not let the people draw water from a nearby spring unless they gave him one person to eat each day. The victims were chosen using a lottery, and one day the town's princess drew the unlucky lot. Saint George was traveling through the town and heard about the princess' plight. He slew the dragon, saving her and all the people of the town.

Saracen

During this time period, Muslims, particularly Arab Muslims, were called Saracens.

scabbard

A rigid sheath made of wood, metal, or hardened leather. It is used to enclose and carry the blade of sword or dagger, both to protect the wearer and to keep the blade clean and sound.

scythe

A farming tool with a sharp, curved blade affixed to a long wooden handle. It was used to cut grass for hay.

sennight

A period of one week, or seven days.

shire

A county in England, typically combined with the name of the shire to form a single word: Nottinghamshire.

sickle

A farming tool with a sharp, curved blade affixed to a short wooden handle. It was used for cutting grain, corn, grass, and similar crops.

sire

The form of direct address used for royalty prior to the 16th century. "Your grace" was also used for royalty and high-ranking clergy.

solar

Inside a castle tower, this room (or suite of rooms) was the primary living area for a lord and his family, and it provided them with some measure of privacy.

squire

A boy in training to be a knight. He would progress from page to squire to knight.

staff

A traditional pole-shaped weapon popular in England during the Middle Ages. It was made of hardwood and was typically 6 to 9 feet (1.8 to 2.7 m) long. It was also called a quarterstaff or a short staff.

stern

The back end of a ship.

Styx

In Greek mythology, a river in the underworld over which the souls of the dead were ferried by Charon.

surcoat

This sleeveless cloth tunic was worn over chainmail. Heraldry symbols were often sewn onto the chest of the surcoat. For example, Crusaders often wore white surcoats with a red cross emblazoned on the chest.

tack

Saddles, stirrups, bridles, halters, reins, bits, harnesses, and so forth. The equipment and accessories needed for horseback riding and for hitching horses to wagons and carts.

tallage

A tax that a lord could demand at any time without giving a reason.

Templar

See: Knight Templar.

tournament

A sporting event that allowed knights to demonstrate and hone their skills. Tournaments also provided an opportunity for knights to build wealth from winnings.

trebuchet

A powerful type of catapult that throws a projectile using a sling attached to a swinging arm. A counterweight is used to swing the arm, giving greater force and speed to the projectiles that are hurled towards the enemy.

trestle table

A table composed of a removable top supported by trestles (A-frame supports with horizontal beams at the top). This type of table could be easily moved around or stored when not needed.

troubadour

A poet and songwriter. Troubadours sometimes performed, but they were primarily seen as composers. They were sometimes from noble families.

Truce of God

Originally a papal edict that was intended to discourage fighting amongst Christians, it also protected Crusaders from attack and allowed them to travel in peace within Christian domains as they made their way to and from the Holy Land.

vassal

When a man swore loyalty to a noble landowner in return for use of that land (a fief), he became a vassal of the lord. A vassal was expected to provide services to the lord whenever needed. A vassal might be required to go to war and fight for his lord. If the vassal could not go to war, he would have to provide a substitute to fulfill his vassalage. Although it is often thought of in terms of lower ranking men, such as knights, anyone could be a vassal. Henry II was King of England, but he was also Duke of Normandy (and many other noble titles). As Duke of Normandy, Henry paid homage to King Louis VII of France; thus, he was also Louis' vassal. The same was true for King Richard; as Duke of Normandy, he was King Philippe's vassal.

vestry

A small room in a church used for storage of items such as vestments, sacred vessels, and other worship-related supplies and accessories.

waning

When the illumination of the moon is decreasing; the time between a full moon and a new moon.

ward

A person who has been placed under the control and protection of a guardian. In 12th century England, if the child of a noble family became an orphan, the child automatically became a ward of the king. This would include unmarried daughters, regardless of their age.

waxing

When the illumination of the moon is increasing; the time between a new moon and a full moon.

wet nurse

A woman who breastfeeds and cares for an infant who is not her biological child.

wheelwright

A craftsman who builds and repairs wooden wheels.

wimple

A medieval headdress worn by women, typically married women. It covered the top of the head and wrapped around the neck and chin.

wound fever

An infection.

Printed in Great Britain
by Amazon

45340880R00192